$4.99 U.S.
$6.50 CAN.

WILLIAM R. FORSTCHEN

72211-5 ☆ (CAN $6.50) ☆ U.S. $4.99

BAEN

FLEET ACTION

WING COMMANDER

THE LAST BEST HOPE OF MAN

Paladin toggled a switch into the burst-signal line. "Green one, green one, this is green two. Am under attack, cover blown, repeat cover blown, get the hell out and back to the barn."

He hit the burst-signal button and the lights in the cabin momentarily dimmed as nearly all the ship's energy was diverted to powering out the signal across the hundreds of light years back to *Tarawa*.

Now even if he bought it, they'd have the information. He realized that in the great scheme of things his job was done, he had uncovered the unsuspected fleet. Within minutes *Tarawa* would have the information and it'd blow the lid right off the armistice when it came out that the Kilrathi were building the ships in clear violation of the terms of armistice. It'd also mean that the war would be back on.

The images still locked on the secondary screen chilled him and he thought again of what he'd just uncovered. The carriers were more than twice as big as anything now in the fleet; the new Kilrathi ships had the power to destroy anything in space.

Worse, the cats undoubtedly knew that their cover had just been blown. The humans' only hope was to fully remobilize before the Kilrathi ships already completed could be moved up into action and meet them on the frontier. If they gained Confederation space with human defenses down, it was over.

The Wing Commander Series

Freedom Flight
by Mercedes Lackey & Ellen Guon
End Run
by Christopher Stasheff & William R. Forstchen
Fleet Action
by William R. Forstchen

WING COMMANDER™

FLEET ACTION

WILLIAM R. FORSTCHEN

BAEN

FLEET ACTION

This is a work of fiction. All the characters and events portrayed in this book are fictional, and any resemblance to real people or incidents is purely coincidental.

A Baen Books Original

Wing Commander is a registered trademark of ORIGIN Systems, Inc. All rights reserved. Used herein under license from ORIGIN Systems, Inc.

Baen Publishing Enterprises
P.O. Box 1403
Riverdale, NY 10471

ISBN: 0-671-72211-5

Cover art by Paul Alexander

First printing, March 1994

Distributed by Paramount
1230 Avenue of the Americas
New York, NY 10020

Printed in the United States of America

● PROLOGUE

"According to the final calculations projected on your holo screens, I think it is evident that over the next eighty days we run the risk of a serious reversal that could set our war effort back by years."

A rumble of stunned and angry growls shook the room. Baron Jukaga settled back in his chair and waited for the storm to settle.

"This is preposterous, an insult," Talmak of the Sutaghi clan snapped, looking around the room as if seeking to find someone to blame and thus sacrifice. "How did we ever get to this state? Our fleets are the finest, our warriors filled with the zeal of *skabak*, the will to die for the glory of Kilrah. By the blood of Sivar, we even outnumber the low born scum in nearly every class of ship. How did this happen!" and as he finished he slammed his fist down on his holo projector, shattering it, as if by so doing the grim figures would simply die.

Baron Jukaga of the Ki'ra clan silently turned in his chair and looked to the end of the table where the Emperor, and his grandson and heir Prince Thrakhath, sat.

"Perhaps our Emperor can enlighten us," Jukaga said silkily, lowering his head just enough to show obeisance, but doing it slowly, thus subtly revealing a disdain and defiance. The Emperor, of course, was not visible to those in the room. Sitting upon his high throne he was hidden from direct view by a silklike screen emblazoned with the three crossed red swords of the Imperial line. Sitting at the foot of the dias was Prince Thrakhath, who shifted slightly under Jukaga's gaze, a soft yet audible growl echoing from his throat as a signal of his readiness to accept challenge,

1

and also in reaction to the insult of directly placing a question to the Emperor.

Baron Jukaga struggled to conceal a flashing of teeth, a revealing of his true hatred for this Emperor whom he believed to be of lesser blood and who had attempted to place the blame for the disaster at Vukar Tag on his shoulders.

He had endured over a year in exile because of that disaster. It was only due to the latest reversals that the other clans had finally pressed for his release and use of his known talents as one who better than most understood the strangeness of human behavior.

The Emperor sensed the challenge and the trap. He stirred uneasily, framing his thoughts. If he answered the question directly, it would be a lowering of himself before the leaders of the eight clans of Kilrah; if he deferred the question to his grandson, the Prince, it would appear as if he were shifting responsibility—and ultimate blame.

"You go too far, Baron," a voice rumbled from the corner of the room, breaking the impasse.

Baron Jukaga looked over at the speaker, Buktag'ka, first born of the clan of Sihkag. The Sihkag were, of the eight ruling families, considered to be of the lowest blood, and as such could usually be counted on to curry favor with the Emperor in a bid to elevate their status whenever possible.

"Your insult to the Emperor is evident," Buktag'ka snarled, coming to his feet and leaning over the table to stare at Jukaga. "It is not the place of the Imperial blood to answer questions. We requested your release from exile for the skills you have in understanding humans and as master of spies, not for the surliness of your tongue, the haughtiness of all of your blood line, nor for the plots you are known for."

Jukaga looked around the table, gauging the response which ranged from nodded lowering of heads in agreement, to rippling of manes in defiance. It was time to change approach.

"I stand rebuked before the Imperial blood and intended no insult," he said, bowing low to the shaded throne. Prince Thrakhath, who sat at the foot of the throne, and was not hidden from view like his grandfather, nodded curtly in reply.

"Let us not ask the hows of it," the Emperor's voice whispered from behind the screen, "there is blame enough for all. Rather let us talk of what now is, and what is to be done."

Knowing he could not press the point, Baron Jukaga lowered his head in reply.

You low born old bastard, Jukaga thought coldly. Everyone here knows that this reversal is your fault and that of your fool grandson. Yet if victory should come it will be you who will sweep the honors around your feet. And even as he thought a concept that was beyond the range of most Kilrathi, rage and intense hatred towards a sworn overlord, he still assumed the posture of obeisance and then slowly rose up to speak again.

"Buktag'ka is right," Jukaga said, "and I accept the rebuke."

He looked around the room, gauging the responses and felt it was best to simply push on with the facts and figures that needed to be presented.

"We do outnumber the human confederation in total number of carriers, fighters of all classes, and heavy cruisers. However, as you can see by the charts projected, we will see no new replacement of carriers of standard design for the next three of eighty days. In the meantime it is projected by my intelligence staff that the humans will have four of their new fleet carriers coming into operations, thus enabling them to form an entire new task force and reach a rough parity with our own carrier forces for the first time in this war.

"This is due to the loss of the construction bays and nearly completed ships in the raids on our construction sites over the last year. First they hit our primary bases on our moon during the Vukar Tag debacle," and he could not resist sparing a quick look at Thrakhath, "and then the two follow-up raids which destroyed three other construction yards."

He paused for a moment, looking around the room, the other clan leaders stirring uneasily. The successful human raids deep within the Empire had been a source of extreme embarrassment for Thrakhath and for the clan leaders. Jukaga smiled inwardly. If anything, the exile after Vukar had enabled him to wash his own talons of any responsibility. In a dispassionate sort of way, he found he could even admire the human who had conceived of the strategy of using light carriers for the strikes. Spy reports, both from their plant high inside the ruling circle of the Administration, and from prisoner interrogation, indicated that it was Admiral Tolwyn who instituted the plan.

"Our shortages," the Baron continued, "are made worse by the fact that within the next eighty days nearly one quarter of our carriers are due for overhauls, resupply, and refitting, with one needing an entire reactor replacement."

"Can't such things wait?" Buktag'ka asked.

"It has already been delayed too long," Thrakhath announced coldly. "The *Ha'Tukag's* reactor is leaking so dangerously that engine room crews have to be suited up and after three duty shifts retired. We might see a total reactor failure if we push her any further. As for the other ships, a variety of minor things threaten to soon become major problems if not addressed. Remember the standard rule is that for every day of flight a carrier needs one day of docking for a variety of reasons. We are stretching that out to almost two to one, pushing our equipment too hard."

He fell silent and Jukaga made a show of nodding his thanks.

"I know the argument is that we cannot afford to move carriers out of action at this time," Jukaga said, "but I believe Prince Thrakhath will tell you we cannot afford not to. Unfortunately the humans, at least for the moment, have found a weak point and are exploiting it, using their new escort carriers to raid deep into our Empire, seeking not to engage in ship to ship combat, but rather to shatter our ships in their construction bays before they are completed and launched. What is even worse is their use of these strike forces to hit our transports and supply ships. Our losses there have been disastrous."

"At least they have paid in turn," Thrakhath replied sharply.

"That is true, my lord, but let us look at those figures. In the last standard year we can be certain that we have destroyed seven of their escort carriers, two fleet carriers and seven eights of other ships. In turn they have smashed eight carriers under construction, destroyed valuable equipment and inflicted thousands of casualties on trained personnel. And perhaps most seriously of all, just under seven eight-of-eights of transport and supply vessels."

He paused and looked around the room and could see the frustration of the clan leaders as they looked to Thrakhath, who was forced to show agreement with Jukaga.

"What sort of animals are these humans?" Bugtag'ka asked rhetorically. "What honor, what glory is there to be possibly gained by smashing a carrier when it cannot even fly? Their gods must vomit in disgust at such craven cowardice."

"I don't think their god sees it quite the same way ours do," Jukaga said dryly, realizing the irony of what he was saying was completely lost on those present.

That was the weak point. In his studies of humans he at least had gained some small understanding of just how alien was their logic, their beliefs, and their concept of the nature of war. To try to translate that understanding to those gathered around him, no matter how intelligent they were, was nearly impossible; the gap was simply too broad to leap.

It was, as well, the weak link in their military. All their previous enemies had been totally destroyed in wars that lasted, at the longest, a little more than four years, and that was simply due to the sheer size of the Hari empire which had to be occupied and destroyed. In such a case, where victory was usually assured from within hours of the first assaults, the need to truly understand one's enemy was moot. The human war was now four eights of years old and still most of those who led the Empire into battle did not truly understand the thinking of their foes.

"With honor, or without, a carrier destroyed is still dead," Jukaga said quietly, "a fact which can not be debated."

He looked over at Thrakhath, and to his surprise actually saw a nod of agreement.

"The real crisis, however, is in our logistical support, our transport ships supplying the fleet."

There were several snorts of disdain from the clan leaders. Such ships and those who served in them were considered to be beneath contempt. Any of fighting age who accepted assignment to one was disgraced within his clan, deemed not worthy to sire heirs for himself, but rather only to sit at the edge of the feasting tables, heads lowered, when boasts of war were shared and arm veins opened to pour out libations on the altars of Sivar. The quality of personnel could be reaildy inferred from this.

"It is a simple fact that, without fuel, food, replacement parts, weapons, and even such basics as air to breathe and water to drink, a fleet is useless. The humans have hit upon the strategy of avoiding direct confrontation and striking instead to our rear, cutting our supplies, destroying our transports, forcing us to detail off precious frigates and destroyers to escort them. Their escort carriers attack and against them even destroyers are outclassed, so that now heavy cruisers must escort convoys. As a result there are not enough heavy cruisers to escort our carriers and our own construction of these new light carriers has yet to come fully on line."

He paused for a moment and looked at the charts projected on the holo screens.

"We have lost over seven eight-of-eights of transports in the last year, along with four yards for their construction. That is our weak point. We have reached the stage where, for the moment, our carriers must leave the front and return all the way to Kilrah to resupply since there are not enough transports to bring supplies to them. As a result, in actual numbers of ships at the front, our strength has been cut in half, and so, in most sectors, Confederation ships outnumber us."

He paused again for effect and saw the cold looks of disbelief, that something as mundane, as undignified as this issue, could actually affect their fighting of the war.

"What I hear is impossible," Yikta of the Caxki clan snarled. "Are you truly saying we have lost the war because of such a thing?"

"The humans have a saying that for want of a nail a horse-shoe was lost, for want of a horseshoe a . . ."

"What is a horse?" Yikta asked.

"It is a beast of war which humans once rode upon," and then he explained the rest of the statement and saw that it had its effect.

"No, the war is by no means lost," Prince Thrakhath finally said, stirring at last. "The Baron tends, I think, to overplay his thinking and chartmaking to scare us."

"But you will not deny that we are in trouble," the Baron retorted.

"Temporarily," Prince Thrakhath said, "perhaps."

"Prince Thrakhath," the Baron said smoothly, "more than six years ago it was you who detailed off all new transport construction to your own Project Hari. Just how many transports and other material has your own clan tied up in that project, while the main battle suffers for want of supplies?"

He paused, seeing the stirring of interest in the room.

"We are not here to talk of Hari," Thrakhath snapped, "we are here instead to hear your own report and ideas first."

The clan leaders looked from Thrakhath to Jukaga and the Baron could sense that more than one finally wanted the truth of this secret project revealed. But first he would drive another point home.

Baron Jukaga nodded to an aide standing in the far side of the room who controlled the holo screen.

The image shifted to a three dimensional map of the Empire and a weaving of orange and red lines.

"Intelligence has found out that the humans are aware of the opportunity that exists for them for at least the next two eight-of-eights days, and are contemplating an offensive to exploit our short term weakness. They will commit their carriers to an opening operation in what the humans call the Munro System. They know we must hold Munro for it is a direct doorway into a number of the shortest jump points into the heart of the Empire.

"Meanwhile, on eight different fronts," and as he spoke orange arrows started to flash, "eight of their light escort carriers, along with raider transports will jump into the Empire, aiming to cripple us from behind and to smash our remaining transport, cruiser construction yards and light carrier conversion centers, while ravaging planetary bases and crippling our few supply convoys still in operation.

"That, in short, is the plan."

The room was silent as the clan leaders studied the screens.

"It is a hideous plan," Thrakhath said coldly, "a stabbing in the back against defenseless positions. It lacks all honor, all meeting of steel blade against steel blade, ship against ship."

"But it will cripple us even in its cowardice," Jukaga retorted and Thrakhath could only lower his head.

The room was silent for a moment.

"And yet," Vak of the Ragitagha clan whispered, unable to speak louder due to the fact that the surgeons had experienced some difficulty in putting his mouth back together after a challenge duel, "if all goes as rumors state regarding this project in the Hari sector, within a year we will see such a growth in our strength as to overwhelm the humans and end this war."

He looked straight at Thrakhath waiting for a response.

"Even here, Project Hari should not be spoken of," Thrakhath said hurriedly.

The clan leaders stirred. The project was nothing more than rumors, its development under the complete control of the Kiranka clan of the Emperor and the Prince.

"These are our brothers," the Emperor announced from behind the screen. "Let it be spoken of."

Thrakhath looked back at the screen behind him as if to protest.

"Speak of it."

Jukaga could see the hesitation. It was known that there were a number of security breaches coming out of the Imperial Palace and the less said about certain things the better. He could see as well that the Emperor was playing a maneuver of showing confidence in the other clan leaders, thus winning favor for acting as if those in his presence were trusted comrades. He could see the effect on Buktag´ka who puffed up visibly and leaned forward to hear.

"Even before these human raids had started," Thrakhath said, "the Emperor in his wisdom had foreseen certain dangers along these lines and thus ordered a tremendous investment of wealth and material into the building of a secret construction yard. It is located in the conquered realm of the Hari on the far side of our Empire in relationship to the Terran Confederation."

He took a holo cube out of his breast pocket and loaded it. Jukaga found this alone to be interesting, that Thrakhath had come to the this meeting fully prepared to reveal the extent of Project Hari. His own people had found out most of its well-kept secrets to be sure and it seemed that Thrakhath had expected Jukaga to force its full revelation at this meeting.

On the main holo screen a map of the Empire appeared, the frontier with the Confederation at the top, Kilrah and the Empire in the middle, and far down at the bottom the conquered space of the now dead Hari, a collection of a thousand stars around which orbited more than a thousand blasted lifeless worlds.

Thrakhath highlighted a single star on the screen deep within the former territory of the Hari.

"Here, for the last five years, a new class of carriers has been tested and developed, overcoming the difficulties of translight jumping of ships above a certain size and mass. These new carriers, what we call the *Hakaga* class, are capable of carrying and servicing our newest *Vatari*-class fighters to be launched next year. With their increased size the carriers have shield generation systems capable of repulsing nearly any weapon the Confederation now has, including their Mark IV & V antimatter torpedoes."

The image in the holo screen shifted and a carrier appeared. The clan leaders looked at it excitedly and then Thrakhath pushed a button on his monitor. Beside the carrier appeared a second image, that of a current fleet carrier. The room echoed with shouts of surprise.

Even Jukaga could not conceal his curiosity. Though he had read the spy reports, the only images he had seen so far were grainy two dimensional shots clandestinely taken by a transport captain in his employ. The new carrier was at least twice the length of the old design, and bristled with six launch bays, three aft and three forward. As the image slowly turned inside the holo field he saw that the vulnerable engine nacelles were completely concealed and armored.

"The first of the carriers is already operational," Thrakhath announced proudly, "and undergoing final testing in the far reaches of Hari space far beyond any prying eyes of the Confederation."

He looked back at Jukaga as if saying that it was also beyond the prying eyes of anyone else.

"What is its capability?" Vak asked.

"When fully loaded it carries three eighties and six eights of strike craft and fighters, launching from six separately contained bays. Its ship defense capabilities include four eights of mass driver quad batteries, four eights of neutron and laser batteries, and six gatling launch tubes for anti-torpedo defense. It has three concentric layers of interior armor, and all six bays are self contained. Thus we can take hits on three, even four bays and keep on fighting, shifting fighters from one part of the ship to the other by internal access corridors. As you can well guess, the material required to build this carrier equals over six times that of a normal fleet attack carrier. In addition we are building more than eighty escort ships of frigate, destroyer and cruiser design. That is why we suffer the transport shortage now. More than two hundred of them were committed to the hauling of all that was needed from the Empire to the far side of Hari."

He looked around the room and saw the nods of understanding.

"I think, my comrades," he said smoothly, "that is why you can also understand why my clan alone took full responsibility for the construction of these ships. We had to maintain the tightest of security. The knowledge of this leaking to our enemies would give them time to analyze our new ships and perhaps find a counter."

He stared defiantly at Jukaga.

"That is why my clan placed such security around the project and kept it hidden for so long."

Jukaga wanted to reply with a challenge, that it also insured the power of the Imperial throne with such ships solely in its hands, but realized that now was not the time, even though the subtle insult to the other clans had not gone unnoticed.

"Then commit it now and block this human offensive," Buktag'ka said, pounding the table excitedly.

Jukaga looked at Buktag'ka and wanted to laugh at the boot licker's enthusiasm.

"That is not the way to win war," Thrakhath replied, an edge of sarcasm in his voice revealing his sense that though Buktag'ka was a family leader, he was still of a lower cast. Buktag'ka quickly looked around the room, hoping for some sign of support and saw nothing but mocking stares and he swallowed his rage.

"In eighty and forty days four more carriers of the

Hakaga class will be ready for their operational tests, in three eighty and forty days, we will have a full fleet of eight and four *Hakaga* carriers fully operational.

"That means we will have a need for over forty eighties of fighter and strike craft pilots. In spite of what the Baron might think, that is why I had fully intended to reveal this information to you today. The first ship's fighter crews were drawn from my clan, but as new ships come on line we will need to draw the best pilots from all clans out of the training academies and off existing fleet ships. All of your *hrai*, your clans, are to share in the glory of this new fleet."

He looked over at the Baron and suppressed a scornful laugh. Though indeed the Baron had pressured him into revealing the project too soon, it was amusing to not let him think so.

"Only then will I release them, when the entire fleet is ready, using them to cleave straight through the human defenses. Our war simulations have gone over the plan repeatedly and our projection is that at least half of these new ships will survive to reach Earth, while in the process smashing the Confederation Fleet in one final climactic battle. Within one hour after gaining orbit above their home planet either the Terran Confederation will surrender or more than one eight and a half hundred of our fighters will deliver antimatter bombs, leaving the planet a burned out cinder.

"The tides of this war have shifted back and forth for more than half my reign," the Emperor interjected, his voice commanding total silence. "Before I return to my ancestors, I wish to see my grandson destroy these low born scum and the ball of offal that they call their world."

"I am moved to joy by this plan of Thrakhath," Jukaga interrupted, "however, it is at least eighty days, more likely two of eighty days till five of the new ships are ready, and three eighty and a half days until the other seven he believes are required for victory are operational. Yet you can all see that even if it is not a fatal blow, the humans will succeed in penetrating our defenses and sowing a wave of destruction within the next five of eight days. In this penetration, they will cripple our logistical support, which will still be needed to keep Prince Thrakhath's new ships supplied in their drive towards victory. If that is crippled the final offensive to Earth is crippled."

He paused for a moment to look at Thrakhath who was forced to nod in agreement.

"We have heard Talmak suggest that the frontier be temporarily abandoned and all defenses pulled into the center," Jukaga said reviewing the earlier suggestions, "but we cannot allow such a stain on our honor, nor can the Caxki clan, which owns many of the frontier worlds, allow it. Our Prince has explained how a counter offensive into Enigma or through Munro towards Earth is difficult if not impossible due to the question of supply, and that the humans might ignore the threat anyhow and still ravage our worlds."

He took a deep breath and looked around the room.

Now it was to the true heart of the meeting. Thrakhath had revealed what his clan had been planning, but no real suggestions as to how to overcome the crisis of the moment.

"You have brought me out of exile saying that with my understanding of humans I might suggest a third way and I have such a way which will bring us victory."

"And that is?" Buktag'ka asked, glad that it was obvious that soon this talk would be over and the mid-day feasting could begin.

"Sue for an armistice and promise peace."

A roar of disbelief thundered from all the clan leaders.

Jukaga waited for several minutes for the anger to die down and thought for a moment that more than one clan leader would call for a blood duel to avenge what they saw as an obscene slight of honor.

"You have been driven mad by your reading of human books of filth and weakness," Buktag'ka roared, coming up to Jukaga's side as if to strike him.

There was a moment of silence as all waited for the ritual first blow to be struck across Jukaga's face and then all turned to look at the screen behind which the Emperor sat.

The Emperor was laughing.

"Tell us your plan Baron, I think I see its merit even though I know the gods will not be pleased."

"But even the gods are not immune to bribery," Jukaga said, a smile of cunning lighting his features. "When my plan works, and is finished, Sivar will be more than pleased with the final offerings."

And in the doing of it, I will be pleased as well, when Prince Thrakhath's victory becomes mine instead, the Baron thought with a smile.

• CHAPTER ONE

Captain Ian "Hunter" St. John crossed through the final nav check point and turned in on attack approach. The lone habitable planet of the Munro system was now straight ahead. A flurry of matter-antimatter bombs snapped across the world, winking brightly even from thirty thousand clicks out, the bombardment suppressing the Kilrathi ground defense systems. He clicked into the Marine channel and listened for a moment as the second and third divisions started their descent into their landing points. Ian switched back to his main channel.

"Red squadron, arm all torpedoes, Blue and Green squadrons, keep close in for support. Let's get the carrier!"

Off his port quarter he saw the Yellow, Orange, and Black squadrons comprising the rest of the attack group fanning out into the standard delta formation, while the red squadron Broadsword bombers lined up for a classic anvil attack, swinging out to hit the Kilrathi carrier on its X, Y, and Z axis.

They were going to lose people in the next couple of minutes, but the light carrier straight ahead was going to be dead as well.

He did a quick scan on to the main tactical commlink net to check in on how the rest of the fight was going, ready to divert part of his attack force, which was damn near overwhelming, if something was going wrong somewhere else.

The Marines were going into their drop right on schedule, no serious opposition, the landing area already saturated by the heavy bombardment from four destroyers and a cruiser which had turned a thousand

15

square kilometers of the primary landing point into scorched rubble. What was left of the Kilrathi bases on the planet continued to glow from the antimatter strikes.

This was a raid on one Kilrathi base which was going like clockwork and that alone was troubling. Across the last thirty years Munro, ever since its seizure by the Kilrathi during the open stages of the war, had been a long standing goal for recapture. Beyond the simple fact that it was once human territory it also stood as the primary approach into the heart of the Empire. Conversely, from this base the Kilrathi stood astride a main jump point terminus into the middle regions of the Confederation and from there the main jump line straight back to Sirius and then on to Earth. It was the front door to both the Empire and the Confederation. A lot of good ships and a hell of a lot of personnel had died in six attempts to retake the planet. Now it was falling like a ripe apple into their laps.

He wondered how the rest of the assault plan was going. This attack on Munro, though crucial, was actually not the primary goal of Operation Red Three. They were to act as a focal point for the Kilrathi to counter-strike on and thus be drawn away from the main thrust of the offensive. Across fifteen hundred light years of frontline that divided the Empire from the Confederation, eight Task Groups, each comprised of an escort carrier, a light cruiser, and four destroyers were poised to leap deep into the Heart of the Empire. Their mission was to strike far into the rear to destroy convoys, shatter bases, and smash construction yards. It was a tactical innovation evolving out of Vukar Tag which appeared to be bearing fruit, a constant harassing of the enemy that some claimed was actually beginning to wear the cats down. He could only hope that the politicians were not about to blow it as latest rumors indicated they would.

"Hunter, we got traffic, vectoring in on 032 degrees your heading true, plus 060 degrees."

Hunter looked at his short range tactical scan and saw the swarm of red blips snap on.

"Blue squadron, you on them?"

"Lone Wolf here, sir, vectoring in, you're covered."

"Get that double ace strip, boy, good hunting."

"Don't worry, you'll get your bottle of scotch off me when I do," Lone Wolf replied. "Wish it was a carrier in my sights instead."

Hunter chuckled to himself. Admiral Tolwyn's nephew was eager for this fight and he could understand why.

"The kid's been going nuts trying to get that strip,"

Hunter spared a quick glance to Griffin, his co-pilot, and nodded. Kevin Tolwyn's escort carrier, *Tarawa*, had joined up with the strike group after the mission had already set out. In the skirmishes leading into Munro young Tolwyn had drawn a blank hand in half a dozen fights and was eager for a kill to round up his number to ten. Such eagerness could get a pilot wasted but Hunter could understand it.

Hunter looked back down at his computer information screen, which showed the other two Broadsword strike groups lining into position. All three groups hit their jump-off marks precisely and started in on the final attack.

"Range one thousand clicks, speed down to 110 kps," and Griffin started the chant, marking off range and speed. The computer could do the job as well, but a machine could always glitch off at a key moment and besides, he preferred Griffin's soft feminine voice.

Hunter watched straight ahead, the planet filling space before him. He could make out a sliver of reflected light, standing out against the blue-green ocean below. The light shifted into a thin pencil-like form.

"Target is turning, following standard evasive maneuver alpha," Griffin announced, "coming about to a heading 002 positive 80 degrees."

"Right on to a broadside target for us," Hunter chortled. That was the beauty of a well timed attack on the three axis points, no matter which way the enemy turned, someone would have a full broadside strike.

A low piercing hum echoed in his headset, the initial locking tone for his torpedo.

"Range fifteen kilometers, closing speed eight hundred fifty meters a second and holding."

He was damn near hanging still in space, sparing a quick glance to his tactical display, filled now with a swarm of blue and red dots. A Kilrathi Gratha heavy fighter flashed by, followed by a Rapier. He heard Jonesy in the turret behind him, stammering out a curse as she snapped off a quick volley. His Broadsword shuddered, damage information blipping red for his rear starboard stabilizer. A spray of mass driver rounds arched up from the carrier as it twisted away, and he nudged up the throttle to follow the ship as it continued to turn.

The tone in his headset started to slide up the scale, signalling that his torpedo guidance system was breaking through the Kilrathi carrier's phased shielding distortion defense, the weapon gaining a secured lock.

The Broadsword to his right disappeared in a flash. He tried not to think about the friends inside. A split second later Jonesy let out a whoop from the rear turret.

"Got the furball bastard. Burn, damn you, burn."

Damn, she was bloodthirsty. But then, who could blame a nineteen year old girl whose brothers were all dead in the war?

The tone in his headset started to warble and then set off three high pitched beeps, the last beep going into a steady tone, indicating that the heavy Mark IV torpedo was locked and armed. He felt his ship shudder as the torpedo broke free from its pylon and streaked off towards the target. Nearly a score of silver blips appeared on his tactical screen, showing the inbound strike. The timing was damn near perfect.

Now was the time to test out the new weapons system.

He slammed up throttle, yanked the stick into his gut and punched straight up, exposing the laser guidance system strapped on to the belly of his Broadsword.

"Have laser lock on torpedo," Griffin announced quietly, hunching over her read-out screen. The new laser system was designed to provide in-bound guidance for the torpedo, the designator locking on to the torpedo's tail. If target lock should be lost, the weapons officer could now guide it in, while also providing evasive for any anti-torpedo missiles and shield jamming by the target's defensive systems. The only problem was that it meant that the Broadsword had to loiter in the target area, belly exposed, until impact.

It might work, Ian thought, but I'd like to take the idiot who designed it and have him fly the wait out with me to see what it's like.

The Kilrathi carrier's point defenses slammed on, miniguns sending out sprays of marble size mass driver bolts. Several torpedoes detonated. Anti-torpedo missiles streaked out from launch bays mounted fore and aft on the ship.

"Still tracking, still tracking," **Griffin** chanted, grimacing slightly and swinging a small joy stick over to put the torpedo into an evasive as two anti-missiles closed. The evasive threw them off and they continued on.

"Still tracking, impact in five, four . . ."

And suddenly it didn't seem quite right. They were using their old single bolt anti-torpedo missiles. Hell, for nearly six months now Kilrathi carriers had been carrying their damn new sub-munitions anti-torpedo missiles which could break into half a dozen shots. The damn things had been a nasty surprise. Ships armed with them were almost invulnerable to torpedo strikes if they could get enough of them out there.

Fleet ordnance had been working like mad to come up with a counter, but so far no one had been able to snag a round for evaluation since they were armed with a timed detonator if they failed to strike a target, thus blowing up anyhow and confounding the munitions experts.

The drama played out in seconds. Four more torpedoes, all of them the older unguided models, went down to the counter-missile strike; it looked like several more were hit by miniguns and then the silver blips converged in on a single point.

"Two, one, got it!"

Space erupted with a brilliant flash as bright as the sun and the carrier was gone, internal munitions stores and fuel detonating in a firecracker string of secondary explosions that ripped the ship apart.

"Scratch one flattop," Ian shouted, comm channel discipline breaking down as nearly everyone came on yelling and cheering. He rolled his ship over, coming in on a banking turn, careful to avoid the edge of the expanding cloud of debris, making sure his gun cameras were running at high gain. A lot could be learned when the holo tapes were played back and inspected—did the torpedo guidance systems function correctly, exactly where were the impact points, were any structural weaknesses revealed as the enemy ship ruptured . . . even ship contents were important.

Several years back one of his old buddies, Paladin, had jumped a light transport and wasted it while raiding inside enemy lines. An evaluation of the explosion had shown a brief single frame image of several space suits blowing out of the erupting hull. It was still a wonder how the holo evaluation crowd had enhanced, magnified and fiddled with the shot and finally figured that the suits were specifically designed for a high radiation high gravity planet. The Hot Pit, a forward base in the Zarnobian System fit the bill as the only military target in the sector that matched up with the suits. A Marine raider battalion was rushed in, set up an ambush, and nailed a landing raid bagging a regiment of elite Kilrathi Imperial shock troops.

Hunter swept past the edge of the fireball, and then turned back towards Munro, ready to offer backup support for the Marine landing operation. The red blips of the few remaining Kilrathi fighters covering the carrier were winking off the screen as the Rapier squadrons finished them off.

Hunter clicked back on to the main commlink channel, knowing that his exuberant cry, "scratch one flattop," the fleet's traditional announcement that a carrier had been killed, had already been received by the combat information control officer and sent up to the other ships in the fleet.

He found the word flattop to be rather interesting, it came from old English when carriers were ships of the seas, but in no way could it ever describe a modern carrier with its bristling array of defenses and landing bays covered over with heavy durasteel armor.

Tradition, how the Navy loves tradition, he thought with a smile.

"All attack squadrons, job well done."

He stiffened slightly. It was the old man himself, Rear Admiral Sir Geoffrey Tolwyn.

"All strike craft return to base."

Return to base? Hell, there was still a major brawl going on down with the Marines.

"Repeat, please?" Hunter clicked in.

"That means you, Hunter, just like everyone else. All attack squadrons return to base," Tolwyn snarled.

"Yes, sir," he said. There was nothing to be gained by arguing with an admiral. But it was certainly strange that the old man would actually allow a voice transmission on his part. A Kilrathi listening post could pick it up, figure out who he was, and perhaps even trace a fleet movement as a result. Tolwyn knew better and it bothered him.

"What the hell is up, Ian?"

He looked over at Griffin and could only shrug his shoulders. This was definitely not standard operation procedure. They had dumped the only capital ship in the sector, now was the time to go after the few corvettes and really smash up any ground resistance and save some grunt lives.

"Say, Hunter."

It was Kevin Tolwyn, Geoffrey's nephew.

"Yeah go ahead, Lone Wolf."

"I just heard the word on *Tarawa's* commlink to our two squadrons covering the ground assault. They've been ordered to break off engagement and withdraw out of the atmosphere."

"Yeah, that's the word. You got any inside stuff? What the hell is the old man up to?"

"Damned if I know, sir."

"Follow orders, then," Hunter replied and then clicked through his channels to make sure that the other squadrons were following orders as well. In the heat of a successful battle like this, it was tough at times to break an action off. There could only be one of two reasons for this, either some major Kilrathi reinforcements had been detected and Tolwyn was pulling in his fighters to rearm, or the other possibility. He pushed that thought aside as absurd.

"Griffin, get us on *Concordia* nav lock."

"Already on, sir."

"Let's go back and find out what the hell is going on."

"Attention!"

The squadron commanders, and section officers called together for the staff meeting leaped out of their seats and came rigidly to attention.

Rear Admiral Geoffrey Tolwyn, strode into the briefing room. He reached the podium, lowered his head for a second and then raised it again to look out at the men and women in the room. He felt a tug at his heart at the sight of them.

"Never, for God sake never, let your people get inside your heart, for your job is to use them, and if need be kill them," a voice whispered to him. It was his old mentor Banbridge's classic piece of advice.

I guess that's what separates me from him, Geoff thought. With Clara and the boys gone this is my family. It was something he never let show, no matter what. He knew that behind his back he was "the old man," which was the gentlest of epithets; usually it was far worse and ofttimes even angry. They never really knew how he felt, especially when he looked into their eyes just before a strike went out, knowing that he was ordering some of them to their deaths. Well, at least that's finished for the moment.

He clicked a comm button which opened the public address channel for the entire ship.

"All hands, all hands, this is Admiral Tolwyn," his deep baritone voice, clipped with the refined touch of an Oxford education, echoing through the ship.

"I have just received the following communication from C-in-C ConFleet, it reads, 'To Tolwyn, commanding, Task Force 45. Armistice agreement and cease fire has been reached with Kilrathi Empire, to be effective upon reception of this signal. All offensive operations to cease immediately and to withdraw to navigation point detailed below. Repeat, all offensive operations to cease at once. Fire only if fired upon. Signed Noragami, commanding, Confederation Navy.'"

He hesitated as if wanting to say something and then lowered his head.

"That is all," and clicked off the comm channel.

He looked back up at his officers who stood incredulous. In the corridors outside the conference room distant cheering could be heard.

"I'm only going to say this once," Tolwyn said quietly. "I'm proud of all of you for the job you've done. In the seven years I've been in command of *Concordia* we've taken out eight carriers, a score of capital ships, countless fighters and bombers, and fought in nine major fleet actions. *Concordia* is not just steel, guns and planes, in fact it is you, it is your flesh and blood and the spirits of all those who've served on her, living and dead."

He hesitated for a moment.

"When it comes time for her to fight again, I hope and pray that I'll be able to count on you all in our hour of need.

"Dismissed."

He started for the door, the room silent.

"Damn, we're going home!" somebody shouted and the room erupted in cheers. Tolwyn stiffened his shoulders and walked out.

He passed down the corridor, ignoring the cheers and the momentary lack of discipline, retreated to his office, closed the door, and for the first time in months poured a good stiff drink of single malt Scotch. Settling back in his chair he started to review the first holo tapes of the strike mission.

The timing was masterful, the strike crews the finest professionals he had ever served with, nearly every Broadsword gaining lock and launching simultaneously. A successful strike like that was even more intricate than the most finely crafted ballet, and in his eyes even more beautiful.

Damn it.

A knock on the door disturbed him and he set his drink down on the table behind his desk.

"Come."

The door slid open and he could not help but allow a slight flicker of a smile to light his features at the sight of Captain Jason "Bear" Bondarevsky standing at attention in the corridor.

"Come on in, Bear. What brings you over here anyhow."

Jason came into the room and stood nervously in the middle of the room.

"We'll wave regs and at least let you have a sip," and he poured out a thin splash of Scotch in a tumbler and passed it over.

"Thank you, sir."

"Have a seat."

Jason went over to the proffered chair by the admiral's desk and settled in. He sniffed his glass and tasted the Scotch.

"Not bad, sir."

"The best, saved for special occasions."

"Like this one?"

"No, not really, I just felt a need for it."

Jason looked down at the floor and Tolwyn could feel the tension.

"Come on, son, out with it."

"Sir, something's troubling me, I thought I better come over and discuss it with you privately."

"You mean this little thing called an armistice."

"In part," Jason said quietly.

"Well, what is it then?"

"Sir, that communication from ConFleet announcing the armistice came through close to fifty minutes before our strike hit the carrier."

Tolwyn exhaled noisily and leaned back in his chair.

"How the hell do you know that, Bondarevsky?" he asked quietly, a threatening chill in his voice. "That message was directed solely to me."

"Sir, *Tarawa* was the back up carrier for this operation. If something should have happened to *Concordia* it would have been my job to assume control of the air strikes. In that situation, I took it upon myself to monitor all Con-Fleet channels and that included yours. Suppose you were hit, sir? It would have then been my job to know the entire picture. I didn't notice it immediately since it was simply decoded and stored in my personal data system. But after the action I was going through the signals to dump them off my system and I saw it."

What Jason was confessing was somewhat outside the regulations but it showed careful planning and foresight on his part. If something had indeed happened to *Concordia* the young officer before him might very well have to take full responsibility for everything that transpired.

There was an ancient cautionary tale told in the service academies, the incident dating back to a war once fought between England and America. In an encounter between an American and British ship the commanding officer of the American vessel was mortally wounded, and the junior officer took him down below deck to the surgeon. In the short interval that followed all the other officers were hit and, without his even being aware of it, the junior officer was now in command. By the time he returned to the deck his ship had already been battered into submission and forced to surrender after barely putting up a fight. The junior officer was held responsible, court-martialed, and found guilty of dereliction of duty, a duty he was not even aware had suddenly come to rest upon his shoulders. The lesson was part of the tradition and backbone of the fleet—there is no excuse for defeat.

Geoff looked at Jason and realized as well that he had made a crucial mistake in not assuming that Jason might very well be listening in.

"And what do you think?" he finally said quietly.

"I lost two crews in that attack, two pilots and a gunner. I'm wondering how their families would feel if they knew their kids got killed after a war was officially over."

Tolwyn nodded and said nothing.

"I don't give a good damn about the furballs," Jason continued, "but five hundred or more of them died when that carrier got cooked. I don't feel too good about that either, sir."

"Neither do I."

"Then why did you do it, sir?"

"I'd rather not say, Jason, but let me ask you a question."

"Sure."

"If this was just another day in the war, how would you feel about taking out that carrier."

"I hate losing people, but trading a Rapier, a Sabre and two of your Broadswords for a light carrier is a damn fine piece of work in my book. I wish it had always been that easy."

Tolwyn nodded.

"That's how I still feel about it, Jason."

"But the war's over. We were hearing the rumors even before this attack started out. Something about a peace party coming into power in the Empire, Prince Thrakhath falling into disgrace, and Foreign Minister Jamison pushing for an armistice. Damn it, sir, they're saying it's finally over and we can go home."

"And do you really believe it?"

Jason hesitated.

"Well, do you?"

"I want to believe it, sir."

"Damn it, man, that's exactly it. You want to believe it. Everyone wants to believe it. But there's a hell of a long stretch between wishing for something and actually seeing it come true. Anyone who believes something simply because it sounds good and he wishes it to be true is a damned fool and that's why I did what I did."

"Sir?"

"This war is not over by a long shot," Tolwyn growled, "and I'll kiss the hairy backside of the first Kilrathi I meet if they can ever prove it differently to me.

"It's too pat, it's too damn straight forward and simple. I remember once hearing a great line about another war, 'this is such madness only an idealist could have started it.' Well, this peace offer is the same thing, only an idealist would be stupid enough to believe it. By God, son, we were finally getting an edge. We stumbled on the tactics of it all thanks to you, realizing just how under-protected and vulnerable their construction sites were. They haven't gotten a single new carrier on line in the last year. They still outnumber us, but they're hurting, hurting even worse with the loss of their transports. We just might be turning the edge in this war, and now the damn fool politicians go for this armistice offer."

"So you disobey orders on your own and decide to keep the war going a little longer."

"The target was there and I took it, a carrier that if we allowed it to get away might cost us fifty to a hundred pilots the next time around," Tolwyn said quietly. "And I think that even you, Jason, who once risked your career to try and save a ship load of Kilrathi civilians, even you down deep agree with me."

Jason drained the rest of the Scotch from his glass and closed his eyes for a moment.

"Yes, sir, I do."

Tolwyn could see the struggle such an answer had created. From most other officers he would have dismissed it as brown nosing a superior but he knew that from Jason it came from the heart.

"Why?"

"Like you said," Jason replied. "It just doesn't smell right. I know that even after Vukar Tag, and the Third Enigma Campaign they still have the edge on us. For the

Kilrathi, war is part of the core of their soul. This intel stuff about a shift in the power structure of the palace. If it's true, the new power behind the throne would have his throat ripped out if he tried for a serious peace after all the sacrifices they've endured. Now I don't know much about Kilrathi psychology other than what I got in the naval college while waiting for *Tarawa* to finish out her refitting, but I know enough that the seeking of peace other than after a total triumph is anathema to them.

"Going for peace is impossible to their mindset. If they were losing there would be only one possible action, a suicidal fight to the end; if they were winning, a fight to ultimate triumph. There is no inbetween. Their society functions primarily through submission to strength, with the one in power gaining complete loyalty by refraining from killing the one who has submitted. But since we are not of the blood, we are therefore inferior, and as such it is impossible to submit to us. There might be exceptions, such as that warrior who serves Hunter, but that was through direct orders from his superior."

"So if the emperor or whomever is behind the emperor orders it, then why not peace?"

"Because the power at the top derives its strength through conflict. They know that if their aggressive instincts are not diverted outwards it will turn inwards and the families will eventually destroy each other. And besides, it's one thing for a lone warrior to submit, but for the highest of noble blood to do so, to submit to someone not of equal blood, is impossible."

"Precisely," Geoff said quietly, inwardly pleased as if a favorite pupil or son had mastered an intricate question.

He felt a flash of warmth for Jason, remembering the relief he felt when he had jumped into the heart of the Empire to pull *Tarawa* out and discovering that the ship was still alive. He felt the warmth as well because it was Jason who had taken his nephew out to war as a spoiled brat and brought him back as a man.

"This whole thing is a set-up, I'm convinced of it; and I

tell you this, Jason, if our government falls for it, all our butts will be in the wringer."

"I best get back to my ship," Jason said quietly and he stood up, putting his glass down on the side table.

"Jason?"

"Sir?"

"What do you plan to do about my violation of orders?"

"If I'm asked about it, sir, I plan to tell the truth." He hesitated. "I have to tell the truth, that you launched an attack after knowing that the initial cease fire had been agreed to. To do anything else would be dishonorable."

Tolwyn smiled.

"You're a good officer, son. I've always been proud of you; I know I always will be."

He extended his hand and Jason took it.

"Let's hope I'm wrong about this armistice, but I know I'm not."

• CHAPTER TWO

Jason Bondarevsky winced from the glare of the lights. Damn, how he hated the press. He had endured "the treatment" before when he had brought *Tarawa* back to Earth for refitting after the raid to Kilrah. The press swarmed over the ship, poking cameras in his face, asking the same asinine questions over and over again, probing far too deeply into parts of the raid he simply wanted to forget. When one had finally hit him with a question about the death of Svetlana, asking how he felt while watching his girlfriend die, he had to be restrained from punching the reporter's lights out, a fleet PR officer, all smoothness and charm, separating the two.

The press madness flared up again when Jason was presented with the Medal of Honor and yet again when the absolutely ridiculous holo movie about his raid, *First to Kilrah*, came out. The film was a humiliating embarrassment, especially since the plot had little to do with the actual raid, spending most of its time focused on his doomed affair with Svetlana, with half a dozen steamy scenes padded in. It still made him boil that the holo spent precious little time on the hundreds of others who had fought, sacrificed, and died with him. He wanted to take the damn money the producer had given him and jam it down the lying scum's throat after seeing the film, which he had been promised would be shot as a straight forward documentary honoring those who had served. The only satisfaction he got out of the whole fiasco was in donating every dollar he earned from the film to a scholarship fund set up for children of the Marines and naval personnel lost in the raid.

And now he was stuck under the lights again, all because he had taken a wrong turn while looking for a bathroom. The same lousy reporter who was far too curious about Svetlana had seen him first and rushed over, the others moving like a herd of cattle when the word spread that "the guy they made the movie about," was present as a staff officer for the armistice conference.

"So whatya think of the war ending? It's Bondevsky, isn't it?" one of them shouted, aiming his holo recorder at Jason's face.

"That's Bondarevsky," Jason said quietly, remembering how his old captain O'Brian had always mispronounced the name.

"Yeah, sorry. So tell us what you think?"

"First of all, negotiations for an armistice do not mean that the war has ended. There's a big difference between an armistice and formal peace," he tried to explain patiently. "Other than that, no comment," and he tried to shoulder his way through the crush.

"Still hate the Kilrathi, is that it? Seems like you fleet officers don't want peace," a sweating beefy faced reporter shouted.

Jason looked back at the fat-faced reporter.

"I'm a captain in the fleet. I'm a professional, I try to do my job and leave the hating to others."

"Even though they killed your lover, that Marine, Susan wasn't it?"

He hesitated, wanting to turn and belt the reporter in the face, or better yet strap him into a tail gunner's seat and take him out for a mission to see what it was really like. Though he hated to do so, he turned away and continued down the corridor, shouldering his way through the crush.

"Military's gonna be out of work, that's what's got them pissed off," he heard a reporter sneering.

He turned, knowing he shouldn't, but he simply couldn't take it any longer. He put a finger into the man's face.

"What have you been doing the last couple of years?"

The man looked at him defiantly.

"Working for the holos."

"Where?"

"On Earth. United Broadcasting."

"While you've been sitting on your fat butt and grinning at the camera I've watched hundreds of thousands die. I've seen entire continents on fire from a thousand warhead bombardment, I've watched carriers bursting silently in space, a thousand men and women spilling out, their blood boiling in the vacuum. I've heard the screams of my comrades as their fighters burned, and they were trapped, unable to eject. I've lost more friends than you'll ever have, you belly crawling excuse for a worm. So don't you ever dare say to me, or anyone else, that we want a war. We know what the hell the price is while all you know is how to stuff your face and bloat your pride."

He turned and stalked off, hearing more than one reporter chuckle and give a word of support, but most of them looked at him with a superior disdain, as if he was an arrogant ignorant child who had just thrown a tantrum.

A Fleet public relations officer slipped in beside Jason, grabbed him by the arm and hustled him along.

"That wasn't very smart, sir," she whispered in his ear, while at the same time smiling to the press, and quickly moved him back down the corridor.

"Go to hell. I'm here as an aide to Admiral Tolwyn, but I'm not going to be insulted."

"Then stick to your job as an aide, things are bad enough as is with the damned press without you making it worse," she hissed in his ear.

Jason forced back an angry retort while the other officer seemed to instantly shift gears, smiling, holding up her hand to the press, repeating that they'd have a story soon enough and finally hustled Jason through a door.

"Next time you need to find a bathroom, sir," the officer said quietly, "for heavens sake, don't wander into the press area. Those bastards are like sharks looking for blood."

"Well, where the hell is the bathroom?"

The officer shook her head.

"No time. The meeting's about to start up again and it wouldn't look good for you, a mere captain, to come wandering in late."

Jason sighed and the officer pointed him to an airlock door.

He suddenly felt self conscious.

"Do I look all right?"

She smiled, reaching up to adjust the Medal of Honor which hung from a blue sash around his throat.

"Fine, sir," and paused for an instant. "And by the way, I'm behind you one hundred per cent with what you said back there, sir."

He forced a smile and went through the airlock and back into the conference room.

For a frontier orbital base the room was richly appointed, with dark wood paneled walls, soft indirect lighting, and even a real oak table taking up most of the center of the room. The chairs around the conference table were all high backed, heavily cushioned and covered in the dark navy blue of the fleet. In front of each desk was a small ensign denoting the rank of the military officers present, and most of them were three and four stars.

The short recess was nearly over and Jason moved to his position sitting directly behind Admiral Tolwyn. He looked over at Hunter, who Tolwyn had picked as his second aide for this meeting, and Ian winked.

"Make it?"

"No and I'm ready to burst," Jason groaned and Hunter smiled.

Why Tolwyn had picked the two of them to serve as his aides at this meeting was beyond Jason. He knew the admiral's regular staff officers were seething over being cut out of this armistice meeting and Jason could only surmise that in part it was an act of friendship, to let him in at an historic moment, but also as a sort of window dressing for Tolwyn to have two of his most decorated and famous officers sitting directly behind him.

He looked around the circular table and saw that nearly everyone was back from the short recess, aides sitting erect behind their superiors who were talking softly to each other, some serious, others chuckling over a shared witticism. Most of the laughter came from the civilian side of the room. A door at the far side of the room opened and everyone rose, the military personnel coming to stiff attention as the President of the Confederation, Harold Rodham, stepped into the room. Jason had first met him at the Medal of Honor presentation and was surprised with how short he really was, something the holo films never seemed to pick up on.

"Be seated, please," Rodham said quietly.

Jason could feel the electric tension rippling through the room.

"I'm prepared to hear any last minute presentations, but I want it done in a calm and logical fashion."

Jason knew that it was futile. In any other setting, without a sea of admiral, commandant and generals' stars around the table he might even have been tempted to speak up but Admiral Tolwyn relieved him of that by coming to his feet.

"Admiral Tolwyn," Rodham said nodding his head.

Tolwyn looked around the room and then focused his attention on the civilians sitting around Rodham.

"You are all well aware that I am the most junior officer sitting at this table; perhaps for that reason it might be best for me, as a front line officer, to review one more time our objections to this armistice which you seem so intent on formalizing."

Jason could see Rodham bristle slightly.

"What you are agreeing to is a freezing in place of all forces until such time as a peace commission can be established, agreeable to both sides, who will then negotiate a permanent cease fire between the Terran Confederation and the Kilrathi Empire. At the same time you are agreeing to a freezing of all construction of military ships, the refitting of vessels currently in dry dock, and the enlistment of new personnel."

Rodham gave a curt nod of reply.

"I find it difficult at best to accept this."

"You're in the military and don't you forget that you are under civilian control, so you'd better accept it," Rhonda Jamison, the foreign minister who had been the key negotiator for the armistice announced coldly. Rodham extended his hand towards Jamison as if to calm her.

"Go on, Admiral."

"I am not a politician, I am a warrior, following in the thousand year tradition of my family who served in the ancient navy, army, and air force of Britain and the space forces of the Confederation. My family has seen the best of those moments, proud of the memory of six Victoria Crosses in our past. Tolwyns served at Waterloo, on the Somme, in the Battle of Britain, at Minsk and the siege of London and shed their blood heavily in this latest war. We have seen the best and we have endured the worst, and sir, I fear that this decision might very well produce the most disastrous defeat in the history of the human race, and perhaps even spell its eventual annihilation."

Jamison sniffed and then shook her head angrily.

"Admiral, we are not discussing genealogy or ancient history, a passion I find many military men are fond of indulging in. We are discussing real politics, the here and now."

"And so am I," Tolwyn replied. "Eighteen months ago I feared that at best the war would simply drag on forever and more likely would eventually lead to our defeat. And then, with new tactical innovations and the latest improvements in technology we appear to have not only reached a balance but in fact, for the first time in thirty years of fighting, appear to have at least gained an edge. We found two weak spots: their logistical support, and their construction. We found the ways to hit at them, to slip past their main battle fleet and we are hurting them. Our intelligence net has detected that some ships are forced to go into action with less than seventy percent of their standard armaments. We've noticed dozens of small signs. The crucial, the absolutely crucial element in this is to keep the pressure on them, not to let it up."

Jason could see the clear division in the room, the military personnel, especially the front line fleet commanders, nodding in agreement, the civilian personnel sitting quietly.

"Don't let the pressure off now, I'm begging you, reminding you that we've lost millions upon millions of our finest to get to this point. Now is when we should be tightening the screws, hitting them all out with everything we have. Until you stopped us ten days ago Operation Red Three held the promise of inflicting serious losses on the Empire — it might have permanently put them off balance.

"Might have," Jamison replied. "That is always part of your military jargon, might have. There was no guarantee. In earlier testimony today you heard Admiral Banbridge state that Kilrathi front line carriers still outnumbered ours by nearly two to one. Simulation studies of Red Three demonstrated that the probability for full success was less than twenty percent, and there was a twenty-five percent chance of a reversal and a loss of most of our escort carriers with little if anything gained. You might take such things lightly, Admiral, after all you would be secure in your heavy carrier, but I lost a son on one of those suicide missions you and your people so blithely send out."

Tolwyn glared at Jamison.

Her loss was well known and she made a point of attacking the fleet whenever possible as a result. He could feel some sympathy for her, but on the other side of the coin was the fact that there was hardly anyone in the room who had not lost loved ones in this war and to accuse him of not feeling that pain was enraging.

He focused his thoughts and pushed on.

"With support it would have worked. But you obviously don't want to give that support now."

"The question is moot," Admiral Banbridge interjected, looking over at Tolwyn, extending his hand in a calming gesture. "Red Three was scrubbed ten days ago and is impossible now to restart. Kilrathi intelligence definitely has the plans by now."

"You just don't get the whole picture, do you, Admiral?" Jamison snapped. "Do you know just how much it costs to build and launch one fleet carrier?

"Seventy three billion and some change," Jamison continued, not giving Tolwyn a chance to interject. "A full compliment of fighters another ten billion. In the last three years we've lost over one and a half trillion dollars worth of carriers and fighters."

"I rather think of it as some fine young men and women that we lost, such as your son," Tolwyn bristled.

Jamison stared at Tolwyn with hate filled eyes.

"You can think of it that way," Jamison replied, "but I and the rest of the government also have to look at the war from a financial light. It cost nearly eight trillion a year to run the war and we have a deficit of over forty trillion. It'll take generations just to pay that off. Shortages are wide spread, in a fair part of the Confederation rationing of everything from fuel to nylon to eggs is in place. You say we shouldn't give the Kilrathi a breather? I think rather it is we who are lucky to have a breather. The civilian population is war weary, Tolwyn and after thirty-two years of fighting I think we have had enough and for that matter the Kilrathi have had enough as well. I'm sick to death of the old military logic of having to waste more blood to somehow uphold the honor of those who are already dead. It's time to let the dead rest, Admiral. Let's finish it now and get on with the peace."

"I find it difficult to accept that a full accounting of the Kilrathi armed forces has actually been reached," Tolwyn replied, falling back on the second position of his argument. "I find it difficult to accept that we are actually allowing Kilrathi personnel into Confederation space as observers and in general I find it difficult to accept that our leaders would be so foolish as to actually believe this entire affair."

The civilians in the room bristled, but Rodham held up his hand and nodded for Tolwyn to continue.

"In the two years prior to your agreement to this armistice we dealt a series of bitter reversals to the Kilrathi. It must have had an impact on their morale. As you know, the young captain behind me," and he paused to nod back towards Jason, "took part in the destruction of six carriers right on the doorstep of the Imperial home planet.

"Now is not the time to call an armistice; now, if anything, is the time to jack the pressure up to the breaking point. I've heard some of you say that we don't really understand the Kilrathi, that down deep they are just like us. I don't think so. Maybe there'll come a day when we can live peacefully with them, but unfortunately it is not now. We must deal with them through strength. All our psy-ops studies have shown that if the Kilrathi have contempt for anything it is for one who displays hesitation or weakness. Even their word for such a person, *tuka*, is spoken with a sneering contempt, a word so insulting that a Kilrathi challenged with such a smear will fight to the death. And I tell you now that we are *tuka* in their eyes if we fall for this subterfuge."

There was an angry ripple in the room and even Tolwyn's superiors stirred uncomfortably.

"Only now are we really starting to learn of their political and social system. Take that information and use it, consider the suggestion formulated by the psy-ops division, plan K-7, which called for specific strikes against the holdings of only one or two families, making them share an unequal burden and perhaps cause a permanent rift triggering a civil war. Now is not the time to stop, it's the time to finish this war on our terms."

Jason could sense the frustration and heartbreak in Tolwyn's voice and looking around the room he saw the division in feelings, some present nodding their heads in agreement, while others sat in silence, their faces like masks.

"We are making the agreement on our terms," Jamison retorted sharply, her voice hard with anger.

"Our observation teams have been granted full access to Kilrathi ship yards as a gesture of good faith to see that no further military construction takes place. They're pulling back their frontier bases and limiting patrols to light corvette-size ships within the demilitarized zone. I've spent countless hours hashing out the details of this with Baron Jukaga and I know that he is just as fervent in his desire to see this war end as we are."

"He is a liar."

A bit startled, all in the room turned to the Firekka representative who throughout the two long days of meetings had remained silent.

Rikik, the flock leader of her world, stood up and cocked her head, looking about the room. The Firekka were something of a strange sight, looking like eight foot parrots one only encountered in nightmares or hallucinations after a few too many drinks. Jason looked over at Hunter, who had helped to save Rikik's life after she was taken prisoner by the Kilrathi and his friend grinned.

"Baron Jukaga is a liar," Rikik announced, looking about the room. "If you humans are so foolish as to believe his words then you are doomed. Remember my planet, the only world we lived upon, was attacked by them for their Sivar ritual. Millions of my flock died, our cities were smashed. It will be a generation or more before we recover. I cannot now believe that you will agree to this foolishness."

"My good friend," Rodham said quietly, smiling as if Rikik were an old companion who might have spoken out of turn. "Remember we too have suffered in this war. It has lasted for over thirty years. More than a hundred colonial worlds, and half a dozen primary planets have been devastated. Billions have died, billions," he paused for a moment, his features pained and Jason knew it was not an act, for Rodham's youngest daughter had been killed during the First Enigma campaign.

He cleared his throat and continued.

"Thirty years of our blood, our wealth, and all our inge-
nuity has been poured into this conflict. Think of what we
could have done with all that we have spent and lost if it
had only been applied to our continued peaceful expan-
sion into the universe.

"Admiral Tolwyn claims that the tide was starting to
turn. I don't think so. We have become like two wrestlers
of equal strength, locked in a hold neither can use to bring
his opponent down, and yet unable to break the hold of his
opponent. How much longer must this go on? Another
thirty years, another generation dead and still no end in
sight, until finally, one day we'll have bombed and burned
and stabbed each other back into the stone age?

"Baron Jukaga has offered a way out, to simply stop the
killing. It is just that simple. We simply agree to stop. I
know you in the military don't like this; you're thinking of
all your comrades who have died and now you wonder for
what? I'll tell you that they did die for something. It wasn't
victory, since that is impossible, but they did prevent
defeat. To call for the war to continue now with the argument that the sacrifice had to mean something is simply to
ask for the pouring of yet more blood on the graves of
those who do not want it."

He hesitated for a moment.

"I do not want my grandchildren to die the way my
daughter has. I think she would want them to live, to grow
up without fear and live in peace."

"They'll die, only it'll be worse. At least your daughter
died fighting, your grandchildren will die having their
throats cut for the Sivar, the way my people died," Rikik
cried, her voice shrill.

"I think that's out of order and insensitive," an aide sitting behind Rodham snapped angrily.

"One can't worry about being sensitive when the issue is
the survival of a nation or of an entire race," Rikik said in
reply. "I'm sick to death of the word sensitivity when it is a
mask for those who wish to advance their own cause at the

expense of others. If the Confederation is foolish enough to take this deal, then I will take the Firekka out of the Confederation.

"And who will protect you then?" Jamison replied sarcastically.

"You did a damn poor job of protecting us when the Kilrathi hit us last time, your fleet withdrawing 'out of strategic necessity,' I think you called it. It couldn't be any worse on our own, and I'll tell you this, there'll be more than one frontier colonial world that will go with us. You don't even see members of the Landreich worlds or the Grovsner colonies here, since they want no part of this peace."

"That's treason," Jamison sputtered, "and if the colonial worlds violate the armistice they will be disciplined."

"No, it's survival and mark my words, there'll come a day when you will choke on the papers you plan to sign here this day. And as for disciplining the colonial worlds, just try it," Rikik said with a cold laugh.

She looked around the room, more than one of the military personnel looking at her and nodding. Without another word she drew back from the table and stalked from the room, followed by her one aide.

"Old K'Kai sure has taught her niece well," Hunter whispered, waving a slight greeting to his Firekka comrade as she followed her niece out of the room.

There was a moment of uneasy silence.

"I think that continued debate on this subject will only serve to cause more animosity and outbreaks," Rodham finally said. "I thank all of you for your input over the last two days regarding this issue."

"Here it comes," Ian whispered.

"I plan to sign the articles of the armistice within the hour and with it establish a bilateral peace commission to work towards a permanent treaty between the Terran Confederation and the Kilrathi Empire. You are invited to join me if you wish. Thank you, ladies and gentlemen."

Rodham stood up and walked out of the room, followed by the civilians and staff.

"Damn them to hell!"

Jason looked over at Admiral Banbridge who flung his memo computer down on the table and stormed out of the room through the opposite door.

Tolwyn turned and looked back at Ian.

"Well, your Firekka friends sure played a damn fine scene," he said with a grin.

"Think they'll really do it?" Jason asked, turning to Ian.

Ian smiled.

"Those birds might not look like much when you first meet them, but I'll tell you this, they make the finest liquor in this corner of the universe and straight or drunk when they make a promise they keep it."

"What about that threat of the colonies not observing the armistice?" Jason asked.

"Let's not talk of that now," Tolwyn said quietly. "Shall we go watch the show?"

Though he hated to admit it, Jason found that he actually did want to see what was already being hailed as the most historic moment in a hundred years, as if all the victories and even the defeats of the war had already become secondary.

Tolwyn stood up and started for the door that Rodham had gone through. Admiral Noragami, head of the Joint Chiefs of Staff came around from the other side of the table and approached Tolwyn.

"Nice try, Geoff, but it was doomed from the start."

Tolwyn nodded.

"I heard that a little something regarding you has just come to light as well," Nuragami said quietly.

Tolwyn merely smiled and Nuragami extended his hand.

"Take care of yourself, Geoff," Nuragami said and turning he went out the opposite door taken by Banbridge. Knowing how Tolwyn felt about the whole affair, Jason was more than a little surprised that his admiral was not boycotting the signing as well.

They passed down a long corridor lined with Marine

security guards and stepped into an open cavernous hall which served as the hangar bay for this deep space base, the vacuum of space on the other side kept out by the magnetic lock field.

How many times have I looked out a bay like that, he thought, sitting inside my fighter, strapped in and waiting for the launch signal? The mere thought of it set his heart racing again. Even though he was glad the fighting had stopped, he knew he'd miss it, the adrenaline rush of launching, the pure joy of flying the most powerful fighter craft ever built. If this peace really did hold, all of that was finished. It was a strange feeling of relief and regret all at once.

"Gonna miss it," Hunter said softly, standing by Jason's side.

Hunter nodded that they should follow Tolwyn, who was slowly weaving his way through the crowd to stand with the small knot of military personnel who had decided to witness the event.

A polished durasteel table two meters wide was the only furniture in the middle of the hangar. On the table, in ornate gold embossed folders rested the armistice agreement with copies in Standard English and Kilrah. To one side more than a hundred representatives of the Confederation were present, easily outnumbered by the hundreds of members of the press. The other side of the table and hangar was empty.

A door on the far side of the hangar opened and a lone Kilrathi emerged without fanfare, dressed in a simple uniform of scarlet and gold. The press turned their cameras on him, several breaking with protocol and shouting questions.

Baron Jukaga turned, looked at them, and smiled, raising his paw in a friendly wave. The press went wild, moving in closer.

"I have a little formality to attend to first," he announced, his standard English nearly perfect and free of the tendency of putting a hissing s on soft ending words and hard k's on most others, "then we'll have a chance to talk later," and his disarming informality caused several of the press to laugh.

Behind him came yet more Kilrathi, these in the more formal garb of high officers and they filed silently past the cameras and lined up behind Jukaga. Jason noticed that there was only one Kilrathi photographer recording the scene as compared to the swarm of reporters from the Confederation side.

"We have reached agreement then?" Jukaga asked, standing by the other side of the table opposite Rodham.

The president smiled, nodded, and pointed at the formal documents set in the middle of the table.

Without hesitating, Jukaga took up a pen, signed the documents, and then slid them back to Rodham, who signed it as well. The two shook and Jukaga turned and looked back at the press.

"Friends, this armistice is but a start. Let us truly come to realize that the universe is big enough for both of us and that a permanent peace can be arrived at. These proceedings are now ended."

A cheer erupted and Tolwyn, shaking his head, looked back at Jason.

"He certainly knows his Earth history with that closing line. Let's hope it isn't prophetic as to who the ultimate winner is."

Jason wanted to ask him to explain the reference but decided to let it pass.

The crowd started to break apart into smaller groups, many heading for the refreshments arrayed along a side wall. Jason followed in Tolwyn's wake and noticed a Kilrathi officer coming up to them.

"You are Tolwyn?" the Kilrathi asked.

"Yes."

"I am Tukarg. I was in command of the carrier *Gi'karga* in what you call the Third Enigma Campaign. I wished to tell you your counterstrike was masterful."

Taken off guard Tolwyn said nothing.

"I also understand you commanded the opening of the recent action at Munro."

Tolwyn still remained silent. From behind Tukarg another Kilrathi appeared and Jason was surprised to see that it was the Baron.

He was not as tall as most Kilrathi and could even be called slight by their standards, though that was still powerful when compared to a human. His coat was a smooth golden red, and from what little Jason knew of Kilrathi blood lines, the coloring was a mark of the most noble breeding. His eyes were dark, almost coal black, but as he approached a flash of reflected light made them appear to glow for an instant with the color of fire.

"A nice quote of MacArthur," Tolwyn said as Jukaga approached. "Did it have some hidden meaning?"

Jukaga laughed softly.

"Maybe a bad choice on my part; I didn't want to imply that it was you surrendering to us."

"I understand you've read a lot of our literature."

Jukaga smiled.

"A hobby I've found fascinating. Your Chaucer's tales are much the same as our own Backrka's 'Tomes of Sivar,' about a group of pilgrims traveling to a holy shrine."

Tolwyn smiled.

"A nice choice of English works to study," Tolwyn said.

"Ah yes, you were born near Canterbury."

"However, the pilgrimage to the tomb of Thomas Becket had slightly different rituals than the blood feast of Sivar," Tolwyn replied.

"Different people, different customs, as they say, but nevertheless I do enjoy your literature."

"You've spent time then studying me?" Tolwyn asked.

"You were an adversary. I heard you led the first wave at Vukar Tag, of course I would want to know more of you."

"So you read Chaucer, is that it?"

Jukaga laughed.

"Amongst others."

"And who are some of the others?" Tolwyn asked quietly.

Jukaga smiled.

"Political, intellectual writers."

"Such as Machiavelli, Sun Tzu," Tolwyn ventured, "or perhaps some pages from the writings of Mao or General Giap and his writings on how to weaken an opponent through means other than war; or perhaps a little Clausewitz or the Alpha Centurian theorist Vitivius the Younger."

"Why those in particular? Is this a recommended reading list?"

"No," Tolwyn said quietly, "just speculation."

"Ah, another mistrustful military man," Jukaga replied, his voice pitched a little louder so that the press who had gathered at the edge of the group could hear better.

"Your assumption, not mine," Tolwyn replied softly.

"Yet another prophet of doom that peace will never work," and he paused for a second, noticing that several reporters and cameramen were jockeying into position to catch the encounter.

"Admiral, aren't we late for our dinner appointment?" Jason said, coming up behind Tolwyn, lying like mad, but unable to think of a better excuse to extract his commander.

"Don't forget, Geoffrey . . ." and Jukaga paused, "May I call you that?"

"My friends do," Tolwyn replied coldly.

"All right, then Admiral. Let me remind you that we Kilrathi have suffered just as much in this unfortunate war. We have lost millions as well. I've heard you people talk about atrocities, but we have suffered them too."

He looked over at Jason and smiled again.

"Though there were some of your warriors who did fight with honor and tried to protect our innocent women and children, even if they were 'furballs' as you so ineloquently put it."

Jason felt uncomfortable by his attention but looked back at him, saying nothing.

Jukaga hesitated for a moment as if not wishing to say something.

"Speaking of atrocities," Tukarg, standing behind Jukaga, interjected.

"Let it drop, it's over," Jukaga replied.

Tukarg shook his head.

"I had clan blood on that ship," Tukarg said coldly and he turned to look at the press.

"We have intelligence information that your Admiral Tolwyn launched an attack against one of our ships after he had already received the report that a preliminary armistice agreement had been reached and that all offensive action was to cease. Such an act is a war crime."

"An honest mistake," Jukaga said as if almost apologizing for Tukarg. "And besides," he said with a forced laugh, "now you've gone and revealed that we had cracked their latest fleet code."

"I'm sorry this has come up," Jukaga continued, "but perhaps there should be an investigation to clear your name."

"There's no need for an investigation," Tolwyn said quietly.

"Oh, then of course you are innocent."

"No, quite the contrary," Tolwyn replied, "I did it because it was my duty. Now if you will excuse me."

He nodded curtly and turned away.

The press swarmed after him shouting questions, shouldering Jason and Ian out of the way.

"Nicely done," Jason said coldly, looking straight at Jukaga.

For a brief instant he felt as if he could almost sense the contempt and then the smile returned.

"I didn't want it to happen. I know how a warrior's blood can get up. It was unfortunate but such incidents happen in war. It was best to leave it forgotten now that it is over."

"But of course," Jason said coldly.

"You were the one who raided our home world, weren't you?"

"First to Kilrah," Jason said quietly, repeating what was now the slogan of his ship.

Again there seemed to be that flash.

"Masterful; I studied it intently afterwards."

"I just bet you did," Ian replied.

"Perhaps we'll talk again someday," Jukaga said stiffly and turning he walked off, the smile returning as he waved to the cameras.

"Come on," Jason said angrily, looking over at Hunter, "let's get out of here, I need to find a bathroom."

Jukaga turned back and watched Tolwyn disappear from view, surrounded by a horde of press shouting questions. Tolwyn's actions had caught him by surprise. It was a convenient way of removing one of the finest fleet admirals of the Confederation and to discredit the fleet as well. And yet it struck him as strange that Tolwyn would allow his passion to get the better of him. It did not fit the pattern at all of a man he had studied so intently. He found that he almost felt sorry for him. How easily he had been destroyed, not in battle, but by a ruse. The ever eager reporters of the Confederation, who would now destroy a man that the best fleet officers of the Empire found to be unbeatable.

Yes, he could feel sorry for him even if he was the enemy, and that realization Jukaga found to be almost troubling.

● CHAPTER THREE

"All engines stop."

"All engines stop, sir. Hard dock to station secured."

Docking a ship the size of an escort carrier was always a bit of a tricky job, and with the maneuver finished Jason sat back in his chair and took a sip of coffee.

He looked around at his bridge crew who stood silent. The speeches had already been made earlier when the rest of the crew, except for the few hands necessary for this final run out from Earth orbit, had transferred off.

There was simply nothing more to be said.

"Secure reactor to cold shut down," he said softly.

He paused for a moment.

"I guess that's it."

The crew was unable to reply.

"Dock yard officer coming aboard," a petty officer announced and Jason nodded.

A minute later he heard the footsteps in the corridor and tried to force a smile. A lone officer came on to the bridge, faced Jason, and saluted.

"Lieutenant Commander Westerlin, commander fleet yard five, requesting permission to come aboard, sir."

He tried to be formal in reply but his voice still caught slightly.

"Permission granted," and returned the salute.

The officer pulled out a small piece of paper and unfolded it.

"By order of C-in-C ConFleet, to Captain Jason Bondarevsky, CVE *Tarawa*," the officer began, and Jason could see he had been through the ritual so many times that he barely needed to read the orders.

"As of the this date, CVE 8 Confederation Fleet Ship *Tarawa* is hereby officially stricken from active list and placed in inactive reserve. Unless otherwise noted in attached form below, all officers and crew are hereby discharged from active fleet service upon completion of all proper discharge procedures and placed on inactive reserves. Signed C-in-C ConFleet."

The officer folded the paper and hesitated for a moment.

"Sir, it's a bit out of form but I also received a note from the Commander of Third Fleet, Admiral Banbridge, which he asked me to read."

Jason nodded, and the officer unfolded the piece of paper.

"Never in the annals of the fleet has so much been accomplished by a ship such as yours. I am proud to have served with all of you. The name *Tarawa* will not be forgotten, God bless you all."

The officer handed the paper to Jason, who smiled.

"Sir, for what's it's worth I hate this job," the officer said quietly. "A lot of the other ships I don't really care about, but your ship, sir," and he hesitated. "Sir, I'm sorry I have to take over this old girl. She's a proud ship."

"So am I," Jason sighed. "Just take good care of her."

"We'll do our best."

He turned and looked back at his crew.

"Time you folks shipped off. I'll be along shortly."

One by one they filed off the bridge, Jason standing by the door and shaking the hand of each until finally he was alone except for Westerlin.

"I'll leave you alone if you want, sir," the officer said, as if he were a mortician withdrawing from the side of a grieving widower, and he silently stepped off the bridge.

Jason walked around the bridge one last time. It had been his bridge for really only a very short time. After the raid on Kilrah the ship had been laid up for a year. It would in fact have been far cheaper to simply scrap her and build a new one from scratch, but public opinion was dead set against it. During that year he'd been stuck Earthside, assigned to the fleet war college for advanced training, finishing up with a brief stint at the Academy to run their latest holo combat simulator training program. But the ship had sailed at last, only to serve in one final brief action before the armistice. Yet, it was his ship, it was in fact, since Kilrah, the only thing he really loved.

He could have stayed longer, but then farewells should never be drawn out. Leaving the bridge without a backward glance he went into his cabin and hoisted the duffel bag off his bed. The room looked sterile now, just another standard ship's room, painted the usual light green, with one closet, a bed, a desk, and a computer terminal and holo projection box. The few pictures on his desk, his brother and himself taken before Joshua had gone off to the Marines, and died on Khorsan, a faded two dimensional image of his mother and father taken on the day they were married, and a shot of Svetlana that one of her friends in the Marines had sent along after her death—they were in his duffel.

He closed the door behind him and walked down the now dimmed corridors. He passed the flight ready room and had a flash memory of his first day aboard, chewing out his new pilots, and passed on into the hangar deck. The Rapiers, Ferrets, and Sabres lined the deck and it felt strange to hear the silence. No engines humming, no shouted commands blaring over the loudspeakers, the hissing roar of the catapult or the thunderclap of engines kicking in afterburners on a hot launch. It was a silence that was as complete and deeply disturbing as if he were walking through a tomb.

He turned to face the bulkhead and the roll of honor listing all those who had died while serving aboard the ship. Coming to attention he saluted the honor roll and then noticed that the commissioning flag which should be to the right of the honor roll was missing. He felt a flicker of anger over that, wondering who had taken it down, and turning started for the airlock door which was secured to the shipyard docking station. Turning the corner, he saw a small line of men and women waiting for him: Doomsday, Sparks (his head of fighter maintenance), Kevin Tolwyn, and last of all Ian Hunter looking strange indeed dressed in civilian mufti, having been already retired from the fleet the day before. The group came to attention, saluted, and Kevin stepped forward to hand Jason a folded flag, the commissioning pennant of *Tarawa*.

"Thought you'd want this, sir," Kevin said with a grin. "Someday you might want to hang it back up again."

"Thanks, Kevin."

To one side he saw a group of technicians, the mothballing crew, who would finish the shut down of the ship for cold storage. Though the government had agreed to the armistice and with it an immediate cut back of fifty percent of the active fleet, at least they were not taking the ships out and simply cutting them up as the Kilrathi had first suggested; the military had managed to stop that mad idea. It had become a major fly in the ointment in the four weeks since the armistice, with the Kilrathi threatening to pull out of the peace talks but so far the civilian government had not budged, though Jamison was screaming for even deeper cutbacks. The inactive fleet was therefore, at least for the moment, secured, the ships hooked to orbital bases for power and maintenance. Rodham, however, had agreed to the ship's crews being paid off and assigned to inactive reserves as a cost cutting measure, a fact which meant that hundreds of thousands of highly trained personnel were being pulled from their ships and demobilized as quickly as ships were pulled from the front and sent to the main bases either above Earth, Sirius, or out at Carnovean Station.

He turned to face back down the corridor and bowed his head for a moment.

"Good-bye, my friends," he whispered, remembering all those who in a way would be forever young, and forever bound to his ship. Fighting back the tears he turned without another word and went through the airlock, his friends following in silence.

✧　　✧　　✧

"Rear Admiral Geoffrey Tolwyn, approach the court."

Walking stiffly, Geoff came up before the court martial officers and saluted.

Admiral Banbridge, as the presiding officer, stood up, his hands shaking as he unfolded a single sheet of paper.

"Rear Admiral Geoffrey Tolwyn, it is the decision of this court that you have been found guilty of disobedience of fleet orders, in that you knowingly attacked a vessel of the Kilrathi Empire after being made fully aware of General Order number 2312A, ordering the suspension of all hostilities.

"It is the decision of this court that you hereby be stripped of your rank and suffer a dishonorable discharge with the loss of all privileges and honors due your rank."

Banbridge lowered his head and nodded. A Marine captain came forward and took Tolwyn's ceremonial sword, which had rested on the desk of the court martial officers since the opening of the trial. He placed the tip of the sword on the ground and held it at an angle. Raising his foot he slammed his heel down on the side of the blade, snapping it in half. The crack of the sword breaking echoed through the chamber and Geoff winced at the sound. The Marine tossed the hilt of the sword on the floor by Geoff's feet and then stepped up to Geoff.

The Marine looked him straight in the eyes and Geoff could see that the man hated what he was about to do.

Grabbing hold of the insignias of rank on Geoff's shoulders the Marine tore them off with a violent jerking motion so that Geoff swayed and struggled to keep at attention. The Marine again looked him in the eyes.

"I'm sorry, sir," he whispered and Geoff nodded a reply.

The Marine turned back to face the court and placed the torn bits of fabric and brass on the desk.

Geoff looked squarely at Banbridge and snapped off a salute, trying not to notice the tears in his old mentor's eyes. Breaking with tradition he leaned over and picked up the broken hilt and blade of his sword, turned, and marched out of the room. After he left a side door opened and a lone figure came through it, bending low and then standing up to his full height.

"Ambassador Vak'ga," Banbridge said coldly, "The fleet wishes to extend its apologies over this incident and as you were informed this morning, restitution will be paid to the families of those killed in the incident. Admiral Tolwyn has been dishonorably discharged from the service in punishment."

"Does that mean that he will now commit *Zu'kara?*"

"*Zu'kara?*"

"How do you say it?" Vak'ga rumbled. "Yes, ritual suicide in atonement for an act of shame to one's *hrai,* I mean family."

"That's not our way," Banbridge replied coldly. "And besides, the carrier he was attacking had also launched a strike after the armistice and Tolwyn could be justified in his action by acting in self-defense. Good God, Ambassador, we've logged more than a hundred such incidents during the first day, and hundreds more since. Shutting off thirty years of war is not easy."

"So that is it?" Vak'ga snapped. "He is simply told to go away with no further punishment? With us, for such a crime, he would not even be allowed the glory of *Zu'kara,* his throat would be slit and his body hung by its heels like a prey animal."

Banbridge bristled.

"I'm sure that would be the case for you," he finally replied, the sarcasm in his voice evident. "As for Geoff Tolwyn, losing the fleet and his rank is the worst punishment imaginable. After all it was the only family he'd had for the last twenty years."

He knew that the Ambassador was most likely aware that Tolwyn's wife and boys had been killed in a raid; most of the holo news reports had played on that theme as a motivation for his spectacular career and his final downfall.

"I lost my family too," Vak'ga snarled, "or didn't you know that?"

Banbridge nodded but said nothing.

The Ambassador turned as if to leave.

"Mr. Ambassador, one question before you go."

"Yes?"

"The issue of POW exchange. A full accounting within twenty four standard days was promised on the day the armistice was signed. We have fully complied and you have not."

"For us it is no issue," the Ambassador replied. "Anyone who allowed himself to be captured has lost all honor, he is *sa'guk*, one who is already dead to his *hrai*. We do not care. I do not see why it is of such great concern to you."

"Because it is, damn it," Banbridge snapped. "We've lived by the agreement on every point. You are already dragging your feet. I demand a full reporting of all POWs immediately."

"Demand? We demanded the head of Tolwyn and you slap his wrist and send him away. We demanded the suppression of your raiders based on your frontier worlds and an apology from the Firekka for their belligerent statements. I will not listen to demands from you in turn on such trivial things."

He turned and strode from the room.

"War was a hell of a lot easier," Banbridge said darkly.

Jason looked up from his drink as Hunter came into the Vacuum Breathers Bar.

The "Vacuum Breather" was one of the favorite watering holes just off the main military base on the moon. It had an old tradition that any patron who had breathed vacuum, that is experienced the hulling of his ship, and survived, received an honorary beer mug with his name on it. The far wall of the bar was lined with hundreds of mugs. The first beer of the day was always free for such an honoree when he came in and his mug was pulled down from the rack.

Gallagher, the owner of the bar, was legendary for his love of the service. He was an old fleet lifer with over thirty years service before retiring, thus his "boys and girls" as he called them, were almost like his own family and he was always ready to loan an extra twenty, or stand a free round.

"Any luck?" Ian asked, pulling his mug down from the back of the room and coming back to settle in by Jason and Doomsday. The barkeep came up, took the mug, filled it and slid it back to Ian who nodded his thanks.

Sighing, Jason shook his head. Jobs, at the moment, were scarcer then a good bottle of Firekka Firewater. There'd been a lead that an old Victory-class transport, a ship that was already out of date when it was mass produced in the first years of the war, needed a co-pilot and flight engineer. When he showed up at the office he already knew it was hopeless. At least a hundred others were there to apply, a few of them old comrades that he hadn't seen since his days on *Gettysburg*. It was a great reunion but no job, the slots filled by the former captain of a frigate and her first officer who were willing to take pay fifty percent below standard. If it wasn't for forty/one hundred benefits — one hundred a week for forty weeks — and free housing in former barracks and training centers, nearly everyone in the fleet would be starving to death.

"How about you?"

"Same story," Ian said with a sigh as he settled down to the bar beside him.

"I always knew it'd come to this end," Doomsday said quietly, and Jason groaned.

"Damn it, man, for years all I've heard you prophesy is that the war was going to kill you. You've got eight campaign ribbons, a medal of honor, two silver stars, the Vegan Victory Award with diamonds, half a dozen fighters shot out from under you and how many kills was it?"

"I lost count after sixty."

"And never a damn scratch," Jason said. "Besides that you cleaned us all out in that poker game last night. You're the luckiest damn pilot in the fleet and the most depressing."

Doomsday sighed, mumbled softly in Maori, and

motioned for another beer for himself and for Ian who nodded a thanks.

"And I lose all my hard won earnings buying you guys drinks."

"Well, at least we're here to drink," Jason replied, raising his voice.

"Yeah, great, brother, beer money for us all from a grateful Confederation," someone announced from the other side of the bar.

A chorus of sarcastic laughter echoed in the room and then fell silent as first one, and then the rest of the patrons of the Vacuum Breathers Club turned and looked at the door.

A heavily built Kilrathi filled the entry way and though his frame was imposing he somehow looked a bit lost and nervous.

"Sire!"

"Oh god, it's Kirha," Ian sighed, coming to his feet and approaching the Kilrathi as he leaped down the steps. He started to drop to one knee and Ian grabbed him by the shoulders.

"Not here," he hissed, "and besides, remember I released you from your oath of fealty."

"But such an oath can never be truly broken, sire," Kirha said.

"Just what the hell are you doing here? It's been years since I've seen you, I thought you were exchanged or something. Why aren't you going back home?"

"I was with the first batch of prisoners to be released last week. It was a sad sight, my lord. Many did not know where to go, what to do, not sure if their *hrai* will still recognize them. I heard I could find you here and thought you might know what to do."

Ian slowly grinned.

"You saved my butt once, my friend, and I must say it's a pleasure to see you again. Come on, let's have a drink."

Kirha came up to the bar, looked at the chairs which had no place for his tail to stick through, and simply leaned against the railing, towering over all the others in the room.

"Hey, we don't serve his kind in here," the bartender growled.

"Listen, buddy, the war's over, or haven't you heard," Doomsday said quietly.

"I don't care, we don't serve him."

"Say, brother, how long you been working in this bar?"

"A week."

"If Gallagher, the owner of this dive, heard you talking like that in his joint he'd throw you out on your butt. This Kilrathi's a friend of ours and that buys him a drink anywhere we are."

"I don't care, I'm not serving him."

Kirha looked around nervously.

"If this will cause trouble, sire, I can withdraw."

"Hey, Hunter, who the hell's your buddy?" a pilot wearing the insignia of a fighter squadron leader on his lapel shouted from the other side of the bar.

"You blokes heard how Paladin and me rescued that Firekka princess?" Ian replied.

Most of the men and women in the dimly lit room nodded their heads, laughed, and groaned. Ian's ability at telling stories of his heroics was legendary in the Vacuum.

"Well, this is the furball that saved my butt. I'd have been dead along with Paladin and that Firekka princess if it hadn't been for him."

The crowd nodded their approval and several came up to shake Kirha's paw, a human ritual which he still obviously found to be disconcerting.

Ian turned back to the bartender.

"So serve him his damn drink."

The man looked around nervously, and mumbled to himself.

"What was that you said about my Cat friend?" a pilot at the edge of the group snarled.

The bartender looked at Kirha.

"Whatya have?" he said quietly.

"Scotch, single malt, make it a triple."

A chorus of laughter echoed around the room, breaking the tension and even the bartender forced a weak grin as he filled the glass and pushed it over. Ian started to slide a bill across.

"Sorry about the mistake, Captain. Keep it, it's on the house," the bartender replied and turned away.

Kirha took the drink up, and bowed to Ian.

"To peace between the *hrai* of the Kilrathi and of Humans."

He downed the drink in a single gulp and a flash of sharp canines signaled his delight. The bartender shook his head.

"I guess you're all right."

"I've waited a long time for this drink," Kirha sighed, and Ian ordered up another round.

"So what do you think of all of this?" Ian asked.

"You mean the peace agreements?" Kirha asked.

"Yeah."

"It is, how do you humans say it, warmed leavings of a male cow."

A ripple of laughter echoed around the room and even the bartender smiled.

"Why?"

"I know of this Baron Jukaga of the *hrai* of the Ki'ra. They are the most ancient of the families, their blood even thicker than that of the Imperial line. Their hatred of the Imperial family is well known."

"How's that?" the bartender asked, coming over, obviously curious.

"Before we gained space, in the Seventh Dynastic War, the family of the Emperor gained dominance over Kilrah, defeating the Ki'ra who were forced to swear allegiance. It surely would have become an Eighth Dynastic war, except for the arrival of the foolish Utara."

"The who?" the barkeep asked, leaning against the side of the bar and pouring Kirha another drink.

Kirha laughed, nodded his thanks and downed the drink in a single gulp.

"The Utara came to Kilrah offering friendship, trade, and peace. They showed us how to make spacecraft, and the secret of the jump points."

Kirha shook his head .

"As soon as we gained space we slaughtered them. They were a weak and foolish people."

Kirha laughed and pounded the bar as if he had just told an hysterical joke. His audience looked at him in silence.

"Some thanks," Ian mumbled.

"It's considered quite funny by us," Kirha said, looking around the room, still chuckling, though finally realizing that his audience wasn't all that amused.

"I guess you don't see the humor."

"Maybe something got lost in the translation, mate," Ian interjected.

Kirha nodded, looking at the bar patrons.

"I see here, yet again a difference between us," he finally said. "To us, such weakness was stupidity so pathetic that it becomes funny. I take it you don't see it that way."

"Something like that," a voice from the back of the room said.

"It is why I, and those still prisoners, roared with laughter when we heard you agreed to this thing you call an armistice. It was an act of weakness. It will cause a loss of face for you, a loss of respect that you have in some way earned by your valiant resistance against the might of the Empire. There is an old Kilrah saying, 'steel against iron is not a testing.' Though we hated you, and wished to overthrow you, still we came to see that our own courage could be honorably tested by matching it against your own. That is the way of finding honor and glory.

"Your leaders have thrown that away. When we come again, it will be with contempt and the slaughter will be brutal beyond your darkest nightmares."

There was a stirring in the room.

"And will you help them out, buddy?" the barkeep asked quietly.

"I am without *hrai*, without country," Kirha said in

reply. "I have sworn allegiance to Hunter; it is now impossible for me to ever go back."

He looked almost mournful and there were even a couple of nods of sympathy from the others in the room.

"You were telling us about this Jukaga," Jason asked.

"Ah yes, Jukaga. With the freeing from our planet and the outward rush to wars with races we had never dreamed existed, our own civil wars became a thing of the past, for at last we had found others to test our steel against. But the clan of Ki'ra never reconciled itself to the fact that it was not upon the Imperial throne, seeing this as the fluke of but one battle lost ages ago. In Jukaga this disdain became more openly voiced with the reversals of our war against you. That is something I suspect your leaders have not given full weight to."

"How so?" Jason pressed.

"The fact that it was Jukaga who made the first overture of peace I find to be surprising. It was not someone of the Imperial line. It means that he has gained enough power to actually allow the Emperor to permit him to be the voice of the throne.

"It is an interesting point of balance. The Emperor must have agreed to this peace because there was some pressure, either from your fleets, or from the other clans, perhaps both. Yet if he allows the peace to continue, without a clear cut victory, he and his grandson the Crown Prince will fall and Jukaga will rise to seize the throne their *hrai* has coveted for so long. Jukaga must know as well that if he seizes the throne, but the war is not then immediately started, he will fall as well, for the drive to killing is so strong in our blood that we will quickly turn upon each other."

"Did anyone from Intelligence ever talk to you Cats about this?" Jason asked.

"Oh many times. They were quite nice, some could even speak Kilrah, a wondrous and strange thing coming from the mouth of a human. We laughed and told them what we thought."

"And the reports were ignored," Ian said coldly.

"There is a game here," Kirha said, "and you humans are, how do you say it, *paki*, pawns, for the power play of Jukaga. I think his wish is to use the peace to somehow then blame the Emperor, eliminate him, and then successfully finish the war himself."

"You sound like you don't like Jukaga."

Kirha growled, his fur bristling.

"He and his *hrai* think my coat not red enough, my blood not thick enough; my own *hrai* is descendent from the Ragitagha," and as he pronounced his clan name his teeth flashed, his mane standing out so that he appeared to nearly double in size and the crowd backed up a bit, looking at him wide eyed.

"The Ki'ra," and he hissed, spitting on the floor, "if they think they can take the throne under the Baron, they must bring a great victory. By the blood of my clan I promise you there will be war again and your leaders are fools not to see it."

"Just like Tolwyn figured it," Jason said coldly, and he heard a lot of angry mutters of agreement.

"Tolwyn, that traitor," a voice announced from the back corner of the room, "they should have shot the bastard."

The room went silent, everyone turning to look at the speaker, who sat at a dimly lit table, surrounded by half a dozen men and women who looked around nervously. Jason could tell instantly that they were outsiders and that reaction he found to be curious. He'd been around military types for so long a group of obvious civilians in a military bar seemed strange.

Nearly everyone who frequented the place now were either the few still serving with the fleet or ex-service, easily identified by the gold star of the army, fleet pin, or fouled anchor pin of a Marine on his collar. There was also an unexplainable something else that so easily set the veteran aside, a bit of a distant far away look, from having seen the far reaches of known space, from having fought, and far too often having seen friends die. The six in the corner were not of the club.

The room went quiet for a moment and Jason finally broke the ice.

"It's a free Confederation, go ahead and speak up if you want to," he announced.

A short portly man stood up and came over to the bar, followed a bit nervously by the rest of his group.

"Doctor Torg's the name," he said, "I didn't get yours."

"I didn't give it, but it's Bondarevsky."

"Oh yes," one of the women behind Torg gasped. "I saw the holo about you. Oh, the girl you loved was just so beautiful."

"The actress didn't look anything like her," Jason said quietly.

"But still it was so sad," and she came up to Jason's side and actually touched him on the shoulder and then looked back excitedly at her friends.

Another woman in the group looked at the excited girl and shook her head.

"Say, Lisa, just back off a bit, OK."

"But he's famous, Elaine."

"I don't think he really wants the attention," Elaine replied.

Jason nodded her a thanks and then looked back at Torg.

"You don't like the Admiral, is that it?" Doomsday growled.

Torg looked over at Doomsday and then turned away, ignoring him.

"Do you know how much this war's been costing us?" Torg asked.

"I think so," Jason said quietly.

"Just under eight trillion a year."

"That wasn't the cost I was thinking of," Jason replied slowly, his voice barely a whisper.

"The Baron is right. Didn't you see his interview on the holo yesterday?"

"We kind of missed it," Doomsday interjected, "so please enlighten us."

"Why, he said that this war was nothing but a conspiracy on the part of the military to get power and make money. The longer the war dragged on, the more power your admirals, generals, and military suppliers got."

"Oh, Baron Jukaga said this," a pilot from the other side of the bar said, "how interesting, and what about their fleet? I guess they're innocent."

"Why, he admitted that their fleet and military had done the same thing too."

"Was this holo shown in the Empire as well?" Kirha asked.

Torg looked up at him nervously.

"I don't know, I guess so. He said that a full report would soon be issued by the Kilrathi-Human Friendship Committee."

"The what?" several patrons of the bar asked in unison.

"Why, it's just a wonderful idea," the excited girl announced as she walked to the far wall to look at the rows of silver mugs. "Doctor Torg is a member of the committee, he's even met the Baron."

"The Baron is organizing a friendship committee that will provide for peaceful exchanges between our peoples," Torg said. "I think he's really quite sensitive to our culture, to a tolerance for multicultural diversity in the universe, and the rights of indigenous peoples of all races to live in peace. I've even arranged for him to speak at my university on Earth about his understanding of our literature and how to strengthen our ties of peace."

"Just wonderful, I can't wait to attend," Doomsday said, the sarcasm dripping in his voice.

"I think you're being too narrow minded in all of this," Torg announced, looking at Doomsday and at the rest of the patrons who were shaking their heads.

"Narrow minded. I hung my hide out on the line for over fifteen years with the fleet and you're saying I'm narrow minded?" Doomsday snapped.

"That's the problem with military types like you," Torg replied with a superior disdain. "You forget to look at the broader issues. This war was a lot more complicated than kill or be killed. You military types just don't see the big picture, that's always been a problem throughout history. I have my doctorate in sociology, I've made a study of this war and the conspiracy of a number of people to keep it going."

"Say, I like these mugs up here," the woman who had been talking to Jason announced, going up to the wall and taking one down. The bar went silent.

"Especially the ones with the gold handle. How can I get one?"

"You get killed in action, that's how. Gallagher gilds the handle of the mug when he hears that the owner bought a permanent piece of space," Jason said quietly, and the woman looked at him wide eyed and then turned pale.

"I'm sorry," she whispered. "I didn't know."

"That's all right," Jason replied softly.

She came back to Torg's side.

"Dave, maybe we should go."

"Just a minute, Lisa."

"Come on, I think we've interfered enough here."

Torg ignored her.

"Listen, pilot, I think I know a bit more about the complexity of this than you do. As a professor it's been my job to study and interpret these types of issues," Torg said. "Just because you got a service pin doesn't mean you own the Confederation. Remember the war's over, friend, so get off the taxpayer's back, get a real job, and get a life."

Several chairs were kicked over and Jason held up his hand as if signalling his friends not to do anything.

"Listen, buddy," Jason replied. "You heard what Kirha said. This whole thing is a sham. The Baron's talking us into laying our necks on the chopping block and he'll be back with the axe. In fact I think some people in this government are so stupid they're even helping him sharpen the blade and drawing the line on our necks for us, and you'll be there to help them."

"Are you saying that President Rodham and I are traitors?"

"No, just stupid."

"If there's a traitor around it's you and people like you," Torg snapped. "It's time to shut the hell up and get behind the government. Those who disagree now with Rodham are traitors."

"I was never behind our government," Jason replied. "I was out in front of it, laying my hide on the line. Maybe you people back here on Earth have forgotten what a real gut-busting war is all about. Yeah, you've paid your taxes for it, bought your war bonds, and lord knows sent enough of your sons and daughters off to die in it."

"You're damn straight," Torg replied, "my wife's brother got killed in it, and more than one of my students, and for what?"

"For what? Listen, buddy, out on the frontier, on the colonial worlds we damn well knew for what. We saw it up front and up close. We knew that if the Kilrathi ever got through the thin line of fighters and carriers our worlds could be scorched to a cinder. I saw enough worlds like that. You folks back here on Earth maybe have forgotten that."

"Not all of us," Elaine interjected. "I want peace, and I'd like to believe the Baron, but I can understand what you're saying, Captain."

"It's Jason."

She smiled and Jason could sense Torg bristling that someone in his entourage was siding with the enemy.

"Then if you want war so damn much, why are you drinking with this Kilrathi?"

Jason started to laugh.

"You just don't get it, do you?"

"Listen, doc," a pilot said, coming up to join the argument. "If I had met this Kilrathi in a fight, him and me out there in the middle of it, I'd have killed him without a second thought and I bet he'd have done the same to me."

Kirha grinned and nodded.

"But that's my duty and it was his duty. I can hate his Empire, I can hate what it does, but I can tell you this, at least the Cats serving in the fleet, the pilots, the crews of the ships usually fought honorably. Imperial legion assault troops, now they're a different breed, but not him, at least I hope not."

"I was with the fleet," Kirha announced proudly.

The pilot nodded.

"And I respect him. At least he shared the same things I did, the fear, the months of waiting, the moments of sheer terror. I have more in common with him than I do with armchair philosophers like you who think you know about war. You professor types kill me. You think just because you get that Ph.D. you're God almighty and everyone is supposed to kneel and call you doctor. Some of the biggest fools I ever met when it came to war and politics I usually found back in the classrooms. You fill your students' minds with a bunch of crap about a world you don't even understand. You don't have a clue as to just how nasty the real universe is, and then you attack those who are protecting you from the darkness that would rip your guts out if it had the chance."

"You're just another ignorant military brute," Torg sneered.

The pilot snapped.

"I spent four years at the Fleet Academy and six years in advanced training. I have the equal of a doctorate in aerospace engineering and nine years of combat tours," the pilot snapped. "As for this Kirha, I'll buy him a drink anytime. As for you, the damn thing is I'll die defending you when this war starts again, and that kind of makes me want to puke right now."

Torg hesitated for a second, unable to reply.

"Let's get out of here," Torg finally announced, looking back to his friends. "There's just no sense in arguing with people like this."

"What do you mean people like this?" Ian interjected.

"You know what I mean."

"No, enlighten me."

"War mongers, that's what you are. You get your kicks

out of it, and then live high on the hog, taking your hundred a week pension out of the taxpayers like me. If I had my way, we'd have ended this war years ago and then spent the money for things that really count and not waste it on your high tech war toys that are good for nothing but killing."

"I thought freedom was worth something," Doomsday interjected. "Enough of my friends died for it. Enough of my friends died so you could come here and play tourist and speak your piece. That's the problem with people like you. You forget all too quickly just how expensive freedom really is and then curse at the very people who gave it to you. No wonder I'm always depressed," and he turned away.

"Now I know where I've heard your name," Torg snapped, ignoring Doomsday and looking back at Jason. "It wasn't that holo movie, it's that you're one of Admiral Tolwyn's hangers-on. He's just the type I'm talking about and he got exactly what he deserved. In fact I agree with the Baron, he should have been executed."

Even as he finished speaking he realized he had overstepped his bounds. Jason stood up and Ian put out his hand to restrain him. The bar went as silent as a tomb.

Torg backed away a step.

"Come on, let's get out of here," he snapped, trying to exit with a display of bravado and contempt and failing miserably.

He turned and headed for the door and then looked back nervously over his shoulder.

"Elaine."

"Go on, Torg, just get out of here. Haven't you done enough already?"

Torg quickly went out the door and then started talking loudly again, denouncing Tolwyn and the military to his followers.

Jason turned back to the bar as Elaine came up to his side.

"I'm sorry, Jason."

"Why don't you just go," he whispered, trying to control the anger in his voice.

"Jason," and she touched him on the shoulder.

He looked over at her, shrugging his shoulder so that she drew her hand away.

"He's a jerk," she said.

"I'd call him something else," Kirha said, and she smiled.

"Listen, Jason. There's always some people like him around."

"Well, he sure seemed like one of your friends."

She laughed softly.

"Like hell. He's a professor on some stupid committee that's supposed to look at turning over some of the bases here on the moon to civilian use. I'm up here on assignment to cover it."

"A reporter?"

"Yeah, a writer of sorts, my magazine wants me to do a story on the project. That's how I wound up with him this afternoon."

"Oh great, another member of the press," Doomsday mumbled.

She laughed.

"We're not all idiots," she replied, "and what you heard from Torg isn't what most people think. Sure, we want peace, but most of us, myself included, are still suspicious of this whole thing. And I'll tell you this, you might have your idiots like Torg ranting and raving on some campus and boring the hell out of his students but he's a joke to anyone with real sense. Nine out of ten people are damn proud of you. My older brother put in two tours with the Marines till he got invalided out and I'm proud of him. Ordinary folks aren't big on talking about it, but they feel it inside," and as she spoke tears came to her eyes.

"Well, the way the papers and holo stations report it, it doesn't seem that way," Jason said.

"You know and I know the full story never really gets told, and didn't your mother ever tell you don't believe everything you read?"

He laughed softly.

"As a matter of fact, she did."

Elaine smiled.

"Look, I've got to go," she said and then fumbled in the bag over her shoulder. She pulled out a card, scribbled a number on the back of it and handed it to him.

"That's my phone number while I'm out on assignment, and the card's my business office. I'll be up here for a couple of more days, maybe we can get together for a drink."

"I'd make a great story, is that it? Ex-hero, what is he doing now?"

"Don't be so defensive," she said quietly. "It's not that at all."

"A pick up then, is that it?"

"You wish," she laughed. "No, just being a friend. That jerk really embarrassed me. Most all of us are damned grateful for what all of you did in the war. A lot of us lost people we know. If we're buying the peace thing it's because we just want the damn thing to stop. The offer's just being a friend, nothing more."

She looked at him and smiled.

"Honestly."

"You know we want it to end too," Jason replied, "but we want it to stop after we know it's really over, and that we or our kids after us don't have to go back out and fight it all over again."

She nodded in reply.

"Just a friendly gesture on my part, no strings attached. OK?" She extended her hand.

"OK," and he smiled softly.

She shook his hand and turned to leave and then hesitated, looking up at Kirha.

"So you really think it's a trap?"

Kirha nodded.

She sighed and left the bar.

Shaking his head Jason watched as she headed out into the main corridor and disappeared around the corner. He had to admit she certainly was attractive, he always did have a thing for very slender brunettes. But then the flash memory of Svetlana hit him and all the old pain came back again. He folded her card up and pushed it under the coaster for his beer. The whole thing with Svetlana was still too close for him to want to even make a try at getting involved again.

"Think what that professor guy said is for real?" the bartender asked.

"If so you'd better learn how to serve Vak'qu, because many of my former comrades will be drinking in this place once the next war is over," Kirha growled.

"What the hell is that?"

"It makes what you call single malt scotch look like *bak*."

"Bak?"

Kirha and Ian laughed.

"It has something to do with old diapers," Ian cut in. "Let's just say Vak'qu will burn a hole right through durasteel."

"Hey, look what just dragged in," Doomsday announced and to the shock of everyone he leaped from his seat and went up to greet a short, almost baby-faced pilot coming through the door.

"Lone Wolf Tolwyn," Jason shouted and went up to join Doomsday in a round of backslapping.

At the name Tolwyn the other pilots and ex-service crowd in the bar got up and gathered around him.

"How's the old man taking it?" and the question was shouted a dozen or more times as Kevin made his way up to the bar and allowed Doomsday to buy his "old life saving buddy," a drink.

"It's been tough on him," Kevin announced quietly. "He's retired to the family estate out on the Shetland Islands. At least out there the press can't get at him."

Kevin chatted with the crowd for several minutes and then caught Jason's eye and motioned for him to break away from the group.

As they moved away Kevin nodded for Doomsday and Ian to join them in a corner of the bar. Settling down around a table which was covered from one end to the other with carved initials and squadron insignia Kevin looked around at his old comrades and smiled.

"My uncle sent me up here on a little, how shall I say, recruiting expedition."

"For what?" Jason asked.

"I can't tell you, because I don't even really know myself, but he's been calling in a lot of his old comrades and personnel to stop by his estate for a visit. He sent me out to round up some of you hanging around out here at the old base. Would you three be willing to drop down to Earth for a day or two?"

"Anything the old man wants," Ian said.

Kevin smiled.

"There's a shuttle leaving in three hours and I took the liberty of booking some seats on it for you and a couple other people I'm looking for. Transfer over to the London shuttle once you get to Earth orbit. Touch down and head to gate 443, there'll be a ground hop waiting for you there. I don't think I need to tell you that this little trip is very private, so let's keep a secure lid on it."

Ian suddenly frowned and looked back to the bar where Kirha was looking over expectantly at him.

"Got a problem," Ian said quietly and motioned to where his Kilrathi friend was sitting.

"What about him?"

Kevin looked over at Kirha and smiled sadly.

"My uncle said that poor Cat might try and look you up. I'm sorry, Ian, security is just too tight on this."

Ian nodded sadly.

"Look, let's do it this way," Jason interjected. "Your family still has that farm back in Australia. Send him there until we finish up whatever it is the Admiral wants."

Ian smiled and then reached into his wallet and pulled it out.

Doomsday, Kevin, and Jason, seeing the dilapidated condition of Ian's wallet and overall financial condition pulled out what money they had.

"That ought to be enough to buy him a ticket. Thanks, lads."

"Look, he can take one of my seats down to London, and then you can fly him to Australia from there. I'll get in contact with my uncle and make sure someone meets us at the shuttle port to take him out."

Ian nodded his thanks.

Kevin smiled and shook hands around the table.

"I'll see you at Windward."

• CHAPTER FOUR

As the London shuttle turned on final Jason found that he had to nearly fight with Kirha for a look out the window. Though he had spent a year Earthside while *Tarawa* was going through refit, he had never had a chance to get to London. He was seeing precious little of it now as Kirha kept leaning over him to look out the window.

"Ah boys, it'll be good to hear real king's English spoken as it should be," Ian said.

"Hell, you're from Australia," Doomsday replied.

"Once part of the same glorious Empire. Look, there's Westminster, beyond that the Tower of London."

"I read they used to cut heads off at the Tower," Kirha said with a note of admiration in his voice.

"We kind of gave up the sport," Ian replied.

"Too bad, I'd have liked to have seen the ceremony. You know it still amazes me how you humans could beat the Empire to a standstill."

"How's that?" Jason asked, finally relinquishing the window to Kirha and settling back in his chair.

"I always thought that you were rather soft, not a warrior's breed, no claws, no fangs, no thrill at the sight and smell of blood."

"We still get by when we have to," Doomsday said.

"Yes, I know, most curious."

The shuttle banked over on to final approach and Jason closed his eyes, the turning and decelerating of the shuttle giving him a nostalgic longing to be in a cockpit again. The shuttle touched down smoothly and taxied to its gate.

When the hatch was popped the warm damp air of London filtered into the cab and Kirha wrinkled his nose.

"How do you breathe this? It's like inhaling water."

"You should try it when a spring fog rolls in," Ian replied. The four travelers pulled their duffle bags down from the overhead compartments and went through the access tunnel into the main terminal. Kirha was, of course, immediately noticed. The basic reaction, which was typical of most people from a metropolitan area, was to act as if he wasn't there, except for lingering sidelong stares. Several people displayed open hostility, and Jason was embarrassed when an elderly man came up and spit in front of Kirha, cursing all Kilrathi for killing his family.

Kirha, displaying a remarkable degree of tact, bowed to the man, offered an apology and then continued on. As they walked down the main corridor of the shuttleport they passed a booth displaying a banner announcing that it was seeking donations for the Human-Kilrathi Friendship Society. At the sight of Kirha several members came out from behind the counter and approached him.

"Ah, friend, so good to see you," one of them gushed.

Kirha looked at them suspiciously.

"How can we be friends? We have not been introduced, our blood lines unknown to each other."

The man hesitated for a moment and then smiled.

"Yes, your ritual of meeting, how clumsy of me." He bowed low. "I am Harrison of the *hrai* Harrison."

Kirha simply looked at him, shook his head, and continued on. Jason looked over at the booth as he passed and saw the other members staring at him.

"You'd think they'd take those service pins off and get back to a real life," an attractive young girl whispered, making sure her voice was loud enough so that Jason could hear. He was tempted to say something but realized it was futile and continued on.

A tall, slender woman with long blonde hair approached the group.

"Captain Hunter."

"Why, yes, that's me," Ian said with a grin. "Do we know each other?"

"No," she said with a mischievous grin lighting her features. "I'm here to meet your friend and escort him to your home in Australia. Everything's been arranged, we have him registered and security cleared."

"How about if we switch things around," Ian replied smoothly. "Kirha can go take care of my business and you can escort me home."

"Not likely, sir," she said with a laugh. "Better luck next time."

Ian shook his head and sighed, looking over at Kirha who was evidently distressed that his friend was leaving him.

"I know I cannot ask you where you are going and why," Kirha said softly, "but I suspect it is dangerous. May Sivar watch over you and guide you through the flowing of blood till we meet again."

Kirha went to his knees and Ian looked around embarrassed as he pulled him back up to his feet and then shyly hugged him.

"Take care, buddy. I'll see you soon. While you're there, try to learn some horseback riding, you'll like it."

"As you command, my lord," Kirha said huskily.

The blonde took Kirha by the arm, looking a bit nervous, and she led him down a side corridor. Ian watched them leave looking somewhat wistful.

"Come on," Doomsday said, "you're not getting sentimental over a Cat, are you?"

"Well actually it's the blonde," Ian replied, but Jason could tell that Ian was actually fond of Kirha and hated to see him go.

"Damn, the sight of a Cat riding a horse," Doomsday said. "I'd pay good money to see it."

Walking to the far end of the terminal, where private craft were docked, they turned down a side corridor and reached their gate. A light Zephyr trans-atmospheric transport was parked outside.

"Hey, it's Round Top!" Doomsday cried, and he raced up to the pilot and grabbed hold of his hand.

"Did you run emotional therapy for that guy?" Ian asked, watching a second display of joyful greeting on Doomsday's part in as many days.

"I guess he got kind of attached to our pups."

"Like hell I'm a pup, sir," Round Top announced, coming up to shake Jason's hand.

"Excuse me, gentlemen."

Jason turned and saw a slender gray-haired man, wearing a simple pair of flight coveralls, approaching them. He looked vaguely familiar and then he realized that it was Tolwyn's old steward from the *Concordia*.

"Johnston, isn't it?" Jason asked, and the man nodded.

"I think you're the last for this load," Johnston announced. "Why don't we get aboard?"

Jason picked his bag back up.

"And might I add, gentlemen, that it'd be best, for now, to drop your old *noms de guerre*."

The group followed Johnston out the door and scrambled aboard the Zephyr. Johnston secured the rear hatch and went up to the forward controls. Putting on a headset he called in to the tower for clearance, powered up the engines, and turned the ship to head for the runway. The Zephyr gained the launch track, did a short fifty-yard roll and then nosed up, soaring up on a sixty-degree climb.

Ian looked around the cabin and checked over the half dozen other passengers crammed into the small plane and realized that several of them looked familiar.

"Vanderman from *Tiger's Claw*, isn't it?" Ian asked, and the old pilot sitting across from him on the other side of the aisle nodded and shook his hand.

"Hell, I thought you bought it when the *Claw* got it," Vanderman asked.

"I got transferred off on a two week furlough the day before she got hit," Ian replied, a flicker of sadness crossing his features at the mention of his old ship.

"Luck of the draw I guess," Ian mused, "if it hadn't been for the furlough I'd have died with the rest of my friends.

"But what about you," he asked, forcing a smile, "I saw

you go down over Draga just before we pulled out."

"I ejected and made it down to the surface, mostly in one piece. Stranded for a couple of years," Vanderman said, "kind of wild and woolly down there, with the carnivores and such."

"I've heard of them," Ian interjected. "It was a famous hunting reserve of the Cats and used for the old rites of coming of age."

"Well, it sure as hell aged me," Vanderman replied, "dodging the local denizens and Kilrathi patrols until a raiding unit dropped in for a visit and I got picked up. I tell you it was an experience."

With that he unbuttoned his shirt collar and pulled out a chain. Dangling from the end of it was a gleaming serrated tooth several inches long.

"I heard the Cats take the tooth of a nalga as a trophy. I got one with a bow that I made and hung on to it, figured if I finally got captured it might make me look a bit better in their eyes. Actually I'm kind of attached to it now."

"It doesn't look like much of a tooth," Ian retorted. "Why it ain't much bigger than my little finger. Now on Farnsworth's World there, you'll get big teeth. I remember . . ."

"The owner of this little gem's got claws bigger than your arm," Vanderman interrupted, "and you got your choice out of which of four heads to pull the tooth from."

Ian, knowing he'd get outclassed in a tale swap, fell silent.

The Zephyr quickly boosted up on a high trajectory jump, so that the breadth of England, from the Irish to the North Sea was clearly in view.

The shuttle reached apogee over Scotland and then started its long curving descent over the North Sea, dropping down through a high bank of dark clouds. Buffeted by the wind the shuttle bounced in the turbulence as it crossed over the cliffs, circled to kill speed, and then touched down hard, kicking on reverse thrusters and jerking to a stop.

"Welcome to Windward, gentlemen," Johnston announced as he walked through the cabin and unlatched the rear hatch. "Move quickly now, lads, it's a bit of a blow out there, and besides, the Admiral's waiting."

As Jason stepped through the doorway the stinging rain lashed into him, the wind driving it in almost horizontally. Cursing he grabbed hold of his duffel and ran towards the dark building barely visible in the driving storm. A portal of light showed where a door was suddenly opened and he ran for it.

Sliding on the wet paving stones he nearly fell on his backside as he gained the door and rushed in, almost knocking over the man holding it open.

"Damn, what a blow," Jason said, wiping the rain off his face and then he realized who was holding the door open and snapped to attention.

"At ease, Jason, remember we're no longer in the fleet," and Geoffrey Tolwyn extended his hand.

The rest of the group came racing in behind Jason and all came to attention at the sight of Tolwyn who smiled and shook their hands.

"Gentlemen, our little meeting was waiting for your arrival. Would you follow me?"

He led them into a semi-darkened library room and Jason was surprised to see real books made of paper lining the walls, something that had not been produced in hundreds of years.

"It's the treasure of my family," Tolwyn said, "some of the volumes go back to an age when England ruled most of the world before the time of flying. This house is nearly as old, and was built in the style of manor homes from an even earlier time."

At the far end of the library a fireplace glowed, and again it caught Jason by surprise. Wood was far too precious on his home world to be used in such a manner, but even as he looked at it he understood the strange almost primal appeal of a fireplace, the smell of burning wood, and the comfortable feeling it provided.

Going through a wide double doorway, they stepped into a broad open room, at the far end of which was yet another fireplace, this one big enough to walk into. Dozens of chairs were drawn in a circle around the fireplace, each of them already occupied and Jason saw yet more familiar faces.

"Hey, it's Sparks," Doomsday announced and the chief fighter maintenance officer from the *Tarawa* got out of her chair and came up to Doomsday, shaking his hand and then Jason's in turn.

"It's like old home week here," she whispered, "pilots, a couple of maintenance officers like myself, ship's computer officers, there's even a commodore of a destroyer group over there in the corner."

"I'd like to get started," Tolwyn announced and he motioned for the new arrivals to grab some chairs.

Tolwyn turned away for a moment and extended his hands to the fire, rubbing them, silhouetted by the flames and Jason felt a flash memory of the hangar deck of *Tarawa* on fire. He closed his eyes and pushed the thought aside, knowing that it'd be back again tonight, one of the worst of the recurring nightmares.

"To start with the old familiar line, I guess you're wondering why I invited you all here tonight."

The group laughed politely.

"We heard about your stockpile of Scotch," Ian quipped.

"Afterwards, Hunter, but business first."

The group settled down.

"It has been four weeks since the formal armistice agreement between the Terran Confederation and the Kilrathi Empire. Starting tomorrow, the peace commission starts its meetings to extend the armistice into a permanent settlement.

"All of us, especially we who fought so hard, and for so long, prayed daily for peace; for only one who fights can truly know how precious peace really is."

He lowered his head for a moment.

"And all of us know what the price might be if this peace proves to be an illusion, which I have feared from the beginning that it really is.

"What I'm about to share with you is level double-A classified information. Though we are no longer in the military I will invoke a military regulation regarding this information which is that the revealing of double-A-level classified information in time of war is a capital offense.

"We are not—" he paused "—officially at war, but I think that the level of classification conveys just how sensitive this material is. If this is something you feel might be over your head, Johnston will be happy to lift you back to London and you'll be back in town in time to catch the evening shows. If you stay, however, I expect a commitment from you to follow through on what I'm going to ask you to do. I called you here because I trust all of you. I'm asking in turn that you trust me and agree to this beforehand."

He waited for a minute and no one stirred.

"Fine, then we understand each other."

He picked up a small hand controller off the fireplace mantlepiece and clicked it. On a side wall a holo projection box hummed to life.

"The figures you see up there were only known at the highest level in the military and in the civilian government on the day the armistice was reached and, according to counter intelligence, were also revealed to the Kilrathi through an as yet unidentified mole."

He waited for that bit of information to sink in and then continued.

"As you can see, it shows actual fleet strength. The numbers in black are ships that were actively on line, the blue numbers were ships in for repair or maintenance and the green numbers new ships projected to join the fleet within the year."

He waited for a moment and then clicked the button again.

"The figures on the right side of the screen show the

Kilrathi fleet size according to the highest level of intelligence and believe me it cost a hell of a lot of lives to get this information."

Jason scanned the figures. He knew the situation was bad, but he had no idea that the margin between Kilrathi and Confederation carriers was as large as indicated. He looked over at Tolwyn and realized yet again just how much the man risked when he took the *Concordia* deep into Kilrathi territory to pull him out. The figures, however, for light craft, especially frigate class and transports were far better, with the Confederation having a significant lead in heavy transport capability.

A low murmur of voices filled the room as the group commented on the figures.

"Now I should add here, that in terms of quality, our technology in fighter craft was showing some significant edges, though they still had it over us in terms of sheer numbers and in firepower, which we offset with maneuverability and the ability to take more punishment, especially with our new upgrades which were just coming on line with the Broadswords and Sabre D class.

"But these are the key figures that I want you to take a hard look at."

He snapped the controller again, and columns of figures in red appeared alongside the Kilrathi column.

"Damn, look at that," Ian whispered, and Jason could only nod in reply.

"As you can see," Tolwyn announced, "from the day of the armistice and for roughly twelve months afterwards not one new fleet carrier was going to come on line for the Empire. Beyond that, it appears as if a significant portion of their carrier fleet needed to be pulled off line for major overhauls and refitting."

He paused for a moment.

"This crippling of their carrier construction is thanks in part to a rather neat job by one of those present here tonight," and Jason nodded a thanks, but wanted to say that it wasn't him, but rather the nearly four hundred

Marine raiders who gave their lives destroying the construction yards on Kilrah's moon that made the difference.

"Six carriers nearing completion were destroyed in the *Tarawa* raid and even more importantly their key personnel and construction equipment went up as well. Intelligence later ascertained that a high level design and engineering team was visiting the moon on the day the raid hit, wiping out some of their top brains. *Tarawa* also showed us a viable tactic for getting at the Kilrathi. You might recall that CVEs *Enigma* and *Khorsan* were reported lost, but no details were ever revealed for security reasons. The truth is that both light carriers were sent on deep penetration raids on carrier construction sites located in the Za'kathag region, killing three heavy carriers that were still being fitted out. Seven more construction sites were destroyed by other means that I'm not at liberty to discuss and in fact I'm not even supposed to know."

He turned away for a moment and reaching over to a wood bin he tossed another log on the fire and then looked back at the group.

"In other words, we had a window of opportunity which was starting to kick in and would have lasted for roughly six months to a year. For a brief period we would have, for the first time in the war, reached front line parity in terms of carrier strength and then the numbers would turn against us yet again. We might have been able to push them to the wall, though, during that time."

He sighed with frustration and lowered his head for a moment.

"Sir?"

He looked back up.

"Go ahead, Ian."

"Just how reliable are these figures?"

"I can't really tell you how we got them, but they're hard core. But now for the tough part, the classified information that only a handful really know about.

"We suspect that the Kilrathi went for this armistice for two reasons, the first the operational concerns created by

their crisis in transport capability, the destruction of heavy
ship yards and the stand down of at least half their carriers
for refit. If that alone was their reason behind the armistice, it would be bad enough. There is, however, the
second issue."

He paused a moment for effect and the room was
deathly still, except for the crackling of the fire.

"We have reason to believe that approximately five
years ago the Kilrathi started the secret assembly of a
major construction yard outside of their Empire's territory
and at this site they are building an entire new class of
ships. If this is true, we can expect that when the fleet is
completed, it might be used to launch a preemptive and
smashing blow to end the war in their favor. The key question concerning this is if indeed this fleet is real. If it is real,
and nearing completion, do the Kilrathi intend to use it to
launch a preemptive strike while we stand down due to the
armistice?"

"What kind of ships and where?" a commodore asked
from the back of the room.

"It's called the Hari," a voice announced from the corner of the room.

"Paladin, damn me, I thought you got killed," Ian
shouted, coming to his feet and running up to embrace his
old friend.

"As usual, laddie, the reports of my death are a bit pre-
mature."

The group roared with delight as the old pilot came up
to stand by Tolwyn.

"How the hell did you get out of that last scrape?" Ian
asked. "They said you were reported long overdue and
presumed dead. Hell, man, you owe me a drink 'cause I
bought a round at the Vacuum Breathers in your honor.
Old Gallagher even gilded your mug."

"It's a wee bit tied up in all of this here talk the Admiral's
giving."

"So what's this Hari?" Doomsday grumbled.

"The Hari Empire," Tolwyn said, "once existed in what

was the realm of space on the other side of the Kilrathi Empire in relation to us. More than two hundred of our years before we first made contact with the Kilrathi, they fought a war with the Hari and annihilated them. So bitter was the struggle that the Hari, in their pride refused surrender and committed suicide."

"All of them?" Sparks asked.

"That's what we've been told by prisoners," Tolwyn said. "It is a vast empty reach of space, a good thirty jump points out from Kilrah. The Hari never knew of the jump points, and traveled at speeds slower than light. They made great ships that could journey between worlds in trips that took lifetimes. When they found a world with resources they multiplied quickly, in a hive-like manner. They quite literally wrecked the planet's biosphere with overpopulation and exploitation of every resource they could find. When the planet was used up, selected members were loaded back aboard their ark ships and moved on, leaving the rest to die. Thus there was little on their worlds worth the taking, the planets they occupied nothing but mined over and scarred barren wastelands when they were finished.

"It's believed that the Kilrathi moved some of their ship construction deep into Hari territory and for at least the last four years have been working on a secret project. This information comes from bits and pieces of a puzzle, made up of thousands of little details we've found over the years—a captured shipping report, a stray transmission coming from where it wasn't supposed to. In part this might explain the anomaly of their transport shortage which appeared to be even more acute than our figures suggested, since part of their transport fleet appears to be committed to hauling material out into Hari territory for the building of this secret fleet."

"Look, sir, if this is the case, then what the hell is our government doing?" Round Top snarled. "What you're telling us is that the Kilrathi called an armistice to get over a potential gap in numbers, and once they've closed it and gotten ahead and get this new fleet ready, they'll come out kicking."

"Prove it," Paladin said quietly, "that's the problem. All I can tell you is, getting into Hari territory reminds me of this lass I once knew who was so . . ." He looked at the females in the audience and stopped.

"As I was saying, it's impossible and believe me, I know. You have to cross all of Kilrathi space, hit into transit jumps that we don't even have charts for, and then go a good thousand light years beyond. I think it's fair to assume that this here system is wired with security from one end to the other. We might be able to put a concealed Kilrathi transport or trader inside their own territory when there's a war on and a lot of traffic to blend in with, but out there, it's military security all the way in and out."

He hesitated for a moment.

"Believe me, I know," he said softly as if recalling a nightmare that still troubled him.

"So how do we know about this then?" Ian asked. "We might just be chasing shadows, our own fears and nothing more."

"That I cannot say either," Paladin replied. "Not even the Admiral here is cleared to know some of it, and remember, I worked for him before, same as you, laddie. All I can say is, the information is good, and a lot of our friends, who are listed as missing, in fact died to find out."

"Well, doesn't the civilian government know this?"

Tolwyn blew out noisily and nodded.

"A week before the armistice was agreed to, there was a meeting with Rodham, Foreign Minister Jamison and the Chiefs of Staff. The information was presented and Jamison said that it was unconfirmed, that the intelligence community and military were conspiring to keep the war going and as much as called the Chiefs of Staff a bunch of liars. Rodham finally sided with Jamison, saying that at best it was rumor, and there were always such rumors that could keep a war going, countering with the statement that Jukaga had claimed the same thing was being done by us."

"So they accuse us of it, and that balances it out, is that it?" Vanderman asked.

"That's about it," Tolwyn replied. "I'd have to add that Jamison does have the weight of history on her side. In the past, in the old Earth wars, there were always such charges of secret bases and construction sites or hidden redoubts. They usually proved to be false," he paused, "but then on occasion they proved to be true."

Tolwyn paused, realizing he could say no more in front of this group, for in fact the Confederation did have several secret projects in the works. Jukaga's accusation had caused a flurry of concern on the part of the Chiefs of Staff and intelligence, but in the end it was surmised that the Baron was merely smoke screening and had not stumbled on any hard information.

A nervous rustle seemed to sweep through the room.

"Damn it, isn't anyone catching on?" someone grumbled from the back of the room.

"Some people are, Commodore," Tolwyn replied. "Call it war weariness, I don't know. I think after thirty years people wanted peace so badly that they were willing to grasp at straws and this Baron knew how to play into it. There was an old American military leader named Marshall who once said 'no democracy can endure a seven years war,' and we've had thirty."

"Admiral, let's get to the point," the commodore replied. "You dragged us here for a reason, and not just so we could cry on each other's shoulders."

Tolwyn smiled.

"You always did get straight to the point, Weiss," and Tolwyn clicked the hand unit once more and the figures in the holo field dissolved to be replaced by a sector map.

"You're looking at the Landreich System."

"What a hell hole," someone growled.

"It's a hell hole all right, in fact one of their favorite planets is named just that," Tolwyn replied. "As you can see from the map, the forward edge of it borders on the Empire, and it's about the furthest you can get from Confederation territory. Most of the worlds haven't even reached G status for colonial outpost ranking."

He hit a couple of buttons on his controller and a number of flashing red and yellow dots appeared.

"Each red dot represents a reported violation of the demilitarized zone by Kilrathi vessels, each yellow dot by Terran or others. Incidents are happening at better than two a day. Back here on Terra they might be claiming peace, and the same on Kilrah, but the frontier regions are just about as hot as ever. There's a lot of freebooting going on, organized raiding cartels are forming and even some free corp units of ex-military on both sides, who have no place else to go, are setting themselves up as petty governments or as raiding groups.

"Now according to the peace agreement, the central government is supposed to patrol these areas," and the group chuckled, "but hell, we could barely do that when we had a full fleet and the war was on. Thirty years of fighting has caused a lot of breaking down out on the edges."

He paused for a moment to throw another log in the fire.

"They might call it rebellious down here on Earth, but from the viewpoint of the frontier governments it's being independent. They know what it's like to live on the edge of total annihilation if the Empire ever broke through, and they are none too pleased with the armistice, since if anything it means that there's no Confederation fleet at all to back them up."

A thin smile creased his features.

"So they're quietly building their own for what they're calling 'reasons of internal security,' and that, my friends, is why you're here."

Jason felt a cool shiver run down his back.

"It might not be much but it's something. I'll not call it an ace in the hole. When you look at the figures I just showed you it's more like a deuce; but at least it's a start, a backup if things turn ugly.

"Shall we say, for convenience sake, that in my current disgraced position I have been forced into a commercial venture in order to make ends meet. I have been approached by a private contractor who wishes to purchase a number of decommissioned ships that could be reconfigured for," and he grinned, "civilian transport. It just so happens that I've located five of these ships in a mothball yard orbiting the moon."

He paused for a moment.

"They're CVEs, light escort carriers, and I need some crews to run them."

Jason broke into a grin.

Prince Thrakhath stood up, extending his arms and groaning.

"So what you are telling me is that you cannot speed up the completion of the fleet."

"No, my lord," and the admiral before him lowered his head to the ground.

"Stand up and stop this groveling, I'm not going to tear your throat out. I need leaders, not dead bodies just because you bring bad news."

The admiral came to his feet.

"It's the problem with the transports," the admiral said. "We simply don't have enough to keep moving the material out to the Hari at the rate you wish for."

"But what about those older ships we decommissioned?" and he almost laughed at the thought of that. The vessels had been ready to fall apart and yet they were checked off by the Confederation observers as first line battle worthy. And even as he thought of it he realized that was precisely why they were useless. The three eights number of jumps required to get to the Hari base exceeded their need for overhauls after every two eights jumps which older ships still required.

"Couldn't we establish an overhaul base at the half way point?"

"It might draw notice. It could be within detection range if they ever slipped deep enough into our territory."

"Do it anyhow, and find a way to heighten security."

"There is another problem as well."

"And that is?"

"Fleet procedures have always been able to provide complete situation updates by burst signal from fleet commanders on a daily basis. Some concern has been expressed that the Confederation, with the rumor that they suspect something in the Hari sector, might turn their attention there and detect these signals. If they can decode enough of the signal it might reveal the existence of the new fleet."

"The range of their detection equipment isn't that good," Thrakhath replied, and then paused, "or is it?"

"We've received a couple of reports over the last year of a new project of theirs to improve their equipment. But nothing is confirmed."

Thrakhath nodded.

"Use courier ships, then."

"It is too far away to be efficient and too dangerous. The tactical, strategic, and operational updates comprise tens of trillions of bits of information right down to the need for a replacement screw. The signals back from Kilrah also send out the key information obtained by our intelligence operatives regarding all new information regarding Earth defenses. If we had to suddenly launch a preemptive strike without warning, the fleet must know on a daily basis the latest information regarding events across the Empire, the demilitarized zones, and inside Confederation space. The fleet in hiding needs this information instantly, and we need to know instantly what its needs are, a time delay of eight and four or more days is dangerous."

"So what do you suggest?"

"Keep the communications open."

The Prince hesitated for a moment.

"How secure is the encoding?"

"Our intelligence indicates that the Confederation was breaking our latest fleet code just as the armistice was reached. However, every five eights of standard days, we changed the code anyhow. We could place our latest one in, and reduce signal traffic to essentials only, keeping the burst signals to under a second each way."

Thrakhath nodded. He could see the admiral's point. If the Confederation picked up signal traffic going in and out of Hari territory, it might draw notice, but then in order to do so, even if they could upgrade their equipment, it would require a penetration into the Empire.

"Do so and inform our counterintelligence to keep careful watch inside the Confederation as to any actions which might indicate that they know something or are planning some action."

"So far we have detected absolutely none."

"There is never an absolute in war, the friction of war always causes a breakdown. You have your orders, now leave me."

The admiral backed out of the room.

Prince Thrakhath settled back down at his desk and then turned to look out the small oval window. In the darkness of space beyond he could see a long sliver of reflected light. *Craxha*, the third of the new carriers to have just completed its first transjump engine testing, was coming back in to dock. Tomorrow the first squadron of fighters, transferred from one of the now drydocked carriers would start to come aboard.

The ship turned slowly, lining up on the drydock pylon which jutted out from the massive orbital base. He sat quietly, watching the maneuver intently.

Docking a ship of such massive size was a difficult maneuver and the commander on board performed it flawlessly.

Good, he had chosen that one well.

He turned away and looked back at his commscreen, intently studying the latest intelligence report provided by the *hrai* spies of the Imperial family.

It wasn't good.

He closed his eyes, silently cursing the Baron. There was no denying that the initial plan of the Baron, to have a temporary armistice, was indeed a good one, no matter how humiliating it might be. Later, once things were finished, the blame for the humiliation could be shifted back to the Baron and away from the shoulders of the Imperial line.

It was the inner intent of the Baron which was disturbing. Already he was trying to marshal support from the other clans against the Imperial blood, while quietly working to extend the armistice far out beyond the original intent. It was obvious now that the true intent was to let the armistice continue, place the ultimate blame on the Emperor, and then somehow seize power himself. When that was accomplished this new fleet would fall into his hands, he would overawe the humans with it and thus secure victory and his own control of the throne.

The alternative, the Prince realized, was to preemptively strike on the humans right now. But the problem was that the fleet was not yet ready for that. It would be at least another six eights of days before the fourth carrier came on line. All battle simulations had shown that the full strength of twelve carriers was needed for an overwhelming victory. Beyond that, the twelve carriers would need more than forty eighties of fighters and, more importantly, trained pilots, for them to be useful. So far he had drawn pilots only from those *hrai* truly loyal to the throne. That was the difficult part of the equation. Far too many of the Imperial Guard pilots had been lost at Vukar, and it would be at least another year before their losses were made good.

If he delayed, his military strength would grow, and the humans would weaken, lulled by the false peace. That they would be so stupid had caused him to lose whatever respect he had once held for them as foes worthy of the testing of steel.

There was the chance as well that some in the Confederation military might try to get the hard evidence regarding the new fleet and its intended target. That they even had suspicion of its existence had been a blow, the information revealed by their all so foolish traitor.

Turning her had been so easy, he thought with a cold smile. Her only son had been captured during the Third Enigma campaign. That was a prize to be sure. Her discontent with the war, and her political ambitions to replace the president were known. The discreet passing of a holo of her son alive, and in confinement had broken her will. To have a Foreign Minister of the enemy working for you was indeed a great thing. She had been promised much and if, when the Confederation was destroyed and she was still useful, they would keep her as a puppet. The only problem with her was that it appeared that she was under suspicion and thus blocked from certain key information, especially regarding the reports of a Confederation secret project to build a new class of weapons. That was a concern as well, for if their side delayed, they might reach their goal and shift the balance of the war. It was another argument against delay, even though every passing day made the Confederation weaker and the Empire stronger.

Yet if he delayed, the discontent in the Empire at the humiliation of peace would grow as well, and be focused upon the Emperor by the maneuvering of the Baron.

It was a balancing act which had to be played out delicately, and he sat in the silence of his war room, lights dimmed, and quietly formed his plans.

Prince Thrakhath returned to his desk and settled back down, punching up the latest reports on his screen. From the ambassador all was still going well. The Confederation government was starting to protest more loudly about the endless minor violations of the truce.

"Look, it's all perfectly legal, you've got the papers, the titles are transferred, now get off this bridge," Jason snapped.

The lieutenant looked down again at the sheaf of papers in his hand and back up at Jason.

"Ah, Mr. Bondarevsky, I've been ordered to have you wait until the peace commission has fully reviewed this matter. You and your people are to leave this ship at once."

Jason turned away and punched into a ship comm line.

"Gloria, how's reactor?"

"Up and cooking, sir."

"Masumi, we on line yet with pulse engines?"

"Can give you maneuvering thrust."

Jason looked back at the lieutenant.

"Mister, if you don't want to go for this ride, you'd better clear the bridge."

The lieutenant looked at him and a thin smile crossed his features.

"Good luck, sir," he whispered, snapped off a salute, and left the bridge.

Jason went over to his old command chair, and sat down, a light puff of dust swirling up around him. He looked around at his skeleton crew which were manning the bridge. Normal ship's complement was just under five hundred personnel — he had only thirty-five. Nearly three quarters of a full crew were either support for the three squadrons the ship would normally be carrying, or for the weapons systems, but even without them, running the ship was going to be a chancy operation. And with only three Ferrets, and a Sabre on board that had yet to be transferred off, he felt very naked.

"The Lieutenant has cleared the landing bay," Sparks announced on the comm, "and is back aboard the docking station."

"Close off the docking collar, Sparks, and disconnect external power."

"Already done, sir, docking collar disconnected, external power cut and withdrawn."

Jason looked over at his helm crew.

"Take us out of here."

A barely perceptible vibration ran through the ship as Masumi tapped into the reactors, lighting up the nuclear pulse maneuvering engines. He felt a cold shiver run down his back.

"Velocity at 225 meters per second," helm announced, "heading 31 degrees, negative 8."

"By God, we're on our way," Jason laughed, coming to his feet.

A cheer went up on the bridge, the crew laughing, slapping each other on the back.

"Ship 2291, respond please."

It took a moment for Jason to realize that the incoming message was for him, the caller using his ship's decommissioned identification number.

The communications officer looked over at him and Jason raised his hand, signalling for her not to open a line.

"Ship 2291, you are in violation of peace commission procedures for title transfer. You are ordered to turn your vessel about and return to the decommissioning yard at once.

"Ship 2291, you are . . ."

"Turn that damn thing off," Jason snapped and the communications officer switched the speaker off.

"Helm, set course for jump transit point 17A and let's get the hell out of here."

"Come on, you two," Jason said, looking over at Ian and Doomsday and they followed him off the bridge.

Picking up a small package he left the bridge and started down the corridor out to the hangar bay. Reaching the bay he paused and looked around. It actually looked big for a change. It was, of course, almost empty of fighters, and it seemed strange to see it like this. He opened the package up and unfolded the commissioning flag of *Tarawa*. He hung it back up in its old spot, next to the roll of honor. A light film of dust was on the honor roll and using his shirt sleeve he wiped it off, stepped back and without any feeling of self-consciousness, he came to attention and saluted.

He heard a light clicking of heels and looked over his shoulder to see Sparks at attention, saluting as well. She came to at ease and smiled.

"It's good to be back with our friends, Jason."

He smiled, realizing that for the first time since he had known her she had called him by his name. It took him a moment to even recall hers.

"It certainly is, Janet."

Her features flushed a bit.

Ian coughed in a very self-conscious manner and nudged Doomsday.

"Come on, buddy, let's go clean up the pilot ready room," and the two left.

"Funny, folks back home called me by my name of course, but you know, I can't remember the last time somebody didn't call me Sparks."

She had changed so much since becoming an officer, the hard edges polished into a smooth professionalism, the dirty coveralls and oil-smudged face long since gone. She was wearing a standard B class jump suit and he realized yet again that it made her look awfully damn attractive. But he had to push that away. Even though they were not part of the Confederation Fleet anymore, he still wanted his ship run by Fleet rules, and one of them was that no personal relationships were allowed between commanding officers and those serving under them.

He lowered his gaze for a second and then looked back and her smile faded a bit.

"Sorry, Jason, I guess we're back to the old routine, aren't we? Funny, I couldn't wait to get back, but I knew if I did, I'd have to give up something to do it, a chance for you."

He nodded. He knew she was interested but maybe it was simply that the sharp edge of pain in losing Svetlana still cut a bit too deeply. The few encounters since her death had left him feeling cold and empty.

Before he could say anything she drew closer, leaned up, and kissed him lightly on the lips, the kiss lingering. Startled, he looked at her and saw the sparkling in her eyes. He suddenly felt so tempted to put his arms around her — but she drew back.

"I'd better get to work, sir," she said, sniffling slightly. "This flight deck is filthy and I'll be damned if I'll allow a launch from it before it's been cleaned up."

"I'm glad Tolwyn let me take you as my maintenance officer, Janet," he hesitated, "and I'm just glad to have you with me as well."

She looked at him, shrugging a bit awkwardly, and went across the deck, leaving him alone.

He exhaled hard and shook his head.

"Captain?"

"On the flight deck."

"We've got a laser hookup from CVE 6 *Normandy*."

"Patch it through to flight operations bridge."

He double-timed over to the flight bridge and climbed up into the empty room. The control positions were all empty and it seemed eerie with not a single soul around. He switched on a comm channel and a holo image formed.

"How're you doing, laddie?"

"Little complaining from the decommissioning crowd, but we're away and clear."

Paladin smiled.

"Even though those papers are nice and legal like, we are bending a couple of the rules a wee bit," he said with a laugh. "I'm coming up now off your starboard beam, *Iwo* and *Wake* and *Crete* are clear as well. How's *Tarawa* look?"

"Everything nominal. We got a bonus of four fighters on board her as well. The mothball maintenance seemed pretty damn good, all things considered, but I feel awfully naked without at least one squadron aboard."

"One thing at a time, laddie. I've got to get off the line now, I'm getting a bit swamped here with calls from those peace commission buggers, and even one now from Con-Fleet. I tell you it'll be right good fun telling an admiral to go to hell. They've got a couple of frigates out at the jump point who might try to stop us, but we've got a dozen lawyers out at headquarters arguing away right now that the sale is legal. Hopefully nobody'll shoot. Hell, by the time they get it resolved we'll be on the other side of the universe. And then what are they going to do, sue us?"

Laughing, he shut down the laser link and the holo screen went dead.

Stepping down from the flight bridge Jason saw the pinpoint of light of Paladin's ship moving against the eternal night of space.

"Captain, this is helm."

"Go ahead."

"Cleared of near Earth orbit, ready to power up to full pulse drive on course heading for jump point 17A."

"Get us out of here, then."

He felt the surge of power rumble through the ship as nearly all reactor power was feed straight into the engines. The ship turned to line up on the jump point and as he walked up to the hangar bay's magnetic airlock, Earth drifted into view, a crescent blue-green ball hanging in the eternal darkness. It gave him a curious sort of feeling. It was, after all, the home world of his entire race, the Russia of his ancestors clearly visible even from half a million clicks out, and yet now, he felt strangely detached from it. He was a product of space, born on a world five hundred light years away. If he had a home, it was this ship, a family, the people aboard her. He knew that this insane adventure he was setting out on was motivated in part by his allegiance to the Confederation and for the protection of the world in front of him, even for the protection of those people who were so ready to reject him and the military that he served. He knew that perhaps that was always the lot of a warrior, to be turned to when trouble loomed, and to be rejected and hidden away when it was believed that peace had returned.

He was fighting for them but he realized as well that if he were fighting for anything it was for his ship, his comrades, and the fleet which they had so loyally served and now faced the most serious crisis in its history, a crisis created not so much by their enemies, but rather by their friends.

● CHAPTER FIVE

In a swirling cloud of dust, Hunter switched off power on his engines, shut down the emergency ejector system, and cracked the canopy open.

A choking swirl of hot dry air rushed into the cockpit, taking his breath away as he unsnapped his helmet.

"Damn, even worse than the outback," he mumbled, standing up to stretch.

A ground crew team strolled over, lazily pushing a ladder as he waited. There was no sense in getting upset by their lackadaisical attitude, this wasn't ConFleet—the base belonged to the Landreich Colonial Air Guard and a crew working in one hundred twenty plus heat had his sympathy.

The crew hooked the ladder against the side of his Sabre and he scrambled down out of the cockpit.

"Where's fleet headquarters?" he asked.

"Over there," one of the crew announced, trying to be heard above the cacophony of ships landing and taking off, and the sudden sonic boom of a Ferret snapping by overhead, the shockwave causing him to wince and instinctively look for cover.

He looked up and saw the Ferret climbing straight up, standing on its tail. The Ferret punched a hole through the high thin overcast and then he was gone, the ship's vapor trail climbing and then winking out as the Ferret crossed into the far reaches of the upper atmosphere. The crew barely noticed the show and obviously weren't running to combat positions.

"Is there a scramble on?"

"Nay, Charlie Boy's just having a little fun."

"Who's Charlie Boy?"

"Why, he's the head of the squadron here."

Ian wanted to comment that at any fleet base punching sonic without a scramble on would have cost Charlie Boy a month's pay and a possible grounding. He had a feeling it was, if anything, a thumbing of the nose at all the outsiders gathering on the base and he started to smile. Hell, he might even like this place after all.

The ground crew looked at him and Ian was suddenly aware his old ConFleet flight suit made him stick out like a sore thumb.

"A lot of you Fleet boys showing up here today," one of the crew drawled.

"The usual gab session," Ian replied. "You know how it is, ConFleet or Colonial, the big wigs always like to have their meetings."

"And I suppose we oughta salute you, is that it, captain?"

Ian laughed and replied with a universal rude gesture.

One of the crew members smiled, reached into a tool box and pulled out a can which was dripping with moisture.

"Have a cold one on us, cap'n."

Ian grinned with delight as he popped the lid. Landreich beer was rated almost as good as the Outback Lager and Fosters of home. He took a long deep pull on the can and then another, draining it off. With a contented sigh he tossed the empty back to his benefactor.

"Ah, thanks, mate, now take care of my ship and by the way, if you don't tell those customs people, you'll find a pint of Vega's best stashed in the carry bag strapped behind my seat and I don't want to find it there when I get back." The crew grinned.

There was nothing like a little gift giving with the locals to make sure that things were taken care of right.

Turning, he started across the landing field, eager to get to the shade. The twin suns of the planet were murder when both were at noon, the red giant and white dwarf combining to cast a strange pattern of colored shadows. He looked around, realizing that this military outpost of the Landreich colonial worlds was definitely at the butt end of the universe. There were a few modern buildings on the base, made of the standard poured plasta-concrete. But most of it, and the small garrison and mining town beyond the base, was made of either adobe or rough sandstone. If it wasn't for the rich titanium deposits underneath the surrounding mountains this world would have been bypassed except for the usual crop of hermits, crazy cults, and freebooters looking for a place to hide. Buford's World they called this place, after the first prospector to land here, but it was more commonly referred to as the Hell Hole. Its inclination of axis was exactly at zero degrees and there was no season except red hot summer with 90 degrees passing as a cool day.

It had but two jump points in the system, one heading away from the demilitarized zone towards the capital world of Landreich, the other leading off on a long lopping pattern through half a dozen uninhabited systems into the flank of the Kilrathi Empire. Both in a strategic and tactical sense it was nothing more than an outpost at the very edge of the war and totally ignored by the main fleets of both sides. Thus space in this region was controlled, if at all, by colonial guards of both sides, and more often by freebooters which, in the eyes of the Confederation, was what the Landreich system was anyhow.

He passed a plasta-concrete bunker, the lid partially open to reveal a cluster of surface-to-space point defense missile-anti-missiles, the latest Sprint 8s, no less. He paused to look in at the crew which was running a service check.

"Got a lot of those, mates?"

"Who the hell wants to know?" and a tech sergeant, wearing the tan coveralls of a colonial guard non-com looked up at him, shading his eyes.

"Hey, just curious, that's all."

"Curiosity like that will get you in the brig right quick," the sergeant growled.

The sergeant turned back to his work and Ian realized that maybe it was best to simply move on.

Tucked into the hangars lining the field was a bizarre assortment of ships. The heaviest was a medium corvette and it took Ian a moment to recognize it as an old Granicus-class, a line discontinued more than twenty years ago. The ship, however, was refitted with a couple of E-8 engines attached to anchor points on the side of the hull, with half a dozen mass driver turrets patched on as well. It was a hell of a smuggler's craft with the firepower of a light frigate thrown in. A number of fighters were on the field as well and it was easy to see which ones had ferried in the staff attending today's meeting, their Confed insignia simply painted over with standard fleet gray.

It was the other ships, however, that caught his eye. It looked like the Landreich was planning to set up a museum, with some of the fighters actual prewar ships of more than thirty years vintage. All of them, however, were no longer spec in any way whatsoever. An early Ferret A had a new engine housing with of all things a Mark 10 engine off an old Falcon light corvette. It looked absolutely absurd, like nothing but an engine with a cockpit up front, with a gatling mass driver gun strapped on underneath. It'd be a hell of a ride, he realized.

Most of the ships were painted Stealth black without identification numbers or even the blue circle and red Saint Andrew's cross of the Landreich. He slowly walked past the hangars, noticing the less than friendly stares of most of the crews. He wanted to take the time to go up and chat, to ask about the specs on the strange array of ships, maybe even try a climb into the cockpits but thought better of it. Ever since the armistice the uneasy cooperation of the Confederation with the colonials was now strained even further. He couldn't blame them, for when the stuff finally hit the fan, it would be the outpost worlds that would get covered by it first.

"Iannn!"

The high pitched voice was unmistakable and startled he looked around, and then noticed a shadow cross over him. He looked up and saw a Firekka hovering overhead.

"K'Kai, how the hell are you!"

K'Kai, folding her wings, landed beside him and moved up close, pecked him lightly on the head and around the back of his neck in what he now knew was a grooming which served as the Firekka equivalent of a handshake. Overjoyed at seeing an old friend he threw his arms around her.

"Last time I saw you was when your niece told the Confederation to go to hell."

K'Kai clicked her beak and he knew that it was the Firekka equivalent of an expression of pride.

"That speech was hers alone, a fine accomplishment for not much more than a hatchling."

"How goes it on Firekka?"

"A lot of harassing raids, skirmishes, ships disappearing, not really outright war, but definitely not peace." She cocked her head and looked at him closely, an act which he always found a bit disturbing when an eyeball the size of an orange aimed in straight at him.

"So you're part of this Landreich colonial fleet?" she asked.

"That's what I'm here for, and you?"

"Sent as a representative."

"Well, I think we're late," and he motioned for her to follow along.

They finally gained the shade of a broad veranda and he drew a breath of relief. Two guards stood at the door and again it struck him how different the colonials were. The men looked sharp enough, with standard M-48 laser rifles on their shoulders. But the uniforms looked like they'd seen better days, the tan coveralls faded from sun and washing, top collars unbuttoned in the dry desert heat. They lacked the spit and polish of fleet Marine guards and he found it appealing.

Both looked with open curiosity at K'Kai.

"Firekka, they make the best drink in the universe," Ian announced, and the guards grinned weakly.

"I take it this is headquarters?"

"This is the place."

"Well, I'm here to see Kruger."

A sergeant stepped out from inside the doorway, took their papers and IDs, then handed them back.

"Down the hall, you can't miss it."

Ian opened the door for K'Kai and followed her in. At least the place had cooling, but it seemed to be barely working. He strode down the open corridor which angled down below the surface, K'Kai at his side. They turned through a double set of blast doors and into the situation room which was packed nearly to overflowing. They were stopped by what he assumed was a security officer, though it was hard to tell by the uniform. He checked their IDs once again and then marked off his and K'Kai's name on a list.

Ian immediately recognized more than one of those present: Jason and Doomsday, who had flown down the day before from *Tarawa*, were in the back corner engaged in what was obviously a heated conversation with several colonial pilots. Sparks, waving a hand computer unit, was shouting at whom he guessed was a supply officer, who in turn was shouting back with equal vigor, and hunched over a table up in the front was a tall gaunt man with sun scorched features and dark eyes. He glanced up at Ian and his gaze seemed to pierce right through him and then, as if he didn't even exist, the man looked back down at a shelf of printouts.

"Say, that's Kruger himself," Ian whispered.

K'Kai bobbed her head.

Technically Kruger was a wanted felon within Confederation territory, having once hijacked his fleet destroyer, which he was in command of, during the early days of the war, when through "strategic necessity," the old C-in-C ConFleet had decided to abandon the Landreich system in the face of a Kilrathi offensive. Using the ship and an assortment of scrounged up freighters and smuggler craft he fought the battle of the Hell Hole, stopping a Kilrathi attack into this sector and according to legend chased them back through twelve jumps.

His own ship was blown out from under him on the last jump through by a Kilrathi ambush and Kruger, with the remaining members of his crew, survived for three years on a planet inside the Kilrathi system, driving the locals nearly insane with his commando style raiding until being picked up by a freebooter who took them back to the Landreich. In the interim, ConFleet had tried him in absentia and found him guilty of mutiny and hijacking of a Confederation warship, a capital offense in time of war. He was hailed, however, as a returning hero by the colonials and elected president of the Landreich system within the year. The election made matters somewhat complicated, presenting the Confederation with the unique problem of having a felon serving as an elected member of the planetary senate and thus being immune from arrest and trial.

Max Kruger had a hell of a reputation and was viewed either as a genius improviser of small unit irregular tactics or a barbarian. In Ian's opinion, he was both. The colonials definitely fought their wars with the Kilrathi, and at times with each other, using cast-off equipment, shoestring budgets, and a hell of a lot of guts. They also fought it with a cold ferocity that rarely asked for or expected quarter. For Kruger there was only one rule of war, ultimate victory.

"Everything back aboard *Tarawa* OK?"

Ian turned and smiled as Jason came up to join him.

"Another hundred crew members signed in last night off a transport that ran out from Sirius. We've got eight more pilots and four Ferrets that were strapped to the transports hull."

"Is that all, we were promised twenty."

"They had some problems getting the four, the peace commission kicked up a royal stink. We're lucky we got what we did."

"It figures," Jason sighed. "That commission really screwed us up."

"What do you mean?"

"That report that we'd have ten squadrons of Rapiers and Sabres, well forget it."

"What the hell happened?"

"The shipment was blocked by the commission. Seems that the Kilrathi ambassador caught wind of the deal, screamed holy hell, and the Baron even got into it, threatening to end all peace negotiations if the ships were allowed to leave Earth system. Rodham, of course, caved in. The three transports, loaded down with fighters and spare parts were blocked from leaving moon orbit. So now we've got to scrounge up whatever we can find around here."

"We've got five escort carriers, and a grand total of twenty-nine fighters and that's it, not counting the stuff the locals have."

More people crowded into the room behind Ian so that he, Jason, and K'Kai were gradually shoved to the back of the room.

"Andrews, everybody here yet?" the gaunt man asked, looking over at the guard at the door.

"Near about."

"Well, damn it, we can't wait, let's get started then."

The gaunt man moved up to a small podium.

"For those of you Confed people who don't know it, I'm General Kruger."

Ian looked around the room and saw the outright admiration on the faces of the men and women wearing the hodgepodge of jumpsuits, assault trousers and vests, and coveralls that passed for colonial guards uniforms.

"First off, I welcome all you white and blue suits into the service of the Landreich," Kruger began. "As already agreed upon, all ships that the Landreich has purchased," and with that there was a ripple of laughter from the colonial personnel, "have been incorporated into our fleet. You will, however, still have your own chain of command, answering to Admiral Tolwyn."

For the first time Ian realized that Tolwyn was in the

room, his nephew by his side. Tolwyn stepped out from a back corner of the meeting hall and raised his hand in acknowledgement. It seemed strange to Ian to see the Admiral not in standard fleet uniform, but in the khaki of a Landreich officer.

Just how the hell did he get out here so fast? Ian wondered, what with Jason's ship arriving only last night into orbit above Landreich.

"Those of you in colonial forces that are assigned aboard former Confed ships will take orders from the duly appointed commander of that ship."

A low groan went up from the colonial personnel in the room.

"We've got to coordinate this effort," Kruger snapped, "so no complaints.

"Any questions?"

The colonial officers looked at each other, mumbled a bit and said nothing.

Kruger nodded towards Tolwyn, who came up to the front of the room.

"Well, I'm glad to see that most of you at least made it out here.

"First off . . ." and Tolwyn was interrupted by the sharp spine tingling wail of a klaxon.

The room went quiet as Kruger raced to a monitor, leaned over it, and then turned back.

"Any pilots with strike craft please man them immediately."

Ian pushed his way out of the room, a stream of colonial pilots pushing around him, Jason, Kevin, and Doomsday falling in at his side.

They ran up the corridor and out into the blazing heat, scattering towards hangars, the high wail of sirens echoing against the surrounding hills. The ground crew, which had so lazily come out to meet Ian when he landed, were moving with a cool precision, unchocking the wheels, the crew chief inside the cockpit, the engine already up and whining, four crew members lifting two missiles up onto the

Sabre's wing pylons. Ian ran to the ladder, one of the ground crew tossing him his helmet which he snapped on, the chief coming down the ladder and clearing it just as Ian leaped on to the third rung and scrambled up, the chief now behind him. Ian saw Jason and Doomsday running past, heading for the Ferrets they had flown down from *Tarawa*.

"Engine green, nav system loaded by combat control, all weapons green with two radar trackers loaded, emergency eject armed and ready, good luck, sir!" the chief shouted, even as he reached over and helped buckle Ian's safety harness on, cinching the shoulder straps tight.

"This is Hunter in Sabre 239A ready," Ian announced to the control tower.

"Will advise, Hunter, ground chief will signal your clearance," the ground control officer snapped and then switched off.

Ian gave a thumbs-up as the chief slid down the ladder and the canopy snapped shut, the green light of airtight lock flashing on. The chief was now out in front of Ian's fighter, hands held high over his head with fists crossed, signalling that the taxi ramp was not yet cleared. The Ferret with the light corvette engine he admired earlier bolted straight out of its hangar to his right, not even bothering to go for the runway and not needing one anyhow as it pitched its nose back, and within fifty yards stood on its tail, flame slamming off the concrete taxiway as it screamed straight up into the sky, riding a column of fire.

To his left he saw the armored bunker which contained the surface to space missiles peel open, the silver tips of half a dozen Sprints pointing straight up.

"Hunter cleared for takeoff, once lifted depart angle nine zero," the control officer's voice crackled in his headset and he grinned with the order to go for a full burn vertical ascent into space.

The crew chief uncrossed his arms and leaped to the side of the Sabre, crouched, and pointed forward. Ian released his brakes, slammed in full afterburners and all aft maneuvering thrusters. The Sabre leaped forward and within seconds he was up past a hundred and ninety clicks an hour. He yanked back on his stick, pulling it into his gut, the nose lifted up and he was off.

Ian toggled up his landing gear as his Sabre pointed straight up into the red sky, the altimeter spinning. Inertial dampening didn't work all that well inside the gravity well of a planet and he started to breathe in short convulsive grunts as the Gs built up. He knew his sonic boom was blasting out across the landscape but it was almost silent inside the cockpit except for the teeth-rattling rumble of the twin Tangent-class engines burning white hot behind him. He punched through the thin clouds and the color of the sky shifted, turning from a deeper red into violet, the first stars starting to appear. He looked to his left to see the curvature of the world and what looked like another Ferret rising up to close on his port wing.

"Combat information, this is Hunter, what's the trade today?"

"Forward scouts report detecting an ionized trail emerging from Jump Point Beta 233. There have been weak radar detects and one laser scan lock indicating a fighter of Kilrathi Stealth design is approaching. Patrol grid is already fed into your auto-nav. If you encounter unknown you are cleared to shoot to kill without warning."

"Just what I wanted to hear," Ian replied as he locked in on the auto nav system and released his controls, the autopilot taking over. Cleared into space, and with fuel scoops closed he continued to accelerate so that within minutes the full sphere of the Hell Hole hung in space behind him.

The attempt to ship fighters to the Landreich was known by the Kilrathi thanks to the peace commission and a scouting attempt had to be expected. At least the colonials didn't fool around with diplomatic niceties, Ian thought. If someone violated their space in a suspicious manner they were taken out, no questions asked.

He scanned the comm channels, listening in as pilots

tersely called out their check points and the search spread outward. The frustrating part of it was that unless they had some really good luck, they could very well pass right over a Stealth and not even know it. The mere fact that the Empire was sneaking a very precious and rare fighter into this sector meant that they had a good idea of what was going on.

He heard a call of a brief contact by Doomsday and then two more by colonial pilots, in each case the Stealth was lost. Punching into his nav computer he checked the three sightings and then overlaid the points into a map of the system.

"Combat control, request break of my standard sweep, wish to investigate region around coordinates 233 by ADF."

"Will advise," and the link clicked off.

A moment later it crackled back to life.

"This is Kruger, good thinking, Hunter; proceed at your discretion."

Grinning, he broke off the auto nav, opened his fuel and maneuvering scoops, and turned. The coded coordinate was the location, at the moment, of the Hell Hole system's largest planet, a gas giant named Thor. The three brief sightings roughly matched a standard Kilrathi evasive maneuver called the reverse claw, and it pointed towards Thor, which would be an excellent place to hide out until the patrols simmered down.

Punching in the new nav coordinates, Ian closed his fuel scoops and within minutes was up over three thousand clicks a second and climbing. Thor was nearly twenty million clicks away and he settled back, nearly dozing off as the Sabre closed, half listening to the commlink chatter as the scrambled forces continued to prowl for the needle in a very big haystack.

Approaching within a million clicks of Thor he finally started into reverse thrust, extending his fuel scoops to create drag. The stray hydrogen atoms found in space impacted on the energy field surrounding his ship and were then swept into the fuel tank. Each strike slowed him down by an ever so minute fraction, which built up with each passing second.

He started a close scan of his instruments, knowing that any sweep radar was next to useless.

"Now where would I go," he whispered, as if he could almost be heard by his opponent and he felt that prickly uneasy feeling, knowing that somehow the Kilrathi was near. He had learned never to discount "the gut feeling." Any fighter pilot who did not believe in the instinctive feel usually didn't live very long.

Too close into Thor, he reasoned, and the passage of the ship would be noticeable as a disturbance in the intense magnetic fields. If he went into the atmosphere he'd kick up the soup and really give himself away. The one advantage of chasing a Stealth, Ian knew, was that he was just as blind, running on scan shut down, otherwise he'd be given away. He spared a quick look at the map of the system. Two moons, one nearly the size of Earth's, the other half the size.

Get into the lee of the orbit of the moon is what I'd do, Ian thought, blocking direct approach from one entire side, hide out and then wait for the patrols to give up before a final run in on the recon sweep.

But which one? If he had had a coin on him he would have flipped it. Ian shrugged his shoulders and started for the smaller of the two, shutting down all scanning systems. He maneuvered so as to approach the moon from the forward side relative to its orbital direction. He throttled back and then came in a mere hundred clicks above the surface, crossing up over the pole and moving down the other side.

Ian punched up a full high intensity burst scan, diverting nearly all ship's power into radar. If there was anyone within a million clicks the radar burst would damn near rattle the fillings out of his head, Ian thought, suddenly wondering if the Kilrathi even had fillings. He waited, watching his screen. The trick was that, even if it didn't detect a Stealth, it just might panic the pilot into thinking that he had actually been found.

There! Just under two thousand clicks away. Damn, he had found the needle!

A faint echo blipped on his screen, the computer working to gain a lock, narrowing the radar beam down and firing off another pulse, this one concentrating nearly all the energy of the previous pulse into a narrow cone. It was enough energy to fry out every circuit on an unshielded vessel a hundred thousand clicks away.

The second burst hit, painting the enemy ship clearly on his screen at a range of eight hundred clicks. The target acquisition computer, upgraded to handle Stealths, threw a laser lock on the ship. The lock hung on and held as the pilot fired up to full throttle and went into evasive.

"Combat control, this is Hunter. Got him! One Kilrathi Stealth, on his tail and closing."

A high pitched whine suddenly cut in on his headset. The Kilrathi had dumped three missiles which Ian's computer told him were IFFs. Ian countered by punching in an IFF scramble. In a full running fleet engagement such an act would be suicide because the moment his transponder switched there was still no guarantee that the enemy missile which had already gained lock would veer away. On the other hand, everything else flying around, either human or computer guided, would assume that he was not on the same side and act accordingly—but out here it was a safe maneuver.

The computer raced through thousands of possible transponder codes, searching for the right one to throw the missiles off, but they kept closing. Ian toggled off a guided bolt in return, which used the laser beam as a guide in to its target.

He continued the chase, running blind. There was nothing to see, only a blip on the screen.

The Kilrathi ship suddenly dropped out of Stealth mode, flashing full visible, and at the same instant Ian picked up a high energy burst signal. The pilot was good,

he realized, never forgetting his mission, even while trying
to evade death. Whatever he was sent here to find out, he
was making sure word got out.

"Combat control, bogey has sent burst signal, repeat,
bogey has sent burst signal."

The first incoming missile closed in. Ian nosed over
hard and then banked back up, the missile jinxing down to
follow and then shooting past. The second and third missiles, momentarily thrown off by his attempts at jamming,
regained lock but missed as well due to the same maneuver. Ian felt the sweat streaking down the small of his back.
His own bolt was leaping forward, guiding straight in.

There was a brilliant flash of light as bright as the sun
and then darkness. It took Ian a second to realize that his
own missile was still a dozen clicks away. The Kilrathi had
self-destructed with a small matter/antimatter warhead,
vaporizing himself and his ship. Now there would never be
any evidence at all of the violation of the armistice since a
missile hit tended to leave a lot of wreckage behind which
could be evaluated later.

Watching the ship, he momentarily forgot what was
now behind him, and suddenly a high undulating warble
sounded in his headphones. One of the IFFs had turned
around, regained lock and was closing straight in.

He punched hard over, aiming straight back towards
the moon, popping out chaff and a noise maker. He turned
his transponder off completely, slamming off all energy
sources.

The damn thing kept closing, following his every turn
and then a high energy ping sounded.

What the hell was this?

"Combat control, combat control!"

"Control here."

"Kilrathi seem to have new prototype weapon. It's
ignoring chaff and noise maker. It registered first as an IFF
missile but the damn thing must have a smart weapon program that continues to recognize its target once locked,"
Ian shouted, realizing that even if he bought it, it was

essential that his friends knew exactly why and learned from it. It was part of the training and it was loyalty as well.

He had no tail gunner to pop the missile at the last second, or wingman to peel it off his back, or the mad confusion of a hundred fighters and ships filling space with metal and energy. He was naked and alone, the IFF following remorselessly, like a cold deadly shark that could kill without thinking or feeling.

He skimmed down over the moon's airless surface, weaving a low sharp turn into a narrow canyon and the missile impacted against the side of cliff behind him. He breathed a deep sigh of relief and then a second warble kicked in, showing that another of the missiles had regained lock as well.

Damn!

The missile was above him, streaking down. He blew his remaining chaff and the missile streaked straight through and closed. He was boxed in.

The warble climbed in tone and then plateaued on a high spine-tingling pitch, the warning of an unavoidable impact.

He yanked his stick back hard, popping up off the moon's surface, then reached between his legs, grabbing hold of the ejector D ring and pulled, even as the explosion engulfed him.

"I think we know why we are here," Baron Jukaga said, his voice quiet, low pitched, his mane lying nearly flat so as to show neither dominance nor submission.

"It is the fault of the *hrai* of Vak," Qar'ka Baron of the Qarg clan hissed, springing to his feet and pointing accusingly across the table.

"Low born scum," Vak snarled in reply, reaching for the claw dagger at his belt.

"Silence!" Jukaga roared. "Damn all of you, I want silence!" and his golden red mane bristled up.

The two stopped and turned, fixing the Baron with hate-filled eyes.

"Jukaga, either one of us could cut your guts out and spill them on the floor for the rats to eat," Vak said coldly. "You of the Ki'ra *hrai* are weaklings compared to either the Qarg, the Ragitagha, or any of the other families."

"And if you did," Jukaga replied smoothly, "then you truly would have civil war and the humans would finish up with what was left."

"Sit down," Baron Ka'ta of the Kurutak clan hissed, "Baron Jukaga is right. Let us listen to him first."

Jukaga nodded his thanks to Ka'ta. At least he knew that the Ka'ta out of all the eight families of the Empire was solidly behind him. It was almost amusing. The Kurutak, along with the Sihkag, had always been viewed as the lowest of the eight, their blood never considered as thick. It was almost a guarantee that when approached by his own clan, the ancient family of Ki'ra, that the Kurutak would grovel over the honor of being treated as equals. It was a mistake the Kiranka, the clan or *hrai* of the Emperor, never realized in their treatment of those residing in the royal palace. In public, of course, the positions of dominance and submission were closely observed during audiences and open ritual, but in private, it was something else, especially when all the other families viewed the Emperor's line as no better than their own.

"This petty feud between the clan of Vak and that of the Qarg is to stop here and now," Jukaga announced. "It is a disgrace that royal blood has been spilled like this in feuds within the confines of the Imperial Palace. Five of the Qarg have died in duels and five of the Ragitagha. It is enough and it is finished."

Vak started to open his mouth and Jukaga extended his paw, talons retracted in a sign of peace.

"It is enough," he said quietly.

"You are not the Emperor," Vak replied, "you have not the power to order me or Qar'ka to stop," and he looked across the table at Qar'ka, whom only a moment ago he would have gladly knifed, for support.

Qar'ka nodded his head in agreement.

The Baron inwardly sighed. The fools, could they not see the weakness revealed in that simple statement? It was something he had learned in his years of study and it had come to him with a crystal clarity. The wars against other races, the ritual of Sivar, were designed above all else as a civilizing factor to the race of the Kilrathi, to quite simply keep them from killing each other. Aggressive combat, the instinct to hunt and to kill was far too close to the surface. Within the *hrai*, the clan and families were controlled by the rigid system of caste. But the clan instinct only extended as far as the clan. Though all might espouse the concept that they were Kilrathi it was only in the face of a prey outside of themselves. War and Sivar were essential for the survival of the race, to keep it from killing itself off and nothing more. It was something he did not discuss, for to even question the divinity of Sivar as nothing more than a social tool would be his ruin.

All the wars had so well served that purpose, the humans, the Hari, the Gorth, Sorn, Ka, and Utara. Thank Sivar for the Utara who in their foolishness had come to Kilrah in peace, gave them space travel as a friendly gesture, and died as a result. If it had not been so, we would have destroyed ourselves when the secret of atomics came into our hands, the Baron thought, even as he surveyed the other clan leaders in the room. Aggressive races rarely survived the move into technology and made it to the point where space offered them an outlet.

He looked around the table. Qar'ka was a fool, Vak not much better; they would not see such things. All they knew was that there was no war for the moment and the pressure within their own *hrai* was building, petty quarreling, long forgotten feuds building to the flashing of claw daggers. And yet, when Vak had turned to Qar'ka and offered him Jukaga as an opponent that they could unite against, Qar'ka was ready to agree.

"The feuding in the palace must stop," Jukaga said coldly, his mane still flushed outward.

"And I say you are not the Emperor to so order me," Vak snapped in reply.

Jukaga smiled.

"Is he really our Emperor?"

There was a moment of stunned silence.

"Are you mad?" Qar'ka asked.

"He and that fool grandson have led us into one too many disasters," Jukaga replied coldly.

"How many of us have lost our sons, the best of our *hrai*, to the terrans? How many of us have listened to our first chosen ones and concubines crying at night, their faces buried in their pillows to muffle the sobs, crying for those lost in this war?"

The other *hrai* leaders lowered their heads and even Vak, who only moments before wanted to knife him, nodded in agreement.

"Vak, you lost your first born of your first litter at Vukar Tag, I know, I saw his gallantry, his heroic death when he tried to ram the enemy carrier. He died *kabaka*, his soul winging to Sivar for his courage."

Vak looked up at Jukaga, his eyes cold with anger at the wasted death of his eldest son. Jukaga almost felt guilty for so easily manipulating him thus.

"He would be alive today, sitting by your side, sharing your feasting cup but for the Emperor. It was the Emperor that ordered the splitting of the fleet and Thrakhath agreed. If all our carriers were there for that fight we would have smashed the Confederation and pressed the war to victory. I was blamed and you now know the lie of that. I languished in exile, expecting at any moment that the Emperor's poisoner would come."

He looked around the room and stood up.

"We must stay united, we must control our *hrai* and stop this petty feuding which threatens to turn the palace into a slaughter pit. Don't you think the Emperor is quietly encouraging us thus to fight against each other, to thus keep us from standing united against him?"

He could see more than one nod of agreement to his statement and smiled.

"Then start the war now!" Qar'ka snarled. "End this

ridiculous farce. We have lulled the humans to sleep, now let us rip their throats out and be done with it."

Qar'ka hesitated for a moment as if not willing to speak.

"We must finish it before the Mantu return," he said quietly, "and take us in the back while we still fight the Confederation."

The others looked over nervously at Qar'ka and then back to Jukaga.

Jukaga nodded and said nothing. Just after the defeat at Vukar, a report had come in from a deep space remote probe, far beyond the edge of Hari space, a probe so far removed that it had taken a year even to bring it in. There was an indication that the Mantu, who had once before invaded Kilrathi space, had completed their war against an unknown neighbor and might very well return. Seventy years past there had been a brief encounter with them, and though the fight had been a draw, it was suspected that the Mantu might in fact be far superior in their weapons technology. They had disappeared, drawing back to fight other foes, but it was always suspected that there would come a day when the Mantu might turn their full attention on the Empire, a concern that deeply troubled Jukaga as he watched their resources being spilled against the humans.

Jukaga turned away and pointed at a long list of figures displayed by a holo projector.

"This war against the Confederation has lasted over thirty years, the borders barely shifting after our first gains. War is not just fighting, it is economics, and resources, and production and morale and perhaps most importantly the learning of the way our enemy thinks. I know some of you might scoff at such concerns but that last factor has been my chief concern and responsibility."

"You and the nobles of your *hrai* have remained safe at home, playing with numbers and reading while we spill our blood," Vak laughed coldly.

"Without the weapons my *hrai* designed and the intelligence my spies and remote devices have gained, you would have been frozen meat floating in space," Jukaga replied.

"He speaks the truth," Talmak of the Sutaghi interjected before Vak could reply. "Now let him finish. If Thrakhath had listened to Jukaga's concerns before Vukar the battle would have turned out far differently."

"The war had become a balanced match without end in sight until now," Jukaga continued. "We almost had the edge until Vukar and their raid to our base on our moon. If it had not been for Thrakhath and the Emperor, as I already said, we might very well have taken Earth.

"Earth, that has always been the key, and Thrakhath forgot that. A human warrior once wrote that in war one must find the focal point that will cause the collapse of his enemy and then throw all resources against it.

"This time I want no mistakes. Give this armistice just a little more time until the enemy is asleep and our secret fleet is completed. Let the fools get used to peace. Let them believe in this friendship. Let our secret fleet continue to be built even as we make a show of decommissioning our current ships. Then we will strike and crush them."

"But the Sivar," Vak replied. "Where is the Sivar to be this year? Our people demand that."

"You have the prisoners that we have kept hidden, do it to them," Jukaga replied coldly.

"Prisoners, there is no honor in that. I still say that in eight eight of days, when Sivar comes, then we should launch our strike and turn the rivers of Earth red with the blood of the slaughter."

"And I tell you that it must be yet five eighty of days. Look at the charts, can't you see the truth in them?" and he pointed to the wall."

"War is not simple numbers, it is blood," Vak snorted.

"Four more carriers at Vukar is a simple number, Vak, and that number is the difference between your first born still floating in space, his body unclaimed, versus his living and breathing this day."

Vak snarled and Jukaga was not sure for a moment if the anger was aimed at him, or at the humiliation over the useless death of a son.

"Listen to me, my *takhars*," and he deliberately chose the word which meant brothers of equal rank. He looked around the room and saw that even Vak was at last willing to listen, unable to argue with the cold facts of numbers.

"Let the plan unfold. When the time is ripe, over a dozen carriers will leap forward, slashing through their near defenseless border region. Before they can even hope to mobilize, we will jump straight to Earth, and there I promise you a slaughter like no other. In our plan we already have our agents at work, weakening their will to fight, ready as well to kill their leaders of war when the time is right. When we cut the heart out of the Terran Confederation, then in the years to come we can go at our leisure from planet to planet, saving some for Sivar, others destroying if they are a threat. Thus we will win, and thus we will be ready as well if our old enemy the Mantu should again return."

He settled back in his chair and waited. Vak looked around the room, saw the nods of agreement and finally lowered his head.

"The feud stops, you have my support," he said quietly.

Jukaga did not allow himself to show his teeth in a gesture of triumph.

"Then I have the promise of all of you to control your *hrai* in the palace."

"It will be difficult, but it will be done," Qar'ka finally said. "But what of your other words about the Emperor?"

Jukaga nodded.

"In the days to come just consider this. He is old, he will not live forever. When he goes to his fathers, Thrakhath will take the golden throne. Given the leadership both have shown, do we truly want them to lead us to our final victory, or even more importantly against the threat of the Mantu if they should return?"

"Are you suggesting the breaking of our oath-sworn word?" Vak asked.

Jukaga slowly shook his head.

"Just that I want you to consider my question, nothing more," Jukaga replied. "Other than that I suggest nothing."

Vak smiled, and for an instant Jukaga was not sure if it was a sign of aggression at himself or towards the Emperor and without another word he got up and strode from the room, the other clan leaders following.

Jukaga sighed with relief as the door closed behind them. How the feuds had truly started was all too evident. The Emperor had manipulated the *hrai* of Vak into feeling slighted at the court rituals by the other clans. He had not intervened when blood started to spill as a result.

It was masterful on the Emperor's part, keeping the clans from uniting and turning their aggressive energy against him. Jukaga closed his eyes to clear his thoughts.

The Emperor by now must see the threat forming. The Emperor must somehow sense that he was actually contemplating the unthinkable, the actual elimination of the Imperial line. If the war was on, such an act would be absolutely intolerable, in peace it might just be successful. The Emperor therefore needed peace to finish the building of the fleet, but at the same time needed war to secure his throne.

Jukaga reached over to a side table and poured himself a cup of wine and quietly lapped it up. And yet there was far more. If he had learned anything from his study of the humans, it was that there was more than one way to win a war. Direct and brutal combat was the only thing the Kilrathi knew and understood. Yet there were so many other ways. It was already evident that the humans were weakening themselves in a foolish bid for peace. A year from now, if all could be kept quiet they would cripple themselves beyond all hope of recall.

If he could eliminate the Emperor and the Prince, and then personally lead the new fleet into Terran space they would most likely capitulate in despair. Thus the fleet would be preserved. For if the Mantu were coming, the fleet, and far more beyond it, would be needed to stop them; a subjugated race of humans, and the vast resources they controlled, would help in that survival. The Emperor was too much a Kilrathi to see that. Brutal all-out war was the only path the Kilrathi had ever understood. It had, for so long, been the fundamental key to their success. Now, it might very well be the path to their destruction, fighting themselves to exhaustion only to then be conquered by others. He even half suspected that this was part of the Mantu plan, for surely they must know what was going on.

The Emperor would have to go, it was that simple, and he found that he could indeed contemplate something that the humans so often practiced in their political struggles but which was unknown to the Kilrathi, political assassination of a superior without direct confrontation and challenge.

As he contemplated he smiled, remembering his favorite readings of the human English author and his play *MacBeth*. It was that reading which had first planted the thought.

Tolwyn. The English race of humans and their cousins the Americans were an interesting study. So violent but also so imbued with a strange idealism. Tolwyn fascinated him, a cultured man, and yet a complete warrior.

He knew that there was something hidden behind the downfall of Tolwyn's career, and his reported move to the Landreich reinforced that. Tolwyn was too honorable to break the old English code of warfare with its bizarre notion of fair play and rules. He was following orders from someone above him, to be removed so he could go to the Landreich. But for what?

Jukaga called up a holo map of the Landreich sector and its jump point pathways into the Empire.

The realization finally came. Tolwyn was being sent out as a spy, to try to find the fleet, and if discovered, his link to the government could be denied.

"Masterful," Jukaga said softly. The information matched into the report he had obtained from one of his operatives inside Thrakhath's military intelligence.

Thrakhath must have surmised this concern as well, and thus sent out a precious Stealth to investigate.

Tolwyn had to be blocked. If the humans found out the truth, the peace would indeed be shattered, the timing of his own plans destroyed. Though he hated to do it, he would have to send a message to Thrakhath outlining his concerns for security and to recommend that it be doubled.

Tolwyn was a fascinating challenge, a worthy foe. Though he would not openly admit it even to himself, he was finding in his heart that the humans were a race he had almost come to like, and more importantly, a race he was even willing to spare in his own quest for power.

"Well look what the birds dragged in," Jason laughed, trying to conceal the fact that he had been sweating out the last twenty hours, increasingly convinced that his old friend had bought a permanent piece of space.

K'Kai, ignoring Jason's teasing remark, led Ian up to the bar. Ian looked around the room with a grin, though Jason could see that the rescued pilot had most definitely had the wits scared out of him.

"Yeah, I know, the drinks are all on me," Ian announced, and a cheer went up from the pilots who swarmed up to the bar. Ian looked around a bit glumly, realizing that the old fleet tradition could be rather expensive.

"I'll have this thing Ian talks so much about, a single malt scotch," K'Kai announced.

The bartender looked at Ian.

"For that kind of sippin' liquor it's ten dollars for a shot."

"Give it to her," Ian sighed, "the bird was the one that rescued me."

The bartender seemed to relax a bit, especially when Jason reached into his pocket and fished out a wad of bills, hard Confederation currency, and tossed them on the counter.

"I don't think you've got much change on you at the moment," Jason said looking over at Ian. "You can pay me back later."

Ian nodded his thanks and called for a Scotch as well, downing it in one gulp. He looked over at Jason and smiled weakly.

"I was scared out of my wits," Ian said quietly. "Maybe I might have been able to dodge that second missile, but it just kept boring in on me. When I popped out of there my ship was already blowing."

Jason could easily see that by the scorching on Ian's flight suit.

"By popping up at the last second I had enough forward velocity to go into a low orbit around the moon. I looped over a mountain range not clearing it by a thousand meters. Every time I circled the moon my orbit kept degrading until finally the mountain range was straight ahead and I knew I was going to slam in. If K'Kai had gotten there thirty seconds later I'd have been splattered. Her tractor beam caught me just in time."

He raised his glass and Jason could see the trembling which Ian struggled to control. Everyone who flew experienced it sooner or later, especially with the life expectancy of pilots being what it was. There was a point though when one too many close brushes simply drained the well dry. If they were back with the Confed Fleet, Ian would have been in to the psych officer and most likely stood down for a couple of weeks of R&R before being sent back in. But there wasn't any time, and in this stripped down fleet a psych officer was a luxury that Kruger would have considered pure idiocy.

"Captain Bondarevsky, Captain St. John?"

The two looked over their shoulders at a colonial officer.

"You got us."

"You're wanted by Kruger."

"On our way," Hunter said, forcing a smile.

Jason looked around at the bar, fished into his pocket and pulled out what he had left and tossed it to the bartender.

"Keep it flowing on me till the money runs out."

The colonial pilots cheered a thanks, as Jason left.

Hunter looked back at K'Kai, and silently nodded a thanks as he went out the door.

The bar was conveniently across the street from the entry into the command post. Following their guide they passed the security guards and went back down into the basement command post.

Kruger and Tolwyn looked up as Ian and Jason came into the room.

"Glad you're alive," Geoff said.

"So am I."

"But you lost a Sabre," Kruger interjected, "a first line ship in return for one Kilrathi Stealth, not a good trade in my book at all."

"Return with your shield or upon it, is that it?" Ian said dryly.

"Something like that," Kruger retorted. "You Confed boys might think it's all right to blow a ship apart or prang one up on a bad landing, get out, and then have another one handed to you, but out here it's different. We're at the butt end of any supplies. With your asinine Confed signing that article 23 of the armistice forbidding the resale of fighter aircraft, a Sabre is precious."

"Sorry," Ian replied, "next time I'll make sure to blow up with my ship."

"At least we know about their new missile," Tolwyn interjected, while pouring himself a cup of tea and motioning for Ian to come over and join him.

"You go too easy on your boys," Kruger said, looking over at Tolwyn. Jason found it hard to suppress a low chuckle.

"Something I say amusing to you, mister?" Kruger asked, looking back at Jason.

"As a matter of fact, yes, sir," Jason replied.

Kruger looked at him coldly and again Jason found himself wondering if his honesty would get him into hot water. Whether Kruger could really discipline him or not was problematic, he was after all a "volunteer" in the Landreich's Free Corp, not even officially sworn in, but he did suspect the gaunt one-eyed leader could make life difficult.

"We've got a little surprise for you two," Tolwyn said, handing a cup of tea to Ian and moving to get between Jason and Kruger. Glad for the excuse to break eye contact Jason focused his attention on Tolwyn.

"What is it, sir?"

"The special equipment we were hoping to get made it out of the Confederation and will arrive here tomorrow. It's the real reason I wanted to get these carriers out here," and he looked over at a frowning Kruger and smiled, "besides helping out our allies in the Landreich.

"Therefore *Tarawa* and *Normandy* aren't going out on forward patrol with the other three carriers."

"Why, sir?" and the disappointment in Jason's voice was evident.

"I couldn't let you in on it till now, but your ship has been selected for the real mission. Let's head up there now, Paladin's moved over from *Normandy* and he's already on board waiting for us."

"What is it, sir?" Jason asked, feeling like a child who was being held back from looking under the Christmas tree.

"Let's just say we've decided to add to *Tarawa* a little something special that just came in."

● CHAPTER SIX

Hard docking completed, Jason followed Geoff Tolwyn to what usually served as the entry bay for his fighters and was now blocked by the side of the heavy transport which was almost as big as *Tarawa*.

The crew worked around him, extending the docking collar through the magnetic field which separated the pressurized flight deck from the vacuum of space. The collar snapped on to the side of the transport and the deck officer turned to Jason, nodding that an airtight seal had been secured. The side of the transport popped open and a thin, nearly bald man, who Jason judged to be in his early sixties, came through.

"So the Cats have been snooping around?" the man asked, coming up to shake Tolwyn's hands.

"They know we're here."

"And they'll be back for a closer look. I think I managed to get here without their knowing and I can tell you what's inside my hold is secure."

Tolwyn looked back at his companions.

"Admiral Vance Richards, I'd like to introduce you to Captain Bondarevsky."

Jason came to attention and the Admiral motioned for him to stand at ease.

"Everyone here's retired at the moment, Captain, so let's cut all the saluting crap."

Jason took Richards' hand, surprised at the firmness of the grip. Tolwyn went down the line introducing him in turn to Hunter, Doomsday, Kevin, and finally Paladin.

"Ah, Vance, tis good to see ya again," Paladin said with a laugh, the two slapping each other on the shoulders. "Did you bring me my new toy?"

"That I did," Richards said, "it's tucked into the forward cargo bay."

Paladin grinned with delight.

Jason watched the familiar greeting with surprise. Admiral Richards, until his retirement only days before the armistice, had been head of military intelligence for the entire Confederation. He was, to the members of the fleet, a shadowy figure, a name without a picture, an individual never seen — though it was often rumored that he traveled into more than one action, hidden away as a staff officer under an assumed name.

"Let's start unloading and get to work," Richards said with an almost boylike enthusiasm, and he motioned for the group to follow him off the deserted hangar bay.

The group started down the corridor back to the bridge and Jason looked back to see a team of black cover-alled personnel emerging from the transport ship, each of them saluting the lone Marine guard by the hatch and requesting permission to come aboard.

"Who are those people?" Jason asked, motioning back towards the stream of personnel filing off the transport.

"That's part of our surprise," Tolwyn said with a grin.

The new arrivals started to maneuver long black canisters from out of the transport, moving them with small hand-held null gravity units. They had a certain look to them, tech personnel he could almost guess out of hand, but beyond that a cold professional look as well.

"Since I am captain of this ship, sir," Jason said, looking over at Tolwyn, "can you finally let me in on what's going on? You've been looking like a cat that just swallowed the canary."

"We're installing a D 3S 5 on board your ship, Jason," Richards said, motioning for Jason to turn into the wardroom off the bridge and indicating that Ian, Doomsday, Paladin, Geoff, and Kevin were invited to join as well.

"Just what the hell is a D 3S 5?" Ian asked.

"Deep Space Surveillance System Five," Richards said quietly, closing the door behind them.

"Something then with signal intelligence, is that it?"

Richards smiled and sat down on the small table that filled most of the room, motioning for the rest of group to sit down. It suddenly caught Jason that Richards was awfully familiar with light escort design, having made it straight from the hangar to the bridge wardroom without a single false turn.

"The sig intel department's been working on this new design for years, in fact they were just getting set to deploy it when the armistice hit. This system was a black project. The only ones who knew about it were the chiefs of staff and several hundred design and research techs working on a base buried inside one of Neptune's moons, and that was it. Security was so tight that the techs were only allowed to bring their spouses and children with them and then were listed as killed in a transport accident."

Jason noticed that Richards had neglected to say if anyone inside the civilian government knew of the project. Chances were not even the president fully understood it, nor perhaps did he want to.

"I should add it is strictly a military project," Richards said, as if reading Jason's thoughts. "I think it's fair to tell you that we've suspected a mole in the inner circle of government for some time now. The money for this project has therefore been buried, and no one else knows about it."

"So what's so important about all of this?" Ian asked.

"Since this war started, signal and photo intelligence has been crucial. From the little bits of information that we've been able to occasionally get, victory or defeat in some of the major battles of the war has often been decided. Vukar started because of a recon survey and in a lot of those missions good people died as a result.

"We've even got picket ships specially designed for the work, and they've been hiding on the edge of the frontier for years, quietly parked in asteroid fields. Hell, some of them are camouflaged to look like asteroids. Gods, it must be boring work, but to the sig intel crowd it's like a giant game, figuring out one puzzle after another.

"The problem is that we're trying to listen in on everything from old sub light ship-to-ship radio communication, through newscasts, right up to fleet command high density translight burst signals. It comes down to hundreds of billions of signals floating around, made even more complicated by old radio waves, signals maybe five hundred years old, drifting by. The Kilrathi, of course, assume we're listening in, so throw in language and coding and you see how complex it gets.

"D 3S 5 might be a partial answer. It's not only the detecting equipment, it's also the analysis software which can sort through these millions of signals, crack codes, figure out which ones have certain things we're looking for and then give them as hard copy to intelligence. When they started the design work twenty years ago, the antenna nets were twenty miles across, it took five hundred personnel to run it, and it needed a ship bigger than a carrier. The early models were, as result of these limitations, well inside Confed Space for security reasons, trying to squeak out information from as much as five hundred or more light years and ten or more jump points from the front. Now we've finally got it down to something we can deploy inside the flight deck of a light escort carrier, with a fifty meter antenna array mounted outside."

"So that's why the other ships got the fighters, leaving us just four, and you wanted them moved to a corner of the hangar?" Jason asked, looking over at Tolwyn.

The Admiral smiled.

"*Tarawa*'s got a different job, in fact the real reason behind our moving out here to the Landreich. The Landreich needed the carriers, to be sure, and some of us wanted to keep a light strike force ready and available on the edge of the frontier. But it also served as a smoke screen for the real mission, the mission you and your carrier have been chosen for. We're going to take our new ears inside the Empire, and get the evidence we need to pull the mask off what they're doing. When we have the proof of what they're doing, believe me, things will hit the fan."

"Just one question then, sir," Ian asked.

"Sure, what is it?"

"How the hell did we get this equipment? It must be worth hundreds of millions."

"Just roughly over eighty billion and some odd change," Richards replied. "What's inside those boxes piling up on the flight deck cost more than the entire *Concordia*."

"So how then?"

"Don't ever ask," Tolwyn replied quietly. "People have died for knowing a hell of a lot less and I suspect there's more than one person who'd be glad to kill all of us if they knew what we were up to."

"And my ship?" Paladin asked.

"Once we off load the equipment to *Tarawa*, we'll leave the Hell Hole and head off to a quiet corner a couple of jump points up, and then off-load your new toy."

"Off-load what?" Doomsday asked, unable to hide behind his usual mask of disinterest and depression.

"A light smuggler craft with Stealth technology," Paladin said with a grin.

"How the hell did we get that?" Kevin asked excitedly.

"Oh, let's just say a Kilrathi Stealth fighter they thought was killed somehow wound up in our hands," Richards replied. "We've yet to really figure out how it works, but we did manage to take it apart and install it in one of our ships and the damn thing actually works!"

"Paladin's going in as our point man on this operation, so we thought we'd give him a little something extra this time around," Tolwyn interjected.

"And its about time, considering what you folks pay me," Paladin replied with a grin.

"Enter."

Bowing low, Vak, baron of the *hrai* of the Ragitagha, slipped into the darkened room, went down on both knees, head bowed to the floor and waited.

"You may arise," the voice whispered hoarsely and Vak came to his feet.

The bent figure motioned for him to approach and sit by his side, an act of great honor, and Vak moved quickly to obey.

"You at least I still know are loyal."

"As always, my Emperor," Vak said softly, not daring to raise his voice much above a whisper. Though the room was supposedly secured and swept, and the walls were mounted with vibration dampeners, it was still possible that something might have been overlooked.

The Emperor touched a control panel by his side and Vak felt the electrostatic tingle of a force field clicking in. Nothing now could hear them, unless a bug had been planted in the very chair in which the Emperor sat.

"We can talk freely now," the Emperor said.

Vak tried to relax.

"I have read the report you sent to me regarding this meeting. They are fools if they continue to follow Jukaga."

Vak nodded.

"I think you should know that you are not the only one to report to me thus."

Vak felt a cold uneasiness. Was this a lie or not? If not, then it meant that at least one other of the eight families had had second thoughts about Jukaga. Could it be that all the others might very well be playing both sides in this? Or was the Emperor truly alone and simply making him nervous, to insure that he told the truth? He tried to analyze this bit of information. He had no love for the Emperor, and that he had led them to the brink of disaster was obvious. But he feared civil war as well, knowing that if it came it would be his worlds that might very well be swallowed up if the humans should attack in the wake of the chaos.

We need the Emperor to hold us together, yet in the needing of him we are destroying ourselves as well, that is the paradox of it all, as Jukaga would say.

"You're wondering who?" the Emperor said with a cold laugh.

"Of course I would wonder such a thing."

"And of course I will not tell you. In fact, you've already

thought I might be lying; I'll leave that for you to meditate on."

"Don't you trust me?" Vak asked, his voice and demeanor showing a genuine concern.

"Don't be a fool, of course I don't trust you. Remember that, Vak, anyone who wears the Imperial crown must learn that lesson first. I did not trust even my own son and in the end I ordered his death. There are times I am not even sure of my grandson, the heir."

He paused for a moment as if the memory did in fact still pain him in spite of his apparent lack of remorse in the years since the execution.

He lowered his head again, growling softly.

"You know that when I go," the Emperor finally said, "if my grandson is not supported, civil war will be the result. My *hrai* has ruled the Empire for centuries; that must continue, for no family will support the rise of another to rule over them."

Vak said nothing.

"But tell me," the Emperor chuckled, "why have you betrayed Jukaga's intentions to me?"

"Because I am loyal sire."

The Emperor leaned back and barked out a laugh.

"Do not play the fool, the real reason. I know you hate my grandson and me, blaming us for the death of your first born."

Vak was taken aback. His first answer had actually been the truth. If loyalty to a sworn oath was viewed as nothing more than a political toy, to be abandoned without thought, then they were indeed truly lost.

The Emperor looked at him closely and finally nodded.

"I believe you actually are loyal."

Vak, feeling insulted that such an issue had even been questioned, remained silent.

The Emperor looked away from Vak. Jukaga, as head of intelligence, had placed his spies not only beyond the borders but within even the palace itself. There was nothing he did not know. Poisoning him would be the easiest answer, but that might very well make the loyalty of Vak and the other family heads waver. The tacit agreement between *hrai* leaders and Emperors had stood for generations: both sides will support the other, neither will attempt to kill the other.

He thought of Thrakhath. He was tempted to recall him from his assignment with the new fleet but then thought better of it. The new fleet was not only the tool for the final offensive against the Confederation, but also a replacement for the home fleet lost in the last two years of campaigns. Three carriers were ready, at the very least six more had to be completed if the next campaign was to be a guaranteed success. He could not afford one more lost opportunity, for it would shake whatever power they had left to the very core and perhaps trigger open rebellion. Yet if they waited, Jukaga in his slyness might very well gain even more power.

It was an amusing question to ponder and he knew if he pondered long enough he would find the answer.

"You know just how munificent my reward might be if you provide me with information valuable enough, including perhaps even the marriage to one of my great nieces. It could very well mean that your family might even thus be in line for the Imperial succession," the Emperor said softly. And Vak smiled.

"Jump transition on automatic sequencing and counting at ten, nine, eight . . ."

Jason settled back into his chair and waited. A cold rush of excitement tingled down his spine. No matter how many times he had jumped he always felt the same, especially when going into hostile space. One of the key tactical points with jumping was the simple fact that you never knew what was on the other side. Inside secured shipping lanes behind the lines there were beacons placed at both points, monitoring traffic, sent up to avoid the possibility of a ship materializing in the same point of space occupied by someone else, an event that always had spectacular results. But beyond that was the question of just who was waiting. Paladin, piloting his new ship which he had named *Bannockburn*, with Ian aboard as his co-pilot, had already gone ahead to scout. The fifteen minutes' wait had passed and now it was time to follow through and the potential for an unpleasant surprise was always there.

He felt *Tarawa* drop away, and there was a momentary queasiness then the flash of rematerialization. He looked over at his navigation officer who was peering intently at her holo display.

"Correct jump alignment confirmed," she announced. "*Bannockburn* reporting in on laser lock."

Paladin's image appeared on the screen.

"This Stealth works like a charm. We found a remote sensor and took it out, it never even put out a signal. Optical scan shows the entire system's clear right up to the next jump point."

Jason looked over at Tolwyn and grinned.

"It looks like we got through. We've crossed from the frontier into the heart of the Empire."

He looked up at his aft visual and less than a minute later his escort CVE-6 *Normandy* came through.

"All ships through," communications announced, "all systems running nominal, *Bannockburn* reports successful take-out of remote drone without detect signal being activated."

Geoff Tolwyn, standing behind Jason, nodded, letting out an audible sigh of relief. Jason found that alone to be surprising; he was used to his old chief being absolutely unflappable.

They were now four jumps into the Kilrathi Empire, tracking down one of the hundreds of transition points leading from neutral territory into the Empire in the one direction and Confederation space on the other. Surveillance drones of course monitored these points, but "accidents" like the one Paladin had just arranged for the drone covering this jump point were easy enough to set up. It could be days or even weeks before a picket ship came out to replace the drone with a new one.

"Let's hit the flight deck and see what Richards is up to," Tolwyn said, motioning for Jason to follow.

Excited, Jason came out of his seat. He had been waiting for days to get a look at what Richards was doing.

Leaving the bridge they went down the main corridor to the forward part of the ship. At the airlock door two guards came to attention at Tolwyn's approach but did not step aside.

Internal ship security was nothing new to Jason but this was different. The two men were not dressed in the usual Marine class B uniform, for after all this was not a Confederation ship any longer. There was something disquieting about the black khaki uniform the two guards were wearing without a single insignia or marking on them. The easy way they held their laser rifles told him that these two were highly trained professionals.

Only seven members of the *Tarawa's* operating crew were allowed on to the hangar deck, Tolwyn and himself, along with Kevin, Doomsday and two Landreich pilots cleared to fly one of the four craft still left in the very forward part of the hangar, and finally Sparks as the one overworked maintenance officer permitted to work on the fighters. Everyone else aboard ship had already been told that the guards had standing orders to shoot first and then ask questions. Jason could tell this was simply not rhetoric, these two would do it without batting an eye.

Clearing the doorway, they stepped out into the hangar deck. Equipment was spread out across almost all the floor space which once was occupied by forty-four fighters. He realized that he was, in fact, looking at perhaps the single largest concentration of computing power anywhere in the Confederation except, perhaps, for the administrative centers of Earth and the moon, and even then he wondered. Banks of storage systems were arrayed along one wall, dozens of holo display fields were already up and running, and he approached one of them, a field nearly half a dozen meters cubed. A technician was standing inside the display field, which showed a three dimensional model of what he recognized as the near space environment around Kilrah. Bright hovering points of light represented the stars, their planets, and transition jump points, with blocks of data appearing above them, the information readable from any angle one looked at it. The technician standing inside the holo display looked almost godlike as she walked about inside it. He was totally mystified by what she was doing as she pulled out what looked like a laser pointer, aimed it at the orange size planet floating in the middle of the field and squeezed.

Another holo field popped into action next to the first, this one a close up of the planet the first technician had pointed at. The entire field was occupied by what looked like a solid ball, its continents covered with hundreds of flashing lights.

"That's Kilrah," Jason whispered.

"Using this, they can lock in on any one of millions of sources even while continuing to scan all other traffic and look for new sources at the same time," Tolwyn replied softly.

Several white overall clad techs gathered around the globe, pointing, talking softly, arguing, and then aiming pointers at particular flashing lights. Behind them, two dimensional flat screens flared into light, streams of data flashing across some, others showing pictures, one of which caught Jason's eye, of Kilrathi wearing heavy leather armor slashing at each other with swords.

Vance came up to the two and nodded a greeting.

"Say, what the hell is that on the monitor?" Jason asked, pointing to the screen.

"A Kilrathi drama from the Gakarg Period."

"What?"

"Their ancient history. They love holos about the ancient wars when the various clans were feuding with each other before the unification. We monitor every such station from Kilrah, their media links are translight signalled throughout the Empire. It cost them a bundle but it helps keep them unified. Watching their stations might give us clues as to internal politics. We have a lot of software tied up with analysis of their popular shows, since there might be some subtle clues as to what's going on based upon the type of entertainment the government is broadcasting. In the last three days we've noticed an increase of Gakarg Period dramas dealing with Emperor Y'taa'gu."

"Who?"

Vance chuckled.

"I never heard of him either. Seems to be an evil emperor who was insane and finally killed by a virtuous warrior in order to save his people. It's worth watching. It's interesting that since the armistice we never see a single drama about the war with us, or any of their previous ones, only ancient history. Their news programs are the same, really tight on war news and only one brief announcement of the armistice and then nothing. These furballs are mighty security conscious on such things, but we still gleam occasional facts; that's why it's worth monitoring."

Lance led them around the holo display of Kilrah, raised a pointer and aimed it at a flashing blue light.

"Blue means commercial communication line," and he nodded back to a screen which was filled with what looked like shipping orders, instantly translated into standard English.

"This D-5 is monitoring everything that's reaching the antenna arrays mounted outside this ship. If it's non-coded it immediately translates it. We have the computers programmed to look for certain things on the commercial channels. For instance, a shipping order for IFF missiles gets tagged into a higher priority slot. We can even look for orders related to just one component of an IFF missile. If certain patterns of shipping develop or if something outside of the ordinary happens, the computer will alert a human operator who then analyzes it and decides if there's something important enough that it has to be kicked upstairs. That's the key job, looking for the little nugget of gold inside the tons of gravel and mud.

"One of the first things that started to tip us off to the

fact that the Kilrathi might be building something was that certain commercial links for the ordering of military parts suddenly went into a new code system, which was changed every eight days. Significant orders for supplies, parts, and shipping became highly classified.

"That started some real questions being asked. The problem was that they shifted this classified work to the part of the Empire out beyond Kilrah, as far from our listening posts as possible. The question of *why* really put the pressure on us to get this D-5 on line and also caused the loss of a lot of good intel people behind the lines. The jump we just completed is the deepest in we've ever been able to take equipment like this. You can see already the streams of data pouring in."

Richards led them over to his command booth and offered a couple of cups of coffee to his guests. Jason noticed that these people seemed to live on caffeine, and a fair number of them were addicted to Ian's habit of tobacco, a practice he found totally mystifying and somewhat disgusting.

"The D-5 can monitor any signal within its six hundred light year range and pinpoint its origin. The hard part is programming it to figure out what is worth looking at out of the billions of messages it picks up every day and then passing it to a human analyst for evaluation.

"The analyst's job is the toughest. It takes someone with a sixth sense to decipher what appear to be unrelated facts but actually are part of a pattern.

"We do the same thing for the media channels, the public communication lines, and of course the military and government lines," and he pointed to the flashing red and yellow lights back on the holo display of Kilrah.

"Those are the tough buggers, a lot of it is burst signalled and highly encoded."

"Damn, there's hundreds of them," Jason said. "Something must be up."

Vance laughed softly.

"Over ninety percent are dummy channels, broadcasting

complete gibberish, total nonsense words that actually tie
up most of our decoding equipment since we're not sure if
it's garbage or the real thing. Sometimes you might have a
burst signal with a million words in it, all encoded, and the
real message is twenty words in the middle, each word
separated from the next by say six thousand four hundred
words.

"Why that number?"

"Remember they have eight fingers and we have ten, so
their numerical system is base eight. We tend to look a bit
more intensely at base eight numerical lines as a result.
What gets frustrating is that they are using at least a dozen
different codes at any given time, with the highest level
material going on what we call Fleet Code A, which tends
to change every twenty-four to forty days. The real messages are hidden in a lot of garbage and we have to wade
through each message and might spend weeks tracking
down promising stuff only to discover it's a decoy.

"Some of their people even have a sense of humor
about it. One message, when finally translated, was a simple 'Hey, stupid, we fooled you,' and another was a long
excerpt from what I guess was a Kilrathi dirty book.
Decoding and translating each of those things took up
time and equipment. We can't ignore a single message because we never know if we might hit paydirt or not. So we
wade through all of this, figure out the real signals from the
fake, then spend a hell of a lot of time cracking the code,
and just when we think we've got it, they go and change
the code and we're back to square one. Then to top it off
they might have a station that's quiet for weeks or months,
and it pops off a lone burst signal then shuts down. Trying
to even figure out where it came from out of a billion cubic
light years of space was nuts until the D-4 model, which
could do a Doppler analysis and at least do a probable
trace."

"I'd go mad," Tolwyn said.

"Some of us do," Vance replied. "It takes a special kind
of person to do this. You fighter jockeys, your battle is one

of skill and wits, but it gets played out in seconds. Some of our battles last years."

Vance smiled.

"I've been in this game for twenty-nine years. I've dreamed all those years of having something like this D-5. With the new antenna array we can pick up bursts from up to six hundred light years out; only a couple of generations back in the system we were lucky to get consistent reads from ten light years away. We used to spend billions on recon drones which would go in, store up data for a week, then send out a burst signal. Once it signalled the Kilrathi would be onto it and take it out. Now this one system can cover an area that would have required thousands of drones.

"The big problem now is that counter intel believes they knew of the D-4 and maybe suspected our D-5. We've noticed a decrease in signal traffic and suspect they're shifting more to courier. So far we've yet to figure out how to read a dispatch pouch six hundred light years behind the lines."

As they continued to talk, Vance led them around the flight deck. Small cubicles had been set up in the center of the room, and hunched over in each was an operator, going through data that the computer felt was of sufficient importance to bring to the attention of a human operator.

"I've got a hundred and three analysts with me on this mission, each of them a specialist and the best in his field with eight or more years of training behind him. There are another forty programmers who feed in the requests and another twenty just to troubleshoot any glitches in the machine."

Jason looked around the room, wondering just who indeed was paying for all of this. He had his suspicions but knew it was best not to ask. What was equally troubling was the matter-antimatter mine that was almost casually brought aboard with the rest of the equipment. It was placed in the center of the room and would be activated if it appeared as if *Tarawa* might be captured. In this case there was definitely no surrender although, technically, they were not even at war.

A technician came up to Vance's side, looked over at Jason and Tolwyn and said nothing. Vance smiled and nodded.

"I think Jenkins here has something to tell me that he'd rather not say in front of the two of you," Vance said quietly.

Tolwyn, smiling, nodded and turned and walked away.

"Hey, we're on the same team," Jason finally said as they went back down the corridor to the bridge.

"Just remember, Jason, if there's no need to really know, then you definitely better not know. Believe me, son, there's a hell of a lot I wish I didn't know at this moment."

Tolwyn looked over at him and smiled.

"Come on, I think it's safe for us to have a short drink, help us unwind. It's going to be a boring float out here until something comes up."

Jason was awakened by a gentle, but insistent shaking.

Damn, what was it now, and then he was instantly awake. The room was dark, there was no klaxon, no attack. He suffered a moment of disorientation, the old dream had come back, the explosions silently bursting across the surface of the moon orbiting Kilrah. Svetlana . . .

"Jason, it's Tolwyn, something's up."

He stood up, rubbing the sleep from his eyes and snapped on the light.

"What's wrong?"

"Nothing, but I want you in on this."

Jason reached into his closet, pulled on a fresh jumpsuit, slipped into a pair of shoes and followed Tolwyn out the door.

It was the midnight to four watch, one officer and four enlisted personnel manning the controls. Actually, the time was an artificial creation, complete to the dimming of all lights aboard ship except in work areas. He looked over at the chronometer; 0308 Confederation standard time and it certainly felt like it. He realized it had to be important if Tolwyn was pulling him out of the sack now. Well, at least it was some excitement for a change. They'd been on station eight jump points inside the Empire for twenty days, the three ships of their fleet rigged down for complete silent running, tucked into an asteroid field in a small system that didn't even rate a name on the charts, only a numbered designation.

Jason followed Tolwyn on to the flight deck and saw a small crowd gathered around a monitor. They quietly approached. Vance looked up and nodded a greeting.

"We've just had a break on cracking their latest A code and we've caught a burst signal from Kilrah but again it was garbled, emanating from the far side of the planet aimed towards Hari. They're only sending this particular burst when this one station is facing towards the Hari system and thus turned directly away from us. We get bounce reflections off of their moon, but the signal is degraded to near gibberish as a result. It's a pattern which seems to be adding up to something. We've also had a couple of partial locks on a burst coming out of the Hari system but it's still beyond our range to get a clear read and fix on it."

"So?" Jason asked, wondering why he had been pulled out of bed to hear what was not any of his business to know anyhow.

"I want to take us closer in," Vance replied casually, as if asking to do a little jaunt from Earth to the moon and back as a Sunday afternoon pleasure ride.

Vance motioned for the two to go into an empty cubicle. He punched up a holo display and then a two dimensional screen on one wall.

"This is why I wanted to get in closer," Vance said quietly, pointing at the holo map which floated in the corner of the cubicle and then to the flat screen where a long string of what appeared to be gibberish, marked by occasional intelligible words scrolled by.

"It's definitely fleet code, their highest grade. We had a twenty-three percent decipher on the last one, then this new code came on line but is being used only by this one station aimed at Hari. It has all the markings of a highest priority fleet code. We got really lucky when one of my people saw a similarity to a code they used nearly eight years ago and pulled it for comparison. We immediately broke a string of words and can do a six percent translation and it's less than twelve hours old. In five or six days I can bring that up to thirty percent and from there comparisons of word groupings, even knowing the writing styles of certain operators and officials, can help us break the rest."

"So why go deeper in now?"

"Because in five or six days I might have enough of the code broken so that we can get some hard core information. When we do, I want to be in position to scoop those signals from Hari and also the signals going out from Kilrah."

"That means getting some place between Kilrah and Hari," Jason said quietly.

Vance smiled again and nodded.

"Do you know what you're asking? Only one ship's ever gone to Kilrah and back, and that's this baby. I don't know how many Confed spy or recon ships have gotten into the area and back, but I bet it's precious few."

"Enough to prove it's possible," Tolwyn interjected. "But you are not going in to Kilrah, you're going to circle the edge of the Empire out to the far side and head into Hari territory."

"You didn't say we, you said you," Jason replied, looking over at Tolwyn.

"I'm taking the jump-capable Sabre on this ship back to Landreich in an hour," Tolwyn said.

"Hell, that's at least a seven day run, it'll be a nightmare in a ship that small. It doesn't even have a head on board."

"Well, if you don't mind, I'm taking Kevin along to keep me company. It'll be a chance for us to catch up on family matters. We'll just have to make do and rough it a bit. One of us can sleep in the tail gunner's slot while the other flies."

Jason smiled, glad at least for once that Tolwyn was

dropping the stiff upper lip routine and allowing himself to show some open attachment to his nephew.

"I'm putting you in command of this fleet. Paladin is being sent out in *Bannockburn* within the hour, doing forward recon and moving ahead of you. His orders are to go straight into Hari territory, to track down their burst signal, monitor it, and if possible close in for a visual check on its location.

"I'm ordering you to go cautiously, feel your way out around the edge of the Empire but don't go beyond extreme burst signal range to a relay drone that I'll make sure is deployed here," and he pointed to a map, which he quickly pulled up on a screen, showing a position four jump points inside of the Empire. "If something should come up, either with you or back home, we don't want you out of touch. I need to go back, some things have come up I've got to attend to and Vance has a little assignment for me."

Vance nodded and pointed back to the screen.

"There's several standard code words imbedded in these signals that we've seen before. They're just like Kilrathi general fleet communications during the war, daily updates on the various fronts that fleet commanders had to be made aware of. I suspect this word 'Nak'tara' that keeps coming up refers to a possible target of interest to those furballs. We're going to try an old trick to see if we can smoke them out. Geoff here has to take the message back personally. It's something I would never trust to a burst signal 'cause it could tip off this whole operation. I don't even want it in writing. It goes out in his head, and he can see to it along with his other business."

Jason looked over at the screen. This system was literally receiving and analyzing hundreds of millions of words, millions of conversations in Kilrathi, all its various dialects, and coded talk, hundreds of hours of video, and thousands of holo images every day. It was analyzing it, and boiling it down for info, and now because of a six percent translation of a half heard signal, he was being asked to jump *Tarawa* to the far side of the Empire. He had wandered into a shadow world of a quasi war which was beyond his ability to really understand. Either they were on to something, or they were all definitely nuts and he tended to think it was the latter.

Baron Jukaga smiled as he read the report. It seemed that both the Emperor and his son were to take the Imperial cruiser out to Largkza, the second moon of Kilrah to attend the yearly ritual of Pukcal, the day of atonement at the famed temple to Sivar located on that planet.

That the two would travel together was interesting in the extreme, a rare breach of security in allowing both the Emperor and the heir to travel aboard the same ship.

It was an opportunity he had to take though the thought chilled him. It was, after all, the greatest sin possible, one even beyond the imagining of nearly all of his race, to strike down a liege lord in secret without direct and open challenge. It was impossible, for to do so was seen as being beneath the contempt of the gods, and beyond that, would usually solve nothing, for without challenge, one could not take the place of the rival destroyed.

And yet I would succeed to the throne in the end, he realized. And as for the sin of it, he thought, I do not believe in the gods, so it does not matter. Even as he thought that heresy, however, he still felt chilled by it. He found it interesting that some humans could believe thus, and therefore deny any ultimate reason for existence, but for one who knew the hierarchy of the *hrai*, the clan, and the Empire with the godlike Emperor above all, it was impossible to contemplate. For was it not evident that in the hierarchy of the living there was also a hierarchy in the universe with the gods above the Emperor so that even in death one would sit with his *hrai* in paradise?

He knew that here again his study of humans had triggered this line of thinking which had taught him just how easy it was to gain power if one was willing to seize it; for after all did not a prince of ability have to reach for power for the benefit of his state?

He would do it, he had to. He looked again at the report. He would have to find a means of placing a small device on the cruiser, no easy task. He realized now that he was committed, and the thought brought him some comfort as he spun out his plan.

• CHAPTER SEVEN

"You know, laddie, I think I'm getting a bit too old for this sort of thing."

Ian shook his head and said nothing, waiting for the jump transit to hit. Space forward blurred and then snapped back into focus, his stomach dropping, flipping over, and nearly coming up his throat. Ian scanned the nav screen, waiting for the locks to set in on the various stars to confirm that they had jumped into the system they wanted. Anomalies in jumps were not uncommon even in the heavily traveled lanes in the heart of the Confederation. In the barely charted jump points beyond the outer border of the Kilrathi Empire it was almost a guess at times where the next jump would lead.

Paladin leaned over Ian's shoulder to watch, the seconds ticking by, finally a confirm light flashed on the screen and both breathed a sigh of relief.

"At least according to what our charts tell us, we're in the right place," Paladin said. "It's a bit hard to tell though. Hell, laddie, we're going down one narrow little road here, we might have passed hundreds of other jump points in between and not even known it. The last time I did this I had to feel my way blind through it all.

"I can tell you this, though, I think we've definitely gone a good bit into Hari territory, and Kilrah is somewhere off there," and he waved his hand vaguely off towards the port side of his ship, "roughly three hundred odd light years away. Where we're heading towards, that signal is sort of this way," and he vaguely waved his hand straight ahead, a gesture which Ian found to be strange and somewhat amusing.

"In the olden days they used to draw places on the map and say, here be'eth dragons," and Paladin chuckled.

"It's a long way back home," Ian said quietly.

"Aye," Paladin said quietly turning in his swivel chair to scan his surveillance instruments.

"Oh, we've got a little company way out here," he announced and pointed to the screen. "Ionization wake coming through here, heading straight for what I think's the next jump point."

"How old?"

"Not very, hard to tell, six, maybe ten hours."

"Could he have spotted us on the other side and jumped out?"

Paladin sat quietly for a minute thinking that question over yet again. One of the problems with this Cat Stealth machinery was the simple fact they were not even sure if it was really working right anymore. At least when *Tarawa* was alongside they could get a very quick and easy read. They hadn't seen *Tarawa* in ten days; it was now a good eight jump points behind them, holding itself at extreme burst signal range back to the edge of the frontier in case it had to get an emergency signal out.

He had figured out by now that the Stealth gear was to be used for only short periods of time, and the drain it made on ship's energy was tremendous. So they had finally agreed to use it only at the moment of jump, and then when the coast was clear to come out of it and recharge their power by running with full scoops open. There was the other simple question as well. The Stealth might work against Confederation ships, but no one had yet to figure out if the Cats had a simple way of detecting it themselves.

"Hard to tell, he could even be hiding somewhere in this blasted system and we don't have time to check it all."

Ian looked over at the chart which showed a dozen planets in orbit around the red giant star of this sector. Information beyond that was nonexistent, nothing on any of the planets, resources, whether they were even inhabited or not.

Paladin pursed his lips for a moment and then sighed.

"Well, laddie, let's power her up, get our tanks full, then close scoops and run to the next jump somewhat straight ahead. It'll take some time, we'll have to sniff it down."

Ian nodded, taking the helm, turning *Bannockburn* and headed towards where they hoped the next jump point was located. It was tedious work, jumping through, snooping on passive listening, and then hunting up the next jump point and moving forward again.

The engines of *Bannockburn* powered up and hours later it was far across the system, zeroing in on the next jump point. Long after their passage, what appeared to be nothing more than a small boulder, floating through the darkness a million kilometers from the jump point, shed its exterior. The Kilrathi light picket ship turned and accelerated away towards another jump point.

"I think he is planning to assassinate me," the Emperor said.

Prince Thrakhath was surprised by just how casual his grandfather was, as if discussing plans for yet another boring court ritual.

His choice of the word *assassinate* was interesting as well. In the language of Kilrah there was no such term, the word having filtered into the language from the Hari during the war of three eight-of-eights years past. For the Hari such disgusting practices appeared to have been their means of selecting who would rule, a chaotic and degrading system that left them ripe for conquest.

"What purpose would it serve?" Thrakhath asked. "After all, I would then rise to power," and even as he spoke the words he felt foolish, realizing that if Jukaga were planning to kill his grandfather, he would be killed as well.

He fell silent for a moment, lowering his head to lap up a gulp of wine.

"We can't simply denounce him," the Emperor said. "The evidence is far too flimsy, a mere hint, an inquiry as to who would be on the security detail guarding our cruiser the night before we leave for the Pukcal, but it fits him and what he has become."

Prince Thrakhath nodded in agreement. There was no denying that Jukaga was far too right in many of his criticisms of how the war had been run. He alone, out of nearly all the Kilrathi, had taken the time and effort to truly study the humans. It was, after all, his assignment as head of spying to learn the secrets of the enemy and how they thought.

That fact in and of itself had been troubling. In the past victory had come so quickly and with such assurance that there was little or no need to study the enemy; they were merely prey to be hunted down and exterminated. The Mantu did not count; their onslaught had come suddenly and with near overwhelming power, and then they had simply disappeared back into the void, apparently threatened by another unknown race. The human war, however, had dragged on for years. The exposure to them had been constant, even to the point of having a city's worth of human slaves right here in Kilrah, some of them even laboring in the subterranean caverns below the palace. Such contact had to, in the end, bring about changes. Jukaga had embraced them in order to understand and thus defeat them. It had thus introduced to him other ways of thinking as well.

But to assassinate? The mere thought of the alien word was repulsive, it was killing without any honor, without challenge. It was done in the dark, without any hope of then picking up the fallen sword of the slain in order to take his mantle of power and honor.

"If we both were killed," Thrakhath said, "there is no direct heir. In the chaos that followed, as head of his *hrai*, he would be in position to take the throne himself by playing off one faction against the other, something which he is a master at."

He said the words softly. The shame of even thinking it was hard to bear. There was no denying the horrifying fact that the seed of his family was weakening. His grandfather had sired many litters, most of them born dead, with but two sons surviving. His father had actually been executed by direct order of the Emperor, his uncle killed in the first days of the war.

He was now the only heir, and not one son had been born to him, a sickly daughter his only surviving offspring from a single litter, and that from a lowly concubine of the second order. It was a humiliation almost beyond bearing. He should have sired dozens of offspring by now. He felt a deep and lasting shame. War was the only outlet left to him to vent his rage over his failure on the mating couch.

There were a number of cousins descending from his grandfather's sister, so many that the chance of blood feud and civil war was the most likely result. Is that what Jukaga wanted, a civil war? He thought of his cousins. It would be easy enough to trigger a dynastic struggle with them, and Jukaga could weave his way through the alliances, weakening the family until finally it would be his own *hrai* that would be the strongest and could then finish them off. It would be a civil war unlike any fought since they had first ventured off their home world over eight eight-of-eights ago.

It was a dreadful thought. He had always assumed that in the passage of years he would either sire a son to succeed him, or, when he was old, he would choose a cousin to sit upon the golden throne. His choice would then ritually kill him and thus take the sword and throne by right of blood.

"We cannot kill him," the Emperor said, "not now. There is first of all the simple fact that his plan for the war has so far indeed worked, degrading as it is. The humans have been placed off guard, our shortage of transports is being rectified, and the new fleet is moving towards completion. If we ordered his death it would upset that plan, and beyond that, appear to be an act of jealousy. The other *hrai* leaders forced his return and the killing of him out of hand would bring their wrath down upon us. There is no denying the fact that, like it or not, his plan pulled us out of a difficult impasse."

Thrakhath nodded in agreement.

"And the onus of such an act we can place upon his shoulders," Thrakhath replied with a smile.

"There is the other fact as well," the Emperor continued. "He heads the operation of our spies. He knows perhaps even more than I do. His operatives are everywhere. Any attempt to take him would be known long before we were ready to strike."

The Emperor stood up and went over to stare at a tapestry hanging behind the throne, which showed an ancient hunt scene, all the time making sure to stay within the stasis field that blocked all detection devices.

Thrakhath looked back at the Emperor, who looked at him sharply.

"Could your fleet take the humans now?" he asked.

"It is not certain. Four carriers are now ready, the fifth in two eights of days."

"Could you win?"

All the variables, all the calculations said that a swift attack with five new carriers would succeed, though there was a slim chance that the losses would be heavy.

"Remember, the humans have weakened themselves," the Emperor said, "and our traitor in their ranks keeps us informed."

Thrakhath nodded. He did not want to take any risks and then he wondered if this peace had made him weak as well. War was risk, that was the thrill of it.

"We can take them with five carriers, my lord. However, we would have to strike with full and overwhelming surprise. Any warning before we cross the frontier could give them time to prepare a defense."

"Then be sure that this unconfirmed report of their having a spy ship in our space is acted upon at once. They are not to get through or see anything, that is still crucial."

Thrakhath nodded in agreement.

"If he makes this attempt and we survive, politically it

would still make us look weak, having first agreed to this disgusting peace and then suffering the indignity of having someone attempt to strike us."

"Then kill him now and be done with it," Thrakhath snarled.

"No. We would never have the evidence we need, he is too cunning for that. Let him make his strike, but then let us shift the blame on to the humans. It will serve a twofold purpose of discrediting his peace effort and help to enrage our own against both him and the humans. I think it is time as well to have a talk with our ambassador in their camp. He has waited too long for his revenge, let him have it."

The radar burst pinged across the screen and Jason sat silent, watching, looking over at his counter electronics officer. She was hunched over her own screen staring at it as if mesmerized. The young woman, she could not have been more than twenty, punched an order into a flat touch screen, absently reaching up occasionally to push an unruly wisp of red hair from her freckled forehead. He felt as if she was not much beyond being a very young child, and the thought struck him as almost funny. He was, after all, only twenty-seven, the youngest carrier commander in the fleet. In any other type of life the woman would have been very dateable. Out here, in this situation, the difference seven additional years of war added was a chasm almost too deep to comprehend. Another ping washed over the screen.

"They're close, they're very close," Vance whispered.

Jason felt that if he went to a topside view port he could almost see the Kilrathi scout ship. A hundred thousand clicks was damn near next door in space.

"Still an unfocused radar sweep," the electronics officer announced.

Another ping hit.

"Doppler shifting away, he's moving past us, sir."

Jason let out a sigh of relief.

"Keep secure for silent running," Jason announced and he left the bridge, followed by Vance.

"I thought you were crazy to land like this," Vance said and Jason looked over at him and smiled weakly.

"Maybe I am."

The move was unorthodox in the extreme. Less than twelve hours ago Vance's team had picked up a series of orders shifting more than a hundred scout and recon ships into the sector they were now occupying and to cover all the surrounding jump points. Apparently something had tipped the Kilrathi off to their presence. His first thought was to run and hide inside the atmosphere of a gas giant but there were none to be found within the system. There was, however, a greenhoused world cloaked in heavy clouds, its surface boiling hot and scored by deep canyons. Placing two light carriers down on the surface under the lip of an overhanging cliff had been tricky. If discovered they would be near defenseless. A light fighter armed with just a couple of antimatter warheads would make short work of them if they were caught and unable to lift off in time.

So far the subterfuge had worked, and with the planet's extremely slow rotational period, Vance had been able to keep a watch on burst signals from the direction of Kilrah, now three hundred and eighty light years away. However, the Hari system was blocked by the bulk of the planet.

The only problem was that the scout ships simply refused to leave and had thus kept them pinned for three days, out of touch with Paladin, wherever he might now be.

"Here we go, laddie, jump in ten seconds."

Paladin cinched up his safety harness and waited. He spared a quick glance over at Ian who sat placidly next to him.

This next jump was totally blind, leaping into a jump point without any idea where they were going. The last three jumps had taken them further than any human had ever ventured before, far beyond the outer rim of the Kilrathi Empire and into the completely uncharted realm of the long dead Hari. The burst signal they were tracking down had fired off again only six hours ago and was very close, in a star system less than eight light years away. They had slipped through the sector using the Stealth, though it appeared as if one of the dozen picket ships they had passed had at least gotten a temporary lock on them. In a couple of seconds he would know if this jump would take them to their goal.

The jump transit hit, blurring vision. The stars ahead disappeared. Paladin swallowed hard and waited. Maybe I'm getting too old for these sorts of games, he thought. Twenty years of fighting is pressing the edge of the envelope just a little too much. He pushed the thought aside, no sense dwelling on it. Besides, what the hell would I do with myself to kill the boredom?

A new starfield snapped into focus and at the same instant the radar detection alarm started to shriek its warning.

He leaned over in his chair, punching the alarm off and turned to look at the readout screen.

"Well, lad, we're being tracked," he announced, trying to keep the fear from his voice. It always amazed him how all the others looked to him as someone with ice water in his veins. If only they really knew just how gut-wrenching the fear could really be.

He watched his screen as optical mounts turned, tracking down the incoming paths of the radar, passively searching out the darkness for the enemy.

"Got one sighted, make that two, now three, the closest standing at thirty eight thousand clicks, a light corvette."

Another high energy radar burst snapped on them, this one a narrow focus beam. It could only mean that the Cats were on to him.

He spared a quick look up at the unknown system they had just entered. The jump point was fairly close into the system's sun, a standard class M. He continued the optical sweep. He'd have a good five minutes before the corvette would start to close. Now that they'd been found out, they could at least do a quick scan before jumping back out and shaking off the pursuit in the system which they had just jumped from.

"Getting an awful lot of sublight radio traffic in this sector," Ian announced. "Trying to get an optical lock on the signals."

Ian, working the long range optical scanners, stayed hunched over his screen. A full radar sweep would have been better, but they would be long gone before the first returns even started to bounce back. The use of the narrow band translight pulse was out of the question. They'd have to drop completely out of Stealth and it'd reveal their true mission to the picket ships.

"Paladin, switch to my screen," Ian whispered, his voice suddenly high and tense.

Paladin switched into the long range optical scan, his eyes straining as Ian spun the optics up to their highest magnification, which could pick up an object the size of a one pound coin from two hundred thousand clicks out.

"My lord," Paladin gasped, "hit the holo recorder switch."

"Already running," Ian replied.

Paladin stared at the screen in disbelief when Ian punched in a computer enhancement with scale gradients superimposed over the image. They were looking at a ship that was at least fifteen hundred meters in length. Several seconds later the computer, now armed with more information, cleared the first image from the screen and replaced it with a higher resolution enhancement, with the beginning of an analysis of what they were looking at.

"Fifteen hundred and eighty meters, estimated half a million ton bulk weight," Paladin whispered. "Range 102 million clicks, orbiting the only planet in the system."

"Dozens of ships orbiting that planet," Ian announced, "coming up now on second screen."

Paladin spared a quick glance over to the secondary images forming, three more ships like the first one, half a dozen more apparently still under construction, a dozen cruiser type vessels that were bigger than the old *Concordia*—battleships he could only guess would be the word for them, drawing the term out of ancient nautical history. Part of the screen was tallying off a count of transports, more than a hundred of them either docked into what appeared to be an orbital construction yard that filled half a dozen cubic kilometers of space, or hovering around it.

The alarm went off again, warbling with a high insistent tone and Paladin turned to look back at his tactical.

"We've got company, laddies. Looks like two Stealths just jumped in behind us. Prepare for evasive!"

"We'll lose the visual lock," Ian shouted. "I don't have a full read on it yet."

Paladin weighed the variables and in less than half a dozen seconds from the sounding of the second alarm he came to his decision. Turning back to his main screen he cleared it of the optical and punched in the order for a translight beam sweep, dropping his ship out of Stealth mode. The pulse went out, even as he swung his ship hard over into an evasive. The first Stealth already had a lock on him and dropped a missile which he assumed was one of the new and more deadly IFFs. Before the missile was even clearly away Paladin popped a scrambler, a decoy pulsing with a standard Confed IFF code and capable of reflecting back a radar image of a fleet light corvette, a counter he had rigged up based upon Ian's unpleasant experience.

Ian looked over at him in surprise and grinned, as the transponder snapped to life. It was a clear give away as to who they really were along with the translight pulse sweep. Seconds later the data came sweeping back in with a high resolution read of the enemy fleet. The first missile at the same time streaked into the decoy and detonated. Two more missiles swept out from the Stealths which were turning to follow *Bannockburn* in its evasive and Paladin punched out another decoy while at the same time launching half a dozen dumb fire flechette bolts from his rear tubes that would fill space behind him with thousands of nail-sized shot that could rip a fighter to shreds if it got caught in the spread.

Even as he piloted the ship he watched the other screen. A green flash indicated that the pulse had been successfully read and stored by the ship's computer.

"Check it!" Paladin shouted.

"We've got good data," Ian replied.

"Load it along with the optical read and our coordinates into a burst signal, aim it back towards *Tarawa*."

"Loaded!"

Paladin toggled a switch into the burst signal line.

"Green one, green one, this is green two, am under attack, cover blown, repeat cover blown, get the hell out and back to the barn."

He hit the burst signal button and the lights in the cabin momentarily dimmed as nearly all the ship's energy was diverted to powering out the signal across the hundreds of light years of space back to *Tarawa*.

At least they'd have the information even if they bought it. He realized that in the scheme of things his job was done, he had uncovered the suspected fleet. Within minutes *Tarawa* would have the information and it'd blow the lid right off the armistice when it came out that the Kilrathi were building the ships in clear violation of the terms. The political ramifications would be explosive, he realized. At the very least Rodham's government would fall. It'd also mean that the war would be back on. He thought again of what he'd just uncovered and the images still locked on the secondary screen chilled him. The carriers were more than twice as big as anything now in the fleet. Even if every ship was still active and on line the new Kilrathi ships had the power to destroy anything in space.

The Cats undoubtedly knew that their cover had just been blown. The only hope was to fully remobilize before the ships already completed could be moved up into action and meet them on the frontier. If they gained Confederation space with our defenses down it was over.

The two missiles hit the second decoy and detonated.

The Stealths dropped out of masking and came to full visual, transferring their energy to neutron guns and laser. A shot lanced into the portside stabilizer of *Bannockburn* and Paladin pulled hard to starboard, lining up a deflection shot on one of his tormentors. He flared off half a dozen more flechette rounds, followed by two dumb fired bolts. The flechette rounds broke open, each deploying a spread of sixty thousand nail-sized shot across a hundred meter wide piece of space. The wave slammed into the Stealth, shredding it to ribbons and the ship silently detonated.

The picket ships were already racing in to join the fray, their speed well up past a thousand clicks a second with maneuvering scoops fully closed.

"Turning in on jump point. Get ready for uncalibrated jump in fifteen seconds!" Paladin shouted.

Another laser burst hit *Bannockburn* dead astern, overloading the shields, cutting into the Y-axis maneuvering thrusters, and Paladin cursed as he purged the thrusters' fuel lines before they detonated.

He spared a quick thought for the message he sent out, hoping that *Tarawa* was at least still alive to get it, otherwise this whole damn thing was for naught.

"How the hell did I ever get into this business?" he shouted even as the jump transit hit.

"We've got it."

Jason looked up at Vance who had not even bothered to knock before bursting into his cabin. The normally unflappable director of intelligence seemed almost giddy with excitement.

"Got what?"

"The signal damn it, the signal. Come on, I'll show you."

Jason followed Vance back down the corridor into the fighter bay. He had a flash memory of the same corridor, running towards the bridge when it was hit by the Kilrathi suicide pilot, killing O'Brian, the first captain of the *Tarawa*, the corridor decompressing when the hull was shattered.

They reached the end of the corridor, the two security guards still requiring that even Vance show ID and undergo a corona laser scan. It struck him as a bit absurd, here they were hiding on a planet's surface, no one could possibly sneak aboard to impersonate Vance, and the man had come down the corridor only a minute before. But he knew that security above all else required no relaxation.

He showed his ID as well and leaned into the corona scanner.

The guards opened the doorway into the bay and saluted, the door slamming shut behind them.

The D-5 team was gathered in a knot around what was Vance's cubicle, and to Jason's surprise he saw bottles of champagne being passed around. He was about to raise an objection to such an open violation of fleet regulations but then realized that fleet regs no longer applied, since officially they were not part of the fleet, and in fact officially did not even exist. Intel people had always struck him as a little strange and he realized that perhaps they needed to blow off steam like this otherwise they would have cracked under the pressure long ago. They were no different than pilots in that respect.

The crowd parted for Vance, patting him on the back.

"Good job, people, now let's finish our party and get back to work, there's a hell of a lot to be done before this mission is finished."

The crowd seemed to immediately sober up and drifted away back to their stations.

"Here's what all the excitement is about. I thought you should know in case anything happened."

"Anything happened?"

"We could take a hit to this bay and our entire team gets wiped out. I want someone off this deck to know what we've just found out. I want you to remember the message but you are to immediately, and forever, forget how we found out."

Jason nodded in agreement.

Vance pointed to a two dimensional screen. On the

right side was what Jason assumed was phonetically translated Kilrathi, on the left long series of white blocks, and occasional words in English which were partial translations of the message.

"When Geoff left he went back, amongst other reasons, to have ConFleet send out a false message which stated that our primary matter-antimatter assembly plant on the moon had been destroyed due to an accidental detonation. As a result no new weapons would be delivered for several months. The message of course was a complete fabrication.

"An hour ago we picked up this message from Kilrah to their Hari base and cracked part of it."

Jason leaned over to look at the screen.

Most of the message was untranslated but one line highlighted in red leaped out at him . . . "Remove target 2778A on moon of *nak'tara* from primary strike list. Accident has destroyed target, . . ." there were several lines untranslated . . . "shortage in antimatter weapons produced from 2778A expected, will update."

Jason looked back up at Vance.

"They took the bait. We broadcast the false message on a code we knew they had already cracked. Their listening post, most likely right in their embassy office picked it up and passed it back to Kilrah. *Nak'tara* means Earth. It means that whatever it is they're preparing out there in Hari is being aimed for an attack straight at Earth. Damn it, the bastards are getting ready to strike."

Jason leaned back in the chair and closed his eyes for a moment. He could understand the elation of Vance's crew. Their job was to get information and they had just pulled out a gold nugget of information unlike anything found in years. They had reason to celebrate. But it meant as well that the armistice was nothing more than a sham. Though he had assumed it to be so from the beginning, there had always been a small part of him that had hoped against hope that maybe the peace was real after all. This was a dark proof that shattered the dream.

Damn all of them, the Kilrathi, the political leaders back home that had led them into this fix, damn all of them.

"Think we should lift off and get the hell out of here?" Jason asked. "We could punch our way through the picket screen."

Vance shook his head.

"And bring back what? One partially decoded message as proof. The peace party crowd would say it was cooked up to restart the war. A lone burst signal does not an iron-clad case make."

"They could be moving at any time now. We should be alerting ConFleet, they'll believe us."

"Son, ConFleet will believe us, but they're the only ones. You've got to remember this as well. We don't exist as far as the government is concerned. There aren't more than half a dozen people off this ship who even know we're out here. How do you think it'd be presented if we go rushing back home and stand up to announce that we parked this ship clear on the other side of the Empire in clear violation of the armistice? The real truth of what we found would be lost in the screaming and protests not only from the Kilrathi but from some of our own people as well. It'd also blow the cover on this D-5 system. That's one of the problems with intelligence. If we make public what we've found, the Kilrathi will figure out just how capable our surveillance is and change their procedures and it might be years before we can break it back down again."

Jason nodded. They'd need something hard, clearly recorded visuals, and even then some people would claim it was a fake out. Hell, the Kilrathi would most likely have to start kicking down the front door before anyone would act.

"So we just sit here and wait."

"Too bad this planet screens us from your friend Paladin. Maybe he might have something by now," Vance replied. "Hell, we're stuck here, unable to move, and one ship out to scout. I doubt if he's even got within a hundred light years of their base."

❖   ❖   ❖

Standing up to stretch, Prince Thrakhath growled softly as he continued to look at the screen which showed the latest intelligence report.

The intelligence report from Jukaga matched that of what his own military chain of command had stated. Jukaga most likely knew that Thrakhath had his own lines of communications, and since the incident took place within a military command district he would find out about it almost immediately.

Someone, almost undoubtedly from the Confederation, had penetrated right into the very system where the new fleet was being constructed. The translight radar sweep could only have been done by a very well outfitted spy ship, as no smuggler could afford to carry such equipment. Beyond that, the ship had been using Stealth masking. The fact that the humans had either learned the secret of Stealthing or captured such equipment was stunning. They were on to something. The question now was whether the information had gotten back to the Confederation and their fleet command. No burst signal could possibly cross such a distance. The spy ship had sent out three burst signals so far, all of them aimed towards the Paghk System, where a suspected ship was still being hunted. But no burst signal had come from that system to relay the message on.

No, Confleet did not yet know.

He turned to a holo projection, ordering up a map of the Paghk system, and then ordered a projection of jump lines and systems back to where the spy ship had been sighted. Next he ordered in a display of where the spy was now located, the position of ships in pursuit and where nearby ships might be located to move in to aid the chase. Finally he ordered a projection of jump lines from the Paghk system back towards the Confederation ship.

The holo field was a maze of blue lines, blinking lights representing ships, and steady yellow lights representing the array of stars which were terminus points for the jump lines.

He studied it intently, shifting, moving in the focus, calling up more data, formulating plans, then shifting the field yet again to examine another part, a side screen scrolling out data on the various ships available.

Yet this was no simple intercept operation. There was a political consideration as well, involving Jukaga, and just what he might be doing in regards to this new situation. As he studied the holo projection Thrakhath developed his plan.

He was interrupted by a paging call. It was the Emperor on an open line.

"It is time that we leave for the ceremony," the Emperor said and then clicked off.

• CHAPTER EIGHT

"We've picked up a threefold increase in signal traffic within the last six hours, chief."

Vance nodded wearily, looking through the report handed to him by one of his assistants. He was exhausted. Against all rules of proper procedure, he had put his people on eight hour on, four hour off duty shifts. He knew exhaustion was cutting into their performance, that it'd be best to give everybody a day off to unwind, but it was getting too hot. Earlier in the day they had made a quantum jump in cracking Fleet Code A, bringing the translations up to nearly sixty percent. It was increasingly revealing the full extent of the conspiracy, ranging from continual updates of military actives and deployments around Earth, but also a thousand other details down to spare part requests, and shipping orders for the transport fleet that was slipping deep out into Hari space, hauling the millions of tons of supplies needed to build a new fleet from scratch. A signal earlier in the day reported the transfer of more than a thousand pilots, their plane maintenance crews and the fighter craft off of carriers in drydock, and thus supposedly deactivated to the reserves, to the new fleet.

Something was definitely up. The Kilrathi were acting, but on what, and for what reason? And now the signal increase.

"We're also getting ship to ship communication increase within this system. Two light cruisers have moved in along with one heavy cruiser just detected."

That made Vance sit up and take notice. He looked at the report that the analyst pointed out on the screen, a real

166

time translation of the messages, broadcast on a low priority code racing across the screen.

"They're setting up for an intercept from the looks of
things," Vance said. "Send a messenger down to Captain
Bondarevsky, tell him to come here at once."

There were times when security got on his nerves. All
communication lines between the fighter bay and the rest
of the ship had been sealed off based upon the near infini-
tesimal chance that a member of the ship's crew, and one
of his own people might collaborate in trying to get information off the ship.

The analyst turned and started for the door while Vance
punched over to his head of Alpha team security, inform-
ing the captain to let the analyst pass into the ship and
return with Jason.

A side channel suddenly leaped into activity on the display screen, originating from inside the system they were
now occupying. It was one of the standard Confleet bands.
But from where?

The D-5 had already locked on to it, a reflected signal
skipping over the horizon of the planet, the message
breaking up. "Just what the hell is this?" Vance whispered,
turning more of the computer's power loose from other
activities to focus in on the signal and enhance it.

It was an audio signal, and he turned on a speaker.

"Green one, Green one, this is Green two over."

"That's Paladin!"

Vance turned to see Jason coming up behind him.

"Green one, where the hell are you, am under attack,
over."

"Where's it coming from?" Jason asked.

"Looks like from directly on the other side of the planet.
Getting some skip through the atmosphere, wait a second."

He typed in a quick order and the D-5 turned one of its
antenna array to aim at the small moon of the planet which
was nothing more than an oversized rock orbiting half a
million clicks overhead.

"Getting a reflection signal from the moon as well, give me a second here . . ." and he punched in another command.

"There, got it. Triangulate the signal as coming from near directly behind us, thirty five million clicks back."

"Straight back towards the jump point towards Hari," Jason said, turning to look at a holo map of the system which one of Vance's assistants activated, a blinking yellow dot showing where Paladin must be.

"We're getting in the clear attack signals from the Kilrathi cruisers, one of them is launching fighters," the assistant announced.

"They're moving in to cut Paladin off," Jason said quietly, looking at the map which was now showing the enemy ships in the sector. Several corvettes were already moving to set up a picket across the jump point leading out towards Confederation space while the cruisers positioned themselves for an easy kill.

"Either they found him out before he got the information, or after he picked it up; it's one of the two," Vance said quietly.

"Why are you telling me this?" Jason asked, suddenly aware that Vance was staring at him in a coldly detached way.

"If he doesn't have the data, and we go up to try and save him, our cover is blown and we'll have to get the hell out. For that matter I wonder if we can get out now considering the hardware they've brought in here."

"Are you suggesting that I do nothing and let them blow Paladin and Ian apart?"

"The mission comes first, Captain."

"And suppose he does have the data we need?"

"I haven't heard it yet, and frankly, son, his chances of finding them were slim to none to start with when we sent him on alone."

Jason looked back at the screen.

"Green one, Green one, am under attack, where the hell are you?"

Jason closed his eyes and tried to focus his thoughts, while Paladin's insistent call for help echoed across the deck.

"Green one, Green one, this is Green two over."

Paladin, exasperated and filled with a frustrated rage, punched the channel off and slammed his fist down on the console.

To have come so far back and now to be cut off. The next jump point out of this system was blocked, and already half a dozen ships which had been pursuing him for days were coming through behind, a fact made worse by the more than fifty patrol craft and three cruisers currently in the sector. The heavy cruiser was already launching its squadron of fighters which would close with him within the hour.

The game was up and *Bannockburn* was about to get fried. As soon as he had jumped, the pickets waiting on the far side plastered him with high energy radar bursts and then threw on laser locks he simply couldn't shake.

Just before they hit him he'd try one more burst signal, feeding every erg of power he had into it, but the chance of it reaching Confed space at this range was remote and made even more implausible by the fact that it was dicey at best if someone had a listening array focused on this region. If only he knew where *Tarawa* was he could transfer the info off and they'd have the power to punch a signal through, plus they would also know where to aim it for an intercept.

"Damn it all to hell, if I get out of this I quit," Paladin snarled. "I'm heading back to Scotland and I'll be damned if I ever let my two feet get off the ground again.

"Ian, you'd better launch now. I'm glad that the Admiral managed to get a jump capable Ferret tucked into this ship's cargo bay. I thought he was a wee bit crazy trying that out. I'm ordering you to break off and try and make it through the jump point. I'm loading the information into your fighter's computers now. You've got to get that information back to Confed territory. *Tarawa's* either gone or bought it."

Ian looked over at Paladin. He knew Paladin was right. The swarm of enemy fighters was closing.

He wanted to say something but couldn't find the words.

Paladin looked up and forced a smile.

"Lift one for me at the Vacuum Breathers Club, laddie. Now get the hell out of here."

Ian turned and headed for the door.

"Good luck, Paladin."

Paladin shook his head and laughed.

Ambassador Vak'ga paused for a moment and looked back at the holo image on his desk. Again he felt the tug of pain and silently cursed himself for still feeling it. After all, the mourning should have ended on the first Sivar after the death of his sons. That was, after all, six years back. But no, the pain had never stopped. His seed was gone and when he died, his *hrai* would die with him.

He thought yet again of the agreement he had made with Prince Thrakhath on the eve before leaving for Earth. When Thrakhath had first suggested it to him his blood had burned with the thought of at last gaining vengeance. But now, it was so cold, there was no rage, no pain, just a detachment, a coldness, as if the goddess had already reached into his heart to still its beating.

The coded message to commit the act had arrived this morning, and soon the pain would stop. At least I will see my sons again, my sons taken from me by the humans. At least we will again embrace and go forth on the hunt with our ancestors.

He thought of the detonator and antimatter explosive buried in his chest cavity. Strange, there will be nothing more of me, nothing to be found to be buried. Fitting perhaps, since there will be no one to mourn me.

The Ambassador walked out of his office, not even bothering to close the door.

❖   ❖   ❖

"How are you doing, Geoff? It's damn good to see you again."

Admiral Banbridge came around from behind his desk, hand extended. Former Rear Admiral Geoffrey Tolwyn grasped it, and to his surprise Banbridge grabbed hold of him in a friendly bear hug. Turning he looked at Kevin, who stood at attention, and smiled.

"I heard you're one of the fleet's best," Banbridge said approvingly.

Geoff smiled broadly at the compliment to his nephew. The long transit back to Landreich, and from there hidden aboard a high speed smuggler craft to Earth, had given him the opportunity, for the first time, to really find out just who his nephew truly was. In the back of his mind, in spite of Kevin's actions aboard *Tarawa*, he still perceived him as a child. That was now dispensed with, their relationship changing to the close bond that can form between an uncle or father, and his son who is now a man.

"Kevin, I hate to ask this, but would you mind waiting for us? My steward will show you a damn nice shower and cook up some food for you."

Kevin saluted and followed the steward into the rear of the small apartment Banbridge had down in the basement of Fleet headquarters.

"He reminds me of you at that age, Geoff," Banbridge said with a smile, as he led his old student into his office and closed the door.

"Glad you're back safe. Have a seat and fill me in."

Geoff settled down into the proffered chair, his old boss sitting down across from him.

"First of all, what the hell was this signal you had me send?"

As Geoff explained Banbridge's features lit up.

"Same trick we Americans once used against the Japanese at Midway with the fake report of a water distillery breaking down. The Japanese picked it up and reported to their fleet that 'target X' was short of water, and by that little trick we knew their next target was Midway. Vance always did know his history."

"Have we had any word yet from out there? Since I left Landreich I've been out of touch."

Admiral Banbridge shook his head and Geoff silently cursed.

"What's been happening back here on Earth?"

Banbridge blew out noisily and reached around to his desk, pulling out two glasses and a small decanter of port wine, pouring out a drink for himself and Tolwyn.

"The damn fools are eating up the crap that Vak'ga and Jukaga keep feeding them. Hell, Rodham has even agreed to a cultural exchange, with a bunch of Kilrathi singers and dancers coming to Earth next month. The damn brie and wine crowd at the capital are eating it up, begging for tickets to the performance. The Chief of Staff raised holy hell about it, pointing out that we'd have over a hundred Kilrathi running around the capital and damn near everyone of them an intelligence operative. He was hooted down by Jamison and told to, 'relax, the war is over.'

"It's nuts, I tell you. Anyone who talks about preparedness, about keeping the fleet appropriations up, is denounced as a war monger."

"And just how is the fleet?" Tolwyn asked.

"Four fleet carriers are still on line."

"Just four?"

"It's worse. Two of them are drydocked at the moment but it's claimed they can be brought back up to operational status within thirty days."

"What about the others?"

"In drydock, reactors pulled, crews on extended leave."

"What the hell for?"

Banbridge sighed.

"Jamison convinced the President, and he convinced the Senate, that if the Kilrathi were going to make a move we'd have plenty of warning and she pointed out that all but six of the Kilrathi carriers had been put into inactive reserve as well. So as a cost cutting measure the carriers were pulled in for major refitting and overhaul. Getting them on line could take up to three months."

"God help us," Tolwyn whispered, draining his glass and then accepting a refill.

"Forty-eight percent of the rest of the ships of the fleet are still on line, the rest are skeleton crewed in reserve. Operationally we're losing our edge. Flight training time for the fighters has been cut by nearly half, even our main battle fleet ships still in active service, our heavy cruisers, are tied off with crews on leave. It'd take weeks, maybe a month to two months to even get one full Task Force Group organized and back on line.

"What's worse is the freeze on construction. We should have had a new fleet carrier and four more cruisers operational by now and a number of other ships started. We tried to get through a government decree requiring all shipyard works to stay on their jobs; that caused a hell of an uproar and some of our best technicians are quitting to look for work elsewhere. Key war industries, which during hostilities were forbidden to strike, are now having walkouts with people wanting higher wages, made worse by what looks like an economic depression due to a freeze on new defense contracts.

"Morale is down in the gutter. The career people are sore as hell. They wanted this thing seen through to the finish. Most of our old line people know that this war won't really be over till we storm through the rubble of the imperial palace and raise the Confederation flag. Anything else is a prelude to defeat. The reservists and draftees on the other hand are all clamoring to get discharged. Hell, senators are getting flooded with letters from parents, wives, and even our own troops demanding demobilization, the old 'bring the boys and girls back home.'"

"I guess it's kind of hard to blame them when you think of it. To them it really does look like it's over."

Banbridge nodded.

"I tell you, Geoff, I think a democratic republic is the only way to run the show; you English are the ones who really invented it and then we Americans picked it up. But there's always been one flaw in it and that is the sustaining of a long-term war. It's hard at times for civilians to truly understand the military; we have a thousand year tradition of always being at odds with the civilians we're sworn to defend. The military at times gets turned into the Greek messenger who gets blamed for simply telling people the truth of how the universe works. People get too caught up in the wish for peace and forget that the law of the jungle is still the law in most parts of this universe, and they don't like it when we try to tell them differently."

"Got any suggestions on how to change it?"

Banbridge smiled and shook his head.

"It's what I've spent forty-three years in the service fighting to defend. No, it's got its problems but I'll keep it."

"That's if it survives one year longer. Don't people realize what the Cats are up to?"

"Oh, a hell of a lot of ordinary people do, especially in the outer planets and the frontier. They've lived on the real edge of the war, sometimes in the middle of it. They know what even a momentary slip of vigilance can do. But the inner system of planets, and especially Earth, have been bearing the financial burden of a war that's been fought several hundred light years and a dozen or more jump points away. I think they're willing to grab at anything if it'll mean peace. We've got an entire generation that's been born and come to adulthood knowing nothing but war played out nightly on the holo screen, and the ruinous taxes to support it; to them peace is a dream as powerful as any narcotic."

"And it just might kill them."

Banbridge sighed.

"The damn media is part of the problem. The Kilrathi have done a masterful job of feeding them selected footage of furball planets bombarded in the war, tearful interviews with widows who ask for peace, the usual propaganda crap. But try and send our own crews in to film freely and the curtain gets slammed down. It seems to be really popular of late, especially on the college campuses, to buy Jukaga's line that the war was a conspiracy of their military and ours to make themselves powerful and big industry rich. The majority of people see through it, but there's enough out there buying whatever they see on the holo to make things a bit hot.

"But enough on that, fill me in on what's happened with you over the last two months."

As Geoff described his arrangement of ship transfers to the Landreich and the mission into Kilrathi space with the D-5 team Banbridge remained silent, sipping on his port, and refilling Geoff's glass when it went dry.

"When I got back to Landreich, that's when things started to get dicey with Kruger."

"How so?"

"He's absolutely furious with the Confed and the blockage of the fighter shipment. At least they were getting a trickle during the war, but the peace commission has shut off any further shipments of war-related supplies.

"I tell you, Wayne, those colonials are absolute masters at cobbling a fleet together and keeping it flying. What they're having an impossible time getting through legitimate channels are the latest high tech fighters, electronics, and ship to ship missiles."

"Legitimate channels?"

Geoff laughed.

"They're still getting some interesting equipment, but don't ask me how."

Banbridge nodded and smiled.

"Spare parts they get from cannibalizing, patching, and making do. They've even produced their own heavy fighters, by taking obsolete three-man patrol ships and jacking on the most god awful bizarre engines you've ever seen. Anyone who flies them deserves a medal of honor just for turning the engines on.

"Now for frontier raiding, dealing with Kilrathi colonial guard forces or even light raiding fleets they could teach us a thing or two. But if the main battle fleet ever hits through there, every planet in the Landreich will be glowing and Kruger knows it. By heavens, Wayne, the way he swore at you, the Chief of Staff and Rodham were a thing to behold."

"Will he stick with us though when the time comes?"

"Only as far as Landreich interests are concerned. Frankly, I think he'd be happy if the Confederation and the Empire blew each other the hell apart and the colonials were the only ones left."

"I just bet that old bastard does," Banbridge said with a smile. "He's the most amazing pain in the butt I've ever known, and also one of the best."

"When do you want me to go back out?" Tolwyn asked. "I think it's crucial that if things go bad that I'm out there with him. I know he sees through this little court martial game I went through. He knows I'm operating covertly for the Chief of Staff and intelligence, and I guess he sort of likes me as a result."

"That's part of the reason you got picked for the assignment, I had a gut feeling he'd see you as a bit of a renegade, and your fighting record was sure to impress him."

Geoff nodded and was silent. There was nothing really to be said. He had been asked to volunteer for the assignment, to deliberately provoke a court martial offense, to seek a dishonorable discharge in order to go into covert operations. It had destroyed his reputation, making him a pariah in his own service, except for the half dozen or so people who were in on the secret. If his old mentor and friend had asked him to kill himself for the good of the service he would not hesitate.

"I do have one question that's troubling me though," Geoff finally said and he hesitated for a moment.

"What about Project Omega?"

Banbridge looked over at Tolwyn in surprise.

"Son, you were never cleared to know that. Damn, if I had known you were on the in on Project Omega I'd never have let you go running off with *Tarawa* the way you did. You aren't supposed to know anything about it."

Tolwyn smiled.

"But I do, and don't ask me how."

Banbridge nodded.

"Still being supported through black funds. This project Rodham does know about, but no one else in the cabinet has been cleared. He agreed to keep it going, I guess in part as a lever to force the Chief into signing the armistice. Rodham thinks Omega is our ace in the hole."

"And how close is it to completion?"

Banbridge shook his head.

"A hell of a lot of snags, six months before we could even fire up the engines on the first ship, a year more likely, though the conservatives are saying eighteen months is a safe bet."

Tolwyn shook his head at the news. There was something ironic about the war that he felt an outside observer would find amusing. The Kilrathi had gone through incredible expense and effort to start the secret building of a new class of carriers, if indeed what flimsy information intel had been able to dig up so far was true. The Confederation was doing the same thing. It was not so much a super carrier along the lines of suspected Kilrathi design, but more a Stealth, heavily armored battlewagon with upgraded shielding that was proof against medium-yield antimatter warheads. There were rumors as well of a super weapon to be carried on the new ship, but that was an even darker secret. They were still a dream, however, and would have no impact on this war, hidden like the Kilrathi construction yard, as far as possible from the battle front.

"Any word yet from *Tarawa*?"

Banbridge shook his head.

"Silent, though forward listening posts have picked up orders pulling several cruisers off from patrol on the frontier to head back in towards the sector *Tarawa* and *Normandy* are operating in. It might be a coincidence."

"I don't believe in coincidence, the Cats must be on to something."

"That's what I thought as well."

"Wish I was back out there with them," Tolwyn whispered.

"Bondarevsky's a good man. If he's in a scrape he'll figure a way out."

Geoff nodded in agreement. Jason had become like the son he had lost. If Reggie had not been killed twenty years ago he'd even be Jason's age.

"When do you want me to go back out to Landreich?"

"The Chief of Staff wants to hear a full briefing from you tomorrow morning," Banbridge paused to look over at his computer screen.

"Speaking of the old man, there's a staff meeting in ten minutes. Why don't you stay here, I'll have my aide get a meal into you, and for heavens sake, Geoff, let's see if we can get you some better clothes."

Tolwyn nodded in agreement. He felt absolutely ridiculous wearing the coveralls of a civilian maintenance worker, and the beard he had grown on the way back from *Tarawa* was itchy as all hell. It was a convenient enough cover for him to slip through the underground parking lot of fleet headquarters. Once he was inside, a Marine security team had ushered him down a private corridor the rest of the way to Banbridge's private quarters. He rubbed his chin.

"Wish I could shave this off."

"You do look kind of ridiculous, Geoff."

Banbridge stood up and grabbed his attache case.

"What's the meeting about?"

"Always curious, aren't you?"

Tolwyn smiled. "Working with Vance kind of rubs off on you."

"That damn Kilrathi ambassador asked for a meeting with the Chiefs of Staff and some of our fleet admirals. He's screaming over a list of grievances about border violations by military patrols, and incidents from the Landreich are top on the list. So just lay low here, there's bound to be some press trying to sneak around, and if they ever saw you, there'd be hell to pay."

Geoff shook hands with his old academy instructor and smiled as Banbridge headed out the door.

Banbridge paused and looked back at Geoff.

"You've done damn good, son; I'm proud of you," and then he was gone.

The aide came in a minute later and offered to lay out some fresh clothes while Geoff took a shower, an offer he eagerly agreed to after weeks in space, surviving the usual water rationing of one minute showers. As he walked past the small bedroom he saw Kevin stretched out on top of the sheets, fast asleep.

"Didn't even bother to eat, sir," the steward whispered. "He stretched out and was asleep like a baby inside of a minute."

"It's been a tough time," Geoff said quietly.

Closing the door of the bathroom he peeled off the grungy coveralls and stepped into the hot stream of water.

He didn't so much hear it as feel it, a vibration slamming through the building. He turned the shower off and from a far-off distance heard a klaxon. Not bothering to towel off he pulled his coveralls on and opened the door. Banbridge's aide was standing alert by the entry into the admiral's quarters and to Geoff's surprise had a laser pistol up and at the ready. Kevin came out of the bedroom, already up and alert and Geoff could see that the klaxon had triggered him into thinking that there was a scramble alert.

"Stay where you are, sirs," the steward snapped, holding his free hand back for them to remain still. "Something's going on."

Geoff felt defenseless, dressed in nothing more than oil stained coveralls. He knew the aide, besides being Banbridge's personal steward, was also a highly trained Marine commando. He'd have to leave things up to him. The aide quietly spoke into a small lapel mike, receiving orders and information back through a tiny earphone.

What seemed to be an eternity passed and then he saw the man visibly pale, right hand clenching tight around the pistol grip.

The aide looked back at Geoff.

"Sir. Admiral Banbridge, the Chief of Staff, and we don't know how many other officers are dead. The entire top floor of the building has been blown apart."

"Merciful God," Geoff whispered, bowing his head.

"I'm going to keep you secure right here, sir. We have had an incident and we don't know what the hell is going on yet."

An incident, Geoff thought. Most of the fleet's top command were most likely dead and it's called an incident.

"Hunter, break off, break off!"

Ian switched off his visual and audio back to *Bannockburn*. The order to abandon Paladin was simply too hard to stomach. The wave of Kilrathi fighters was now less than five thousand clicks off and closing in fast, their maneuvering scoops popped wide open to break after the high speed run in from the cruiser that had launched them. There was a slim chance that he might be able to pop off the two fighters on the forward left edge of their sweep, thereby punching a hole through for Paladin to follow.

He could imagine that Paladin was swearing a blue streak at the moment, but to hell with him if he didn't want to be saved.

Ian turned in towards the approaching fighters, toggled up his IFF missiles and dumped them off in a long range spread to stir things up. The missiles leaped forward and several of the approaching Kilrathi fighters pulled into sharp turns. As soon as the tail of the nearest one was exposed Hunter fired off an infrared tracker which instantly locked on to the fighter's engines which were glowing white hot from the high speed approach. The missile slammed up the exhaust nozzle of the fighter and detonated.

First kill of the new war, he thought grimly.

Within seconds the fight was on, several Dralthi fighters peeling off to swing in on Hunter, while the forward edge of the strike, six Grikath fighters, pushed straight on towards *Bannockburn*. Paladin let loose with his remaining salvo of flechettes and then toggled off a battery of IFFs from his gatling mount missile launcher. Space was a mad confusion of explosions and Ian pulled a tight turn to try and shake off an incoming infra tracker, firing off a flare, which the missile went for, detonating silently a kilometer behind him.

A Grikath shot directly across his starboard bow and with a perfectly timed deflection Ian nailed him solidly amidships and turned inside of the Cat, firing three more rapid mass driver rounds into the Grikath which blew apart.

He spared a quick glance at his tactical display and saw that the Kilrathi cruisers were spread out into an open sweep, coming up behind the wave of fighters in case there was anything still to be finished off. Behind them more than a dozen patrol craft and a light frigate were coming in as a second wave, while from the other direction half a dozen patrol corvettes were closing, pushing *Bannockburn* into the trap. A wave of fast moving fighters was moving ahead, above, and below to close the trap.

With a sickening finality he realized the futility of the gesture he had just offered. The game was up. He switched back on to Paladin's channel.

"Not looking good, buddy."

"Hunter, break free, make the run, I'll provide support."

"Like hell, they're on me, now run for it and get that damn information out, otherwise this whole thing is useless."

"Hunter, damn it, get the hell . . ."

"I think its the other way around, buddy, I'll cover you, now run for it. When you get to the Vacuum Breathers, buddy, lift the first round for me."

"Hunter!"

He punched ahead of *Bannockburn*, moving to break up the forward screen so Paladin could slip through.

A spread of half a dozen missiles leaped forward from

the next Kilrathi attack group, the new IFF and radar trackers. Ian swallowed hard and keyed up his own transponder to draw the missiles in.

The warbling tone in Ian's head set clicked to a steady hum, increasing in pitch. The incoming were all locked on to his ship. He pulled up hard, leading the missiles away from *Bannockburn*.

"Pop out, Ian!" Paladin shouted, and then there was another voice on the radio.

"Green two, Green two, this is Green one, strike on the way."

Ian started to reach down to pull the ejector D ring when he saw a fighter lining up to hit *Bannockburn* from above.

He dropped the ring, lined up on the target and toggled off the one missile strapped beneath his fighter. Even as it streaked away he knew the game had finally caught up with him at last. He bit down hard on his cigar and closed his eyes.

Six Kilrathi IFF's impacted across the stern of Ian Hunter St. John's Ferret.

Jason leaned over the tactical display on the screen, watching as *Normandy* launched her fighters. Already one of the cruisers was turning back around as he cleared the north pole of the planet at an altitude of three hundred clicks, just barely skimming above the edge of the atmosphere, accelerating fast.

If only I had a full bay of fighters, he cursed silently, we'd swamp them under. *Normandy* had already launched her full load of fighters, twenty, and Doomsday along with two other pilots had taken out the remaining three fighters in his own bay. He could already sense that this was going to be a ship-to-ship action and he didn't relish the idea of facing a cruiser head on with a light escort carrier.

"Knew you wouldn't leave me in the lurch, laddie."

Paladin's wavery image appeared on the screen.

"You certainly brought along enough company, Paladin."

"Aye, that I did. Get ready for a coded burst, unscramble it and you'll see why."

Seconds later the signal came through and Jason turned to watch his communications officer decode it. He started to see the holo read out and turned to one of his watch officers.

"Get down that corridor fast and tell those gorillas guarding the door to send Vance up here on the double!"

"Fighters are breaking off from attack on Paladin, returning to cover cruiser," the combat information officer announced, looking back at Jason.

They must have detected the burst signal and realized we're carrying the football now, Jason thought.

"I already got it on our system," Vance said, coming on to the bridge and Jason realized that with the gear down in the fighter bay Vance would already know.

"Look at the size of those damn ships," Jason whispered, and he looked back at Vance who was intently studying the screen.

"Should we send the signal?" Vance asked.

Jason looked back at the holo. Their cover was fully blown now. He knew that was the end result the moment he made the decision to come up and save Paladin. He knew as well that if Paladin had come back empty-handed he would be in very hot water for having blown the mission cover just to save a friend. But then again it was extremely difficult to argue with success, and his decision would now be viewed as the right move and the personal reasons for Paladin and Ian forgotten.

The Kilrathi already had a visual lock on his ship. Within seconds they'd known the type and model and would quickly figure out it was *Tarawa* with *Normandy* right alongside. The antenna array atop his carrier would definitely tip them off as well as to the mission of his ship. If not for the information they had, it would be a diplomatic explosion. There was no sense in giving the Kilrathi the first jump on that front. If the information was released after the Kilrathi started screaming about the border violation the information might be dismissed as an attempt to cover up.

"Send it out now," Jason said.

"Good decision, son," Vance said with a grin and he turned back towards the flight deck. A minute later Jason noticed the momentary flicker in the ship's battle lighting as the translight burst signal went out, repeated a minute later by a second burst for good measure.

All three cruisers had now come about and were closing in, the ranging indicator marking down the rapid drop in range. The forward spread of *Normandy's* fighters closed with the Kilrathi fighters launched from the cruiser and the fight was on. The edge on skill was clearly on the side of the colonial and ex-fleet pilots, deployed out to take on the heavy cruiser and its lighter escort.

One of the cruisers, however, pushed on through and Jason felt the cold sweat start to streak down his back as he sat on the bridge, waiting for the Kilrathi cruiser batteries to open up. He had never fought a carrier in a head to head engagement and he longed for a joystick and throttle, rather than the cumbersome relaying of orders.

The first volley of missiles spread out from the lead cruiser, even while the second one in line exploded from the direct hit of a torpedo spread from a Broadsword.

"We've got four incoming warheads," the combat information center officer announced, "blowing chaff, flares, and radar noise makers."

"All weapons fire," Jason announced, struggling to keep his voice calm.

Mass driver cannon mounted forward went into action, a volley of torpedoes leaping out from the forward launch tubes. The range was below a hundred kilometers and closing.

"Helm ten degrees to port, fifty degrees down." He started a curving turn downwards and then countered the order, bringing his carrier straight back up towards the underside of the rear cruiser.

"Torpedo attack diverting," combat information announced, "regaining lock on *Normandy*."

Several Kilrathi fighters raced across his bow, dropping missiles, the weapons impacting on the forward shield.

"*Normandy's* in trouble!"

Jason turned to look back at his communications officer and then toggled over to a damage display of his sister ship.

A torpedo from the first spread impacted on his sister ship's bow. Forward shielding was gone. Two colonial fighters on close in escort maneuvered and rammed two of the next spread of torpedoes coming out from the Kilrathi cruiser while *Normandy* fired a spread in return.

The torpedoes crossed each other's paths and seconds later *Normandy* and the enemy cruiser fireballed, the two ships so close that the explosion merged into one vast expanding cloud of white hot flame.

A colonial fighter came through the wreckage, spinning wildly. The pilot, however, was still able to maintain some control and he aimed his craft straight in at the cruiser in front of Jason. Punching on afterburners the modified Ferret slammed straight into the Kilrathi bridge.

"Damn," Jason whispered. Within seconds he had seen three colonial pilots go kamikaze.

The enemy cruiser started to rupture along its bow, internal explosions detonating off from the blow. Half a dozen fighters swung in front of the cruiser, matching speed so as to hover, and ignoring the defensive fire they poured mass driver rounds into the ruptured hull. The cruiser started to disintegrate, mass driver rounds punching clean through the hull and the ship detonated, taking another colonial fighter with it.

The explosion from *Normandy* was still spreading out and Jason realized he had just under twenty strike craft out there, some of them still engaged in eliminating the rest of the fighters, others moving forward to provide cover for *Bannockburn,* or pursuing the light corvettes and patrol craft.

Jason left the bridge and headed down the corridor to the fighter bay, stopping before the ever present guards and waiting impatiently until they brought Vance out.

"I want your gear torn up and moved out of the way for fighter recovery," Jason said.

"What?"

"You heard me, Admiral. I've got twenty fighters out there, some of them undoubtably hurt and I plan to recover them."

"Jason, it'll take days to disassemble the D-5. Most of it is hard wired into the floor."

"I'm sorry, sir, I don't have days, for some of those ships I might only have minutes. D-5 has to be moved."

Vance started to bristle.

"Son, there's billions of dollars' worth of equipment in there. Enough money to buy a couple of hundred fighters. Tell your pilots to eject and we'll pick them up."

"I'm sorry, sir, that's not the way it's going to be. Those are colonial fighters and I'm not going to go back and tell Kruger that we ditched them to save a surveillance computer which has already done its job. Beyond that, if we don't have those fighters for the run back home, I don't think we'll make it. We've put a real burr in the ear of the Cats and they'll want our hides as vengeance. This is going to be a running fight all the way home."

"Listen, son, I hate to pull rank, but I think you should know I'm a full admiral in the fleet."

"I know that, sir, but I am captain of this ship."

Vance looked at him appraisingly and after a brief span of seconds, which to Jason seemed like an eternity, a thin smile creased Admiral Vance Richards' face.

"Aye aye, sir. I'll have a landing area cleared."

Jason inwardly breathed a sigh of relief.

"Thank you, sir," and he headed back to the bridge.

"Message for you, sir."

Jason nodded and went over to the communications officer and saw that Paladin had established a laser link.

"Thanks, laddie."

Jason sensed that something wasn't right.

"Are you all right?"

Paladin nodded and then lowered his head for a second.

"Jason. Ian's gone."

Jason felt as if he had been punched in the stomach. He stood silent.

"I told the lad to run for it, he stayed to get me out instead. They burned him with a missile spread meant for me."

"Damn it all to hell," Jason whispered.

"Aye, lad, damn all of it," Paladin sighed.

There was a moment of silence and then Paladin finally stirred.

"By the way, did you get the message out?"

"On its way."

"I think the old proverbial manure is about to hit the fan when that arrives."

"It's only just started," Jason replied coldly, remembering the holo display of the new Kilrathi carriers. He realized that chances were they might already be heading to Earth. The armistice was a fraud as he always knew it was, and by falling for it, the Confederation might very well have lost the war. But for the moment it was hard to think of that. He had just lost one of his closest friends and that was all that he could grasp.

"Sire, there has been an accident."

Jukaga looked up from his desk at the aide who was bowed low, trembling.

"Go on."

"Sire, we've just received a burst signal that the Emperor's personal cruiser suffered a reactor detonation, and that all aboard are lost."

"Oh, really, how tragic."

The aide looked up at him, confused by his tone.

"You are dismissed," and he turned away, barely able to hide a flashing of teeth in satisfaction. So it had worked as planned. Getting a reactor fuel tube aboard, with the tiniest of pinholes drilled into it, had been a chore. The fuel rod had been a trick thought up years ago, the idea being to have smuggler craft carry it into the frontier region and sell them off, with the hope that the rods would eventually wind up on Confederation ships. The rod would then rupture in the white hot heat of the pulse engine reactor and cause a chain reaction detonation. The idea never worked, but he always remembered where they were stockpiled while everyone else forgot. It had taken a little maneuvering of computer shipping files to get it into the right place, knowing that the Emperor's ship never left Kilrah without an entirely new load of rods on board.

He smiled. Yes, that had been masterful, and it helped when one of your own deep agents worked on ship maintenance. Fortunately, the poor fool never even really knew what he was doing, which made the plan leak-proof.

A moment later there was a flurry of angry roars in the corridor outside. As he stood up the door slammed open.

Prince Thrakhath strode into the room.

Baron Jukaga knew that in spite of all his effort at self-control his mane was bristling with fear. He struggled to bring it under control.

"Surprised to see me?" Thrakhath growled.

Jukaga stood, speechless and then finally recovered.

"I just heard of the tragedy, the Emperor?"

"Better than you had hoped for," Thrakhath snarled.

"Whatever do you mean, my Prince?" Jukaga replied, angry with himself that there was the slightest of tremors in his voice.

"That is for you to figure out," Thrakhath stated coldly.

"I don't understand what you are moving towards."

Thrakhath stood silent, eyeing him coldly. He could see the Baron regain his self control. What was enraging was the simple fact that the Emperor, through intuition or information had suspected that his ship would be destroyed, but as to how it would be done they had never figured out, and still did not know and most likely never would. His only real hope had been to so startle the Baron as to make him say something foolish and incriminating and that, Thrakhath could already see, had failed. It was obvious now that the Baron will claim that he was being blamed unjustly. If directly accused, the other clans might very well rally to his side as they had once before after Vukar.

Thrakhath snarled angrily, seeing that his bluff had failed.

Thrakhath, still glaring at Jukaga, waited for him to speak.

"What are these two reports I just received," Jukaga finally said, motioning to his comm screen, "regarding a bombing on Earth and that the spy ship was located too late before it sent a burst signal out?"

"It means that we have to move for war now."

"That is madness," Jukaga snapped, regaining his full composure. "The plan called for another four and a half eight-of-eights of days."

"Impossible now," Thrakhath replied. "Many of the humans are already blaming us for the bombing, and with the information regarding our fleet it means a renewal of war."

Thrakhath smiled.

"And an end to your weak scheming."

"What is the truth about this bombing?" Jukaga asked coldly.

"Oh, undoubtedly one of their own did it and then will blame it on us. Perhaps the attempt on the Emperor can be linked to it."

Jukaga hesitated.

"They would never do that, kill their own military leaders like that. There's more to it than that."

"Are you accusing me?" Thrakhath snapped.

Jukaga looked at him coldly but knew it was best to back off.

"And how did this signal get out? We suspected the carrier was in that system and we knew that their scout ship was running back towards it. How could this have happened? There should have been a carrier and a full cruiser squadron there."

"And are you accusing me of a fault in that as well?" Thrakhath asked quietly.

"You don't understand at all, do you?" Jukaga finally replied. "If we had but waited the year, they would have fallen into our hands, weak and divided. Now, they will feel nothing but rage at a betrayal of their trust, they will fight with a fanaticism you have never seen.

"Remember I warned your father and uncle of this back when the war started and they so foolishly decided to open with a surprise attack."

"Then it is your job to disarm them of this fanaticism, and if you fail and they do not submit . . ."

"Then what?" Jukaga snarled.

"I will annihilate their worlds and no one will be left alive, no one, and you will be responsible."

• CHAPTER NINE

"Show that transmission from *Tarawa* on the main holo."

"Big Duke" Grecko, the Marine general of the Joint Chiefs and the only survivor of the explosion, settled back painfully in his chair. Geoff Tolwyn looked over at him anxiously. The bleeding from the lacerations to his back and neck had soaked through the bandages and his shirt, staining the khaki a dark red. Geoff wanted to say something but knew it was useless. Grecko was a Marine, and would bite the head off of anyone who tried to show sympathy.

The wonder of it was that Grecko had survived at all. He had walked out of the meeting with the ambassador in disgust, threatening to resign his commission, and was down the far end of the corridor when the bomb went off. The explosion had ripped Grecko's left arm off. Fortunately it was an artificial arm which had replaced the one lost at Vukar and the plasti limb absorbed the blow from a shattered support pillar which would have killed anyone else.

Grecko started to move his shoulder, as if the lost limb was still in place, swore vehemently and then clumsily used his right hand to scratch his neck.

"I'd leave that alone, sir, there's still some shrapnel in you," an attentive medic standing behind Grecko said.

"I didn't ask for your advice, son, and besides I don't think your security clearance allows you to be in here, so get the hell out."

"I've got my orders to stay with you, sir, until you report to the hospital."

Grecko looked to the Marine guard standing at the door.

"Sergeant, either escort this pest out of here or shoot him, I don't care which."

Geoff smiled sympathetically at the medic, who looked flustered as he left the room, mumbling that all Marines were nuts.

"Nothing a good shot of whiskey and a couple of minutes with the tweezers can't cure," Grecko snapped, still scratching his neck.

The holo screen in the middle of the room activated and Grecko studied it intently for a long silent minute.

He picked up a secured phone and punched in a number.

"Mr. President, this is Grecko, are you still in the building, sir? Good, I think you need to come to my office at once," and he hung up.

He looked back at Geoff.

"We're really in the barrel this time, Geoff. Are you sure that this stuff Vance just sent is the real goods?"

"I wasn't there when he got the data," Tolwyn replied, "but you know Vance even better than I do, sir. He wouldn't have sent it if it wasn't genuine." Grecko nodded grimly.

"We've got five admirals and seven generals dead in the morgue downstairs, a hundred and thirty one other key personnel gone as well, a military half dismantled and now this," and he viciously pointed at the holo as if it were something he could vent his rage on.

Grecko shook his head wearily and Tolwyn could see that the man was struggling to control the pain, both physical and emotional. Geoff felt it as well. He had just lost his old mentor and one of his closest friends and many other comrades whom he had served with through the years.

"How does this all fit together?" Grecko asked.

"The armistice, I think we had that figured from the beginning," Tolwyn replied. "Now we know it was to buy time so they could reorganize and concentrate on finishing their super carriers. They know that we now know and I guess that's where this bomb plot figured in, to decapitate our high command, sow confusion and then strike hard straight at Earth."

"How long before that fleet could get here?"

"If they were fully ready to move, flank speed could put them across the Empire in twelve, fourteen days. From the frontier to Earth, another ten days. Even if we had full resistance up, I think those carriers could cut through inside of two and a half weeks from the time they cross the demilitarized zone. Remember, just before the armistice we wargamed that one out, the assumption of a surprise attack with our own defenses down. With these new carriers, it doesn't look good at all, sir."

Grecko exhaled noisily.

"According to what Banbridge briefed me on just this morning, it'd be at least four months to bring the fleet back up to full pre-armistice strength.

"Damn all to hell," he snapped.

The door to the small conference room opened and President Rodham stepped in, followed by Foreign Secretary Jamison.

Grecko stood up as did Tolwyn. Geoff still found the nickname "Big Duke" amusing since Grecko barely stood over five two. His pugnaciousness, however, more than made up for his shortness and more than one Marine or fleeter had found himself on his back after making a comment.

"How are you doing, Duke?" Rodham asked, looking at the Marine general's torn and empty sleeve in surprise.

"Nothing like getting shot in a plastic arm. Didn't hurt a bit."

Rodham nodded and then shifted his gaze to Tolwyn.

"What in hell are you doing here?" and his features went cold.

"He was here today as a personal guest of Admiral Banbridge when the explosion happened," Duke replied.

"You have no security clearance," Jamison shouted. "Grecko, get this man the hell out of here right now! I wouldn't be surprised if it turned out that he had something to do with this bombing."

"No, sir, he isn't moving."

Jamison turned on Grecko in surprise.

"Rear Admiral Tolwyn," and Geoff was surprised to hear Grecko use his official and former title, "was acting under the direct orders of the Chief of Staff when he violated the cease fire order, with the intent of thus having a cover to subsequently engage in a covert operation."

"If that bastard were alive right now, I'd see that he was stripped of his rank," Jamison snarled.

Grecko stiffened.

"That bastard, as you call him, ma'am, was my closest friend. I'd like to suggest, ma'am, that you go down to the morgue and tell what's left of him that he's a bastard."

"General, would you explain Tolwyn's presence here?" Rodham asked, stepping between the two as Jamison leaned forward, ready to explode.

"The Chief of Staff suspected the armistice from the beginning, sir and asked Geoff to volunteer for a covert mission. If the mission were undertaken by someone already dishonorably discharged it would give us," and he looked coldly at the President, "plausible deniability if something went wrong. Geoff organized the transfer of some of our demobilized assets to the Landreich where the equipment could be kept on line and then went out on a deep reconnaissance mission inside the Kilrathi Empire. He returned from that mission and arrived here only minutes before the bomb went off."

"We've just received an official protest over that escapade," Jamison snapped. "The Kilrathi are screaming their heads off claiming that five of their cruisers were hit in an unprovoked attack and destroyed."

"What about *Tarawa* and *Normandy*?" Tolwyn asked anxiously.

"They claim they got one."

"Not a bad exchange," Grecko said dryly. "The Kilrathi must be damned embarrassed, but *Tarawa* only reported three confirmed kills for the loss of *Normandy* and I'll take their word over the furballs'."

"They're claiming the right, as provided in the armistice, to hunt the other one down and have requested information regarding the ship's location."

Jamison looked over at Rodham who nodded sadly.

"The Kilrathi have demanded information regarding the ship's location and destination. If we refuse to provide that immediately, a condition of war might be declared."

"Tell them to go burn in hell," Grecko said.

"And besides," Tolwyn said quietly, a smile creasing his features, "those ships are not of Confederation registry."

"Look, General, the armistice is hanging by a thread," Rodham replied, ignoring Tolwyn. "First the violation of their territory and then this terrorist bomb plot to kill the ambassador and make it look like the Cats did it by killing some of our people as well."

"Are you trying to tell us that some of our own people did this bombing?" Tolwyn asked, incredulous that such a suggestion could even be made.

"Well, it's one serious possibility," Rodham replied, "and we have to look at all angles."

Tolwyn was about to come back with a rather angry and very obscene retort, but Grecko held his hand up for him to be silent.

"Sir, I would appreciate it if you took a look at this holo display and the data printouts. We just received it as a burst signal relayed in from *Tarawa* less than a half hour ago. Their mission was to follow up our suspicions regarding Kilrathi construction inside the Hari sector," and Grecko pointed to the three dimensional projection, in the middle of which floated the images of the Kilrathi super carriers.

Rodham went over and looked intently at the carriers, requesting that the computer rotate the images and then provide data on mass, length, armaments, and projected fighter carrying capacity.

Tolwyn watched the President closely and could detect a paling of his features and more surprisingly a nervous tic at the corner of his eye. It was obviously a hell of a shock for the President, but he had little sympathy for him at this moment, still remembering how not so long ago the head of the Chiefs of Staff, with tears of frustration in his eyes, begged for the armistice not to be signed, warning of what would be the end result. Noragami was now dead as a result.

"Is this genuine?" Rodham asked quietly, now examining the map which showed where the fleet was and projected times of arrival into Confederation territory if an offensive were launched.

"The data was burst signaled from *Tarawa*, located here," and Grecko pointed at the map showing the last reported position of the carrier. "The data was obtained from a deep reconnaissance probe which ventured into Hari space."

"On whose orders?" Jamison asked. "I was never informed of this escapade. Remember, I am the Foreign Minister and if you were contemplating a violation of the armistice I should have been informed."

"On the orders of the Chief of Staff," Grecko said coldly, not even bothering to turn.

"Is there a chance this is falsified information?" Rodham asked, and Tolwyn could detect the slight note of hopefulness in his voice, as if wishing that the entire problem would simply be shown to be a hoax.

"It was sent in personally by Admiral Vance Richards, sir, and that's good enough for me."

"Richards is out there — I thought he retired?"

Grecko merely smiled.

"What you've committed here is outright mutiny," Jamison snarled. "If the rest of the Joint Chiefs were not already dead I'd demand their resignations as I am now demanding yours."

Grecko turned slowly and stared at Jamison.

"If you were not a lady," he said coldly, "I'd loosen your teeth for what you've done to us. If you want my resignation you can have it, but only after we have a full investigation of myself, the Joint Chiefs and more importantly of you.

Would you care to see the file military intelligence has on you and your suspected cooperation with the Kilrathi in return for your son?"

Jamison turned towards the President.

"I want him fired as of this minute and Tolwyn here put in jail pending an investigation."

Rodham looked over at Jamison in confusion and then slowly sat down, turning to look back at the holo.

"Your report on the false signal and the Kilrathi message regarding the antimatter warhead plant, does that fit into this?"

"It fits right in, sir," Grecko replied.

"Sir, you are looking at the beginning of a full scale offensive with an upgraded fleet," Tolwyn said. "In less than a month the Kilrathi will be above Earth demanding our surrender if we're lucky, though if past practices are any indication they'll flatten us with a full antimatter warhead bombardment and then come down to gloat over the wreckage and tear out the throats of the survivors with their claws when their next Sivar ceremony comes around."

Rodham nodded slowly and closed his eyes for a moment. Jamison started to speak and the president held up his hand for silence. He finally turned and looked over at Tolwyn.

"You were the best fighting admiral in the fleet, Geoff. Banbridge told me more than once that he wanted you to replace him as commander of Third Fleet when he retired."

Geoff lowered his head, saying nothing.

"Admiral Tolwyn, I am officially pardoning you for the incident at Munro. As of this moment I am reinstating you as a full admiral in command of Third Fleet, with the mission of organizing defenses against the anticipated Kilrathi invasion. General Grecko, I am appointing you the new head of the Joint Chiefs of Staff in command of all Confederation forces."

"Just what the hell is this?" Jamison roared.

"Secretary Jamison, I expect your resignation as Foreign

Secretary effective immediately and also advise you that you will face an investigation. I have refused to believe the allegations made against you for too long. I think this matter has to be looked into." Jamison's features flushed.

"Harry, you can't do this," she said quietly, her voice full of menace.

"I am the President of the Confederation, and I can damn well appoint and fire my cabinet as I see fit."

"And have me as the whipping boy for this situation? Like hell. Your charges against me are nothing but a smokescreen to shift blame. It was your decision to sign the armistice."

"Based upon the information you provided to me regarding Kilrathi political intentions."

"You're the president, Harry," she snapped coldly. "The buck stops here, remember."

Rodham lowered his head, nodding sadly.

"Yes, it does. I fully realize that," he whispered. "And that is one of the reasons I demand your resignation. Admiral Richards presented me with a report more than six months ago, indicating that you might present a security risk since the capture of your son and that the Kilrathi might be in contact with you for a possible deal."

"Are you calling me a traitor?" Jamison roared.

"Not yet," Rodham said quietly.

"You want my resignation, well you can go to hell. Make it a public firing in front of the press, and believe me, my side of the story will be told as well."

She looked around the room angrily.

"I'll see all of you in hell," and she stormed out of the conference room.

Rodham watched her go and wearily he turned back to face Tolwyn and Grecko.

"I'm sorry, Duke, you and the other officers were right."

"Even if we turn them back, Mr. President, a lot of good youngsters are going to die in the doing of it. We had them, sir, we had them on the ropes and we could have crippled them. Now it's the other way around."

"You don't need to remind me, Duke."

"I do need to remind you, sir," Grecko snapped back. "It's always been this way. The civilians start to forget just how dangerous the world, or the universe really is. They start to believe their fantasies, and then in the end it's the kids on the front line who pay for it. Well, sir, on this little folly the human race might very well become extinct before it's done."

Rodham started to speak and then stopped and looked away.

"After I take care of Jamison, I'm resigning as President," he said quietly. "Vice President Dave Quinson never did support this idea; he was as much as public about it. I think he could help rally our people better than me."

"I think that's a good idea, sir," Duke replied, his voice cold and even.

Rodham stood up and looked back at the holo display.

"You know, Jamison will make this an ugly fight. It might slow down our mobilization. I'm therefore issuing as my final executive order a full mobilization of the fleet, along with wartime governmental control of the economy. Jamison is most likely running to the press right now so I'd better act first. When I resign my cabinet will have to resign as well. Maybe it'll clear the deck for Quinson."

"A smart move, sir."

Rodham nodded again and extended his hand.

"I'm sorry, Duke. Sorry for everything."

Wayne hesitated for a moment and then shook hands.

Harold Rodham, shoulders slumped in defeat, turned and walked out of the room, not even noticing the salute of the two officers behind him.

"I guess his heart was in the right place," Geoff said quietly.

"You know what they pave the road to hell with," Duke replied, "and frankly, Geoff, I think we're all on a greasy slope aimed straight into the fiery pit."

The Emperor, in an unusual gesture, ordered the screen removed so that he was fully visible to those who sat before him. As the two Imperial Guards drew the screen back the clan leaders went down on their knees, foreheads touching the cool turquoise inlaid floor of the audience chamber.

"Raise up your heads, return to your feet," he said, and they did as commanded.

"I wanted you to gaze upon me, to dispel any lingering doubts as to my continued existence."

They stood silently, furtively looking from one to the other, but most of them finally turned their gaze upon Jukaga, who stood in the middle of the group, staring straight at the Emperor.

"You have heard the rumors, and they are true," the Emperor said. "Someone indeed attempted the most heinous of all crimes, a crime so loathsome that there is not even a word in our own tongue to describe it, so that we must borrow this word from corrupt and downcast races."

He fell silent as if waiting, and the silence dragged into long uncomfortable minutes, as if he were waiting for one of them to throw himself upon the foot of the throne in supplication.

No one moved.

"He shall be found out," the Emperor finally said coldly. "Now let us discuss the war."

The group visibly relaxed.

"The fleet made jump fourteen days ago from their base, within hours after being discovered, and is moving at flank speed to the front. It will arrive here at Kilrah later today."

"Then it has begun," Vak breathed, trembling with excitement and a low murmuring of growls filled the audience chamber.

The Emperor nodded.

"We have placed blame, both for the bomb in their headquarters, and for this other loathsome act, upon the humans."

"Could it not be," Jukaga replied, his voice soft and even, "that both bombs were indeed acts of humans?"

"I heard a report that you yourself said that the bombing of their headquarters could not have been done by them," the Emperor retorted.

"It is a mere conjecture," Jukaga replied, "for I have not heard any admission that we planted the bomb in their headquarters and thus wrecked the peace."

The Emperor smiled. Both he and the Baron knew the real truth, yet neither could admit it.

"I expect, Baron, that you will continue to keep them divided as long as possible. Even now they still argue, though, before they shut our embassy down and arrested the staff, we had information that they were mobilizing."

"What of our spy?"

"We have lost touch with the embassy and thus no longer have direct contact. It is assumed that she is gone."

"And what of the human embassy here on Kilrah?" Vak asked.

"I ordered their throats torn out this morning," the Emperor said coldly. "In public we are blaming them for the bombing of my cruiser. It is a convenient excuse now to treat them all as they deserve: total annihilation, total destruction of every world they inhabit."

Jukaga looked up at him in shock.

"That was in violation of the rules of war and of the agreement," Jukaga snapped.

"What rules of war?" Vak retorted. "There are no rules with such beasts who have lost whatever shred of respect we once held for them. They are lower than prey and should be exterminated without thought or mercy."

The Emperor laughed coldly.

"I am sick to death of this human scum and the potential for corruption that they present to us. I am therefore issuing the following order: all human prisoners that we still hold as well as slaves are to be slaughtered. Secondly, the new fleet is to be armed with thermonuclear weapons that are clad in strontium. These heavy weapons, when detonated in the atmosphere of a planet, will make it uninhabitable. They shall be annihilated."

As he finished speaking he looked straight at Jukaga while the others in the room roared with delight.

Jukaga looked around at the clan leaders and for the first time truly felt as if a distance had opened up. If his plot had succeeded, even now they would be turning to him for guidance. Now instead they were eager to close in on him for the kill. But there was more. He felt a cool distaste for what the Emperor now proposed. Though he wanted to see the humans humbled and defeated, he found that of late he was feeling something far more, what could almost be called, if not a fondness, at least the beginning of a respect. He knew he was falling into a trap, that if one studied his enemy long enough, and came to know him, in the end one would find things, beliefs, and individuals one could identify with. What the Emperor was now proposing was monstrous.

"Such an action will arouse them to a frenzy," Jukaga said. "They will fight as they have never fought before."

"They are animals to be hunted," the Emperor replied.

"No, my lord."

A stunned silence filled the chamber at his direct contradiction to the Imperial word. He did not care. How could he even begin to explain what he knew, the countless examples of humans, motivated to fight without thought of self, fully willing to die fighting rather than submit.

"Terror will not breed submission as it did with others," Jukaga said quickly. "It will instead create a wish, as the humans put it 'to take one of the bastards with me.'"

The utterance of an obscenity, which to the Kilrathi was the most foul of insults shocked the other clan leaders.

"Do what is assigned to you, Baron," the Emperor replied sharply. "Convince them to submit. Now leave me!"

Baron Jukaga backed out of the room, barely inclining his head.

Jason "Bear" Bondarevsky opened his eyes as the distortion field from the transit jump settled down and looked over at his navigation officer.

"Alignment correct, star lock confirmed, jump was on the mark."

"Tactical," and he turned in his chair to look at the officer hovered over the holo display of the sector.

"*Bannockburn* in position eighty nine thousand clicks dead ahead. Too early to tell yet, sir, on passive optical sweep. At jump transit our pursuers, three corvettes and one frigate, were forty-two thousand nine hundred clicks dead astern and gaining at eight point two clicks a second."

Jason nodded. There was time to scout around before worrying about the back door.

"Flight deck."

"Doomsday here, sir."

"How are the birds?"

"All fighters ready and armed, just give us the prey."

"What about munitions?"

Doomsday gave his usual glum look.

"Enough for one more strike, sir. Eight torpedoes are all we have left for ship busters. The fighters will have to sortie with half standard missile and mass driver round bolts."

"Stand by."

"Paladin on laser lock, sir."

Jason looked over at the communications officer and nodded for her to put it on the main holo.

"How goes it, laddie?"

Jason smiled. Even though he was technically the commander of this two ship fleet, he knew Paladin would never follow protocol of address and the fact was refreshing.

"Fighters are up and armed. Damage control's repaired the hull breech in the port engine room."

"And Vance?"

"Madder than hell. Seems Sparks broke one of his computers moving it out, said something about the machine costing just under half a billion. Sparks frowned, then said he could dock her pay if he was upset, but she had fighters to service."

"Good for Sparks. She's a rare lass," Paladin laughed and then his features went glum.

"We've got some trade up ahead, lad. Another cruiser just came through from the jump point leading back to Kilrah with two destroyers leading. Looks like standard tactical for more coming behind. I tapped into their comm channel and they're madder than hell and lookin' for blood."

"Can we run past them to our jump point?"

"Just barely."

Jason punched into the engine room.

"Shovel on the coal back there. I want full thrust, fuel scoops closed."

"Close the scoops and we'll run her bone dry by the next jump."

"Just do it."

He switched back to Paladin.

"Let's get the hell out of here, and hope they don't have more waiting at the next jump."

"Laddie, from the looks of it I think the whole Empire is gonna be stirring to fry us."

"Let's just hope Kruger figures a way to get us out of here."

• CHAPTER TEN

Admiral Geoffrey Tolwyn stood up and walked to the front of the room. He looked down the length of the conference table and felt a cold twinge of pain. So many familiar faces were gone, killed in the bomb attack. It felt strange now to be standing before this group; after all it was Banbridge's job to run Third Fleet. He suddenly felt old and very lonely. He pushed the thought aside.

"Good morning."

He paused, reached into his breast pocket, pulled out an envelope and opened the letter. A paper letter such as the one he was holding was a wonderful gesture out of the past, part of the old traditions that the military still hung on to.

"By order of the JCS, Admiral Geoffrey Tolwyn is appointed commander Third Fleet as of this date, with the primary mission of meeting, engaging, and destroying any hostile invasion into Confederation space which is directed towards the inner system of worlds. You are authorized to employ any means necessary as outlined in Emergency Decree 394 issued this date by the President of the Confederation. Your command will include 3rd Destroyer Group, Commodore Polowski commanding . . ."

He paused and looked back up at the group.

"Anyhow, all of you are listed here," he said quietly, "and if you aren't listed, I'm taking you anyhow," and the room echoed with nervous laughter.

Geoff activated the main holo screen which displayed the new Kilrathi heavy carriers, while a side screen displayed the surmised position of the fleet and its possible route into Confederation space.

A low murmur of voices filled the room as the dozen group and squadron commanders, representing the ships and Marine assault regiments under his command examined the data.

"Our task is to meet and stop this force before it gains the inner worlds of the Confederation."

"Just how many fighters will these ships carry?" Lyford Beverage, commander of the First Cruiser Squadron asked.

"We're working off of only one intelligence sweep, a long range optical examination followed by a translight radar burst, so our data is sketchy. Our evaluation team believes they carry four launch bays, and perhaps six. It's hard to tell, since all the ships were aligned identically at the time we swept them so we don't have a full examination from all angles. Given the mass of the ships, our best guess is two hundred and forty fighters, scout and bomber craft, perhaps three hundred. Close analysis of the scan detected five of the ships emitting infrared signatures for functional reactors. The other seven were cold."

"Good lord, Geoff, if five of those things are coming at us that means we'll be facing upwards of fifteen hundred attack ships," Rear Admiral Allen Zitek growled from the back of the room, his speech computer making him sound almost robotic. Zitek had been badly burned years before leading a squadron against a Kilrathi carrier. It still amazed Geoff what the surgeons could do if a man could be brought in while still alive.

"Don't forget that the Kilrathi had a minimum of nineteen other standard carriers and at least twenty heavy cruisers that carried thirty fighters each. That comes to over three thousand seven hundred additional strike craft."

There was a chilled moment of silence.

"What about logistical support, supplies, and training from the Kilrathi view point?" Duke Grecko asked from the back of the room.

"That's the one hope," Geoff replied. "We now understand

the mystery of their transport shortage and their occasional
shortages of missiles. They were straining their system beyond
the max to keep the war going and at the same time building
this new fleet in secret. I've handed this data over to intelligence analysis, and I'm stilling waiting for the full report. My
gut feeling on it is that they couldn't fully do both. I think they
stripped some of their best squadrons off their front line carriers during the armistice and shipped the personnel out to the
new ships, replacing them with new recruits. The burst signal
from *Tarawa* already indicated a thousand fighters transferred
off ships that had been put into their inactive reserve. I'm
certain we'll see their best shot from the new carriers, which
will be fully loaded for combat. The rest of the fleet will be held
in a secondary support role or open action on other fronts as
diversions."

"That still would leave a minimum of fifteen hundred
strike craft on five carriers coming straight at Earth, not to
mention what looks like close to a hundred escort ships,"
Zitek replied. "And just how many fighters will we have to
meet this?"

"We can have five carriers fully on line within two
weeks, with forty one escorts, carrying a total of six hundred and eighty-nine strike craft."

"Just five?"

"Actually, only two are on line and fully operational at
the moment," Geoff said shaking his head.

"With crews working around the clock and cutting a lot
of corners, I expect to see three more carriers ready to join
the fleet by the time the Kilrathi penetrate into Confederation space. It'll be forty-five days, more like sixty, before
our remaining carriers will be on line again."

"Jamison was brilliant pushing that deactivation
through," Grecko snapped and Geoff could only nod his
head in agreement.

The political arena with Jamison standing in the center
was now one of absolute chaos. Less than twenty-four
hours ago Rodham had announced the existence of the
Kilrathi super carriers and the assumption that Earth had

been directly targeted for attack. He then called for the Confederation Senate to renounce the armistice and to mobilize for a renewal of the war, closing with his resignation as president. Minutes later the vice president was sworn in and delivered a sharp rousing speech, demanding that the Kilrathi open their border for full inspection of the new fleet or face offensive action. It was all a bluff on Quinson's part, but it at least sounded good. The Confederation had been thrown into a state of panic by the announcement, with every holo reporter scrambling to put their spin on the issue, which ranged from "we've been stabbed in the back by the Cats," to "the evil military was pushing for a war." The situation was further stirred up by the Kilrathi reply that the bombing of headquarters and the attempt on the Emperor's life were part of a military coup by pro-war officers and that they were totally innocent of any wrong-doing.

At first Geoff had naively assumed that this had closed the deal, that the Senate would vote for war and that the new president's declaration of a full military emergency would be observed.

Jamison had triggered near chaos instead. First she refused to resign, even though Quinson had appointed a new Foreign Minister. Next she accused the military of conspiring to renew the war, a position that the Kilrathi were pumping out through their propaganda agencies.

The result was that the Senate had still not declared war, wavering, some even adopting the Kilrathi line, and demanding that the military unilaterally disarm.

Quinson had stood firm, however, evoking executive right to order the military to mobilize for emergency action. The one restraint, however, was that such an emergency did not give the fleet the right to take offensive action. Tolwyn had actually fallen into a shouting match with the Senate military committee over that point, wanting to free his two light escorts that were operational for a spoiling and recon raid into Kilrathi space, but he had been held back.

"Sometimes it really bites to be in the military," Polowski snapped from the back of the room. "I'd just love to get Jamison onboard my ship as a forward turret gunner's mate when we charge those carriers and let her see what her peace loving friends have done while we slept," and there was a chorus of approval.

Geoff held up his hand for silence.

"Remember, we are the military. Civilian politics is outside of our control and like it or not that's a tradition we must observe. It's our job to defend the Confederation from the attack we all know is coming, and I'm counting on you to give it everything you have. Some really big damn fools got us into this fix. The hell with them, push them out of your minds. I want you to focus on the billions of innocent people who will be under the Kilrathi antimatter bombs and the survivors who will face their knives if we fail. The existence of the human race now hangs in the balance."

He paused for a moment. The words had come out of him, not planned at all. In any other setting he felt they would have sounded worn. But it was the simple truth: the actual existence of his entire species rested in their hands. One wrong move on his part and it might all be over with. All of it gone forever, two thousand years of England gone, a cold silence of death, of extinction.

I can't dwell on this, he realized. It'll drive me insane if I do, so stay focused on the job and nothing else.

He switched the holo screen to a map of the inner core of planets and the jump lines leading out to the frontier.

"The Kilrathi have three main lines of approach, all of which finally come in here," and he pointed to a blue white star from which radiated a number of jump lines. "Here at Sirius and the jump point behind Sirius the shortest routes of jump lines come together and then from there straight back to Earth. By the shortest route, jump line alpha, it's ten jump points from Sirius to the frontier, four back to Earth. The next route, beta is twelve jumps to the frontier and delta is thirteen. All the other routes meander back and forth. For the Kilrathi I think they'll be so confident of their strength, and also concerned about not giving us time to rearm, that they'll come straight on in.

"I propose to meet them in front of Sirius."

"Geoff, that abandons several hundred inhabited colonies further out," Polowski said quietly, "my own home of Planet Warsaw being one of them."

Tolwyn nodded.

"There are eighteen major jump points leading across the frontier and several dozen other jump points running parallel or zigzagging back and forth. Before the armistice neither we nor the Kilrathi had the strength to simply go charging in, saying the hell with our rear and leaping towards the jugular. They now do. We lack the strength of a major counter strike and even if we did have it, it'd be weeks before we could even begin to move it. By then it'll be too late. In addition they can hold a number of their standard fleet carriers in reserve as a reaction force to counter even light escort raiders the way we had been using them in the past. We have to fall back and concentrate what assets we have. If we try a forward defense they might swing around us."

"Why not an offensive, Geoff? Split them off the way we did at Vukar Tag," Grecko asked from the back of the room.

"It won't work this time, sir. Even if we took what we had right now and shot it straight in, their older carriers acting as a reserve would stop us cold, while the new fleet would just continue on into Earth. Second, they'd see it for what it was, an effort to split their offensive. They'd ignore it and still bore straight in. What we have to do is seek a meeting engagement with their main fleet and stop it, that's the only viable option left open to us."

"So what about my home planet?" Polowski asked.

Geoff paused for a moment. The cold hard word for it was "abandon" but he could not bring himself to say that, or even really admit it to himself.

"Mike, the Kilrathi have two ways to run this offensive.

The first is to break through our forward defenses, then spread out and start ripping the colonial worlds to shreds. Every day that they do that is one more day for us to rearm and they know it. The second way is to come charging straight in, figuring they can mop up the colonies at their leisure after the core planets have been destroyed along with the fleet.

"I'm betting on the second method. It's sound militarily and it's what we would do: kill the home world and inner planets and end the war. The only advantage we can hope for is to stand and defend as close to our main base as possible, thus stretching their line of communication while we can continue to pour into action whatever ships come on line at the last minute. It is the one classic advantage of the defensive: the ability to fall back upon your base of supplies, and it's our only hope."

"Easy for you to say," Mike replied. "My entire family's out there on Warsaw, two jumps from the frontier."

"Can you propose any other alternative given what we have?" Geoff asked, his voice filled with a genuine concern. He knew he couldn't simply order men to abandon their homes and families. They'd have to be willing to do it with the hope of final victory and then rescue, no matter how slim the chance.

Mike looked down at his memo pad and then finally shook his head.

"You're right, Admiral, it's the only way," and there was a soft chorus of agreement.

"I wish we could inform the governors and presidents of the various colonial worlds of our strategic plan, though for security reasons it is obvious we cannot. For that matter, gentlemen, no one outside this room is to have any knowledge of what our strategy is."

"That'll give precious little warning to whichever worlds are in the way of the fleet," Zitek said. "Even if they're coming straight on, they'll still dispatch some cruisers on the way in to scorch the planets directly in their path. They'll have to, they can't afford to leave potential bases in their rear. Nearly every one of those outer worlds has at least one base on them, the major systems garrisoned with troops and orbital bases. They could stand against raiders, but not against what they'll be throwing in."

Geoff nodded grimly. It meant that millions in the outer worlds might die. He could only hope that those who could get out of the way would, heading to remote areas of their world to wait out the attack. At least most of the worlds were sparsely populated, with a lot of room to hide. In the early days of the war the outer regions, except for the Landreich on the flank of the Confederation, had been devastated, and billions had died. The region had yet to recover. It wasn't until Sirius was reached, inside the area never touched by the war, that the major inhabited regions were located.

He could only hope they had dug their shelters deep enough to survive bombardment.

"So the colonies are a write off?" Duke asked quietly, obviously wanting to make the fact absolutely clear.

"Local guard units will be given the discretion to stay, but I want everything here for the major showdown," and he pointed at Sirius, hanging in the middle of the holo. "Sirius is where the decision will be made."

"What about the Landreich and Kruger?" Polowski asked.

"I'll ask them for help and for the release of the escorts we signed over to them, but I doubt old Kruger will be amused that once again we're pulling a withdrawal due to strategic necessity."

He could well imagine the explosion that would be created when the burst signal reached Kruger on that one.

"Gentlemen, I want the fleet fully loaded and ready to move within four days."

The men looked at him incredulously.

"Geoff, it'll be eight, more like ten days before we get all our personnel back in aboard ship," Zitek replied. "Even our active carriers had half their crews on leave. Some of them are at the far end of the Confederation."

"You'll find a clause in Emergency decree 394A that allows for the drafting of emergency replacements off civilian ships, and retired personnel if need be for the duration of the emergency. Use it, shanghai your crews if necessary, but I want full ship's complements inside of ninety-six hours. Now let's get to work." The admirals and Marine officers filed out of the room. Geoff looked back down at his memo pad, ready to feed in a long series of orders. Looking up he saw that Duke had stayed behind.

"Something's wrong, isn't it?" Geoff said, sensing that there was bad news coming.

Duke nodded.

"I just got a signal in the clear from Kruger."

"Go on."

"He told us and I quote 'you created this mess, you solve it. Go to hell.'"

Geoff chuckled sadly.

"Doesn't the damn fool realize," Grecko snapped, "that if the Confederation goes down, the Cats will turn on him next?"

"If he comes to help us, he'll get hit from the rear. It's the old classic problem of frontier militia being called up to serve with the regulars—do you leave your homes open to attack by marching off somewhere else?"

Geoff paused, realizing that there was something else to the message.

"You're holding something back, Duke, what is it?"

"He also reported, in the clear, that *Tarawa* has failed to return and is assumed lost."

Geoff remained standing, staring straight at Duke.

"Damn this war to hell."

Eyes wide with excitement and with the thrill of the hunt, the Emperor turned to face his grandson.

"Magnificent, simply magnificent," he growled, turning back to look out the forward view port of the cruiser that now served as the Imperial ship. Less than a kilometer away, the Kilrathi Fifth Fleet of the Claw passed by in

review. The light frigates, corvettes and three destroyer
groups had already passed. The last of the heavy cruisers
was just passing to port and now the first of the new carriers, *Hagku'ka*, came into view.

Every fighter had been launched and moved in formation ahead of the carrier, three and a half eighties of
fighters arrayed in eight V formations. The bow of the carrier came into view, the heavy durasteel forward edge
studded with quad mounted mass driver guns and anti-
torpedo launch tubes. Three launch decks, one on either
side and one topside opened into the vast interior of the
ship, which was mostly comprised of the huge hangar bays,
workshops, and armament storage areas needed for the
fighters.

Internal bulkheads had been double layered, compart-
mentalizing the ship so that even if the forward end was
shattered all the way back amidships, the aft half could
continue to fight. Three belts of armor sealed off the outside of the ship from the interior so that if a torpedo did
penetrate the phase shielding and outer layer of armor, its
detonation would not burst into the vulnerable inner
decks and fuel storage areas. Sealed internal access shafts
even allowed for the transfer of fighters from one bay to
another for launching if a bay opening were shut down.
Just aft of amidship three more launch bays were mounted
pointing aft, in the same configuration as the forward half
of the ship. The six *Yatug* class engines were actually buried inside the ship, wrapped in heavy armor, their exhaust
vents tunneling through thirty meters of ship before
reaching open space. If a spread of missiles were closing
from astern, the engines could be throttled off and the
exhaust vents slammed shut, the missiles impacting impotently against heavy durasteel. The shields could then be
retracted, or if need be blown clear and the engines,
unharmed, fired back up.

The first carrier passed, followed by four more and the
Emperor watched, speechless. So this was the culmination
of years of secret planning and the stripping of the best

resources of the Empire. All for this, a fleet of ships unlike anything ever before seen in this sector of the universe. When the war with the humans was done, such ships could even stand against the Mantu, if they should dare to return.

"Grandson, with this fleet victory is ours."

"Remember, my Emperor, the fleet is but half the size we planned," Thrakhath said cautiously. "Victory should not be counted until the blood of the prey is in one's mouth."

The Emperor nodded, realizing that his enthusiasm had taken hold too deeply. He was still shaken by the murder attempt. It had been his dream to see at least one ceremony of Sivar in the burned ruins of Earth, for he knew that it would not be much longer before his ancestors finally called.

"Bring me victory," the Emperor finally said, "that is all I ask. You should take Earth in time for Sivar, we will celebrate it there. Be sure that it is ready for my arrival."

"Yes, my Emperor."

"And as for Jukaga, have you found anything more?"

"Three have died under the question, none have spoken. His path seems to be secured. If we put him directly to the question, the other clan leaders would again object. That path is closed as well."

"Then take him with you on this expedition," the Emperor said quietly.

"Grandfather?"

"You heard me. I've summoned him to this ship, he is in the next chamber. He is to go with you."

"He is head of spies, it is not his role to be a fleet warrior."

"He is a clan leader, a post of honor with the fleet he can not refuse. I think you will know what to do with him once battle is joined."

"It might be dangerous having him with us," the Prince replied.

"You will find a way," and the Emperor turned, motioning for a guard to open the door into a side chamber.

✦   ✦   ✦

Baron Jukaga entered, looking around cautiously. When summoned to the cruiser he had not known what to expect, and now the moment had come.

"Arise, my Baron. Was not the sight of our fleet wondrous?"

Jukaga stood up again.

"Wondrous."

"And what of the Confederation government?"

"Their senate still debates. It was reported however that two carriers sortied from their main base above their moon with a third to soon follow, and that the shipyards are working full time to prepare those in drydock for launching as well. Even though their government debates, their new president is acting quickly, with declaration of war or without. There have been forays by the Landreich into our territory, but no deep penetrations."

"I cannot even begin to comprehend how they function," the Emperor replied.

Jukaga nodded as if in agreement.

And that is why you never won, you old fool, he thought coldly.

"I have a new assignment for you, Baron."

He waited, tense and expectant.

"You go with the fleet to speak to their leaders one more time before we strike."

The Baron nodded. Would they simply arrange "an accident?" That now seemed to be the path.

"I am master of spies, my Emperor. Would not one of your warrior leaders be more appropriate?"

"You know this species of prey the best. It is your voice that they know, let them hear it one more time before we strike. You seemed disturbed by our ultimate plans, let us see if you can convince them to submit and thus save this species you seem to like so much."

He looked around the room, which was filled with the leaders of the new fleet. He was trapped and could not refuse.

"As you command it, my Emperor."

The Emperor turned away back to his grandson.

"Your plan is set, then?"

"Yes, my Emperor. The fleet will head towards the frontier at flank speed. Refueling tankers will accompany them so that we may move swiftly without need of deploying fuel scoops. The Second Fleet of the Claw, with four of our older carriers, will join us before we reach the frontier and make the first penetration, thus shielding our main fleet as long as possible. The Fourth Fleet of the Claw, with three carriers, will sortie towards the Landreich to pin down any forces they might have there, preventing them from shifting against our flank. The First Fleet of the Claw, with three carriers, will make up the reserve. The other carriers have been stripped of their crews and pilots for the Fifth Fleet and will be held in reserve."

"That is ten carriers," the Emperor said quietly.

"You know the shortage of trained pilots has become serious. Either our best pilots went with our new carriers or else the new fleet would be manned by pilots with no combat experience. It will be a year before we have enough fully trained pilots and fighters to bring the older reserve carriers back to operational strength."

The Emperor nodded grimly.

"So let it be," he said, turning away. "Now bring me victory."

• CHAPTER ELEVEN

Weary with exhaustion, Captain Jason Bondarevsky strode across the landing field towards the command post with Admiral Richards behind him. Stepping onto the veranda he coldly eyed the two Landreich guards at the door.

"I'm here to see Kruger."

"We have no orders to let you pass, sir."

"To hell with your orders, I want to see that son of a bitch now," and he moved to shoulder his way past the guards.

Caught by surprise they backed up slightly and then physically moved to block the doorway, one of them grabbing him by the shoulder.

"Listen, sir, don't make me get rough about this," the guard snapped.

"Get the hell out of my way right now, mister."

"Hold it, Jason," and he looked back at Richards. "They're just following orders."

The guards looked to Richards with some relief. They obviously knew that Kruger would skin them alive if anyone got past. They knew as well who it was they were trying to stop, and even if he was Confederation, he was also a first class hero.

"Sir, if you stay put, I'll go in and get my captain," a sergeant growled, coming out of the doorway to the aid of the two guards.

"Well, damn it, go get him," Jason snapped, and the sergeant turned and went into the building.

Jason paced up and down the length of the veranda, angry at everything, his mood made worse by the searing heat of the Hell Hole. He could feel the moisture draining out of his body, barely cooling his skin before evaporating.

He looked back at one of the guards.

"You know something, corporal, this planet of yours truly sucks."

The corporal showed the faintest of smiles.

"I fully agree," he whispered.

No longer able to get mad at the man, Jason turned away.

"Admiral Richards, Captain Bondarevsky?"

Jason turned back to see a very young captain, wearing commando fatigues and barely out of his teens, in the doorway. Though the man was shorter than him by a good half a foot, and skinny as a rail, Jason could tell from his eyes that he was deadly.

"President Kruger is expecting you, sir, come on in."

Jason nodded, grateful to be stepping out of the blazing heat of the twin suns and into the dark cool corridor. He followed the captain down into the below ground bunker, the captain leading him through the blast doors into Kruger's small and austere office. The captain withdrew, closing the door behind him.

Kruger looked up from his desk.

"Care for a cold one?" and he motioned to a refrigerator.

"Don't mind if I do," Richards said, and he went over to the refrige and pulled out a beer.

Jason looked at the Admiral angrily and then back at Kruger who sat behind his desk, smiling.

"Well, young captain, out with it."

"We monitored that signal reporting the confirmed loss of *Tarawa*, *Bannockburn*, and *Normandy*," he continued. "Just who the hell do you think you are to do that?"

"Last time I checked I was president of the Landreich, son. Just who the hell are you?"

"An officer in the . . ." he paused. He was, in fact, not an officer in Confederation at all but rather on leave, serving the Landreich forces.

"You are under my orders, young captain, and need you or not, I'll put your ass in the clink till this planet turns into an ice ball if you ever talk like that to me again."

Jason stood silently, still seething with anger.

"How about that beer, Jason?" and Richards came back to his side, holding an open container.

Jason stared at Richards, expecting support, but Richards merely smiled.

"But the emergency decree. Three-ninety-fourA is mobilizing all fleet personnel, and that includes me and my ship," Jason finally replied.

"Jason, we are officially listed as missing in action, presumed dead," Richards replied, "and I think our host intends to keep it that way."

Jason looked back at Kruger.

"I have your carrier and the others," Kruger replied. "We can make this happen one of two ways, young sir. Either you continue to command your ship under Landreich colors or one of my people will. I'd rather have you do it. You know the ship better than anyone else, and besides that, you're damn good. You managed to bring her out in one piece."

"No thanks to you."

Kruger smiled.

"You're here, aren't you? Therefore, any effort expended on my part to pull you out would have been a waste."

Jason felt ready to explode again. He had made a fifteen day run out, pursued all the way to the frontier. *Bannockburn*, the only Stealth light recon ship in the fleet was finally turned around and sent back on auto pilot with Paladin cramming into a light shuttle sent over from *Tarawa*. The momentary delay created by the supposed counterattack had gotten them through the final jump with a very angry Paladin cursing the entire universe over the loss of his ship.

He had not been able to snatch more than two hours' sleep at a stretch throughout the entire retreat and all he really wanted now was for someone at whom to vent his rage for being left out in the cold after doing his mission. A barroom brawl might even serve the bill, and then a good drink followed by a long sleep. And beyond that, there was still the pain of losing Hunter.

Richards, without waiting for the offer from Kruger, settled down on a sagging and threadbare sofa, which obviously doubled as Kruger's bed, and took a long pull on his beer.

"You know something, Kruger," Richards said, "I got holy hell over the fact that you hijacked that destroyer from my squadron and went gallivanting off."

"Vance, that was thirty years ago."

"Well, I got a reprimand in my file thanks to you, and wound up a desk jockey in intelligence."

"Consider that beer as payment then. You most likely would have had your butt blown off by now if I hadn't worked your transfer for you like that. There are very few old destroyer skippers floating around. Besides, last I heard you loved intelligence work."

Richards chuckled and held up the container in salute and then looked back at Jason.

"Settle down, son, the old man did the right thing. He didn't have the assets to pull us out, it was that simple. You did a damn masterful job getting out on your own. So damn good I think Kruger here owes you a decoration."

"I hereby award you the Order of Nova with diamonds and promote you to commodore," Kruger said sarcastically. "My adjutant will send you the award and paperwork when he gets the time. It's a nice looking piece of tin, you'll like it. Does that settle it?"

Jason could see that he wasn't going to win but still didn't know what to do.

"I want to rejoin the Confederation fleet with my ship."

"Impossible," Kruger snapped. "I need you here, and here you're staying."

"Look, son," Richards said, suddenly serious. "It's a ten day transit back to Earth at full speed. You'll arrive back to the inner worlds with just twenty fighters on board."

"None," Kruger growled. "Most of them are mine anyhow, and I'm requisitioning the rest."

"All right then, none, and no munitions, because even if Kruger did let you go I doubt he'd spare one IFF missile out of his stores to refit you."

Kruger nodded and said nothing.

"The battle shaping up back there, wherever it is they're going to fight it, might already be over. Meanwhile, we can expect a major sortie by the Cats straight in here to pin us down. You could very well run from one action to the other and miss both. It's that simple."

Jason had already heard the argument once before from Richards just before loading him into the Sabre for the trip from orbit down to the Hell Hole. He'd been too damn angry over the abandonment and then from the signal reporting him dead to think. He realized now he could no longer argue the point.

"Damn you," he said quietly, looking back at Kruger. "All right, you won. You've got me."

"I'm so honored that you would volunteer to join me," Kruger replied with false sincerity.

He took an old style printout report and held it up.

"This is our latest intelligence report. Three Kilrathi carriers are moving to the frontier and are expected to cross it momentarily, with an estimated eighteen escort ships. They're moving straight at Landreich and will make planetfall here in this system within eighteen hours."

"And your response?"

"Meet them and beat them, it's that simple."

"Four escort carriers going head to head against three Kilrathi fleet carriers?" Jason asked. "At best we've got a hundred fighters on board our ships."

"Eighty seven."

"They'll have over three hundred. We'll be frozen meat an hour after the action starts."

"Do you have any better ideas?"

Jason looked at the President. Though he was still

simmering with rage he could not help but wish that it had been Kruger who had been running the Confederation instead of Rodham. They wouldn't be in this mess now if it were.

"No, sir."

"Then get back to your ship. We leave here in six hours."

"What about the Confederation, sir, what's happening there?"

"The usual screw-up. The only positive sign is that Geoff is heading Third Fleet. They moved out five days ago, and have kept radio silence since."

"Admiral Tolwyn commanding the Third? What about Banbridge?"

Kruger told him of the bomb plot, the pardon, and the political confusion that still gripped the Confederation, along with the growing panic.

Jason took it all in, wishing more than ever he could be back under his old commander for the showdown.

"If Geoff stops the invasion, it'll be a miracle," Kruger said.

"And if he doesn't, what about you then?"

Kruger smiled, the first time Jason had ever seen him do it.

"We'll survive. It's what we've been doing for thirty years, with precious little help from your Confederation, I might add."

"It's official, gentlemen, a state of war now exists between the Kilrathi Empire and the Confederation. Four old style carriers crossed the frontier four hours ago, and the Senate passed the declaration."

He looked around at his bridge crew on *Concordia*, flagship of Third Fleet.

"All signal traffic from Station Hanover and the Hanovian System was lost forty-five minutes ago, the last report stating they were under heavy attack."

"Good God, there's two million people on that world," a staff ensign whispered.

"There were two million people there," Geoff said.

Geoff saw a young communications technician lean over his desk, covering his face, and he inwardly cursed, realizing that Hanover was most likely the boy's home. He wanted to say something, to apologize for his lack of tact, but knew he couldn't. The cold reality of what they were facing had to be driven home.

The bridge was silent, more than one turning to look at the boy as he muffled a sob and then sat back up, his features pale.

"We're going to lose a lot of worlds in the days to come," Tolwyn said, "a lot of worlds."

"Communications, put laser locks on the other ships in the fleet, pass the information, and order all ships to continue silent running."

He turned and retreated back to his wardroom. Sighing, he settled down into his chair and looked at the holo map. They were now positioned three jump points ahead of Sirius in towards the frontier. The Kilrathi had yet to show their main fleet. The carriers could be a diversion, or the vanguard of the main assault.

Damn, to be able to use full size carriers as a vanguard, while he had to husband the five ships that would be under his command, that is if *Saratoga* and *Leyte Gulf* could get up in time to join his other two ships. He ran a quick question into his nav system and the answer coldly blinked back at him. If the Kilrathi came on at flank speed, they'd get to Sirius a day and a half before the other two carriers could join up.

He looked at the three dimensional map, pausing for a moment as a new signal burst in, updating the situation. Three more red blips appeared, the three tentatively identified as cruiser squadrons, crossing the frontier. Far off to one side, over by Landreich, a thin red line was already traced deep into Kruger's territory, two definite and one probable carrier moving fast towards the core worlds of Landreich.

Which was the main assault? The carriers at Hanover

could be a feint to draw him in, the main fleet following behind one of the three cruiser squadrons. If he had the strength, that would be his approach, hoping to draw the enemy forward, then flanking by a side jump line, cutting him off from the rear.

He sat back, hands clasped, pondering, wishing he could somehow penetrate the fog of war. The Kilrathi had shut down nearly all military channels and kept silence ever since the burst signal from *Tarawa* got through, except for the nonstop bombardment of propaganda. The mere fact that signal traffic was nonexistent showed just how well planned the operation was. In the ordinary sphere of war, it was impossible to maintain operations for long without a steady flow of information.

Masterful.

I've got to buy a little time till they show their hand, but at the same time I need to wiggle a little bait, bringing the main assault on myself.

It was almost a foregone conclusion that Thrakhath was in charge of the main fleet. He was always bullheaded, and when he believed himself to have the upper edge, arrogant. Thrakhath never really gave a damn about taking territory; he wanted battle, to close with his enemy and destroy him.

He'll come straight in and dare me to stop him. He was behind the carriers.

I need to show confidence, aggression, he thought, not let them think we're already whipped.

Geoff punched in to his bridge officer.

"Pass the word to the fleet. We jump forward to the Warsaw system and will move at full speed to meet the carriers head on. Get Admirals Ching and Bjornsson on laser."

He turned the channel off and within seconds felt the vibration run through the ship as the helm officer called for full engine thrust.

Ching's image materialized on a flat screen, the bridge of his carrier, *Moskva*, in the background, followed seconds later by Bjornsson, commander of *Verdun*.

"We're going up to bloody nose them a bit and get their attention," Geoff said. "It'll be three on four, and with luck we'll buy enough time for our other two ships to get into position."

"Tough move, Geoff," Ching said. "They could be flanking in behind the cruisers."

"They're diversions. Thrakhath will come straight on in, looking for a fight."

"I hope you're right, Tolwyn. If not, they won't be too happy back on Earth if those super carriers get there and we're out chasing shadows."

Tolwyn laughed grimly.

"If they do, we won't hear the complaining for long."

"It's a risky move, Geoff," Bjornsson said, her features grim. "If we lose a carrier that'll leave just four to face off against the big ones."

"If we don't slow them, there'll only be four anyhow in front of Sirius when they arrive. It's a risk I'm willing to take though."

"Glad you're running this one, Geoff. This isn't just a battle, it's the whole shooting match."

"Yeah, thanks. If there's ever another time, remind me to retire first."

The two admirals laughed softly and signed off.

Again the thought crept in. The old rhetoric of the battlefield, how the fate of civilization depended on what happened next. It had been used by his ancestors when they had stood at Agincourt, Waterloo, the Somme and against Hitler and Zhing. In most cases it was just rhetoric; this time it was for real. He realized that if he allowed himself to dwell on the outcomes it'd cripple him, and he pushed the fear aside. There would be time enough for that later.

Another update flashed on the holo, a blinking purple light, showing that action had started in the Landreich. It had taken hours for the signal to travel, even at burst speed. Three carriers of the Kilrathi fleet now confirmed against what a colonial militia could put up. Their chances were next to nothing, he thought, just about the same as ours.

❖   ❖   ❖

"Ten seconds to jump and counting at nine, eight . . ."

Jason punched in to the deck flight officer.

"All fighters prepare for launch!"

"Two, one, jump initiated."

The phase shift of the jump field kicked in, space in the forward and aft screens disappearing in a wavy haze. Jason swallowed hard, the momentary nausea of jump taking hold, as *Tarawa* and everything inside of it winked out of existence at jump point 324C and then rematerialized seconds later half a dozen light years away, back into position in the Hell Hole system.

The screen shifted, star fields returning to view.

"All ahead full, move it!" Jason shouted and *Tarawa* surged forward. Not five seconds later *Gallipoli* appeared behind him in nearly the exact same space he had just been occupying, followed seconds later by two more escort carriers.

The maneuver was insane. Standard fleet procedure was to have at least one minute intervals between jumps. The actual point of rematerialization was problematic, never occurring at precisely the same spot, and if a ship in transit should come out of jump in the same space occupied by another vessel no one in the two ships involved would ever even realize that their existence had suddenly winked out in a white hot explosion.

"Launch all fighters, launch all fighters!"

A hazy shimmer appeared in the forward screen.

"Helm hard to port, up ninety degrees!"

Tarawa shifted, turning, as a destroyer of the Landreich fleet materialized out of jump less than four hundred meters ahead.

Jason was nearly knocked from his command chair and at the same instant a bank of red lights started to flash at the damage control desk.

"Ship hulled starboard side, sections twenty-two through twenty-four. Decompression hull breach!"

Internal bulkheads had already been sealed for action

stations. Jason looked over at the damage display board. Three sectors of the outer hull were gone, crew quarters. He could only hope no one was still in there. He waited, watching to see if the breach would rip down the length of the hull or burst into the heart of the ship. It held.

"What ship was that?"

"Destroyer *Blitzkreig*, Kruger's flagship, sir."

"Damage?"

"Part of her port rear stabilizer gone. Hull integrity holding."

"Then the hell with her, get the rest of those fighters out!"

He turned back to tactical display and drew in his breath.

Kruger was either a genius or a madman, the next five minutes would tell—so far the plan had worked.

Directly ahead, at less than a thousand kilometers, were the three Kilrathi carriers, moving in line abreast formation. Kruger had met them ten hours earlier as they jumped into the Hell Hole system, fought a brief skirmish, trading a corvette and two fighters for two destroyers and nearly twenty fighters of the Cats and then fled, the enemy in hot pursuit.

They had jumped out of the Hell Hole System, come to a dead stop, and then turned, jumping straight back into the system they had just fled.

The Kilrathi, assuming they were chasing a beaten and far weaker foe, had recovered nearly all their fighters in preparation for jump in pursuit. Forward of the carriers by three hundred clicks was the outer screen of frigates, which would, according to standard doctrine, jump through first to secure the next point in preparation for the carriers to follow.

Range to the forward ships would close in under a minute.

Doomsday gave the thumbs up to the deck launch officer. She saluted, crouched down low, pointing forward, and the senior deck officer in the launch control room hit the catapult button.

In under two seconds Doomsday was clear of *Tarawa*, full afterburners roaring, even as *Tarawa* turned to avoid colliding with Kruger's flag ship. Doomsday banked hard over, skimming past the destroyer with less than a dozen meters to spare, and took a deep breath as he shot clear.

His heavily modified Sabre, with side-by-side pilot and co-pilot seats crammed in, and a single heavy Mark IV torpedo slung underneath shook with the 110% power surge. Grinning, he looked over at Paladin who was flying the right hand seat as weapons officer.

"Here we go again, laddie," Paladin said calmly, though Doomsday could tell that the old pilot was miffed that there weren't enough fighters in the fleet for him to get one of his own.

"Weapons check?"

"Torpedo armed and ready, now give me a target."

Doomsday spared a quick look down at his tactical screen. The forward string of frigates were less than a minute away, the first of them already slowing, turning to move in across the carriers. Less than thirty seconds behind them the three carriers were starting to come about.

"All hell's about to break loose," Paladin chuckled. "These two fleets are about to go straight through each other.

"There's the rest of the strike," Doomsday announced, pointing nearly straight up, and he edged his stick back, climbing a thousand meters to tuck himself in under a Broadsword's belly, giving himself a little more protection from the heavy strike craft's gunners.

"We're going for the middle carrier," Doomsday said quietly.

"We'll go for his port launch deck, you take the starboard one, lad," the Landreich pilot of the Broadsword above them replied and Doomsday clicked his mike twice as an affirmative.

"Hang on, crossing through the frigates!"

A crisscrossing of neutron bursts, laser flashes, and mass driver rounds snaked out from the Kilrathi picket line. Doomsday held steady on his course, working for an early fix and lock on the center carrier, which was now full broadside and starting to come around astern.

"Launch bay hits are out," Paladin announced. "Go for main engines."

A Landreich fighter, moving ahead of the two, winked into a fireball and disappeared. They shot through the wreckage, Doomsday wincing when a bloody smear of what had once been the pilot smashed into his forward canopy and spun away into the darkness. The blood seemed to be a dark omen and he started to breathe hard, fighting down the sense of premonition and Paladin looked over at him.

"He was already dead, laddie, already dead."

Doomsday gulped hard and shook his head. He pulled open his helmet visor, wiped the sweat from his face. He reached into a breast pocket and pulled out a short cigar and clamped down hard on it, chewing the end.

Ian had given the cigar to him long ago. He had never smoked it, but somehow, for this mission he felt it was a talisman and he brought it along.

They shot under the belly of a frigate, the two attack craft shuddering as they skimmed through the high energy field of the ship's fuel and maneuvering scoops.

"I have target lock," Paladin announced calmly, "and counting at thirty seconds, twenty nine."

Doomsday hated torpedo launches more than anything else. It required the fighter to stay on a straight and steady course for thirty seconds until the torpedoes' guidance and arming systems cut through the high energy shielding of the target, decoded the shield phasing, and then countered the phasing so that it could penetrate for the kill.

The carriers were now clearly visible in space, three silvery masses less than fifty clicks ahead, the ships completing their turns, engines winking white hot. Three

Landreich fighters darted past Doomsday, their afterburners flaring, diving straight in, loosing a string of infrared guided missiles. The shots would not penetrate but their explosions on the carriers aft shields would momentarily blind the point defense systems.

"First fighters coming out," Doomsday announced, able to clearly see the pinpoints of light leaping out from the Kilrathi carriers.

"The furballs are a bit late today. Caught them with their pants down this time, that is if the buggers are wearing pants."

The pin points of light disappeared, and Doomsday knew that meant they had turned and were coming straight back towards him.

He caught the first hum of an IFF locking on, and then three more. Taking over defensive systems control from Paladin, he launched one of the new noise makers, hoping it would distract the missiles. The Kilrathi carrier seemed to fill all of space in front of him and he felt that if he closed any further, he'd run straight into it. The sweat was soaking his back and he found himself silently praying.

A modified Ferret, stitched on to what looked like old twin Sabre A engines, slammed past, diving straight into the emerging fighters. Several flashes of light appeared, fighters being killed, though Doomsday could not tell who had bought it.

"Ten seconds, nine, eight. Signal lock on, phase counter lock on, warhead armed, three, two, one . . . it's away!"

Doomsday felt his ship lurch as the ten meter long torpedo dropped from the underbelly pylon, its engine flaring to life. He looked up and saw a Landreich craft above him dropping his spread of three Mark III Torpedoes as well. Breaking his ship hard to starboard, Doomsday nosed straight down and then spun over, keeping his belly turned towards the carrier so that the new laser torpedo guide could maintain lock. Paladin stayed hunched over the weapons screen, ready to take over manual guidance of the torpedo if Kilrathi jamming should throw it off course.

Doomsday spared a quick glance at his tactical as half a dozen red blips closed in.

"She's closing, closing," Paladin chanted softly, punching in a guidance command as the torpedo lost lock for a second, his guidance laser firmly tracking on the torpedo's tail. The fact that Kruger had half a dozen of the new ship-to-torpedo laser guiding systems in his munitions inventory had surprised Doomsday, who figured it was best simply not to ask how they got into Landreich hands.

"Closing, closing . . . impact, laddie, we got 'em!"

Doomsday punched in an aft visual and saw an expanding fireball of light erupting from the carrier's main engine bank. A second ball of light snapped as one of Doomsday's torpedoes slammed into the explosion. Four of the Landreich's old obsolete Scimitars darted in towards the carrier's tail, disappearing into the inferno, two of them reemerging from the fireball seconds later and as they pulled out, a solid ripple of explosions shuddered across the carrier's stern from the missile spread they had launched, now that the aft shielding was overloaded and down. The entire aft end of the carrier suddenly disappeared in a white hot light.

Doomsday watched the Scimitars, amazed yet again at the suicidal tactics of the Landreich pilots, flying fighters that should have been on the scrapheap years ago.

"Fuel igniting, she's going!"

The explosion burst out, the blast wave washing over Doomsday's Sabre, shuddering it as if from a direct hit. He lost sight of the two surviving Scimitars, who were simply consumed in the ball of light, the enemy fighters pursuing them disappearing as well.

"Look out ahead!" Paladin shouted, and Doomsday looked up to see a frigate turning directly in front, her gun mounts shifting, tracking straight down on him, preparing to fire a full broadside at near point blank range.

"All weapons fire independently and at will," Jason announced calmly, standing now and pacing behind his row of bridge personnel, who remained hunched over their tactical, communications, damage control, and fire system holo displays.

He looked up at the main holo battle screen, watching the converging line of blue and red dots. A blue dot, representing a light frigate winked out, followed an instant later by two red dots to either side, one of them a cruiser, the other a destroyer.

"Landreich frigate just detonated her reactor pile, crew has ejected," the tactical officer announced calmly.

"These people are insane," Jason whispered, realizing that even if the crew had ejected, a bridge team would have had to stay on board to time the detonation.

The explosion cut an opening straight through the middle of the Kilrathi defense line deploying aft of the three carriers. All of the strike fighters from the four escorts had already launched and were inside the picket line, engaging the carriers. A dozen fighters disappeared within seconds, caught by the crossfire between the picket line and carriers, hundreds of blinking yellow dots marking the crisscrossing paths of missiles. Bright green snaps of light flared inside the holo display, detaching from half a dozen fighters.

"Torpedoes are launched and running," tactical reported.

"All ships close and advance on carriers, follow me."

Kruger's image appeared on the command screen only long enough to pass the order then disappeared.

"Helm, lock on Kruger's ship, follow her maneuver."

Kruger turned in, racing through the opening created by the Landreich frigate's sacrifice, and within seconds every battery on *Tarawa* was engaged, trading shots with Kilrathi frigates, and destroyers to either side.

Jason suddenly imagined that he could almost hear a bugler blowing charge, the way the Marines still did when their landing craft went in on an assault, as they raced straight towards the three carriers. It was madness; they were about to close and trade broadsides with capital ships at point blank range. The center carrier in the holo flared, exploding outward.

"Scratch one flattop!" tactical shouted, and Jason looked up at the visual, watching the explosion, then back down at the holo as two fighters, his own, emerged out of the fireball. A Kilrathi frigate turning towards *Tarawa* moved in front of the fighters, its guns turning to fire.

"All weapons, train on frigate, port side!" Jason shouted.

Turrets swung about, fire rippling out from *Tarawa*, the frigate swinging her guns back on *Tarawa*, ignoring the two fighters as they raced between the two ships.

A shuddering explosion ran through *Tarawa*, battle lights winking out for a second, a gust of acrid smoke filling the bridge, red lights coming back on again in the now shadowy gloom.

"Main generator off line, emergency back up, shielding down to seventy one percent."

"*Tarawa*, close it up, hit the carrier to starboard."

Kruger's image appeared for only a second and was gone again.

The fleet flagship was out forward of the charge, a Kilrathi cruiser angling in, opening with a spread of missiles. Flare, chaff, and noise makers streamed out of the destroyer and the two ships traded fire. Behind the flagship the four escorts, moving in two lines of two, stormed through the maelstrom, while frigates, corvettes, destroyers, and fighters swirled about them.

Another shudder ran through *Tarawa*, damage control shouting out a report, red lights blinking on his screen. Jason could barely hear the officer as the explosions echoed through his ship, the concussion nearly bringing him to his knees. The Kilrathi cruiser shot past, unable to turn in tight enough to run parallel.

On the port side the still expanding wreckage of the blown carrier continued to swirl out and then was astern. Kruger arced his destroyer directly across the stern of the carrier they were pursuing, lashing out with a volley of torpedoes and missiles at near point blank range.

Landreich corvettes raced past the escort carriers, closing in on the prey, two of them fireballing from the strikes of Kilrathi fighters, the survivors launching torpedoes, most of which were shaken off by the carrier but three impacting nevertheless. Four more of the corvettes disappeared.

"Her shielding's down!" tactical shouted.

Jason felt as if he were about to explode with excitement. The battle had lost all semblance of tactical maneuvering, the old standard of fleets launching fighters at long range, and capital ships rarely if ever coming within ten thousand clicks of each other, was gone in the mad confusion. He thought of Nelson at Trafalgar, charging into a broadside exchange with the French and Spanish, and felt that if Tolwyn were here the old man would be proud.

The Kilrathi carrier was less than fifteen hundred meters ahead.

"Fire on her, fire!"

Simultaneously the four escort carriers opened fire, hundreds of mass driver rounds and neutron bolts, from the anti-aircraft batteries, now slamming into the stern of the enemy carrier. Explosions rippled, jagged fragments of metal hurtling off into space. *Tarawa* raced down the length of the carrier, stitching the side of the ship with everything she had, while *Gallipoli* turned to cross the T of the Kilrathi carrier astern. The Kilrathi, however, were firing with everything in return, and explosions rocked *Tarawa*. Jason felt as if the frenzy of battle had torn into the heart of his soul. He stood rigid, wanting to roar with both rage and delight. More than one of the bridge crew had broken discipline, pounding the sides of their monitors, screaming curses, oaths, encouragement, and whooping with joy at the destruction.

"*Gallipoli*'s going!"

Jason looked up at the aft visual and saw his sister ship splitting open as if she had run straight into a buzz saw that was tearing the ship apart from stem to stern. The fuel cells astern ignited and the ship fireballed, her flame washing over the topside stern of the stricken enemy carrier.

They darted past the ship, turning to starboard while the Kilrathi carrier edged over to port and started to dive.

"Tactical report!"

"Enemy carrier suffered multiple hits, computer counting two hundred plus hullings, secondary explosions igniting, three of five engine pods destroyed."

"Damage control?"

"Sections one, three through five portside hulled, midships port mass driver gun mounts destroyed, main generator still off line, shielding down to forty-two percent, holding steady."

Jason looked back at the tactical.

The enemy carrier was turning hard over to port, now moving away at a right angle, debris trailing out behind her as she struggled to accelerate. The other carrier was coming around to flank the stricken ship. The enemy picket line was now racing full back, coming abreast of their two surviving carriers and moving to pursuit.

"Helm, prepare to come about for a second strike," Jason announced, and his crew looked up at him, startled.

He knew it was madness, but they had not finished the carrier off and he'd be damned if it was going to get away.

"All ships follow me."

Jason looked up at Kruger's image and then back at tactical.

Kruger was moving straight away from the engagement, heading back towards the Hell Hole.

"Get me Kruger," Jason snapped.

The old man's image reappeared, looking annoyed.

"Let's finish 'em, sir, he's crippled."

"We killed one, we crippled another and lost one escort," Kruger snapped. "Go back and we'll lose the rest of our escorts just to finish a kill. We want him crippled. They'll have to protect him. Bondarevsky, I'm breaking the engagement. We got what we wanted, they'll run for home now. Hell Hole is still under bombardment and that's our main priority now."

"Aye, sir."

The image winked off.

Jason took a deep breath, realizing that the excitement of the charge and the lust of battle had clouded his judgment.

"Belay helm over, lock on *Blitzkreig* and follow."

He could see that some of his crew were disappointed while others took a sigh of relief.

"Damn good, I'm proud of all of you," he announced and then settled back into his command chair.

He looked up at the chronometer.

It was less than six minutes since they had jumped through, undoubtedly one of the shortest fleet actions in history. Kruger had lived up to form, shattering an invasion, killing a carrier, and crippling another. He had certainly taken them in harm's way.

The question now was, what would Kruger do next?

"Signal all fighters, return to your ships for recovery."

Admiral Tolwyn stood silently, watching the display screen.

It had been a standoff for more than a day. They had met the four enemy carriers just inside the Warsaw system, his fleet and theirs arriving at opposite jump points almost simultaneously.

He had raced to cover Warsaw but the Kilrathi carriers had held back, staying close to the jump point.

The question had been whether to close and engage, or wait. It could be that they were holding at the edge of the jump point, waiting to lure him in and then the main Kilrathi fleet would jump through. A listening post inside the next system had managed to get out a brief burst signal, reporting the transit of more than thirty escort ships and then had gone off line. It could only mean that the main fleet was coming up fast. Yet if he did advance and close for action there was a chance to meet the enemy three on four, with the possible edge that the pilots aboard the enemy ships were not their first line Guard fighters.

He had opted for action, but with the stipulation that

his carriers would not close within ten million clicks and engage at long range only with fighters.

The action had been inconclusive throughout the day, with the loss of thirty-eight fighters in exchange for two hits on a carrier with moderate damage, and three enemy frigates destroyed in return for one hit on *Moskva* and a destroyer lost.

But now there was no longer a question as to Prince Thrakhath's strategy. He was indeed coming straight on.

For the last hour, the jump point covered by the carriers had disgorged destroyers, frigates, fuel tankers, and supply ships. And now at last the first of the new carriers had emerged.

His intelligence officer passed up a continual stream of reports, the hazy images from *Paladin's* recon scan, replaced now by clear optical and radar images passed up by light Ferret recon fighters moving back from the edge of the fleet.

Tolwyn continued to pull back, his fighters coming in to land, a screen of escort ships guarding the sterns of the carriers from enemy fighters, while dropping out a spray of porcupine mines to slow the relentless advance of the enemy fleet.

A fourth carrier appeared and then a fifth, each of them identical, each of them terrifying.

"Sir, we are receiving a hailing from the Kilrathi fleet."

"What?"

The communications officer looked back at his console for a moment and then turned again to Tolwyn.

"Confirmed, sir. It's an in the clear translight signal from their fleet."

"I'll take it in my office."

He left the bridge and stepped into his wardroom. He spared a quick glance at a mirror. The circles under his eyes would tell of his exhaustion but there was no helping it.

He settled into his chair and punched the holo screen to life.

"Go ahead, comm, patch it in."

The image of Baron Jukaga appeared.

"Ah, Admiral Tolwyn, our intelligence reports said that you were in command of Third Fleet. My congratulations on your promotion. We have always admired you as perhaps the best of the fighting admirals of the Confederation."

"What do you want, Baron?" Geoff replied coldly.

"Your surrender."

"I'm a military man, not a diplomat, Baron. Direct your inquiry to President Quinson. I'm sure he will tell you to go perform a certain impossible anatomical act."

The Baron chuckled.

"You humans and your sexual obsession. So strange, we must discuss the differences some time. But I am asking a military question, Admiral. I'm not demanding the surrender of your Confederation, merely your fleet."

Geoff replied with what he assumed the President would have said.

"Such crudity, Admiral, it's not becoming of one of your breeding and education. You and I are alike in our study of human warfare. It creates a bond between the two of us, a bond I should add that I feel is even stronger towards you than to many of my own species. It would be distressing to see you defeated and dead."

"You assume too much, Baron. Do not worry about my death until it is accomplished, but instead worry about your own."

"Touché. But come, can't we reason this disagreement out?"

Geoff laughed coldly.

"My government was stupid enough to believe you once. It'll be a very cold day in hell before we believe you again. This time the fight's to the death, no quarter asked or expected."

"A shame you put it that way."

"No, I want it that way," Geoff snarled, angry with himself that he was losing his temper. "You murdered one of my closest friends in your bomb plot. I heard as well about your attempt on the Emperor. I'm surprised they didn't rip your guts out for that, you *utak*."

He deliberately chose the Kilrathi word used to describe the lowest caste member of Kilrah society, the cleaners of privy pits for fertilizer, one considered so untouchable that it was a defilement if his shadow even touched the shadow of anyone of a higher class.

He could see that the word caused Jukaga to bristle.

"I'm surprised the Emperor even allowed one such as you to live. I've heard that assassination is all but unknown in your society. It seems you learned it from us. You know nothing of us. You learned but the worst and learned none of the best. You are beneath the contempt of both my race and yours."

He noticed a change in Jukaga's demeanor and his image disappeared.

"Communications, what's going on?"

"Signal shifted, sir, coming back in, on a fleet scramble line."

Jukaga's image reappeared on the screen.

"I feel more comfortable now, Admiral, talking without anyone able to listen in on my side for the next several minutes. May I have your agreement that this conversation will be kept strictly between us?"

"I can't promise that," Geoff replied.

"Then at least do not let it be shared with my own people. I've managed to have the signal scrambled from here but soon it might be compromised."

"I agree then, it will not get back to your side."

"We don't have much time to talk, Admiral. I want to give you a warning. I was supposed to do this anyhow but I want you to understand that my concern in this is genuine."

"Go on then."

"If you do not surrender your fleet, Prince Thrakhath has declared that this shall be a war of *gatagak'vu*. How do you say, a war of total eradication."

Geoff felt a cold chill.

"Has it not always been thus?" he finally ventured.

"No. This is different. He will not only slaughter everyone — man, woman and child, but he will also slaughter the very worlds you live on through the use of high radiation doses. Nothing will be left, nothing. Your home, your Earth, with all its long history, will be dead, uninhabitable, lifeless."

His words trailed off and Geoff was startled to realize that Jukaga's voice was filled with remorse.

"You wanted us destroyed, enslaved, why your concern now?" Geoff asked.

Jukaga smiled and shook his head.

"That is not your concern, Admiral Tolwyn, only my own. I therefore implore you. Surrender. If you do, I will ensure that you and your warriors are treated with honor, that your Earth will continue to live."

"Better to die as free men then live as slaves," Geoff replied coldly.

Jukaga nodded, a smile lighting his features.

"As any true warrior would reply," he said quietly, "as I knew you would reply."

"Then there's nothing more to be said."

"I have been told to advise you that you have twenty four of your standard minutes to reply. If not, the planet you call Warsaw will cease to live."

"Go ahead and do it now," Geoff replied coldly, "but by God, Baron, tell Thrakhath that if he does, there'll come a day when we'll come back. If it takes a hundred years, we'll come back and we'll watch Kilrah as it's burned to ashes."

"Good-bye, Admiral," Jukaga said quietly and he started to reach over to switch off his screen. He paused and looked back up.

"I'm sorry," and then his image disappeared.

Shaken, Geoff sat back in his chair. He had just condemned more than twenty million to death.

"God help me," he whispered and he lowered his head for a moment, offering a silent prayer for forgiveness and strength.

He stood back up finally and went back out on the bridge.

"Warsaw, now five million clicks astern sir," the helm officer announced.

"Make course back towards Sirius, order destroyer squadron three." He paused. "No, make that squadron two, to form rear guard using maneuver delta for delaying action."

He settled into his command chair, watching the tactical. The enemy carriers, masked by more than a hundred escorts, continued their relentless move forward, while one of the older carriers, escorted by a cruiser squadron, broke away, turning towards Warsaw.

"Get me Mike Polowski on laser link," Geoff said quietly.

Seconds later the commander of squadron three appeared on the holo screen. Geoff felt as if the commodore were in the room with him. His features were pale, jaw quivering.

"I've got bad news for you, Mike."

"I can see it, Geoff."

"I'm sorry. They demanded the surrender of the fleet. If we didn't they said they'd hit your home world."

Mike lowered his head.

"You did what you had to do, Geoff. God help me, I would have done the same. Anything else, sir?"

"It's going to be bad, Mike. They're going to radiation-bombard it as well, killing the planet and everything on it."

Mike's jaw started to tremble and he turned away from the screen for a moment and then finally looked back, his eyes filled with anguish.

"Why? It's not even a military target."

"To make an example of what's to come."

Mike stood silently, unable to speak.

"I'm sorry, Mike."

Polowski nodded silently and then his image winked off.

"Give me full optical power on Warsaw, patch in to their planetary defense."

The orbital base commander appeared on the side screen, while optical locked on the planet. It still looked peaceful, an illusion since with visual scan it now took more than two minutes for the image to reach him.

"White Wolf, this is Warsaw defense. We are under attack. As per your orders, primary station has been abandoned. Civilian population are in shelters. All ground to space missiles have been expended.

"White Wolf, this is Warsaw defense. We have high speed incoming! We have . . ."

The image snapped off.

Geoff watched the optical scan in silence, and then the first blossom of light snapped across the northern continent's surface. Seconds later hundreds of snaps of light erupted, blanketing the continent, the snake-like chain of islands in the southern hemisphere erupting as well.

"We are picking up thermonuclear air bursts in the five hundred megaton range. The nukes are emitting strontium ninety," the tactical officer announced, her voice hard-edged with rage.

"The bastards," Geoff whispered, "the damn bastards."

It had gone even beyond genocide. The planet was seeded with enough strontium 90 to wipe out the entire biosphere. The Kilrathi were destroying an entire planet simply as a demonstration of what was to come.

"I know why you're here, Captain, excuse me, I think I made you a Commodore. Anyhow, Commodore, you're wasting your time."

Without even waiting for an invitation Jason went over to the refridge in Kruger's wardroom, pulled out a container of beer and popped it open.

"Help yourself," Kruger said quietly and then paused, "you deserve it."

"You did well out there," Jason replied.

"Not good enough," and Kruger motioned to a flat screen projecting an image from a drone probe that was circling above the main airfield and town on the Hell Hole, at least what was left of it.

"Four antimatter warheads and one thermonuclear airburst loaded with strontium ninety. The world's a write-off."

"The bastards," Jason hissed, looking at the radiation read-outs. There had been an unwritten and unspoken agreement between the two sides since the start of the war, that no matter how grim the conflict was, the deliberate destruction of life-bearing capability of a planet was beyond the limits. It had been in part a self-serving rule for both sides, for both sides hoped for ultimate victory and with it the worlds inhabited by their foes.

"We just got this burst signal from the Confeds," and he switched the screen.

It was an official government news service report on the opening action in the Warsaw system and Jason watched, seething with rage as an optical scan showed the annihilation of Warsaw. The report finished with a demand from Baron Jukaga, delivered in the most sincere of voices, as if he were on the human side of the conflict, calling for an end to hostilities through the surrender of the Third Fleet. The closing comment came from President Quinson, a wonderfully crude response, delivered before a packed Senate meeting, and as he said the words the Senate came to its feet, roaring their support.

"I actually rather like Quinson," Kruger said, turning the screen off. "Too bad he's going to get his ass kicked."

"At least he'll go down fighting."

"A gallant gesture but useless in the end," Kruger said quietly.

Jason spared a look over at the holo tactical display.

"The Cats have pulled back?"

"Into the next system already. I've got a squadron of destroyers in pursuit. They're circled around the crippled carrier like a wolf pack defending its pups. Just what I wanted, they're shaken and are afraid of losing a second carrier."

"Now what?"

"Ah, what you came to hear."

Jason nodded.

"Stay here. The bastards will be back. We know where seven of their old carriers are now, rather six, thanks to the kill your pilots helped put in. That still leaves at least ten unaccounted for. They might hit us from another direction at any moment."

Kruger paused and looked up at Jason.

"Go on, I'm expecting to hear it. Even old Richards on that frigate I gave him is mumbling about it."

"Head for Sirius or Earth. Look, I'll admit when I first got here I didn't think much of your Landreich fleet and pilots. But by God I'll admit it now, they're the best I've ever seen. Brave to the point of suicidal."

"Sometimes I even have to ask that," Kruger replied quietly. "A trade-off of a couple of lives for many."

"They might help tip the scale."

"First of all, action will be joined there by then."

Jason nodded.

"But it still might be going on and we could help."

"And while I go running off what about my own people out here? You're proposing that I leave the planets and orbital colonies of my system defenseless and go riding off to help the Confederation? Your Confederation was willing to write us off thirty years back, and they did it again this time. Why the hell should I care?"

"Because the Confederation needs you, needs your leadership and your pilots."

Kruger snorted with disdain.

"Oh, solidarity of race against the Cats, is that your next pitch?"

"I knew that wouldn't work," Jason replied. "But you know damn well that when Earth and the inner worlds fall, it's finished. What happened to Warsaw will happen to them. The Kilrathi are on a killing frenzy and they won't stop. They've levered the war up another notch. When they're done in there, they'll come out here and follow you and your people no matter where you flee."

Kruger said nothing, as if having heard the argument too many times before.

"So you won't go?"

"You guessed it."

"Will you release me and my people, give us at least *Tarawa* to head back?"

"No."

Jason had already calculated the chance of doing a Kruger on Kruger, of hijacking his carrier out of the fleet and knew it was impossible and useless. Nearly all the pilots and over half his crew were Landreich. Kruger had shrewdly made sure that none of the carriers had a majority of Confederation crews on board.

"You just can't forgive, can you?" Jason asked coldly. "Thirty years ago the Confederation made a mistake and I'll admit you made the right move in response. You know enough about me to know I did the same thing. I led a mutiny against an officer who ordered us to murder Kilrathi civilians and it would have destroyed my career if it hadn't been for Admiral Tolwyn.

"I went through hell because of that, but I never blamed the Confederation. I blamed the bastard who forced me to mutiny. For thirty years you've been carrying a grudge and because of your damned stupid blind pride you'll condemn humanity to death.

"I'm not going to mutiny against you, Kruger, but when the Kilrathi finish with you, if I'm still alive, I'll spit on whatever is left of you."

Without waiting for a reply Jason Bondarevsky stormed out of President Kruger's office.

• CHAPTER TWELVE

The two inhabited worlds of Sirius glimmered in the aft screen, showing themselves as two pale green points of light in the middle of the holo display of the system. Geoff jacked up the magnification level of the holo and the further of the two planets disappeared. On the far side of the holo display a nearly solid swarm of red blips were arrayed in five large clusters. Hundreds of smaller red lights, Kilrathi strike fighters and interceptors, were moving ahead, coming straight in at his own thin blue line, behind which were positioned four large blue dots. In the middle region of space between the two groups, two V wedges of small blue dots were aiming straight in at the heart of the enemy fleet.

"Strike forces crossing into Kilrathi controlled space," a voice whispered.

The Combat Information Center, buried in the heart of *Concordia* was almost like a tomb, encased in a double layering of durasteel, illuminated by soft diffused light and the shimmer of holo displays and flat screens. Outside a battle was raging, in here, where the decisions were being made, the cool professionalism of his staff made it seem almost like an exercise. Yet, as he spared a glance from the holo and looked around the room he could see the grim determination. After retreating through three star systems, and impotently witnessing the annihilation of the worlds he had been forced to abandon, Geoff Tolwyn had finally turned his fleet about. The Battle of Sirius had begun.

"Blue Squadron, this is Lone Wolf. Close it up. Remember, we want the big ones, nothing else, so cover your Broadswords."

"Lone Wolf, this is Round Top, read me?"

Kevin Tolwyn smiled; it was his old comrade from the *Tarawa* days.

"Where are you, Chamberlain?"

"Right above you in Broadsword Two off *Moskva*, so be sure to cover my butt, son, while I win the glory."

"With you all the way, Round Top."

Kevin tightened the grip on his joystick, his Rapier G jiggling slightly from his nervous hold on the stick. It was certainly the biggest strike group he had ever flown with, more than two hundred and fifty fighters and attack bombers launched from four carriers. The extra fifty heavy strike craft from *Saratoga* were missed, the carrier still half a system away with a main engine fuel pump acting up. Two hundred and eighty fighters were being held in reserve as protection for the fleet carriers and as a second strike wave.

Kevin looked down at his tactical display. Straight ahead the individual blips of enemy fighters, corvettes, frigates and destroyers had merged into a solid wall of red.

He clicked into a side band to the main fleet communications line. A real time image of Gilead, the second inhabited planet, was being transferred out to the fleet even while the battle was about to be joined.

He was past the point of rage. The planet flickered on his screen, bursts of five hundred megaton thermonuclear warheads, clad with strontium, detonating high up in the atmosphere, destroying yet another world. The image winked off, replaced by his uncle.

"This is Tolwyn. Good luck to all of you and good hunting."

The image winked off and Kevin smiled. Typical Brit understatement.

The forward edge of Rapiers, Raptors, Ferrets and Hornets, running ahead of the attack wave, slammed into the opposing wall of opposition defending the Kilrathi heavy carriers.

From out of the red wall dozens of blinking orange dots appeared, aiming straight in at the attack force.

"All right, Blue team, we've got incoming antimatter area strike," the strike leader announced. "Let's bring 'em up."

The strike force diverted from its straight in approach, turning up at a ninety degree angle relative to the orbital plane of the Sirius system. The area bombardment missiles started to turn to follow, the range closing. The first one winked into a white hot ball, dozens more detonating, catching half a dozen fighters at the back of the strike.

The squadrons nosed back over, following the strike commander, slicing in through the explosions, and as they came out the opposite side, the Kilrathi fighters were upon them.

Kevin fought down a moment of panic. The largest action he had ever been in was at Munro, a cakewalk attack on one carrier. Even the Academy holo simulators had never been programmed to handle the number of enemy fighters now coming in on him.

It was impossible to sort out which target to lock on. Hundreds of IFFs streaked across space and within seconds dozens of ships on both sides were exploding. The Broadsword and Sabre gunners sent out sprays of shot in every direction as wing group size attack waves by the Kilrathi came in. The four light corvettes escorting the attack dropped out sprays of chaff, jammers, and flares. The first wave passed and Kevin, ashamed, realized he had not fired even a shot.

He looked up at the Broadswords he was escorting. One was gone, another turning out of formation, spinning, its port engine blown apart, its starboard engine apparently jammed at full throttle. Its crew ejected and the ship spun away, exploding seconds later.

From out of the confusion a wave of Dralthi, Krants, and Gratha, flying nearly wing tip to wing tip, came sweeping in, forward cannons firing.

"Blue three, there's our Cats. Let's break 'em up."

He edged his throttle forward, leaping ahead of the Broadswords, lining up on the lead Dralthi and putting a dumb fire bolt straight into the furballs' canopy, blowing the top of the enemy fighter apart. The enemy attack broke apart, three Dralthi dead, and Kevin came around, seeing that his number three man was gone. There wasn't even time to ask.

"Keep moving in, close in maneuvering scoops," the strike commander called. "We want the carriers!"

Kevin swallowed hard, passing the order on to his squadron, and he closed scoops in.

It was no longer possible to pull the tight-in maneuvers. It was going to be a straight in high speed run.

Blasts snapped around him, missiles detonating, his number five pilot ejecting from her fighter as it crumpled up in a ball of flame.

He pulled in close under the bellies of the Broadswords he was escorting.

The outer row of enemy picket ships was straight ahead and their barrage opened up, two of the escorting corvettes taking multiple hits and disappearing. As they shot through the line of Kilrathi frigates and destroyers, more than a hundred missiles were dropped by the furballs, slashing into the squadrons, the two remaining corvettes blowing out more sprays of chaff, jammers, and flares. The curtain of distractors diverted most of the missiles, but enough found their mark and more than two dozen Confederation fighters and bombers were gone.

Kevin pulled open his visor and wiped the stinging sweat from his eyes. His back was soaked with sweat, the suit coolant unable to evaporate it off fast enough. His mouth felt dry, as if he had swallowed a ball of cotton and he suddenly understood why Ian had developed the revolting habit of chewing on an old cigar while in a tight spot.

Straight ahead on his tactical were five large clusters of red. He no longer needed to use the screen. Even from extreme range he could already pick out a thin sliver of reflected light.

"Bombardment groups one and two, take center

carrier," the strike commander announced, and Kevin could see on the comm screen that the leader's ship had been hit, smoke in the cockpit making him barely visible, "three and four carrier to port, five and six to starboard. Range nine hundred clicks, open maneuvering scoops, full reverse thrust for deceleration in ten seconds."

"Got that, Lone Wolf?"

"Straight in we go, Round Top. Make it a good one, buddy," Kevin replied.

"Nothing less will do."

"Three, two, one, decelerate!"

Kevin pulled his maneuvering scoops wide open and slammed in reverse thrust, instantly slowing his fighter, which shuddered to a near stand still less than fifty clicks out from their target.

A swarm of Kilrathi fighters closed in on them.

There was a flash of light forward off the carrier's bow and Kevin realized that someone, driven by rage, had simply tried to ram the enemy ship. Such a maneuver at full closing speed was nearly impossible to do and the fighter had deflected off the side of the carrier's heavy shields.

"I've got initial torpedo lock," Round Top announced, "and counting at thirty, twenty nine . . ." The other strike craft that Kevin was protecting joined in with their own announcements of initial lock.

They slowly drifted in towards their target and Kevin felt as if his heart were wrapped in ice. The ship was massive, more than twice the size of any carrier he had ever seen before. He could barely spare it a glance, however, as hundreds of enemy fighters swarmed in upon them.

Within seconds he had lost the rest of his squadron in the mad melee as he twisted and turned his fighter, struggling to stay alive while at the same time desperately attempting to cover the Broadswords as they hung near motionless, waiting for their torpedoes to gain full lock.

Broadsword after Broadsword disappeared in white-hot explosions. Three Krants lined in on Round Top, his countdown still echoing in Kevin's headphones as he weaved into them, crippling one with a dumb-fired flechette spray, and destroying a second with a stream of neutron bolts cutting into the fighter's engine mounts.

The third stitched a flurry of rounds across the portside gun turret of Round Top's ship, and Kevin caught a glimpse of the gunner's body shredding to pieces, his canopy bursting into shards from the strike.

"Keep 'em off me," Round Top shouted. "Ten seconds and counting."

The strike squadron had drifted to within eight clicks of the carrier and what appeared to be a solid wall of mass driver rounds snaked out from the ship's bow, blowing three more Broadswords apart. Kevin struggled with his stick as a shudder ran through his fighter, starboard shielding overloading and a laser hit sheered off the last meter of his wingtip.

He turned inside the laser beam, blowing out reflective chaff which temporarily blinded the laser's target lock, the beam skewing across his bow, cutting a gouge into the forward durasteel armor.

"Three, two, one, it's away!"

The fifteen surviving Broadswords out of the thirty in the strike group launched their torpedo loads. Round Top, along with half the remaining ships, were armed with the laser lock guidance and they turned upwards, making sure that the laser emitters were pointed at the torpedoes.

The space between the attacking fighters and the carriers turned into an insane explosion of anti-torpedo missiles, dogfighting ships, and point defense blasts from the Kilrathi carrier.

"We've got lock, we've got holding lock," Round Top shouted.

Kevin turned his fighter to circle around Round Top and saw yet another swarm of Kilrathi fighters cutting in, dropping a wall of missiles on the surviving Broadswords.

"Round Top, evasive, evasive!"

"Can't! We still have lock, three seconds, two, one . . ."

Kevin screamed with rage as five missiles detonated across the top of his friend's Broadsword. The ship simply disappeared.

From off his portside wing he saw four torpedoes impacting on the carrier's bow. In the silence of space it seemed somehow surreal, as if a holo movie was being played out. For a brief instant the carrier disappeared behind the exploding curtain of antimatter warheads. He waited for the secondary explosions to begin.

"Scratch one flattop," someone screamed on the commlink. "We've got the bastard!"

And as he waited, the carrier emerged from out of the fire. Its forward bow, and for nearly a hundred meters back, was a twisted wreckage, but the ship continued to purposefully move forward.

Making sure his gun cameras were still on, Kevin turned in towards the carrier.

Wreckage was trailing off from the bow of the ship as he raced in and he could see fires flaring inside the ruins of the forward portside launch bay. He crossed up and over the top of the carrier and then suddenly the anti-aircraft defenses of the carrier kicked back on.

She still had internal power — it was impossible after four torpedo strikes!

Jinxing to throw off the gunners, he raced down the length of the ship, passing one of the aft launch bays. He locked his camera into a laser designator and swung the designator in on the bay. On his small comm screen he caught a quick glimpse inside the ship. Another fighter was coming down the launch ramp, afterburners flaming. Internal lighting was still on and launch crews were purposefully working, some of them still picking themselves up, shaking off the aftereffects of the torpedo hammer blows. The image disappeared as he flashed across the stern of the ship.

He looked up and saw that more than a dozen Kilrathi fighters were streaking in to pick him off and he went into a violent spin, cutting down over the stern of the ship, his fighter bucking and shuddering as he got caught in the exhaust plume of the carrier.

He punched through into the fleet comm channel.

"White Wolf, this is Blue One. No joy, repeat, no joy, carrier still running after four torpedo hits. Catch my video transmit."

He sent the signal through and then looked at his tactical.

Space was dotted solid with red, with only an occasional blue dot. The strike force had shot its bolt and been destroyed, and the Kilrathi Fleet continued on in.

Sick at heart, Admiral Tolwyn silently watched as the action reports came in. He coughed again, wiping the tears from his eyes. The Combat Information Center was still filled with smoke, the air filtration plant still off line from the torpedo hit to *Concordia*.

"Message from *Moskva*, sir."

"Put it on main."

A young woman, blood trickling down from her forehead, appeared in the flat wavery image.

"Where's Ching?"

"Dead, sir. Last hit took out the bridge."

He nodded silently. Damn.

"Sir, we have to abandon ship, all engines are dead. We're moving on inertia and one bank of maneuvering thrusters only. Secondary generators are going off line, hull integrity lost in sixty-three percent, remaining bulkhead are leaking and will rupture with one more hit."

"Get your people into the escape boats. I'll have Polowski stand by to pick up survivors."

"I'm sorry, sir."

"You fought her well, lieutenant, you fought her well."

He looked back at the action reports that streamed in across the monitors.

Two of the new carriers and one of the old ones had been hit in his strike. The old style carrier was gone, but the two new ones still appeared to be relentlessly moving forward. In return, all four of his carriers had been hit. *Verdun* was lost with all hands, and now *Moskva* was finished. *Leyte Gulf*, which had only joined him this morning, had one bay down from a direct hit. Of the more than four hundred and eighty strike craft and bombers he had launched three hours ago, less than two hundred and twenty were still able to fly. Worst of all was the loss of Broadswords; less than a quarter had returned. Estimates of Kilrathi fighter loss stood at just over seven hundred. He knew the figure would be cut once the debriefing teams had a chance to look at all the camera footage.

In short, he had lost.

He looked at the status plot boards. Only twenty-nine Broadswords and twenty modified Sabres were armed and ready for a second strike. Already the Kilrathi were sending up their next strike wave which was even stronger than their first as they shifted craft over from defensive to offensive operations. He turned back to his strategic communications officer, who was burst signal linked back to Earth.

"Latest reported position of *Saratoga*?"

"Still six hours twenty-one minutes short of jump point 3A."

Geoff looked back at his main nav screen. Jump Point 3A, the connecting link back from Sirius towards Earth was an hour behind him.

Saratoga would never come up in time to help repel the next attack, let alone be able to aid in a second strike.

"Signal all ships by laser link. We are withdrawing from Sirius."

His bridge crew looked around at him startled.

"We'll be swarmed under in the second strike. If I thought we had a chance of hitting them back hard enough, I'd do it. There's no sense in dying for no reason."

"What about Sirius, sir?" a helm ensign asked angrily. "Damn it, sir, that's my home."

"Son, it's finished whether we stay here and die, or leave. We need time to repair damaged planes, get *Leyte's* port launch bay back on line and prepare a second strike. *Saratoga* will nearly double our heavy strike fighter strength if we fall back on her."

The ensign looked around, realizing he had spoken way out of turn to a full admiral. He started to open his mouth again and was restrained by his section lieutenant who took him by the shoulder and turned him away.

Gilead, the smaller of the two worlds, was already flaming ruins. Sirius Prime, thirty nine million clicks to port, was now wide open and already a section of Kilrathi cruisers was turning towards it. He didn't even want to think about how many people were down there.

"Helm, turn us about. Let's get the hell out of here," he snarled.

"Recall those cruisers now!"

Prince Thrakhath turned to gaze coldly at Baron Jukaga.

"Growing soft, my good Baron?"

"Your senseless barbarism will only arouse them further. You've made your point, now spare the second planet. Show mercy and it still might weaken their will."

"Terror breeds terror, Baron."

"Terror can also breed fanaticism and hatred. Your demonstration at Warsaw did not intimidate the humans, instead it caused them to stop their internal bickering and unite. You know nothing of humans. Senseless bombardments of their civilian populations have always tended to unite them. The deliberate destruction of entire worlds with radiation will cause them to fight us tooth and nail to the death rather than surrender."

"And that's what you wanted, wasn't it, surrender?"

The Baron attempted to control his loathing and rage.

"You are a barbarian," he snapped. "We could have undermined them, let their natural weaknesses play into our hands. You have gone on a rampage and destroyed eleven of their worlds so far, and their fleet is still intact."

"We just crippled it, or weren't you watching?"

"They still have fight left in them. Remember, Prince Thrakhath, the new fleet is to serve two purposes: one to win this war, and second to prepare us for the Mantu if they should ever return. You are now gambling that fleet in your drive for vengeance on the humans."

"Not vengeance, extinction."

Sickened, the Baron turned away. He knew now that the accusations were right. Study one's enemy for too long and in the end you might come to admire them. He did not admire the humans, the very essence of his nature prevented that, but he could acknowledge them as something more than mere prey to be slaughtered. His plan, if it had been allowed to be played out, might very well have resulted in a near bloodless victory, a Confederation completely divided, lulled by peace, and then psychologically overwhelmed when the dozen new carriers appeared. It all suddenly became very clear.

"You allowed that recon ship of the humans to slip into Hari space and then allowed it to escape. You wanted the peace ended, didn't you?"

"In spite of your claims of intellect, Baron, you are often rather slow at figuring things out."

"You wanted this war to end in a blood bath. You were the one who triggered the bomb in the human headquarters."

Prince Thrakhath smiled.

"You were never a prisoner of the humans. I was. You have not lost comrades to them, I have. I shall rise to the Imperial Throne, hailed as the conqueror of the humans and winner of this war, while as for you . . ." and he leaned over, touching a button on his console.

The doors to his wardroom were flung open and four Imperial Marine guards stepped in.

"Escort the Baron to his quarters and make sure he is very comfortable."

"Are you arresting me?"

Prince Thrakhath shook his head.

"Let us say that there are certain questions to be asked

of you later, once the battles are completed and I am secure in my victory."

Baron Jukaga smiled coldly.

"Don't underestimate Tolwyn and his people. They are not finished yet."

"They soon will be, Baron," and he laughed coldly as Jukaga was lead from the room.

"How are you, Geoff?"

Geoff looked up in surprise as "Big" Duke Grecko walked into his private quarters.

Geoff started to get up from his cot and Duke motioned for him to relax while he pulled a chair around and sat down across from Tolwyn.

"What the hell are you doing out here, Duke?"

"Can't keep the Marines in port when the action starts. I'm not interfering out here, Geoff, but I thought I should come out and have a look. "

"You got the after action report then?"

Duke nodded glumly.

"It was relayed up to my frigate a couple of hours ago."

"I screwed up, Duke. I should have fallen back from Sirius and then held here with *Saratoga* joined in for the strike."

"You couldn't abandon Sirius without a fight. Civilian morale would have gone off the deep end."

"So we lose two carriers and still lose Sirius."

"At least you bloodied them."

"One old carrier destroyed, one damaged and one of their new carriers reported heavily damaged, but no kills on the new fleet. Which is what I wanted."

"We're reporting that big carrier as dead for now," Duke said quietly.

"I never liked doing that."

"Sometimes we have to, and for all practical purposes it is dead at the moment."

"So what do you want, Duke?" Geoff asked, cutting straight to the point.

"I'm ordering you to fall back on Earth."

"What? Hell, Duke, if they break our line there they'll fry Earth in a matter of minutes."

"I know, but we've been busy. By the time you pull back, *Lexington* and *Ark Royal* will be on line."

"How? The jump engines on *Lex* and *Ark Royal* were fully out for realignment, and core reactors had been dumped."

"If we're fighting inside the home system we won't need jump engines and both ships have one reactor back up and running."

"They'll be sitting ducks."

"They'll be sitting ducks in the dockyard anyhow. At least they can still launch fighters."

Though neither one said it, they both knew as well that the two additional carriers would serve as targets, forcing the Kilrathi to spread out their attack.

"Mars is the closest planet in towards the jump line," Duke continued. "We've packed every landing field there full of every damn fighter, trainer, and even civilian light craft."

"You've got to be kidding. I stripped out every good plane and pilot before I left. Put what's left into space and they'll die like flies."

Duke nodded.

"And the Kilrathi will burn up ammunition while some of our people still get in for another strike."

He knew it was better than a desperate stand out here with no hope of winning. If he stood now, it'd only delay the inevitable by maybe a day or two at most.

"Our psych analysis people tell me that even if you abandon this key jump point, Thrakhath will not spread out into the inner worlds until he completes his kill of you and Earth. The bastard hates your guts, according to psych, for too many humiliations. He wants your hide almost as much as he wants Earth. He'll follow you straight in."

"You know, Duke," Geoff said quietly, "even with the additional material and manpower, they still have us. You saw what happened to my last strike, and those boys were the finest pilots in the fleet."

"I know, Geoff, I know. But there's one more idea I sort of cooked up on my own, that might help things out."

"What?"

And as Duke told him, Admiral Tolwyn came to his feet.

"You're mad, Duke, that's senseless murder. You're bloody mad to even think of it."

"And that's why it might work," Duke said with a cold smile.

"My lord Thrakhath."

He turned to look at a holo display of his bridge captain.

"The latest report, sire."

"Go on."

"The human fleet is turning about, retreating back towards Earth."

"Are you certain?"

"Yes, my lord."

That caught him slightly off guard. He had thought that Tolwyn would make his final stand here. One system past Sirius, eight jump lines diverged outward into the inner worlds of the Confederation and also back outwards towards the frontier. Control of the next system would be a major victory in and of itself. Yet he was abandoning it now without a fight. Damn him.

"Latest intelligence report?"

"Three carriers still confirmed with their Third Fleet. Intelligence is still working on their latest code but we have picked up a civilian channel reporting that a carrier left its Earth base six hours ago, and that a second carrier is moving up to join the fleet. The signal was from one of their news stations, and its coding simple to break."

"The stupid fools."

"Our latest damage report?"

"*Tarvakh* is still contending with internal fires, all three forward launch bays are closed. *Yu'ba'tuk's* main shield generator is still off line and one launch bay closed."

"Secondary shielding?"

"At ninety-one percent, expected to upgrade to ninety-three within the hour."

"Fighter losses?"

"Heavy, sire. Seven eight-of-eights and two eights today. Eight eight-of-eights and five eights total."

Not good at all. The Empire could invest all it wanted on new carriers that were next to indestructible, but at the core, it still came down to having fighters that were equal to or better than the latest Confederation designs, and pilots who were trained to fly them. It had always been the weak edge. Except for the handful of Stealth fighters possessed by the Empire, fighter design and pilot training had never fully kept up with that of the humans. The emergencies of the last two years had forced them to repeatedly reach into the academies and throw half-trained cadets into action—where most of them died within a matter of days. The survivors were tough, but there were always too few.

He looked at what he had left and made his decisions.

"Order *Tarvakh* to transfer her remaining fighters to my flagship. That will make good on our losses. Detail off," and he paused to look at the status of the three surviving older carriers. "Detail off *Notakgak* and *Darthuka* and their support ships to escort *Tarvakh* back to the Empire. Both the retreating carriers to transfer their heavy strike squadrons to this ship as well. Order the flanking cruiser squadrons to join us in the next sector forward. Their fighters will equal those we lose from *Notakgak* and *Darthuka*. Order the fleet to move up to flank speed in pursuit. When we reach the next jump point send the first wave of light corvettes and minesweeps through first, followed by cruisers in case they are waiting in ambush."

The officer bowed in reply.

"The cruiser squadron detailed to the main planet of this system has suppressed the planetary defenses, my lord. They are awaiting orders."

Prince Thrakhath smiled.

"Annihilate the planet, and then we go for Tolwyn and Earth."

• CHAPTER THIRTEEN

Transjump completed, Prince Thrakhath stood up, expectant. A tremor of excitement coursed through him. Involuntarily his talons extended and he felt saliva filling his mouth. He waited, heart racing as the jump point confirmation flashed across the main screen of the battle bridge. Optical scanners swept space and then finally locked on to what the Prince was seeking. Magnification and computer enhancements kicked in and the image zoomed in, expanding.

Earth floated in the middle of the screen. A growl of triumphal shouts echoed on the battle bridge, a total breakdown of discipline that he was willing, at least this once, to ignore and forgive, as his own howl of triumph mingled in with that of his crew.

"Signal the fleet on an open channel," Thrakhath roared and his communications officer opened the line.

"Today we shall watch Earth burn. Long live the Emperor and the Empire. Standard battle formation, advance full speed ahead!"

"They're starting to advance," Duke Grecko said quietly.

Geoff Tolwyn said nothing, intently studying the long range tactical display, as the information was relayed in by a line of picket ships pulling back ahead of the Imperial Fleet.

The advance came straight on with a defiant certainty. There was no elaborate maneuvering, no attempts at tactical ploys. The Kilrathi main battle fleet came on in a solid mass, arrogant in its overwhelming power.

"I'd better get to my ship," Duke said.

"Your tactical plan is suicidal, Duke. Ship-to-ship fighting isn't a Marine job. Leave it to the fleet. And by God, Duke, boarding is something straight out of Nelson and Trafalgar."

"I'll be damned if we're sitting this fight out, so don't argue with me about it."

Geoff looked over at him, smiled, and took his old friend's hand.

"All right, it just might work. But you know, Duke, the proper place for the Head of Joint Chiefs is back at headquarters on Earth."

Duke sniffed angrily.

"Look, Geoff. Up until they decided to make me a hero after Vukar I was a line officer. Being in command of the whole show was never my plan. I'll be damned if I hide in a bunker while my grunts are fighting for survival. Anyhow, I've always wanted to lead a battle like this."

"Leading men in a desperate battle, against impossible odds?" Tolwyn said with a smile. "What are you, the reincarnation of Patton?"

"Don't let anyone in on the secret, Geoff."

"Take care, Duke."

"God speed and good hunting, Geoff. I'll see you at sundown."

Geoff laughed softly and walked his commander off the bridge and down the corridor to the starboard launch bay. Fighters were lined up down the length of the deck, crews going over last minute checks, armament teams finishing up loading, and repair crews off to one side, struggling to salvage and bring back into the fight craft damaged in the Battle of Sirius.

A Marine landing craft was on the launch line, pilots standing by the open door, talking with the launch officer. At the sight of Grecko approaching they stiffened, came to attention and saluted.

"At ease, boys. Fire the engine up and let's get to work."

Geoff saluted Duke, who looked back at him and smiled.

"Give 'em hell, Geoff," and then he was gone, the entry hatch closing behind him and snicking shut.

Geoff stood back from the launch line as the deck launch officer stepped up forward and beside the Marine landing craft. She held her hand to her earprotectors, waiting to hear from the senior launch officer that Marine 1 was cleared. She saluted the pilot when word of clearance was passed, crouched down and pointed forward. The landing craft started forward, clearing the airlock, then kicked on full afterburners and, turning to starboard, disappeared.

Thirty million clicks beyond the airlock Mars hovered in the darkness, a bright point of red light. Thin lines of reflected silver light moved past the airlock, hundreds of light civilian ships heading outward, with several hundred Marine landing craft moving in the middle of the formation.

Geoff felt sick at heart watching them and turned, heading back up the corridor. He was already late for the final briefing and he moved purposefully down the main corridor into the pilot quarters and ready room.

"Attention!"

Geoff came into the ready room, his features set, and reached the lectern. He looked out at his pilots.

Nearly half the faces were new, many of them cadets pulled straight out of the Academy to replace the losses from Sirius.

God, we're sending children out now.

"At ease. Be seated.

"I'll keep this short, we don't have much time. You'll be pleased to know that *Lexington* has just cleared dry dock, carrying fifty-seven fighters. That'll give us five fleet carriers for this action."

Actually he knew it was almost meaningless. *Lexington* was coming up with just a little more than half her complement and running on secondary reactor power only. It was nothing more than bait, moving ahead of *Concordia*, *Saratoga*, *Ark Royal* and *Leyte Gulf*. With three hundred additional fighters sortied up from Mars and Earth orbital bases, there'd be just over six hundred fighters, half of them with green crews who'd never seen action beyond a flight simulator.

"You know your missions. Blue Three, you're flying Combat Air Patrol over the carriers. Blue Two, you're escorting in the Broadswords."

He could see Blue Three was less than amused, getting stuck in a purely defensive role. Blue Two knew what was going to happen to her but didn't display a flicker of emotion. The Kilrathi would turn their full fury on the Broadswords and Sabres, and with less than eighty making up the strike and eighty escorts, the chances of any of them coming back was nil.

He hesitated for a second.

"Blue One, you have the second strike escort slot. It's going to be grim. You have to remember what the final objective is, and remember that they're all volunteers out there."

His nephew looked up at him and forced a smile. Geoff paused and looked over at the tactical display flickering in the briefing room's holo.

The Kilrathi Fleet was still staying together, coming straight in at a range of twenty million clicks and closing. Thanks to simple orbital mechanics, Mars was the closest planet to the jump point, with Earth seventy million clicks behind it.

The huge colonies on the moons of Saturn and Jupiter were on the far side of the system. The only settlement areas now being overrun were in the asteroid belt and had already been abandoned.

"Pilots, man your planes," Geoff said quietly and he saluted first as they came back to their feet.

The pilots and crews stormed out of the room. The usual banter and bravado was gone today. They were silent, some obviously frightened, all of them filled with a grim determination. He felt he could have made a bit more of an emotional appeal, but knew that was nothing but crap. Every one of them knew that this was no ordinary battle. If this one was lost the Kilrathi would be above Earth within hours.

Kevin came past him, helmet tucked under his arm. His nephew slowed, looking at him out of the corner of his eye.

The hell with protocol, Geoff thought as he stepped forward and put his hands on Kevin's shoulders.

"I've never been prouder of you, Kev. Now take care of yourself."

Kevin looked at him, his eyes bright.

"It's an honor to be with you today, sir," he said, trying to control the tremor in his voice. Geoff let go of him and the boy followed the stream of pilots out the door.

"Launch all fighters. Let us finish this hunt."

Prince Thrakhath turned away from the screen, a tingle of excitement coursing through him as the fighter launch klaxon sounded through the ship.

Before him stood the Baron.

"You do not look thrilled about our impending victory, Baron."

Baron Jukaga merely snarled, looking at the Prince defiantly.

"I have one final little assignment for you, Baron."

"Go on then, what is it?"

And as Thrakhath told him the Baron's eyes went wide with shock and rage.

"It is useless, senseless. The Emperor ordered you to preserve the planet for the next Sivar."

"There are a hundred other worlds to choose from once this is done. A squad of Imperial Marines will now escort you to your ship, Baron."

Baron Jukaga looked coldly at the Prince and then spat on the floor.

Prince Thrakhath merely laughed in reply as Baron Jukaga was escorted from the room.

"My lord, there are significantly more ships than intelligence indicated."

Thrakhath looked back at the main screen and ordered the forward picket ships to send back enhanced optical scan. He waited for the visuals to be returned, watching the display of the two fleets being deployed. More and more blips of enemy ships were appearing, moving out from behind other ships which had been masking them. He had his suspicions as to what the new ships were and did not feel overly worried. One of the advantages of having had an embassy team on Earth was the ability to conduct reconnaissance. It was made even better by the fact that their own Foreign Minister had become a traitor. Too bad she was under arrest.

"They're civilian ships, my lord. Numerous light craft, personal ships, light business ships of corvette size, shuttle craft, and civilian interplanet transports."

Thrakhath nodded.

"They're throwing everything in as a screen to waste our weapons on. Order the outer wave of fighters to ignore them and to concentrate on the incoming Broadswords and Sabres. Once their offensive capability has been smashed we can turn our attention to this chaff they throw out and destroy them."

"We're also detecting Marine assault and landing ships, my lord."

Thrakhath stirred, ordering that this new sighting be highlighted on the main display. Several hundred of the blips started to blink bright yellow.

What were they up to?

"A diversionary effort, my lord?"

He looked over at his chief tactical officer.

He still had over seventeen hundred fighters at his disposal, almost all of them already launched and moving towards position. The first offensive strike wave was already committed, four hundred strike craft moving out past the outer line of picket ships with four eights of corvettes and light frigates in escort. Long range Confederation patrols were already moving to intercept, a pitiful six eights of fighters.

He was holding back over a thousand craft, assuming a more defensive posture than in the last battle. One of his carriers was gone, another slightly damaged. He would absorb and totally destroy the offensive strike, eliminating the final threat. Then he would smash through with a totally annihilating second strike, smashing whatever was left of the enemy fleet. They could no longer retreat and regroup; they would have to stand and die.

But the Marines? What were they for? To draw fire, obviously, while the last of the Broadswords went in.

"Still concentrate on the Broadswords," he said. "Then we slaughter the rest."

Kevin tried to purge the anguish, to block it out. His friends, his comrades were dying. Flickers of light filled space straight ahead and to starboard a hundred and fifty clicks away. The Broadsword strike was going in. His tactical screen traced the attack. The first wave of Broadswords, what few were left, was slowing, hovering. Going through the agonizing thirty second countdown to launch. And one after another their transponders winked off, the blue blips replaced by brief flashes of light and then disappearing.

He switched to strike two's main comm channel.

"Ten seconds, nine, keep 'em off, keep 'em off . . ."

"I can't eject, I can't get out, oh God I'm burning . . ."

"Six on your tail, Maria, break, break . . ."

"Yellow three, torpedo lock failed, am . . ."

The signals became fewer, space ahead flashing with hundreds of points of light.

The second wave, going towards the carriers, was straight ahead, slashing into the storm of defense. A hundred Kilrathi fighters were now hitting into his own attack column and ships were dying, but the main blow had not hit yet.

"Blue One, we've got company coming."

Kevin tore his attention away from the dying attack and saw a wave of fifty fighters coming in from above and slashing into the column behind him. He held course, looking over his shoulder.

Nearly a thousand craft were spread out around him. Off his port quarter he saw a civilian transplanet liner trying an evasive and disappear in an explosion after a single burst of neutron bolts from a light fighter.

It was suicide and he had to harden his heart to the realization that was precisely what the pilots flying the civilian craft had signed on for. They were nothing more than sitting ducks, unshielded, totally defenseless. Having been given pressure suits and rescue transponders, the pilots were told to bail out if things got too hot. But they were serving their purpose. The first waves of Kilrathi fighters, wading into the hundreds of targets, had become drunk with the thrill of killing. He watched as a flight of Krants shot right through a line of Marine transports, not even bothering to fire, racing ahead to smash a cruiser size liner, a dozen fighters tearing into the defenseless ship until it split apart. And each fighter that took thirty seconds to line up and fire on a useless ship was one less fighter engaged in the real fight, while the hidden weapon drew even closer.

"My lord, we might have a tactical analysis on what they are doing."

Thrakhath looked over at his tactical officer.

Even as the officer started to offer his analysis the truth of what he was saying sunk in.

"All fighters strike them now! Strike them now. Order all carriers into full evasive!"

"Here we go! All ships pick your targets. If you can't get to a carrier, nail a cruiser. Charge!"

General Duke Grecko leaned forward, looking over the shoulder of his assault craft pilot. A recorded charge blared on the assault craft's loud speaker and Grecko grinned with delight.

Behind him, in the aft personnel bay, a hundred assault

troops cheered, thumping the butts of their laser rifles on the floor of the ship.

Space around him was pure chaos. Hundreds of Kilrathi fighters were swarming in, escort ships moving to intersect the attack. Dozens of ships and assault craft were vaporizing every second in the slaughter, so that he thought for an instant that his plan was exactly what Geoff, and for that matter everyone else from the President on down, had declared it to be: pure suicide.

The only advantage he could now see in being head of the Joint Chiefs of Staff, was that he didn't have to convince anyone — he simply had to give the order, and then go.

A civilian liner twisted in front of him, blocking the rush of three incoming Dralthi, diverting their shots. His own pilot dived under the liner as it exploded and then lined back up on their target.

"The carrier, go for the carrier!"

"We'll never make it. Let's nail the destroyer to port!"

"Damn it, son, I'm the general here. Anything less than a carrier is an insult, now move it!"

Kevin weaved his way through the melee, moving up to protect an assault wave of twenty Marine landing craft, a full brigade of troops packed inside. They were breaking through.

A Kilrathi destroyer was moving in towards the group and he saw three of the landing craft turn towards the destroyer. The destroyer's defensive batteries nailed two. The third closed in, letting loose with its ground bombardment armaments which leaped across space, exploding across the bow of the enemy ship. The rounds were designed for area suppression, not shield and hull penetration, but they nevertheless blinded the ship. The landing craft swung across the top side of the destroyer, matching speed and then slammed down on its main cargo hatch. Explosive shape charges mounted to the bottom of the landing craft detonated, blowing the destroyer's main access hatch open.

The landing craft edged forward, gaining magnetic lock on the destroyer's hull. No matter what the ship now did as evasive, the Marine assault craft was glued to its side like a lamprey eel on the side of a fish—and it was just as deadly.

The back hatch of the landing craft blew open and assault troops streamed out, wearing magnetic-soled shoes and swarmed in through the ruptured cargo door, firing RPGs, miniguns, and assault recoilless flechette launchers.

Kevin shot past the destroyer.

The damn plan just might work!

The seventeen assault ships ahead pressed in, Kevin now riding herd above them. He tried to ignore everything else: the hundreds of ships fighting and dying around him, the total chaos, as all tactical formations were lost. Kilrathi fighters, now fully committed to this new threat, swarmed in, space so thick with them that he witnessed half a dozen collisions between turning fighters, their own ships, and Confederation craft.

Five of the Marine ships disappeared, a full battalion of five hundred men winking out of existence. In any other situation their loss would have been viewed as a disaster. Here, with the final desperate defense of Earth, it was the mere incident of a second's time. Three Jalthi turned in on the group, ignoring Kevin. He slashed two out of existence, while the third took out three landing craft and then broke hard down and to the left, disappearing.

The Marine craft pressed on in, dodging past a lumbering cruiser, with the lead landing craft pushing up and over.

"Come on, take it, just take it before you're all killed," Kevin thought, wanting to scream at the assault unit's commander. The cruiser fell astern, taking out three more craft as they shot past, with a mass driver burst shutting down his own aft shields and slicing deep into his armor. Six craft were left and then he saw the target straight ahead as he looked up after dispatching yet another fighter—a Kilrathi heavy carrier turning in evasive.

The carrier, with a mix of twenty civilian and assault

ships behind it, was going through a slow, ponderous turn, its aft, top, and bottom batteries all engaged, slaughtering their pursuers. Within seconds the twenty ships were gone.

They were racing straight in on the carrier. The six craft he was escorting opened fire, sixty area suppression bombardment missiles blanketing the ship's bow.

"Fighter following me, we're going for their topside forward bay, match speed and give us suppressive!"

Startled, Kevin looked at his comm screen. It was Duke Grecko on a laser link line.

The order was insane and yet he followed it. He leaped ahead of the six landing craft, even as two more of them exploded, then slammed in reverse thrusters, coming to a dead stop fifty meters in front of the launch bay.

Kevin toggled through every weapon he still had, dumping out IFFs, dumb fire and then mass drivers. The spread exploded across the airlock bay, which shimmered and glowed red, part of the concentrated blast kicking through the shielding, blowing apart a mass driver turret above the bay. Two landing craft came streaking past and headed in. An explosion rocked his ship, spinning it over in a cartwheeling pivot away from the carrier. A quick scan of his instruments told him the worst and he reached down between his legs, grabbed hold of the ejector ring, and pulled.

"Switch IFF transponders now!" Grecko roared.

The pilot flipped the switch to the preprogrammed Kilrathi IFF, which intelligence claimed would get them through the airlock if they activated it at the last second before the deck officer could toggle the channel to a different frequency.

He closed his eyes as they hit the field. If intelligence was off, the landing craft would not be able to handle the head-on collision and would vaporize on the shield.

An explosion rocked the ship and he was slammed forward by a jarring blow. He opened his eyes. They were skidding down the length of the flight deck, the Kilrathi launch crew scattering in every direction.

"Blow rear hatch!"

The rear hatch swung open even as the landing craft continued to skid down the deck in a shower of sparks.

Duke, unbuckled from his jump seat, stood up clenching a laser gun and started for the rear.

"Let's kick ass!" he roared.

The Marines closest to the hatch were already up, leaping out the door, rolling on the deck, coming up and firing. Grecko hit the back edge and jumped, deliberately rolling on to his new artificial arm which could take the blow better. Gaining his feet he nailed a furball pilot coming at him with a drawn pistol, cutting him in half, then dropped a ground crew coming out from under a Krant.

The landing craft skidded to a stop and Duke raced towards it. He looked back at his other landing craft. It was on its side, burning, survivors struggling out from the wreckage.

"Get that mine out now! First platoon with me on the advance. Second platoon knock out their launch bridge and secure a perimeter, then help any survivors from the other landing craft. Third platoon escort the demolitions team."

Duke looked around, trying to figure out where to go next. Intelligence had never said anything about the internal layout of the ship. But then again, what the hell did intelligence know about these damn ships anyhow, other than that they were big? The only plan they had was to board and then get as deep into the ship as possible.

He saw an oversized door. Hell, they were all oversized given the size of the Cats. Flight deck personnel were fleeing through it and it looked as good as any.

"First platoon, let's go!"

He raced for the door, firing as he advanced, dropping Cats, their bodies piled up at the entryway. He hit the corridor, started to step in, and then ducked back from a flurry of laser shots. Two of his Marines leaned in, firing a suppressive spray while a third held up a minigun. The explosive roar of the gun drowned out all other sound, filling the corridor with fire, smoke, and a hundred rounds a second. Another Marine threw a concussion grenade in; it detonated and they waded through. Each door that they passed was kicked open and a grenade dropped in.

They reached the end of the corridor which broke into an intersection of four hallways radiating outward.

"We have to get down, damn it, into the guts of the ship!"

He sent sections running up each of the corridors and thirty seconds later a runner came back.

"Access hatch to lower levels, sir, this way."

"First section, first squad, secure this point. Get the demo team up here and move them in after us."

He looked back at the rest of his team.

"I'm getting too old for this crap," he grinned. "Come on, let's go!"

"My lord, they've boarded the ship through the topside launch bay!"

Stunned, Prince Thrakhath looked over at the ship security officer.

It was madness, absolute madness. And brilliant. Why could he have not seen that in desperation this would be a final tactic?

"How many Imperial Marine guards are on board?"

"A security detachment of fifty, my lord, not counting your own security squad."

"Where are they heading?"

The security chief toggled through a schematic of the ship and traced out a line.

"They're moving down into the second level already. Reports are sketchy."

"They're going to set mines and blow them," Thrakhath said coldly and he looked over at his damage control officer.

"What can they do?"

The damage control officer looked at him wide-eyed.

"All our calculations of damage containment were

based upon external torpedo and missile strikes. Our armor is layered, through several sectors of the ship, strongest outside, with two internal belts. Into the core, there's no armor at all, my lord."

He paused.

"If they blow a demolition charge in the middle of the ship, the armor will actually act to contain it, making the damage far worse." He swallowed hard. "It'll destroy the ship, my lord."

Prince Thrakhath roared with anger, slamming his fist down on a console.

"Get everyone who can carry a weapon forward. Block them off!"

The security chief ran from the bridge.

"Boarding parties now reported on two other carriers, my lord, as well as twenty-nine other ships."

"And the enemy fleet?"

"Still holding position, my lord. Two of their carriers have been destroyed, all the others damaged."

"Press the attack, press it in!"

Prince Thrakhath looked back up at the main tactical display. Hundreds of his fighters were now circling around his carriers, nearly all of the enemy strike waves destroyed. There was nothing for them to go after, their armaments expended in the mad shooting match.

"Order all on defensive to prepare for second strike on enemy carriers."

The combat commander looked up.

"Their armaments have nearly all been expended, my lord."

Prince Thrakhath growled angrily. If he landed them and any of the carriers were destroyed by the boarders he'd lose his pilots.

"Order the fighters to hold until boarders are disposed off, then land and rearm."

He looked up at the internal security display and saw a white line tracing the enemy attack into the second level of the ship.

"I'm going to the forward launch bay," he announced coldly. "The attack to finish their fleet I'm personally leading."

He started off the bridge and then paused.

"Order the cruisers to break through and finish Earth now!"

In anguish Geoff Tolwyn watched the flickering two dimensional image on the tactical display. All holo displays were now off line as was primary shielding, jump engines, and port launch deck. *Concordia* had survived two more torpedo hits and was crippled, barely able to make twenty percent speed.

The offensive strike waves had simply disappeared into the heart of the enemy fleet. He knew some successes were made, with more than a dozen frigates, destroyers and cruisers gone. But the carriers were still intact. Whether any of the boarding parties had even gotten into the heart of the fleet was merely a guess at this point. The computers handling the hundreds of comm channels was down, as was burst signal link to Earth.

They had fought the enemy offensive strike to a standstill. Not fifty of the enemy fighters out of the four hundred that had come in had survived. Two more of his carriers were gone, the surviving three damaged, with *Lexington* threatening to blow from internal fires—and there were still close to a thousand enemy fighters left along with a hundred escort ships.

But what was worse, far worse, was the cruiser squadron that at the opening of the action had flanked far out to port by more than five million clicks and was now plunging straight in towards Earth, scoops closed and up to flank speed. Not even his fastest ships could close with them now. The light picket line of a cruiser section, Earth orbital defenses and moon ground based defenses and a handful of obsolete frigates would have to stop them. It had been assumed that at least one section of enemy ships or more would go for a straight breakthrough under the screen of the fleet-to-fleet action. Earth was on its own now.

He thought for a moment of a distant ancestor of long ago, who, when contemplating the invasion and destruction of England, announced that even if England fell, the Empire, and with it the fleet, would still continue the fight.

England. No, he didn't want to think of that now.

"Get me Polowski on laser link."

The image flickered on the screen.

"Mike, they're going to come in to finish us off. We still need to keep our carriers alive. I want you to close and see what you can do to knock them off balance."

"What I've been waiting to hear," Mike replied, his voice sounding distant and strained.

"Take care, and God's speed to you, Mike."

Mike did not even reply. Seconds later Destroyer Squadron Three leaped forward into the attack.

Duke Grecko, his good arm shattered by a blast from a grenade, sat against a bulkhead wall. A lone runner came back from the point squad.

"The bastards are insane up there. At least a hundred of them charged when we hit the next deck. It was hand to hand."

The runner was panting hard.

"Your platoon?"

"Finished, sir," and she paused. "I got out because Lieutenant Flory sent me back just before they overran us."

"It's all right, Marine. How long before they get here?"

"I lasered the door shut, sir. Not more than a minute or two."

Duke brought his laser up with his artificial arm at the sound of running. From around a corner a Marine appeared, gun down low, ready to fire, and relaxed at the sight of Grecko. He looked back and waved on his unit and came up to Grecko.

"Demo team reporting, sir. How's it up ahead?"

"As far as we're getting, son."

"Only three levels down, sir. Can't we get one more?"

Duke looked at the young woman who had been on point.

She shook her head.

"Then it's right here, son," and as he spoke the survivors of the demo team and the platoon escorting them came up, pushing a steel crate, maneuvering it with null gravity handles.

"Open her up," Duke said quietly, and the team lowered it down, popping the lid open.

Duke looked at the detonator for the thermonuclear warhead.

"All right, now get the hell out of here. I'm giving you five minutes," and he reached over, first arming the device and then turning the timer on.

The demo team looked at him and grinned.

"Let's go, sir."

"I'll be along in a minute," Duke said quietly.

The surviving corporal of the team hesitated.

"That's my job, sir."

"I'm not going to play hero, son. Now get the lead out of your butt and that's an order. I'll be along shortly."

The Marine looked at him, hesitating. A thin smile creased his features. He saluted and then turned, heading back down the corridor, leading his team with him.

Duke settled back against the wall and sighed. He simply couldn't admit that he was played out and exhausted. Perhaps the president was right, he had never really recovered from his wounds taken at Vukar. He should have stayed at his desk rather than running off to play commando. Since someone did have to stay behind, just in case the Cats got through and knew how to disarm the weapon, it might as well be him.

"You all right, sir?"

He looked up. It was the young woman who had been on point.

"Marine, get the hell out of here."

"Like hell, sir," she said quietly. "I'll hold point."

He smiled sadly.

"I thought you might want some company," and her voice was almost childlike.

"What's your name, Marine?"

"Jenny McCrae, sir."

"That's my girl's name too," he said, a fatherly tone evident in his voice. "She's with the Fourth Marine."

He didn't want to think about that now. She was somewhere in the assault.

"I know, sir, we went through boot together. She was awfully proud of you."

"Really? I wondered. I haven't seen her in years. Her mother and I . . ."

"I know, sir. It's all right though."

They heard the door down the corridor burst open, a thundering roar filling the corridor. He looked down at the chronometer ticking off on the bomb. A minute forty-five to go. The squad just might have made it back by now and gotten off.

I'll give them a few more seconds.

The first Cat turned the corridor and Jenny dropped him. And then a swarm of them came on. He started to slam his fist down on the firing button when a solid blow knocked him off his feet, slamming him against the bulkhead. He tried to get back up, barely seeing the Kilrathi Imperial Guard trooper closing in on him from behind.

The Cat fired again, stitching a burst across his chest and the world started to go warm and hazy.

He looked up and saw Jenny standing over him. She looked like his daughter, or was it his wife, or mother—filled with gentleness.

She looked at him, a smile lighting her innocent face, and then her fist slammed down on the ignitor.

Kevin Tolwyn flung his hand over his visor as a sun ignited before him.

They got it!

He knew he was getting dosed but he didn't care. Not

now. The entire top forward half of the carrier was engulfed in the fireball, the lower and aft parts of the ship tumbling down from the shock of the explosion. The rest of the ship appeared to hold together for a brief instant and then fractured open, the engine cells igniting, the fireball racing outward. Another flash detonated to his right followed by half a dozen more. He guessed that two of them were cruisers; the others, he wasn't sure of.

But two more of them were heavy carriers! The glare of the explosions filled space across hundreds of cubic kilometers. His dose meter clicked off, beeping an alarm. He didn't care. He just didn't care anymore. They had finished the bastards.

He closed his eyes, feeling at peace.

Stunned, Prince Thrakhath turned his fighter around, looking back at his flagship as it blew apart, a dozen clicks behind him.

He knew that those on the deck had thought him a coward for leaving the ship, seeing through his excuse that he was going to personally lead the next wave into battle.

Well, they were dead now and he was still alive.

His heart filled with mad rage as more detonations let go, two more of his prized ships disappearing, and he howled with insane fury.

The explosions died away. He scanned through his tactical.

He still had one old carrier and *Craxtha* intact.

He punched into *Craxtha*'s main channel and called in, the commander of the ship obviously startled.

"We feared you were dead, my lord."

"I was off ship, preparing to lead the next strike."

"Sivar be praised. She guided you thus, my lord."

"The status of your ship?"

"She is fully operational, my lord. We repelled all boarders — my fighters stopped them long before they closed."

He could detect the pride in the commander, as if he

were saying that the other ships were lost through negligence.

"Yes, of course, praise to Sivar. Order all heavy strike fighters from all ships to land on your carrier and rearm immediately for a killing strike on the enemy fleet. We will still win this action."

The commander hesitated.

"We have reports of an incoming strike of enemy destroyers, my lord. And besides, you are talking about turning around over five hundred strike craft on this one ship."

"Your ship is designed to handle that. Now pass the order. Let the remaining fighters and our escorts block the destroyers."

"As you command, my lord."

Thrakhath turned his fighter in towards *Craxtha*, which within minutes was surrounded by swarms of fighters who were lining up for recovery on the six launch bays.

Thrakhath cut into the front of the landing pattern and came in, touching down in the forward portside landing bay.

Inside the hangar deck was mass confusion, the bay crammed from one end to the other with fighters. Fuel lines were snaked across the deck, armaments lockers were open and torpedoes were being hoisted out. Crews struggled with long energy cables, hooking them into ships, recharging neutron guns, batteries, and shielding systems.

There was no semblance of order: pilots and ship crews from the other three heavy carriers milled about, most of them in obvious shock at the sudden reversal.

Thrakhath stepped out of his fighter and instantly the deck went silent.

"Keep working," he snarled. "We will still finish the scum before this day is done."

He felt the ship start to heel over, the starfield outside the entry lock shifting. He could imagine the confusion this sudden maneuver was causing with the hundred or more fighters and strike craft still lined up for recovery. Angrily, he strode across the deck into the launch officer's operations office.

"Put the bridge on," he thundered.

"What are you doing up there?" he shouted. "We need to get these fighters in as soon as possible and turned around."

"Five destroyers have broken through the inner screen and are coming straight in on us."

"Enemy carrier turning away, sir."

"Keep on closing," Mike said calmly.

He looked over at his helm officer and smiled.

"Just like the Battle of Leyte Gulf," Mike said.

"I was thinking that," the helm replied. "One of my illustrious ancestors commanded a cruiser there. We should have won that day."

Mike nodded.

"Torpedo room."

"Torpedo room, sir."

"Have lock yet?"

"Twenty-two seconds and counting, sir."

Mike looked back up at his tactical. Of the twelve destroyers in his squadron only four were left. There was a flash of light on his main visual and he realized he was down to three.

"Hell of a day to be a destroyer skipper," and then he focused back on the enemy carrier, a dozen clicks ahead as it turned hard over, now presenting a full amidships shot and then started to present its stern.

A swarm of Kilrathi fighters shot in, stitching his destroyer with everything they still had. Four of them elected to simply come straight in, one of them kamikazing through the shield as it struggled to recover from the repeated hammer blows. The kamikaze hit just aft of the bridge, blowing into the center of the ship, knocking Mike to the deck. Decompression alarms sounded off, the damage control board sparkling with red lights.

"Torpedo room."

"Twelve and counting, sir. What the hell happened back there?"

"Never mind, just get those birds launched."

Another string of fighters swooped in, concentrating on the bow of the ship.

"We've lost lock, sir. Torpedo guidance control off line."

"Damn it!"

To his right, *Roger Young* launched its torpedoes just before blowing. The spread of a dozen rounds leaped forward.

"Helm, follow those torpedoes in," Mike shouted, and then he reached over, punching the abandon ship alarm.

"This is the captain speaking. If you wanna see your families again, you've got thirty seconds to get to the escape pods and the hell off this ship!"

He looked over at his helm and fire control officers.

"I hate to ask this of you two."

"It's all right, sir," the helm officer said. "This time the family wants to be on the winning side."

Mike looked at the rest of his team.

"You heard me, get the hell off this ship."

They hesitated.

"Damn it, you fools. You've got something to live for, now move it," and he grabbed hold of his damage control officer and pushed her towards the door.

She looked at him, wide-eyed, torn.

"For God's sake, Elaine, you've got kids back home. Now move it!"

She struggled to hold back the tears and then, turning, ran down the corridor to the nearest escape pod, the rest following.

"Helm, follow those torpedoes in."

"Aye, sir."

Mike stood, watching the screen, ignoring the fighters that swarmed around his ship. A staccato series of hammer blows blew the main generator off line, dim emergency battle lamps coming back on. All but two of the torpedoes launched by *Young* were gone as well.

"Torpedo room, still with me?"

"Still here, sir. Figured we should hang around for the fun."

"Get ready for blind fire. Set fuses at point one seconds!"

"Point one seconds, sir?"

"Shut up and do it!"

"Point one seconds, sir, and we'll see you in hell."

"Helm, do your job right. Bring us in on the landing bay an instant after *Young's* birds hit."

The helm officer grinned as he delicately worked the controls, weaving the destroyer in, as it came up directly astern of the enemy carrier.

The carrier's point defenses tore into his ship and he felt her dying, letting go.

"Helm, full speed ahead now!"

He felt the final surge of his ship thundering under his feet.

"Torpedo room, ready, ready, fire!"

The one surviving torpedo from *Roger Young* hit the carrier's aft starboard launch bay and blew, distorting the phase shielding. An instant later a dozen more torpedoes fired at point blank range detonated.

The last thing Mike Polowski saw were his own torpedoes blowing less than fifty meters ahead of his own ship. He thought of the warm hills of his now dead world and smiled as the blast wave blew his ship apart. The forward momentum of what had been the aft end of his destroyer, however, continued on, even as it died, adding its thousand tons of mass into the detonating firestorm of the torpedoes impacting against the carrier's overloaded shields. Most of the mass was repelled away, but the aft end of the ship, engines still pulsing, even as the ship ahead of it vaporized, continued onward, driving through the shattered hull, pushing before it fragments of bulkheads, decking, and those few still on board. The engine mounts, made of solid durasteel, were all that was left a hundredth of a second later as they impacted through the landing bay's airlock.

Several dozen tons of molten durasteel blew into the vast hangar bay, vaporizing flesh, cutting into fuel lines, igniting ammunition, and ripping open the hundred and three fighters being readied for launch.

The entire bay exploded in a white-hot fireball of destruction.

Prince Thrakhath staggered through the wreckage and onto *Craxtha*'s main bridge. The room was choked with smoke, half the bridge crew dead or wounded, open fires still licking out of shattered equipment. The ship's commander was dead, slumped in his chair, the top of his head gone.

"Who's in command here?"

The crew looked at him, stunned.

"I think I am now, sir," and Thrakhath saw the green tabs of damage control on the officer's collar.

"Can you save her?"

"We've lost two aft bays, my lord," the officer reported. "The explosion started in starboard aft bay, then leaped through an open access elevator to topside bay."

"Why was it open?"

"The commander ordered it. They were out of torpedoes in the lower bay. We were shifting them down from above."

Thrakhath looked back at the commander and silently cursed. If he were still alive, he would have him executed on the spot for such stupidity.

"Two of our main engines are gone as well, sir. We're lucky the main fuel cells didn't go up. I'm purging out the three cells closest to the fire right now. I've also ordered all armaments in the aft topside bay dumped overboard."

"Do that and we have to run with scoops full open!" Thrakhath roared. "We'll lose whatever offensive capability we have left. With half our remaining armaments gone, we're finished!"

"Sire, if you don't like what I'm doing then execute me and do it yourself," the officer snapped. "We're lucky to be alive as is. If we don't purge those cells now they'll blow. It's an inferno back there."

Thrakhath stood silently, looking over at the flickering display on the damage board and finally lowered his head.

"Tell me what we can still do."

"We still have more than five hundred of our best fighters out there, my lord. They have no offensive strike capability left; they're mostly light fighters. I think it's time we landed them, my lord, to get our pilots back. We won't have enough room for them, so the craft will have to be dumped overboard as fast as we recover them."

Thrakhath looked up at him, unable to speak.

"It's time to go home, my lord. We've done all we can do today. One more hit and we'll lose this ship as well. We've got to save our pilots now, my lord. There'll be over a thousand of them on board here. They'll still give us victory once we've repaired this ship, and the rest of the new carriers come on line."

Thrakhath looked around the bridge. He knew the young officer was right. He had to save his pilots; he had lost too many already.

The only satisfaction left now was the fact that within a matter of minutes the cruiser squadron would close on Earth. At least with Earth destroyed, this would still be a victory.

"Launch fighters now!"

Jason Bondarevsky leaned forward in his chair, wishing now more than ever to be back in a fighter.

The first fighter, piloted by Doomsday, cleared the bay.

The blue-green home of his race filled the forward screen.

The run in from jump point 12Y, the line leading back towards the Landreich, had been with scoops fully closed. Kruger had even committed the ultimate madness of doing the final jump at full speed. A third of the fleet had missed the jump point completely, forcing them to decelerate, turn around and come back in. They were now several hours behind. They were the lucky ones. Two frigates had only achieved partial jump, hitting the point as fast as they did. Part of the two frigates had come through, the other part had simply continued on back in the last system. The crews never knew what hit them, their molecules spread between Alpha Centuri and Earth.

The maneuver, however, had gained them precious time, and moving at a good fraction of the speed of light they had closed from the jump point to Earth in under three hours.

They were too late for the main battle, but the threat closing in on Earth was all too obvious and Kruger had ordered them in to head it off.

He could only hope that they would be there in time.

Baron Jukaga watched as the three escort carriers came up over the northern pole of the planet, a spread of fighters leaping ahead of them.

He had but one cruiser left with him, seven falling to the inner defense line. The other two cruisers had turned to bombard the naval yards of the Earth's satellite, the bright flashes of explosions tearing through the military bases and construction yards spread out on its barren airless surface and in orbit above it, smashing dozens of ships of the fleet including the carriers still caught in drydock. Both were destroyed by point defenses but they had successfully smashed a military target — an action which, at least for the moment, had filled him with pride.

That, at least, he approved of. It was a target worthy of being hit, a fitting vengeance for the raid on the moon of Kilrah.

He stood silently behind the cruiser's captain, ignoring the Imperial Marines standing to either side as his guards.

"We'll only have time for one pass," the commander said quietly, looking up at the tactical display in rage. They had detected the small fleet of escort carriers and destroyers only minutes before, the enemy ships coming from the direction of another jump point at full speed with scoops closed.

"We have first target solutions and locks," the captain announced. "After our first hit and destruction of their defensive centers, we drop the thermonuclears.

"First wave, antimatter warheads ready for firing."

The commander grinned, looking over at his weapons control officer.

"For the glory of Kilrah, the Emperor, and the Empire. Fire!"

Baron Jukaga watched as the first weapons leaped forward, tracking downward, racing in towards the North American continent and Northern Europe.

"Incoming fighters!"

"No!"

Doomsday screamed with impotent rage as he saw the heavy antimatter rockets streak away.

A light screen of enemy fighters, launched from the cruisers, moved to intercept, and with a wild frenzy Doomsday slashed into them, killing them with a mad insane glee, while behind him, four modified Sabres lined up for the first torpedo launch.

The torpedoes leaped out, tracking in on the first cruiser, and seconds later detonated. Kruger's fighters swarmed in, slamming the cruiser, which appeared for a second to collapse in on itself before bursting asunder. The comm link was filled with mad screams of hatred and rage as the strike team turned towards the other cruiser.

Down in the Earth's atmosphere Doomsday could see pinpoint winks of light as point defense systems fought to knock down the incoming wave of more than a hundred missiles. And then there was a flash of light over the center of the North American continent. It looked like Chicago going up, followed seconds later by a dozen more: Pittsburg, Boston, Miami, Quebec, then across in Northern Europe: Amsterdam, Berlin, Stockholm, Constantinople and Paris. Other flashes detonated over the primary control centers for Earth's American and European space defenses at Omaha, Rio, Tripoli, and Kiev.

He started to close towards the next cruiser, knowing in his heart that it would be too late.

"We have incoming, still closing."

The commander looked up at his tactical screen and could see that within less than a minute he would be under attack.

"First strike report?"

"Primary strategic defense centers over target areas destroyed, ground to space anti-missile defensive system seriously damaged except for point defenses."

"Second weapons load," the commander announced with a cold glee. "Prepare thermonuclear strontium clad weapons for air bursts."

He looked back at the Baron.

"We might not have the pleasure of first pounding their cities to rubble, but we'll poison them all anyhow. In a month their world will be a charnel house."

"And you call this victory," the Baron hissed. "May Sivar spit on you."

"No, I call it revenge," the commander said coldly and he turned away.

Behind him he heard the cold laughter of his guards who stepped forward to look at the screen.

"Weapons ready for launch."

The commander held up his hand, talons extended.

Baron Jukaga lunged forward, grabbing at the commander's holster and pulled out his pistol. The commander turned, wide- eyed, even as Jukaga brought the gun up, jamming it up under the commander's jaw and squeezed the trigger. The laser burst streaked through his head, the top of his skull erupting, a boiling mass pouring out.

The Marine guard to his left started to turn, startled, and Jukaga dropped him in turn. He then swung about, killing the weapons officer, the blast knocking him backwards and away from the firing switch.

A stunning blow knocked Jukaga to the deck, and he realized with an almost detached emotion that he could no longer feel his legs. The shot must have severed my spinal cord, he thought, even as he brought his gun up, toppling the other guard over.

Jukaga lay back, wide-eyed, looking at the rest of the bridge crew. One of them tried to lunge for the firing panel and he dropped him and then two more. The two surviving bridge crew members stood still.

"You filthy traitor, Sivar will roast you in hell forever," one of them hissed.

Jukaga laughed softly. It was all such a wonderful joke, he realized. Just what was a traitor to a traitor, and who exactly had he betrayed? It was an interesting logic question to be certain.

He looked up at the main visual screen.

Earth actually did look beautiful; in a sense far more beautiful than Kilrah.

And then the explosion of the impacting torpedoes washed over him.

Stunned, Prince Thrakhath sat alone in the wardroom of the *Craxtha's* now dead commander.

The long range opticals showed the end of the drama. Their moon bases were totally shattered, but that was not the ultimate prize. Less than three eights antimatter warheads had hit Earth. The final wave of thermonuclears had never been launched.

He looked at the status reports of his losses. But one more carrier here and we could still press through to victory. But one more carrier.

All the ifs started to play out in his mind. If only he had waited but five eights more days, he would have had his sixth ship, but Jukaga had to be contended with.

He looked back at the visual, glad at least that Jukaga was dead.

Another explosion shuddered through the ship and he held his breath, waiting. The explosion rumbled away.

A piping call sounded and he connected into the bridge. It was his chief navigation officer.

"Go on."

"Sir, your orders. With the engine speed we now have, we'll only be able to make it to the next jump point with less than four eights of minutes to spare ahead of those new ships coming up from Earth orbit."

Thrakhath nodded silently. They had at least crippled the human fleet: three of their five carriers gone, the third exploding only minutes ago, at least three more smashed at the moon base along with the construction yards and several eights of other ships. Nearly two eights of their major cities were now smoldering ruins. He could still pull back, his one remaining older carrier covering him, repair the damage sustained on his two surviving heavy carriers. His precious pilots would be brought back as well to fly once more off the new carriers still coming on line. If he stayed now, chances were good that they would finish this carrier off, and everything would be lost, including himself.

He looked back at the screen.

"Order the fleet to retreat," he hesitated. "The battle is over."

• CHAPTER FOURTEEN

Geoff Tolwyn, in spite of his exhaustion, forced a smile as the shuttle craft door swung open. He walked forward, extending his hand as President Kruger, followed by Jason, Paladin, Doomsday and Richards, stepped down.

Kruger hesitated ever so briefly and then took Geoff's hand.

"Damn it all, Kruger, thank you."

"I'm rather surprised myself that I did it," Kruger said. "It was your young commodore there who just kept badgering me until finally, to shut him up, I said all right."

Geoff looked at the group and though he was afraid to ask he had to.

"Ian?"

Jason shook his head.

Geoff sighed and then came up to shake Jason's hand.

"How are you doing, sir?" Jason asked.

"A terrible day, Jason."

Jason hesitated and then finally asked.

"Kevin?"

"Missing in action," Geoff said quietly.

"He might still turn up, sir."

Geoff nodded, unable to reply.

Jason looked around at the smoke-filled flight deck.

"Looks like it was kind of rough here."

Geoff couldn't even reply. He had lost three carriers, *Lexington* finally succumbing to internal explosions, and over seventy percent of his pilots. First reports indicated that the Marines had suffered over ninety percent casualties. Duke Grecko was confirmed as dead, his landing craft crew telling what happened. As for the civilian pilots, their casualties were almost at one hundred percent. The primary bases on the moon were all gone, as were the drydock yards and three carriers hangared there. The casualties on Earth, he didn't even want to think about that. The only bright spot was that for some reason the Cats had not launched a wave of strontium clad thermonukes. England had been spared as well, though it seemed at the moment to be an almost selfish thing to think about.

Geoff led his guests down to his wardroom and without even asking, pulled out a bottle of single malt Scotch, six tumblers and poured out six very stiff drinks, draining the bottle dry.

"To our comrades," he said quietly, and they silently drank the toast.

Geoff settled back in his chair and looked around.

"If this is victory," Geoff finally said, "I sure as hell would hate to see defeat."

"You stopped the bloody Cats at least, sir," Jason replied. "Hell, three of their super carriers blown apart, more than half their best pilots gone, forty other ships crippled. I heard the report coming in that they're dumping fighters off their carrier as they retreat, not even enough room to haul them all out."

Geoff nodded, fighting an exhaustion that had all but robbed him of any ability to do anything beyond sitting in silence and staring.

"I heard about Polowski, sir," Doomsday said.

Geoff looked over at him. When he had ordered Mike in, he knew in his heart that Polowski would get his revenge and die doing it. If the Cats had miscalculated anything, it was that. They had pushed the intimidation a notch too far, and rather than terrorize it had aroused every pilot, spacer, and Marine in the fleet to a willingness to die rather than submit. He suspected that Jukaga had realized that but it was obvious that Thrakhath never would.

The war had changed, changed far from anything that

either side had ever anticipated. The manipulation of the human desire for peace had backfired, their collective rage turning the enemy back, though at best it was a Pyrrhic victory.

The Cats still had seven more heavy carriers close to completion. If they came on again, he dreaded to think what would happen. They had shot their bolt in turning back the attack. Perhaps the new dreadnought-class battleship under construction on the far side of the Confederation might reverse that, but in his heart he doubted if it would be ready in time to repulse the next attack.

All he could be certain of now was the fact that those who had survived this attack would stand united to the end. He could even see that in the eyes of Kruger, who, upon seeing him, lifted his glass in a salute.

"To the Confederation Fleet," Kruger said.

"And to comrades gone," Paladin replied softly.

"Admiral Tolwyn."

Geoff looked over at the comm screen, dreading that it was yet another battle report stating that the Kilrathi had turned about and were coming back.

"The Kilrathi?" he blurted out.

"Their carriers have already jumped through in retreat, sir, still trailing abandoned fighters. Cruisers are now jumping out as well. Picket squadrons are reporting no further action."

He let out an audible sigh of relief. The battle was really over.

"Admiral, sir, you're wanted on the port flight deck."

"Why?"

"Don't know, sir. Launch officer requested your presence, that's all."

"On my way."

Geoff stood up, his knees suddenly weak and Jason rose from his chair coming up to his side.

"I'll go down with you, sir."

Geoff smiled a thanks and looked back at his guests.

"There's another bottle in the cabinet. Finish it off," he said quietly.

"Best advice I've had in weeks," Doomsday replied even as he reached into his pocket and pulled out the chewed on remains of the cigar Ian had given him.

"Geoff, for heaven's sake," Kruger interjected, "would you order him to get rid of that god-awful cigar? It's enough to turn my stomach."

"Hell, he's still officially Landreich," Geoff replied. "He's your responsibility, not mine."

Doomsday pulled out a lighter and puffed the cigar to life, Kruger, Richards and Paladin cursing him while they poured out another drink.

Geoff left the wardroom and headed back to the launch deck, pressing up against the wall as a med team came past, bearing a stretcher, a bloody towel draped over the body's face.

Geoff watched it silently as they passed.

Jason reached out, and put his hand on Geoff's shoulder.

"No matter what you might think, you did good, sir. Earth is still alive, the Confederation still lives."

"And how many did I lose, Jason?"

"I once asked the same thing after Vukar Tag, sir. It's the nature of war, you told me. Even when you win, it still breaks your heart and will crush your soul if you let it."

"And you call this winning?"

"It's a damn sight better than what the Cats wanted. You turned them back and you brought us time."

Geoff nodded and then continued on, reaching the flight deck. The launch officer was by the door.

"I thought you should come down here, sir. We just brought some casualties in."

Geoff looked at him, confused, as the officer pointed him over to a flame scorched landing craft. Its back hatch was open, pilots and Marines, most of them wounded and still in their pressurized flight and combat suits, being helped out.

Geoff looked back at the launch officer who smiled and nodded.

Geoff ran to the back of the landing craft, Jason at his side, and climbed in.

On the flight deck was a bundled up form, two medics working over him, one holding an IV, another injecting an anti-radiation dose straight in through his suit.

Geoff knelt down by their side.

A blood-stained medic looked up and she smiled softly.

"Picked him up an hour ago. He caught a hell of a dose, sir, over four hundred rem. He's gonna be a sick fighter jockey for awhile but we got him anti-radiation dosed in time. He'll be all right."

Geoff nodded and looked over at Jason.

Kevin Tolwyn opened his eyes and saw Jason first.

"Hi ya, Jason. What the hell you doing here?"

"Came to save your ass, boy, that's all."

Kevin smiled weakly and then saw his uncle kneeling by his side.

"Did we win?" he whispered.

Admiral Geoffrey Tolwyn nodded, no longer able to fight back the tears.

"Yes, son, we won."

THE BEST OF THE BEST

For *anyone* who reads science fiction, this is an absolutely indispensable book. Since 1953, the annual Hugo Awards presented at the World Science Fiction Convention have been as coveted by SF writers as is the Oscar in the motion picture field—and SF fans recognize it as a certain indicator of quality in science fiction. Now the members of the World Science Fiction Convention— the people who *award* the Hugos—select the best of the best: *The Super Hugos*! Included in this volume are stories by such SF legends as Arthur C. Clarke, Isaac Asimov, Larry Niven, Clifford D. Simak, Harlan Ellison, Daniel Keyes, Anne McCaffrey and more. Presented and with an introduction by Charles Sheffield. This essential volume also includes a complete listing of all the Hugo winners to date in all categories and breakdowns and analyses of the voting in all categories, including the novel category.

And don't miss *The New Hugo Winners Volume I* (all the Hugo winning stories for the years 1983–1985) and *The New Hugo Winners Volume II* (all the Hugo winning stories for the years 1986–1988), both presented by Isaac Asimov.

"World Science Fiction Convention" and "Hugo Award" are service marks of the World Science Fiction Society, an unicorporated literary society.

The Super Hugos • 72135-6 • 432 pp. • $4.99 ☐
The New Hugo Winners Volume I • 72081-3 • 320 pp. • $4.50 ☐
The New Hugo Winners Volume II • 72103-8 • 384 pp. • $4.99 ☐

Available at your local bookstore. If not, fill out this coupon and send a check or money order for the cover price to Baen Books, Dept. BA, P.O. Box 1403, Riverdale, NY 10471.

NAME: _____

ADDRESS: _____

_____

I have enclosed a check or money order in the amount of $_____

POUL ANDERSON

Poul Anderson is one of the most honored authors of our time. He has won seven Hugo Awards, three Nebula Awards, and the Gandalf Award for Achievement in Fantasy, among others. His most popular series include the Polesotechnic League/Terran Empire tales and the Time Patrol series. Here are fine books by Poul Anderson available through Baen Books:

THE SHIP WHO SANG IS NOT ALONE!

Anne McCaffrey, with Margaret Ball, Mercedes Lackey, and S.M. Stirling, explores the universe she created with her ground-breaking novel, *The Ship Who Sang*.